Bravo, I won
(Bravo j'ai gagné)

Monique Dubois

Bravo, I won *(Bravo j'ai gagné)* © **Monique Dubois, 2020**

Book and cover design by Monique Dubois
ISBN: 978-1-940012-50-6

Other books by Monique Dubois
One day you will come back
These moments of my life

Preface

The winner takes it all was written by Benny Andersson and Björn Ulvaeus for ABBA in 1980, the French version with lyrics by Charles Level was released as *Bravo tu as gagné* in 1980 by Mireille Matthieu. This novel turns the tables as to who takes all and considers themselves the winner, hence, *Bravo, I won* or *Bravo j'ai gagné*.

Contents

A new Barclay

I received a notice in the mail in early August of 1979 that my new plane was ready. It had been ferried from the factory in Kansas to Reims, where they had been stripping out the ferry tanks and cleaning the plane up. The first plane I had bought was actually built in Reims, but the new one was a larger model and not built in France, so it had to be ferried over the Atlantic from Kansas. I had been staying with my mother, Maman to me, reflecting the fact that she is French, and her partner, Portia, at their villa on the Riviera since the death of Ian, my husband of only four years. He had been killed in a traffic accident in Kenya where we were living. He was with the British High Commission there and had gone close to the Uganda border to talk to an agent about the imminent collapse of the Idi Amin régime. The régime had in fact collapsed and Uganda was now essentially under Tanzanian rule for a while. To introduce myself, I am Fiona Hartley, née Barclay, I consult in the fields of economics and computer science. I have been successful as a consultant and can now pick and choose the projects that I want to take. Maman had persuaded me to stay with them for a while following my departure from Kenya. Ian's death had hit me hard and after cleaning up a few projects that I had been working on had decided to take a few weeks off, I had taken her advice and gone to stay with them. She and Portia had been concerned that I would sink into a depression after Ian's death. I could still easily have done that. I missed him, I missed his grin, I missed his touch, I missed hearing him talk to me, I missed his presence in bed, I missed making love with him, I just missed him. Staying busy for a few weeks had been good, I had had little time to brood, but, now I was at a loose end and wondering what to do next and how to move on with my life.

Maman and Portia came with me to Reims, we took the train to Paris and stayed the night there. SNCF was supposed to be improving the service from Lyon to Paris with what they were calling TGV, *Train à grande vitesse*, and which was supposed to be capable of speeds up to 200mph. They had a couple of test beds running, but we did not get the chance to ride on one of them. So, we settled for trundling along at much lower speeds and broke our journey in Paris. We had a place to stay in Paris. When my grandmother had died, Maman inherited her flat and kept it. The flat was in the centre of Paris, close to the Seine and to Notre Dame. As flats go in the centre of Paris it was very spacious with three bedrooms and various other rooms. I had stayed there quite a lot in recent times when my consulting business took me to France and had enjoyed spending time with my grandmother, Mémère to me. She was from Tahiti and had married my grandfather, Pépère to me, when he had been stationed in Tahiti as part of the French Government there. When they first returned to Paris from Tahiti, I gathered that their accommodations had not been so grandiose, but as time went on and Pépère moved up in the government they had been able to afford this flat. So Maman did not grow up there, but like me, she had stayed there a lot and now she owned it. After our night in Paris, we took a taxi to the Gare de l'Est and found the train to Reims. The ride was not that long and we were in Reims by ten. Another taxi took us to the factory.

The factory people were ready for us and we were taken and shown the plane. It was a Cessna 206 Stationair, with seats for six, if you counted the pilot. My first plane had been smaller with seats for only four and Ian and I had flown all over Kenya in it. While Maman and Portia were entertained by some of the factory people, I walked around the plane with a representative and the instructor pilot, Gerard, whom I had met before when I had been to Reims to see my first pane being built. I poked, prodded and checked the exterior of the plane, from wings to elevators to wheels and the propeller. It was new, but it had just come across the Atlantic, an interesting series of hops from airport to airport, with long over-water periods. I asked about issues that had cropped up on the ferry ride and was given a short list of four items. The factory rep assured me that those items had been addressed and everything was now fine. I wanted to see the paperwork and scanned through the documents quickly and took comfort in the diligence of the Reims people. I opened up the engine compartment and looked over the engine inside, it looked good, but the only way to really check that was to start it up and run it. I opened up the luggage compartment and was pleased to see the tie-down kit that I had ordered was there. Inside the plane, the ferry tanks were gone and the interior had been cleaned and aired and the seats looked clean and new. I climbed in with Gerard and we reviewed the instruments and navigation systems. It was essentially the same as the panel on my first plane, with a few small changes. I had had the manual for a while so tapped on each instrument and control in turn and named them, while the instructor nodded. We went through the pre-start checklist, then we started the plane. I listened to the engine and ran it up and down, it sounded good, nothing untoward that I could detect. Then we ran through the other checks, then got clearance to taxi.

In the air I discovered that the Stationair handled a little differently than the Skyhawk, but nothing that was in any way disturbing. We flew up, around, down, up, left, right, down, up, around again, did two bumps and circuits, did a stall and a recovery, stopped and restarted the engine, then came back into land.

"This is a nice plane," I told Gerard.

"It is," he agreed. "Where will you keep it?"

"Biggin Hill," I said. "But for the moment I'm staying in France, so we'll fly today to an aerodrome near Orléans."

"Why Orléans?" he asked.

"My sister-in-law runs a vineyard near there," I explained. "We're going to pay them a visit."

"What happened to your Skyhawk?" he asked.

"I sold it," I said. "I thought about ferrying it from Kenya to France, but decided against that. I got a good price for it and decided to buy something a little bigger."

"Why did you leave Kenya?" he asked. This was a question I knew I would be getting from people I had met but did not know that well, so had thought about my answer a lot and had decided that the best way for me to answer it was to be straightforward. I needed to accept the fact that Ian was dead and that I would have to create a new life for myself.

"My husband was killed in a car accident," I said. "We were in Nairobi for his job, so when he died there was no reason for me to be there."

"I'm so sorry," Gerard said. "How are you managing?"

"Good days and not so good days," I said. "Today is so-so, Ian would have liked this plane."

"It is a nice plane," Gerard agreed. "Shall we go in and finish all the paperwork?"

"Fine," I agreed. We went in and I signed the acceptance forms for the plane, it was now mine, registration number G-GTTF, so I was going to be golf tango tango foxtrot. I found Maman and Portia, they were in a conference room listening to an earnest young man extol the virtues of Reims Aviation and Cessna. When I joined them, he suggested that we have lunch before we departed. That sounded like a good idea, so he led us to the company cafeteria where we were treated to a rather nice lunch. I think he was trying to sell Maman and Portia on the idea of buying their own plane, but they were both masterfully non-committal.

After lunch, we thanked our host and went out to the flight line where the plane was. I asked Gerard if I could get a full tank of fuel and he slipped back into the building and a minute later a fuel bowser appeared. The driver got a step ladder and opened the tanks and filled each. I was prepared to pay, but Gerard waved it off, telling me that it was a parting gesture from Reims and Cessna. Fuelled and ready, I took the bags that we had and stowed them in the luggage compartment. They were small enough, just enough for a couple of days. I asked who wanted to sit up front next to me and Maman and Portia tossed a coin for it. Portia won the toss and told Maman to sit in the front. Aboard I went through a safety briefing with them and then busied myself with the various checklists. Ready to go, we started up and got the appropriate clearance and taxied out onto the company runway. It was actually a municipal field that served Reims, but there was no commercial traffic, just the plane factory and some local flying clubs. In the air I made contact with the relevant controllers and was passed from one to the other until we passed Orléans, then we said goodbye and I did my visual flight approach into the Cosne-sur-Loire aerodrome. James was waiting for us and I let him take the bags while I tied the plane down. It had become a habit of mine to tie the plane down wherever I went, one never knew when the winds might pick up and move the plane. James was my younger brother and he had married Charlize Cillie from South Africa and essentially married into the family business that was winemaking.
"Good flight?" James asked.
"Good," Maman said. "How is Charlize, the baby must be due any day now?"
"She's fine," James said. "Her Ma is here and you're right, it must be soon, any day now, and add to the fun her Dad is here as well, along with Hansie and the family."

4

"Well, we'll try and stay out of the way," I promised. James drove us to the château that was part of the vineyard. I had always been impressed with that, it was an actual château, not quite as ornate and imposing as the château at Sully-sur-Loire, but still very nice. The château had been a little dilapidated when they had taken over the estate, but over time they had restored it to its former glory and it truly was beautiful. The château had been adapted to include a storage facility for bottled wines and a tasting room and shop. I loved the place, it had a moat, but much to my regret, no drawbridge, but instead a permanent bridge. It had I do not know how many rooms and they had all been restored, thanks to the efforts of James and Charlize's father and brothers. I have no idea how many hours they each put into making it first habitable, then elegant. It certainly worked as a tasting room and shop and James and Charlize even held tasting events there. I suppose, lunches and weddings might follow in time to provide a steady cash flow.

At the château, Charlize was there to greet us, her mother, Anna, and sister-in-law, Clara, in attendance, and James was right she looked as if the baby could come any minute.
"How are you, Charlie?" I asked.
"Well enough," she said. "I feel like a whale now and am ready for this to be over."
"No issues, no problems?" I asked.
"She's doing fine," Anna assured us. "I will be soon, very soon." Well, I supposed Anna would know, apart from her own three children she had an army of grandchildren, so had seen this many times.
"We shouldn't bother you," Maman said.
"You're no bother," Charlize assured us. "I need the loo, again!" She left and Anna then gave us chapter and verse on how things were.
"It will be tonight or tomorrow," she predicted.
"How's James managing?" I asked.
"Like most men," Anna laughed. "Terrified, anxious, not sure exactly what to do, wanting to help, but not sure what to do. He'll be fine if he doesn't faint."
"Is this going to be a home birth?" Maman asked.
"No, we're planning to take her to La Charité," Anna replied. "In fact, judging by the look on her face, we should take her now." She called for James, then the three of them left. La Charité-sur-Loire was quite close,

only a few miles to the south, so it would not take them long to get there. Now, all we had to do was wait.

"Are they gone?" John, Charlize's father, asked as he came into the room.

"They're gone," Maman confirmed.

"Well, let's hope it's not too long," he said. "Nice to see you all again, how are you doing, Fiona?"

"Good days and not so good," I confessed. "Today should turn out to be a really good day. Clara, where are Hansie and the kids?"

"They're out in the vineyard," she replied. "Hansie's trying to keep them out of the way for a while, give me a break too. I'm thankful for that. It's been a bit chaotic with the move and with Charlie so close. Brigitte, Portia, shall we go and make some dinner?"

"I was wondering," John started. "We've sold the South African business and bought more here and will be buying in the States, and could use some help with a model for the business we're buying there and what we're thinking about for new plantings."

"I'd be happy to help," I said. "Give me something interesting to do while we wait."

"If you two are going to talk business, then Portia and I will make dinner," Maman announced. "Some wine with your discussions?"

"Thanks, Maman," I said. "See what they have and find me a nice white, John?"

"That would be good," he added. Maman and Portia left and John then showed me the figures he had of the operations they had either bought or were buying. The bought one was in Aix-en-Provence and the other was in New Mexico, and I remembered James talking about New Mexico and its rivers and mountains. The model that John was interested in was essentially the same as the ones I had already done for their French and South African operations, it was just a question of modifying it to fit the new criteria.

"Are you concerned about Charlize?" I asked, as John's mind seemed to be wandering.

"I suppose I am," he admitted. "With the boys it was different, yes, I was concerned that all went well with Anika and Clara, but Charlie is my baby and I worry about her a lot."

"I'm sure she'll be fine," I said.

"I'm sure she will," John said, grinning ruefully. "She's certainly done a wonderful job here, we've decided that she should go to New Mexico. Hansie is here to manage this winery and Frikkie is in Aix-en-Provence. It was a lot easier to get immigrant visas for France than the States, particularly for South Africans. The Cillies came from France originally, from La Rochelle, so we're just coming back."

"Are you two ready for dinner?" Portia asked.

"We are," John said. "I'm having difficulty concentrating on what Fiona is telling me, so dinner is a good idea."

"Charlize will be fine," Portia assured him.

"I know, but that doesn't stop me from worrying," he said.

"Well, eat something," Portia suggested. "You may be up late tonight."

We were joined by Hansie and his three, and the noise level jumped a few decibels. They ranged in age from eleven to sixteen, and it seemed to me that their appetites were insatiable.

"So where is this vineyard you're buying in the States?" I asked John, between bites of my dinner.

"It's near a town, if you can call it a town, called Pecos, which is on the Pecos River, would you believe?" John replied. "They over-extended and got themselves with too much debt, but the operation is otherwise sound and the harvests have been excellent, and the wines are really rather good. We want to establish ourselves in New Mexico and look for more properties to buy, either just land that we plant ourselves or going concerns."

"Where is this Pecos?" I asked.

"East of Santa Fe," John explained. "It's not far off the 25 freeway. It's in the northern part of the state, about an hour and a half from Albuquerque."

"How many acres?" I asked.

"About 50 planted," John said. "But there's another 200 acres that could be planted, there's water from the river and growing conditions are not bad. Growth is limited because land is limited to what's along the river, because it sits in the middle of a national forest, so if you like the wilderness, this is the place, the general lack of more available land is why we're also looking elsewhere."

"When does the purchase close?" I asked.

"Should be soon now," John said. "I'm going over in two weeks to settle everything."

"Who manages it before you can get Charlie there?" I asked.

"I will," John said. "Actually I was wondering if you'd come with me. I'd like to take another last look at the books before we agree the final number?"

"I would be happy to help," I promised. The prospect of a trip to the States was exciting, I had never been, so it would be a new and novel experience. Further discussion was halted when the telephone rang.

"It's James," Maman announced. "It's a girl, 3.2 kilos, both doing well."

"We should go," John said. I think we all agreed with that sentiment, so cleared up the kitchen quickly locked up the house and drove to La Charité. There we were shown to the appropriate room and told not to be long and not to tire the new mother. James and Anna met us at the door, then we saw Charlize with her daughter. I think the hospital staff were horrified by the number of visitors, there were eleven in all, including James.

"Isn't she beautiful?" Charlize said. Well, I had not had much experience with babies, but they had all struck me as singularly not beautiful, but wrinkled, red, with little or no hair.

"She's wonderful," I said, echoing the comments of the other members of the family.

"James did wonderfully," Charlize said. "He didn't faint, but I may have broken his fingers I squeezed so hard during the contractions."

"May we hold her?" Maman asked.

"Of course," Charlize said, handing over the baby to Maman. "We've decided to call her Fiona Anna." That did choke me up, I now was an aunt, had a niece, and she was named after me. Maman passed Fiona to Portia who then passed her on to me. I had watched how the others had held her and did not drop her or allow her head to droop. I did my part then quickly passed her on to John, who was delighted. He and Anna looked at each other and smiled, I think it was some kind of private moment between the two of them. A nurse then came in and shooed us all out, telling us that we could visit again the next day, during normal visiting hours, and that the next time, there should be fewer visitors. We said our farewells to Charlize and Fiona and went back to the château, where James broke out some champagne so that we could toast the new baby.

"That was quick," Maman commented.

"What do you mean?" I asked.

"Well, labour can go on for a while, so this was very quick," she said.

"Shorter than mine with any of my three," Anna added.

"Shorter than any of mine," Clara added.

"It was amazing," James said. "But Charlie's right, she did crush my hand a bit, I think I've got the feeling back in it now. Anyway, here's to Charlize and Fiona Anna." We all raised our glasses in salute and welcomed the newest Barclay into the world. I know that Americans would be horrified by Hansie and Clara's three also got to toast Fiona. They had after all grown up with wine and wine making and had been introduced to it early and now all could do a good job of tasting and identifying different varietals.

"Fiona Anna Barclay, Fab," I mused. "Well, it's better than it could have been."

"What do you mean?" James asked.

"Well, it could have been Lab, Gab, Jab, you name it, at least Fab is reasonable," I commented.

"Sometimes I think you've got the weirdest mind," James laughed.

"Only sometimes?" Maman asked.

"Well, I've got a niece named after me, so I can't be that bad," I said.

"You're not," James assured me.

"Well, I'm for bed," Anna said. "I'll see you all at breakfast, then we can decide who bothers Charlize tomorrow."

"When does she come home?" I asked.

"Thursday," James said. "Apparently that's the normal time for post-delivery. I'll see you all in the morning."

I went to bed with an atlas and found New Mexico and then Pecos. It looked like it would be worth a visit, it was in the hills, mountains, and not too far off the main road to make travel difficult. I wondered what kind of wild animals they got there. I supposed deer of one type or another, perhaps coyotes, even bears and mountain lions. Well, I would see in a couple of weeks when I went off there to visit. I needed a visa to travel to the States, and wondered if that would be easier to get in Paris or London. I started nodding off to sleep with images of deer browsing away at grape vines, wondering if in fact they would eat them. I also wondered about my new niece, what would she be like, what kind of world would she grow up in, where would she grow up, would she like me, would I like her. I knew very little about the development of babies and children, how much weight did they gain a week, when did they start to crawl, when did they start to walk, what kinds of sounds did they make before learning to talk, so many questions, to which I was sure that there were studies and distribution charts that I could consult. It was hard to imagine James as a father. He had been a pest when we were growing up, as I am sure all sisters view their younger brothers. But as he had grown up he had become more tolerable and by the time he went to college, we actually got on fairly well. Charlize had changed him too, gone was the carefree James of before, now he was still fun, but a little more serious, and since working with Charlize to run the vineyard and winery he had become positively responsible.

Breakfast the next morning was ready when I dragged myself downstairs. Anna had been up early and had cooked up all kinds of things. I settled for a smallish breakfast and looked for coffee. Maman had made the coffee and brought me a cup.

"How are you today?" she asked.

"Fine," I said. "I'm happy for Charlize and James, happy that there were no problems with Fiona and that both are doing well. It's weird talking about Fiona, I'm so used to being one of the few Fionas that I know. Why was I called Fiona?"

"Your Dad and I both knew Fionas and we both liked the name, so you got stuck with it, it's originally Irish or Scottish and means fair, so Fiona the fair is a bit redundant," Maman explained.

"Who's going to see Charlie this morning?" I asked.

"James, naturally, and I'm going with Brigitte and Portia," Anna said.

"Then, this afternoon perhaps you can go with John?"

"Where's Hansie, Clara and the kids?" I asked.

"They're all out in the vineyard getting things ready for the harvest," Maman said. "No rest for that family, they'll have to work."

"Where's James?" I asked.

"He's talking to your Dad on the phone," Maman replied.

"How is James this morning?" I asked.

"Proud as they could be," Anna laughed. "That will be one spoilt little girl unless Charlie takes a firm hand."

"I talked to Dad," James announced as he joined us. "You're never going to believe this, he's set up a trust fund for Fiona, so that she'll have money at university and afterwards."

"That's very nice of him," Maman said. I could see a competition brewing there, if Dad could set money aside for Fiona, then so could Maman, the question I am sure she would have loved to ask, was how much?

"She's very lucky," John said.

"I'll say," James echoed. "Mom, you and Dad were always generous, but you made us work for a living."

"Of course," Maman said. "It made you independent."

"Where is Dad?" I asked.

"In California," James said. "That business he has there, where is it Torrance?"

"Torrance it is," I confirmed. It was also a business I had invested in. Dad had put up most of the money in the form of loans, but he had taken an equity position, and he had talked me into doing the same, so that I had ten per cent of the equity in the firm. It was one of five companies that I now had positions in, all about the ten per cent mark. The company in Torrance was unimaginatively named Torrance Aerospace, then there was the ceramics factory in Luxembourg, Luxasiette, the clothing company of Rachel Adams in Kensington, the furniture company, Krevati, in Loudwater, and the whisky distillery, Glen August, in Fort William. The only one I had yet to visit was Torrance, which might just be moot as the company was currently in the process of being sold, so perhaps I could combine the trip with John with a trip to California. I would have to talk to Dad about that. Dad and I expected an offer soon on the furniture factory, in fact, there were three interested parties. That was the whole point of taking an equity position, if and when the company was sold, then the equity holders should benefit, and in this case, it looked as if we would, multiplying our initial investment by a factor of twenty. I would be happy about that and was pondering what to do with this largesse when it came, perhaps the wine business would be an opportunity.

"Are we ready?" Anna asked of James, Maman and Portia. She received affirmatives all around, so they left, leaving John and me to man the fort. The tasting room was still open and it was possible that we would have casual drop-in customers. There were two full-time employees who normally worked in the tasting room, but one had called in with a cold.

James had taken the call earlier and told me that she really did sound horrible.

John and I were busy that morning. I had thought that there might be one or two casual visitors, but it was a fairly constant stream. There were always four to six people in the tasting room and we were kept busy. Most of the visitors were English or American, but there were a few local French people, well perhaps not local as they came from the far-flung parts of France. We did sell quite a bit of wine, some taking away a bottle or two, but quite a few taking cases. We were relieved at lunchtime when the afternoon crew came in. Anna and the others came back from the hospital, they had been shooed away by the nurses, who probably just wanted to do all the things that needed to be done, like changing bed linens, cleaning, checking on the condition of the patients.
"Well, Charlie just wants to come home," James said when they arrived.
"I'm not surprised," John said. "Probably too much regimentation at the hospital. Here at least she can come and go as she pleases."
"They're both okay?" I asked.
"Fiona is thriving and Charlie is doing well," Anna said. "They can come home the day after tomorrow. So, how was your morning?"
"Busy," I replied. "I was surprised by the number of people stopping at the tasting room."
"That's because we got a good review in one of the snob wine journals," James said. "Our wines got good marks and the tasting room itself was made out to be some sort of fairy tale castle."
"Well, that's good for business, isn't it?" I asked.
"It is," James agreed. "We brought lunch with us from town, so dig in, then I need to go out and actually work."

After lunch, John and I drove into Le Charité and visited with Charlize and the baby. We were limited in time, apparently afternoon visiting hours were more tightly controlled than the morning hours.
"How are you, Charlie?" I asked.
"I'm fine," she replied. "I'm a bit tired and Fiona wants to feed every two hours, so sleep is a challenge. I'll be better off at home, less distractions, less people milling around."
"Maman told me that it was quick," I commented.

"So everyone tells me," Charlize said. "But, I've seen workers in the vineyards at home give birth and then go back to work only a few hours later."

"Did you want a boy or a girl?" I asked.

"It didn't matter to us," she said. "All I wanted to be sure of was that all the fingers and toes were there and that everything was normal."

"Why Fiona?" I asked.

"Because of you," Charlize said. "You've been an inspiration to me and, no matter what James might tell you, he loves you a lot."

"Well, thank you," I said. "I'll try and be a good auntie."

"I'd rather you were an Auntie Mame," Charlize laughed.

"I could teach her to fly," I thought. "I wonder how old she'd have to be to reach the rudder pedals?"

"Not too soon," Charlize pleaded. "If you teach her to fly, then she'll want her own plane, and she can't even sit up on her own yet. So, Dad, Ma tells me that you've recruited Fi to go with you to Pecos?"

"*Ja*," he said. "She can run through the numbers with me and also take a look around the place. James should stay here with you and it's a bit too soon for you to be flying off to the States."

"Well, you know what to look for Fi," Charlize said. We chatted for a little longer then the nurses showed up and visitors were shooed away. We said our goodbyes and drove back to the château.

"When Charlie and James go to Pecos, there's no château there," John laughed.

"Is there a house on the property?" I asked.

"A log cabin," John said. "It's nice enough, but a little different to the château, they'll have to decide if they want to live there or somewhere else."

"Where's the other vineyard you bought?" I asked.

"It's near Aix-en-Provence," John replied. "There's about 300 hectares all planted, so it's a pretty big operation. Your Dad put together a financing package that let us do it."

"Let me take a look at that," I said. "Dad's packages tend to favour Dad, so read the fine print very carefully."

"We did that," John laughed. "And there was quite a bit of back and forth before we both finally agreed."

"Is there still the chance of taking an equity position in the Pecos winery?" I asked.

"I'm sure that can be arranged," John said. "If you take some, then it will make things easier for us."

"How did you get your money out of South Africa?" I asked.

"That was the biggest challenge," John admitted. "It helped that the buyer is a US company, so they were prepared to pay us outside the country, we just needed to finalise all the details."

"What's the yield like on the Aix-en-Provence property?" I asked.

"About 50 hectolitres per hectare," he said.

"So, about 555 cases," I commented.

"About," he agreed. "The total yield on the property is about 167,000 cases a year."

"What about New Mexico?" I asked.

"Not so big," John said. "Yields about 500 gallons per acre, or about 210 cases per acre, so a total of just over 10,500 cases, if you go back in history to the 1880s, they reported yields of up to 350 US gallons per acre in the New Mexico vineyards, but there were also reports of up to 1,500 US gallons per acre."

"That seems a lot," I said.

"Does, doesn't it," he said. "The economics work at 500 gallons per acre, but if we were able to improve yields even a little, things get a lot better. Planting more would also be good, the stripping, straining and pressing equipment can handle an expansion of another 50 acres, then we'd have to start adding equipment. For settling and fermentation and maturation we'd have to add tanks, but the assemblage and packaging lines could handle things. Adding another 50 acres beyond that means more of just about everything, including buildings to house the extra tanks. But all that is in the future."

"Why ask Charlize and James to go to New Mexico, why not Frikkie or Hansie?" I asked.

"Hansie and Frikkie are both good at managing existing operations," John explained. "But for something new, or to start up a new operation, Charlie is the one, she has always been more adventurous and more capable of adapting to new circumstances."

"But isn't it a bit of a step back for her to go to a smaller vineyard?" I asked.

"Not as I see it," John said. "Yes, Pecos is small, but we're looking to invest in New Mexico and she's the best of us to do that. She'll be able to manage the Pecos property and look for something else, and if we buy bare ground, she's the one to supervise preparation and planting and construction of facilities."

"Are you happy with your new granddaughter?" I asked.

"*Ag man, she's just lekker,*" he said, grinning from ear to ear.

"So, this is seven now?" I asked.

"*Ja,* seven," he confirmed. "Johannes, Daniel, Anna, Emily, Piet and Koos, now Fiona, but this is the first in your family?"

"It is," I confirmed. "We're thin on the ground as far as family goes, Dad was an only child and Maman had a sister, but she was killed in the War, so there's only James and I. There are some cousins of Dad and Maman, but we're not in any kind of close contact."

"So, not many Barclays out there?" John asked.

"Not in our family at least," I confirmed.

"I was sorry to hear about your man," John said. "I liked Ian, he was a typical Rhodie, but smart too. I would have enjoyed a bush trip with him, he was a really jacked up *ou.*"

"I miss him," I said. "I'm dealing with it, but there are times when I want to just show him something or tell him something."

"*Ja,*" John said. "My brother Piet was close to me and he was killed in Italy in the War and it was different when he didn't come back."

"I'm sorry to hear that," I said.

"Well, there's one new Barclay here now, and life does go on," John said.

"It does," I agreed. "I know I'm supposed to say how beautiful she is, but do all babies look like that?"

"They do," John said, roaring with laughter. "I can just see you echoing all the coos about how beautiful she is, but thinking my puppy was much cuter and what is that wizened-looking thing?"

"What about yours?" I asked.

"Hansie was not bad, Frikkie and Charlie were *lelik* looking things, but they turned out not so bad, hey?" he replied.

"True, if *lelik* is what I think it means," I said. I seemed to recall Ian using the expression once or twice when he was talking about things one would hardly describe as pretty or beautiful.

We arrived back at the château with John still chuckling about my lack of enthusiasm for babies in general.

"What's so funny?" Anna asked.

"Just something Fiona said," he replied.

"Well, are you going to tell us, or are we to be left in the dark?" she pressed.

"It was just something about babies," he parried.

"I suppose she doesn't think they're that pretty," Maman interposed.

"You said it, not me," he said, throwing his hands up in surrender.

"Fiona was never one to be diplomatic," Maman laughed. "I shudder to think how many diplomatic incidents she caused when she was in Nairobi."

"Maman," I protested. "I was really good, I never caused offence or even raised eyebrows."

"Charlie was *lelik* when she was born," Anna said in my defence. "But she turned out to be really beautiful."

"She did indeed," I said. That is something I could not argue with.

"You were no picture," Maman said to me. "But to me, you were just beautiful, I had carried you around for nine months, so when you decided to join the world I was delighted and it wouldn't have mattered what you looked like, you would have been beautiful to me."

"Even warthog mothers probably think their piglets are beautiful," Portia laughed.

"So, now I'm a warthog?" I asked.

"Sometimes," James said when he came into the room. "How's Charlie and the baby?"

"Just fine," John assured him. "She's expecting you after dinner."

While we waited for Charlize and Fiona to come home, I took the opportunity to fly to Cannes to go to Maman's villa and collect the rest of my luggage. It was time to get back to work and re-enter the human race. My mourning period was essentially over, but I knew that there would still be occasions when I would be reminded of Ian, and that those times might be sad. I swear it took longer for the taxi to go from the airport at Cannes to Maman's villa than it took me to fly from Cosne to Cannes, well, perhaps that is a bit of an exaggeration, but the flight only took just over two hours. I had packed all my bags before leaving to collect the plane at Reims, so all I had to do was load them into the taxi and return to the airport. I was back just after lunch and found John waiting for me. He had been detailed to come and pick me up and, fortunately, had not been waiting long when I landed. He helped me unload the plane, then I tied it down and we went back to the Château. I gave Maman the mail that had been sitting at her villa, for which I got little thanks as most of it was bills. James did make some snide remarks about the amount of luggage that I had, but I had been at Maman's villa for a couple of months, so had needed a few clothes.

Charlize came home with Fiona on the Thursday as promised. She and James had already set up a bedroom as a nursery with easy access to their own room. I spent time with her as she fed Fiona, burped her then changed her nappy.

"Phew," I said, the first time the nappy came off. "Does it always smell like that?"

"It's the milk," Charlize replied. "Think about it, no solid food, just a high protein, high-fat food, if you ate just a diet of milk, you'd also be pooping through the eye of a needle."

"I suppose," I agreed. "Well, I suppose if you can stand it, so can I. How do you change the nappies?" Charlize showed me how to clean Fiona, then dress her in a clean nappy and where to pin it in place. There was a technique to it.

"How did you get so good at this?" I asked.

"All those nephews and nieces, I learned how to do it," she explained.

"You don't use disposables?" I asked.

"I think if we were travelling I would," Charlize replied. "But we can launder the nappies here and not just throw the disposables into the rubbish to sit for a thousand years."

"Happy?" I asked her.

"Very," she said. "Fiona is lovely and I'm thrilled and James is on the moon, I'm going to have to watch him or he'll spoil Fiona terribly."

"I can see that," I said. "You know that Dad set up a trust fund for Fiona?"

"I know," she said. "I can't believe it, he put two million, pounds not francs, into a fund that she can access when she's twenty-five, but not before. Hopefully, by then she'll have some judgement and common sense and not go through life as a wastrel."

"I'm sure you and James will bring her up better than that," I said.

17

"When are you and Pops going to Pecos?" she asked.

"I think he said in a couple of weeks," I replied. "I need to get a visa for the States and see who's going to book the travel, your Dad or me."

"He'll do it," Charlize said. "It's company business and he's taking you as a consultant, using the agreement we already have with you."

"I need to tell him that I may also go to Los Angeles," I said. "I'm going to talk to Dad about visiting Torrance Aerospace."

"I'm looking forward to getting back to work," Charlize said. "I haven't been able to do much this past month except numbers and office stuff. I need some help with that Macintosh you gave me, I have some ideas about some programs I want."

"I'm sure I can do that for you," I promised. "Don't do too much too quickly, let James do it."

"He can help Hansie the vineyard stuff," she said. "But he's not that well versed in the models you did for us, it's something I should take the time to make sure he understands."

"What do you think about moving to the States?" I asked.

"It will be exciting," she said. "A new challenge."

"You wouldn't rather move to Aix-en-Provence?" I asked.

"Maybe," she said. "But, that's already planted out to the maximum, in New Mexico I can plant more and look for either more land or a going concern that we can buy."

"Have you been to Pecos?" I asked.

"I have," she said. "I went with Pops about three months ago, just after we came to Nairobi for the funeral."

"What's it like there?" I asked.

"Small town, in the middle of a national forest, lot of Spanish spoken, there's a monastery near there, they get snow in the winter, more than here, it's not that far from ski areas, so we can ski there," she said.

"How do you get there?" I asked.

"Fly to Chicago then either Denver or Albuquerque," she said. "Denver means a longer drive, but there's better air service, Albuquerque is closer, but less air service. What I saw of Albuquerque I liked. The closest larger town than Pecos is Santa Fe, bit more arty than Pecos, old town, but nice."

"How far from Denver?" I asked.

"About five and a half hours," she said.

"And Albuquerque?" I asked.

"About an hour and a half," she said. "The drive from Denver is pretty through the mountains from Trinidad to Raton and the one from Albuquerque is pretty from Santa Fe."

"Trinidad?" I asked.

"Don't ask me," she laughed. "I wondered when I saw the sign."

"Well, I should let you put Fiona down and get some rest yourself," I said.

I left Charlize to her nap and joined the rest of the family. Actually, we were thinning out, Maman and Portia were planning to leave and go back to the Mediterranean and I needed to go to London to get a visa. I asked Anna how the others were adapting to the changes since they moved from South Africa to France.

"The children quicker than their parents," she said. "They all took lessons in French before we came, and I would say that Anna and Emily speak better French than the boys, but the boys are more prepared to just give it a go, even if they're not exactly sure what to say."

"And you?" I asked.

"I took French in school, but only remember a little, but I have been taking classes with John, I'm learning," she said.

"Are you happy you moved here from South Africa?" I asked.

"For the most part," she said. "I was sad to leave, but, the children will have a more secure future here. Things are heating up in South Africa, and there will be change, the white government is on borrowed time and when the change comes, I'm not sure how well it will be managed."

"Will you live here or in Provence?" I asked.

"I think Provence," she said. "The winters can be dreary here. I should get something on for dinner, Hansie's tribe will be here soon and we'll do better if they're fed and watered."

Maman and Portia left for the Mediterranean and that left me with the new Barclay family. Fiona was demanding, but I suppose that is true of newborns, they need feeding and caring for around the clock. As long as Charlize was breastfeeding the demands on her would go on. At least when solid food was introduced she would get some time to herself, but for the moment it was two-hour intervals between feeds. I helped Charlize with the computer programs that she wanted and wrote a few more for her to manage inventory as well as the planting aspects of the winery. We also spent some time with John, Hansie and Frikkie, going over the computer models and programs that I had written. I did get to sit in on a meeting of the partners as they talked about the business structure. They were kind to me, I think under normal circumstances it would have been conducted in Afrikaans, but for my benefit, they all spoke English. The partners were John, Hansie, Frikkie and Charlize and they had decided to create a holding company in Luxembourg and then create subsidiary companies in the Loire Valley, Provence and Pecos. I had researched this for them and showed them the tax benefits of this structure. Luxembourg was one of those little advertised havens for, as it was known in the financial world, tax efficiency. In more basic terms that meant paying the least amount of tax possible. It was interesting in that none of the spouses were partners, just the patriarch and the children.

I took my leave of the Barclays and flew to London, to Biggin Hill where I planned to keep my plane. I had made arrangements with them already so they were expecting me. I had to check in with a customs and immigration officer there, but again, I had given notice that I was arriving and he was waiting for me and stamped my passport and quickly glanced over my mountain of luggage, more interested in whether or not I had cases of wine with me than whatever might be in the bags. I used to have two passports, a regular one and a diplomatic one. Ian had been a member of the legation in Nairobi and when we travelled on official business I used my diplomatic passport, but after Ian's death I had had to surrender that passport as I no longer had any claim to it, using the diplomatic passport had been nice while I had it, not the least for which was that the immigration line in most countries was usually shorter. Now, without it, I would be just an ordinary mortal again, not entitled to any privilege.

My flight over from Cosne-sur-Loire to Biggin Hill had been short enough, just over two hours, half an hour of which was crossing the Channel, from Dieppe to Hastings. At Biggin Hill I had booked and paid for hangar space, so found a nice man with a tug who towed my plane to the hangar and we parked it. I shut everything off and locked up the plane. I had used a limousine service quite a few times to travel in and out of London, so had called them to have a car waiting for me. The driver had seen me land, I had provided them with the tail number of my plane, so they knew what to look for. I had just finished closing up my when the car pulled up outside the hangar.

"Dr Barclay?" the driver asked. It was a young lady, resplendent in a grey uniform with a peaked cap.

"The same," I said. I had decided to go back to being Fiona Barclay, I did not want to forget that I was until recently Fiona Hartley, but it seemed to me that if I was going to start my life again, I needed to stop reminding myself of what I had lost.

"I'm Tiffany, your driver," she said. "May I take your bags?"

"Thanks," I said. There was actually quite a bit of luggage as I had finally decamped from France to return to my own flat in London. Tiffany had a Range Rover, Tuscan blue, and she loaded all my luggage into the back. One of the odd things about the Range Rover is that it only had two doors, so, the easiest thing to do was sit in the front, rather than in the back like Lady Muck. Tiffany, judging by her accent was Scottish, I would guess about five feet eight, slim build, jet black hair, worn pulled back in a ponytail. She had on a short skirt which showed off a pair of legs that most women would have envied. It was difficult not to stare.

"To Cadogan Place?" Tiffany asked.

"Yes, please," I said.

"A good flight?" she asked.

"I landed in one piece, so yes a good flight," I joked. "But it was nice coming over from France, the weather was good, skies clear, so a nice view of the coast as I came in."

"Is it your plane?" she asked.

"It is," I confirmed. "It's very convenient for flitting between here and France."

"You have business there?" she asked.

"I do," I said. "But it's time to come back and get back to work here. And you, have you been driving long?"

"Just over three years," she said.

"Do you enjoy the job?" I asked.

"I do," she said. "I get to meet interesting people and sometimes I get to drive people quite a long way out of London, so that makes a change from fighting London traffic. Have you been a pilot long?"

"Same as you, about three years," I said.

"Is it hard to learn to fly?" she asked.

21

"No," I said. "Flying is easy, the hard bits are landing and knowing what to do if something goes wrong."

"That must be very scary," she said.

"My instructor took great delight in switching things off and making me work out what had happened and how to recover," I said.

"Can you fix the plane yourself?" she asked.

"I learned to fly in Kenya, so had to be self-sufficient, there aren't always airports around when you might need one," I said.

"Kenya, that must have been nice," she said. "My partner and I were thinking of doing a safari there next year, but maybe that will have to wait."

"You should go," I told her. "It'll be an experience you won't forget."

"Did you go on safari while you were there?" she asked.

"Quite a few times," I said. "Each trip was different and each one was exciting." We chatted back and forth for the journey, which was nice, because it made it go quickly.

"Well, not long now," Tiffany said as we crossed Chelsea Bridge. She was right, from the bridge to Cadogan Place was not that far and we were there in about ten minutes.

"Let me help you with your luggage," she offered.

"Thank you," I said. "There's a few stairs, so quite a bit of lugging up to do." Between us, we hauled all my luggage up the stairs and Tiffany stood by until I had the door open. When she said goodbye, I did give her a reasonable tip. She had been pleasant to talk to, and had helped me with my luggage. I know that was her job, but she had done it with grace and charm. My flat was a little musty, it needed airing after standing closed for a few months. I threw open the windows and decided that unpacking could wait. There was some mail by the door, but most of my mail would have gone to the service that I used to take messages for me and receive the mail. They had been forwarding all that to France and I had taken care of most of it. I looked around the flat and there were boxes there that had arrived from Nairobi, all the treasures that I had had shipped back. They could also wait. There was a notice from the Rover people that my Land Rover had been collected from the docks and was sitting in their workshop waiting to be collected by me. I had decided to bring my Land Rover back from Kenya, rather than buy a new one, so had arranged for it to be shipped back. I had a garage ready for it in a mews close to my flat, so should at some time collect it.

I was on my own. When Ian had died, Maman and Portia had come out to Nairobi, then they had stayed with me for a while in London while I finished the various projects I had had going at the time, then I had gone and stayed with them in France, now I was back and it was just me. Living alone again was going to take some adjustment. I had lived in my flat alone before Ian had moved in with me. Then, shortly after that we had got married and moved to Nairobi, now Ian was gone and I was back to living alone again. On the plus side, since Thatcher and the Conservatives had won the General Election in May, things were really looking up on the income tax front, so the monies I now made would not be taxed at the iniquitous rates that Callaghan had imposed.

Pecos

For the next two weeks, I was busy. I answered correspondence, I collected my Land Rover and garaged it, I had meetings and agreed to three new projects, I worked long hours and had to discipline myself to break for meals. If I did not eat I was not going to be able to do anything, so my local bistro got a lot of business. I went to the American Embassy in Grosvenor Square and got a visa, a business and visitor's visa, good for six months and allowing multiple entries. I talked to Dad about going to Torrance and it seemed that it was just not the right time, the sale was far advanced and the whole idea of a visit was rather pointless. He had been busy with the sale of Krevati and that sale had closed very quickly. That had netted me £200,000, even after the tax people had taken their pound of flesh. Given that the country was plunging into a massive recession, it amazed me that anyone would pay that much for a business. Perhaps they had a better crystal ball than I did, or they just really wanted the business and were prepared to pay, setting themselves up for a much higher market share when the economy turned around. The £200,000 together with what I had already saved and made on the stock exchange would put me close to my first million, imagine that, a million pounds, even though Callaghan was doing his best to make sure that people like me did not succeed. I could see why Grandpa Barclay and Dad had amassed so much money, by judicious investing they had managed to create small fortunes. The return from the Krevati business was very good for me, I had only put in £10,000, so was delighted with the expected return. I offered up some £25,000 for an equity position in the winery in Pecos, but there looked for dividends rather than an expected upside from a quick sale. John formed a company in the state of Nevada, Cillie Wines US, and my £25,000 got me 2.5% of that company. That was the vehicle that John was going to use to make the Pecos acquisition and potentially more. I had unpacked all my boxes from Kenya and now had mementoes around the flat. I had also taken a life drawing I had of Ian, done by an artist we had met on Colonsay, and framed it and hung it in my bedroom. I had considered the living room, but even I got visitors on occasion and they might not appreciate the art. I also framed Ian's doctoral certificate and decided that I would also do mine, so had all three framed and hung them as well.

John called me with the details of our trip to Pecos. We would fly BA to Chicago, then Continental to Albuquerque, stay the night there, then drive up the next day to Pecos. On our return, we would drive north to Denver, stay the night there, then fly to Chicago on Continental and pick up the BA flight there back to London. The arrangements seemed fine to me, but then there was the big question, what to wear. It was now September and the weather was still quite warm in the daytime, but beginning to cool down a little overnight. Something told me that jeans and a jacket were probably going to be more use at the vineyard than skirts and blouses, so I packed accordingly. For the journey itself, that was still the days when people dressed up a little for flying, so searched through my wardrobe for something comfortable, but also elegant. I went with a tailored suit, trousers and jacket in dark grey, with a tyrian blouse, grey shoes with a small heel, and matching grey handbag. I kept the jewellery to a minimum, just some simple gold studs in my ears. John assured me that it would not rain in Pecos in September, but in case it did, I did throw in a foldable umbrella. In case it got cool overnight I added a pullover to the pile. I did decide to take my briefcase, I had in it facts and figures that John had given me about the winery and expected to add more, and I had some work for one of my other projects.

The day of our flight to Chicago I had the chauffeur service collect me from my flat and was delighted to see that it was Tiffany again.
"Off again, Dr Barclay, where to this time?" she asked.
"New Mexico," I replied.
"That's in the States, isn't it?" she asked.
"It is," I confirmed. "One of the western states, between Colorado and Mexico."
"Colorado, that's skiing isn't it?" she asked.
"Yes, pretty good I've heard, this is my first trip to the States, so it will be interesting," I said.
"Which airline?" she asked.
"BA, please," I said.
"So, Terminal 3," she said. "We'll get you there in no time." She did indeed get us there in record time, she weaved in and out of the traffic in

London, then once out onto the Chiswick Flyover then the M4, she sped along, showing me what the Range Rover could do. I was impressed by her driving skills and again could not help but look at her, but as I did I was uneasy, what was it that I was feeling. At Terminal 3, I checked in and was told that my seat had been assigned for me. I assumed that meant that John had already checked in and reserved the seat for me. He was to meet me in the departures hall, as he had flown over from Paris and was in transit. Through immigration, I scanned the crowd and wondered how I would find John in the multitude. He found me, he had been waiting by the way in to the departures hall and had seen me.

"Fiona," he said. "How's things?"

"Good," I replied. "And you, Charlie, Fiona, is everyone well?"

"All fine," he reported. "Fiona's gaining weight madly."

"How's Anna?" I asked.

"Proud as only an *ouma* can be," he laughed.

"And you?" I teased.

"*Ag*, man, she's just a delight, I'm looking forward to when she can walk and talk, then we can do more together," he said.

"And James, how's James?" I asked.

"Busy," John said. "It's harvest time, so he's out in the vineyard every day, with Hansie picking, they've got helpers, and they're pretty good, but they both like to keep an eye on things. Frikkie is also picking in Aix-en-Provence and that's going well."

"Where's Gate 28?" I asked.

"Just down there on the right," he said. "I've been here just over an hour, so took a look around."

"With all the strikes going on, I'm surprised that BA's actually flying," I commented.

"We must have picked a good day," he said. "Shall we go to the gate?"

At the gate, an officious agent examined our boarding passes and allowed us to pass and board. She was probably one who felt that BA was not paying enough, so take it out of the customers, the ones that pay the bills, and her salary, no matter how small she felt it was. On board it was a little better, at least they smiled. John had got us seats on the left-hand side of the plane, row three, A and B. John wanted the window, so I took the aisle. We took off and headed north over Scotland. We were served lunch, which I have to say was actually a better service than I had been used to on my trips back and forth to Nairobi. Perhaps because the Chicago route had more competition, and it was also flown by the big Trans World Airlines as well.

After lunch, I settled down to some thinking and pulled out the materials for one of my projects and started to jot down ideas. I became aware of someone hovering at my shoulder and looked up to see a man standing there looking at my papers.

"That's some pretty serious maths," he said. "Excuse me for looking, but I've never seen anyone actually do that before, what it's for?"

"It's a distancing model," I explained, wondering as I said it if it would also apply to people on planes intruding on another's space and thoughts.

"What does a distancing model do?" he asked.

"It predicts the fall in business for retail companies based on how far the customers live from the shop," I explained. "It's used to plan where to place new shops."

"Oh," he said. "Would it work for sand and gravel?"

"It, or a modification of it would," I said.

"Are you staying in Chicago or going on?" he asked.

"Going on," I said. At this point, John woke up and was looking at the man with great interest, probably with not the best intentions.

"Oh," the man said. "Well, if you get time in Chicago, here's my card, I'd love to talk to you about models for the economics of sand and gravel and aggregate production. I'm Richard Berg, by the way." I looked over the card and it said, Richard Berg, CEO, Dundee Materials, with an address and telephone number in Chicago.

"As a rule of thumb, the economics of sand and gravel operations tend to not work beyond about thirty miles," I said.

"How did you know that?" Richard asked.

"She knows a lot," John interjected.

"Seems like it," Richard said. "Say, I didn't get your name?"

"Fiona Barclay," I said, proffering my card.

"Wow, Dr Barclay, are you with some university?" Richard asked.

"No, I consult for clients," I said.

"Doctor of what?" Richard asked.

"Economics," I said, picking one of my three.

"Is he bothering you?" a woman said as she came up to join him.

"No, it's fine," I said.

"This young lady is an economist and does models for businesses," Richard explained, showing her my card.

"Oh, and I suppose you're trying to hire her?" she asked.

"No, well, maybe," he said. "But, you know it would help us to decide what to do about improving the bottom line and where and when to open up new operations."

"Let me explain," the woman said. "I'm Barbara by the way, Richard is the CEO of Dundee and its materials business stretches across the northern tier states with pre-mix concrete plants, quarries and gravel pits all over and we're looking to improve what we do and where."

"I've not looked at construction materials before," I said. "The only work I've done in the mining business is asset valuations for ore reserves."

"Are you staying in Chicago?" Barbara asked.

"No," I said. "We get off this plane and onto another."

"Well, if you've time, call us," she said. "We've got some decisions to make. Now, Richard, we should leave Dr Barclay and stop bothering her."

"Well?" John said. "What do you think?"

"I think look up Dundee Materials and see if they're any size and worth talking to," I said. "How soon can Charlie and James move to Pecos?"

"Anna insists that they let Fiona get a little bigger first," he said. "So, I'd say three months at the least."

"Isn't this rather a lot to be taking on at once?" I asked. "The new winery in Provence and this one in Pecos?"

"Possibly," he agreed. "But the Loire is well under control and Hansie can manage that well enough, Frikkie had told me that the Aix property has no issues and he's well into picking, the only one that has some issues is Pecos."

"Why?" I asked.

"You'll see when we get there," John said. "Dale wants out quickly."

"Why is there something wrong with the winery?" I asked.

"No, it's his other interests that are the issue," John explained. "He's got a ski resort in Utah and he's been funnelling cash from the winery to build the ski resort and the ski season opens in a month or two, so he wants to be there."

"So, what are you going to do?" I asked.

"As I told you, we're going to close the deal, say goodbye to Dale, then, I'm going to run it until Charlie and James move," he said.

"Oh," was all I could say. I thought about that for a bit. John could obviously run the Pecos winery, he had run their South African wineries on his own until his children had grown, so the small operation in Pecos should be simple enough for him.

"Where are we?" I asked.

"Somewhere over Canada," John said. "We've passed Greenland and are coming down over Canada, should start down in an hour or so." John was prophetic as I heard the engines throttle back and we started our descent into Chicago. We joined the landing pattern and went out towards the west, it seemed to me that we were going halfway to California, but eventually, we did turn and go back into land. On the ground, we said goodbye to the crew and walked down the steps and across the tarmac to the international arrivals. I would have thought that an important airport like Chicago would have had something more impressive for foreign arrivals. Perhaps in time, they would actually build a new terminal just for that. Immigration and customs were fairly quick then we found a transfer desk for Continental and dropped our suitcases with them, then went looking for the gate to take us to Albuquerque. John did the smart thing, to me unusual in a man in that he actually asked someone. We were told terminal 2 concourse D. So, off we went. We found the gate and had about an hour or so to wait, so we waited and people watched and speculated on the occupations and journeys of all those who passed us by. We saw the crew arrive and board, all dressed in quite smart tan and maroon suits. When we boarded the plane was smaller than I had expected, it was a Boeing 727, nice enough, but not the wide comfort that the larger jumbo jets offered. I wanted to see America, so persuaded John that I should sit by the window. The crew were very nice, compared to the BA crew, they were positively friendly. I think they were speculating on the relationship between John and myself and I think I had been cast as a second wife, those that are commonly known as trophy wives, much younger than the husband and good to look at, but little else. Perhaps that is judgemental and a simplification, but I had seen it myself in Kenya when our paths crossed those of some of the tourists. The service on the Continental flight was excellent, small plane or not, they did really well with what they had.

Our flight took us out over Illinois, Iowa and Kansas, it seemed to me to be a never-ending series of farmlands, it was so different to flying from London to Nairobi where one would cross desert and dry lands. I was intrigued by circles on the ground, then realised that I was looking at irrigation circles. Eventually, the farms became more intermittent and then some hills and mountains appeared, just about the time that the pilot said that we were beginning our descent into the Albuquerque airport. I could see from the window a motorway, or as John reminded me, a freeway. My review of a map before told me that this was the I-25 that ran from Albuquerque to Denver. It was also the route we would take to get to Pecos. We did our twists and turns to get into Albuquerque and my first impression was that the airfield itself was huge, but that the airport terminal was actually quite small. John pointed out that the airport shared the field with an air force base, which perhaps accounted for the sheer size of it. We thanked the crew, deplaned, and then went looking for our bags. They had made it, which was gratifying, I had not wanted to go traipsing around a vineyard in a tailored suit and heels. We had a rental car reserved, actually, a Chevrolet Blazer, which struck me as something akin to a tank. Compared to my Land Rover, it was big, but I suppose easy enough to drive, being an automatic. We stayed the night at a hotel close to the airport and I consulted the map to see where we would go the next morning. John had been before and was one of those people who having been once would always to able to get there again, without the use of a map. He did bring out one gadget that he had brought with him, a radar detector, or Fuzz Buster as they were known. The speed limit was 55 and it quickly struck me that that would become tedious, to say the least on the huge distances in the States.

The next day I dressed in jeans and a denim shirt and put on work boots, that seemed more appropriate for Albuquerque and would be much better for touring a vineyard. We paid our bill and checked out of the hotel and started on our drive north which took us through the centre of Albuquerque and then we passed a sign that said we were entering a reservation. John explained that there were several Indian Reservations close to Albuquerque and that we would go in and out of them, which we did, I think I counted four different ones. The area was much dryer, more uniformly brown, much more like Kenya than the farmlands we had flown over. The road then started to go up hills, then down hills, then up again, until we came to the outskirts of Santa Fe. Past Santa Fe, the scenery took on a much more pleasant aspect, there were hills and trees, lots and lots of trees, all conifers of one type or another. At a place called Glorieta, John left the freeway and took another road that led to Pecos. We entered Pecos and drove to the winery. The owner, Dale Black, was waiting for us and after I was introduced, suggested that we take a tour.

We walked the vineyard itself, then the processing facilities all the way from stripping and pressing to ageing and bottling. It was not the winery that Charlize currently ran, but it looked in good condition and the numbers were good enough, except for debt service. I saw what John had been talking about, Dale had been using the winery to fund his ski resort and had overburdened the winery with debt. The sale price of the winery was essentially the debt. When I looked at the numbers, the debts amounted to what I would have valued the winery at in terms of land, other assets, intangibles and goodwill, so it did make sense. It would not have been viable if the price had been based on the assets of the winery and assumption of the debt, that would have been untenable. The total price was $800,000, well over ten times earnings before taxes, but that was because there was a lot of debt service, the interest on which was considerable. The $800,000 was for an asset sale which was made up of $475,000 in equipment and buildings, $137,500 in inventory and $180,000 in land value, and $7,500 in cash, goodwill and such were just thrown in and not allocated values. John seemed happy with the numbers and we took a private minute to confer and I told him that I agreed with him. John and Dale shook hands on the deal and the actual close was set two days later at the offices of Bank of the West in Albuquerque. That gave us a day free to contemplate the transaction, explore the area or do nothing.

We took another tour of the place, this time with an inventory list and I quickly ticked off all that we saw. It was all there, picking bins, stemmers, crushers, presses, pumps, fermentation tanks, storage tanks, barrels, and a bottling line. We also looked at the cellar and checked off the number of barrels ageing and the bottled wine awaiting shipment. Again, it was all there. Dale invited us to the tasting room, which was a small building near the gate to the property and which, in my opinion, could stand some dressing up. I wondered how much traffic there was in the tasting room. Pecos was a little off the beaten track and New Mexico itself was not the most populous state, so to get traffic some advertising would be necessary. Charlize would manage that, it was one of her many skills. We also met with the staff that Dale had, the winemaker, the cellarman and the office manager. John had met them before and they were all staying on, relieved I think that the company was going to be in new hands, and hands that not only had wine-making experience, but was solvent. We took our leave of Dale and journeyed back to Santa Fe to the hotel where John had made us a booking.

The La Fonda was an interesting-looking building, I suppose one would call it southwest style. It was a sprawling hotel rather than a tall one, but it was nice and centrally located. I rather liked Santa Fe, it had a charm about it and I thought that I would take a walk about the town centre, John gave me a map and suggested dinner at seven. I took my walk and found a shop that I liked and bought myself a pair of western boots, a suede jacket and suede shoulder bag to match and a black broad-brimmed hat, a hat with a flat brim, not curved up at the sides like a Stetson. My boots had more of a square toe than the classic cowboy boots, but they suited me and I liked them, which I suppose was the main thing. The next big question, should my jeans be tucked into the boots, or worn outside. I had seen examples of both, so decided for the moment to just wear the jeans over the boots.

The next day, we had the day to kill. All was set for the close and John was eager to get the keys, and to carry on with the picking and pressing, but that would not start until after the close, so we had to wait.
"Like the boots," he said, when I joined him for breakfast.
"Nice aren't they," I agreed.

"What shall we do today?" he asked as we ate breakfast.

"Could we take a drive and explore a little?" I asked.

"*Ja*," he said. "I've done some driving around, but there's a lot of the state yet to see. We've seen the Rio Grande at Albuquerque, we saw the Pecos yesterday, why don't we go and find the Canadian?"

"Is it a bigger river than the Pecos?" I asked.

"No idea," he admitted. "We should go and take a look."

"Okay," I agreed. "Do you have a map?"

"*Ja*," he said. He spread out a map on the table and pointed to it. "We're here in Santa Fe, we drive east to Las Vegas then north to this place, Wagon Mound, we leave the freeway there and head towards this place, Roy. We'll cross the Canadian on the way there. Then we'll drive down towards this place, Mosquero, with any luck we'll find something there for lunch, then we find this place, Trementina and cross the river again, then back to Las Vegas and back here, how does that sound?"

"Like an adventure into the wilds of New Mexico," I said. "Looking at the map, it's not the most densely populated part of the state. I suppose there are petrol stations along the way?"

"I know there's a couple at Wagon Mound, because I've stopped there before," he said. "We'll take some food and water anyway, in case there's nothing on the way."

I joined John in the lobby of the hotel, dressed and ready for our expedition. I had on jeans, a burgundy shirt and the suede jacket I had just bought, and my new boots. I finished it off with my new hat and my aviator sunglasses. I think I looked very fashionable, but I am not sure if anyone else would have agreed, but it suited me. We did a little shopping for food and drink, then set out on our adventure. The drive from Santa Fe to Las Vegas was delightful. The road wound its way through hills and forests until we reached Las Vegas, then the scenery became more plains-like, with only scattered trees and much more grassland. John used his Fuzz Buster and we sped along, somewhat secure in the knowledge that we would get some warning of police radar. We were passed a few times by other cars, who clearly had somewhere to be in a hurry and we saw none of them pulled over by the police, so perhaps the police were busy elsewhere. I imagined that this part of New Mexico could be bleak in the winter, there was little to stop the wind that I was sure would blow. We did see antelope near the road. John had seen them before and identified them as pronghorn antelope and he informed me that they could run very fast and had been known to race cars on the smaller roads. Wagon Mound, when we came to it, was just a small village with the requisite petrol stations and a school. We filled up and then set off to find Roy. We passed the hill that gave the village of Wagon Mound its name and came across a historical marker that told us that Wagon Mound was on the old Santa Fe Trail. I suppose I could image covered wagons moving across the plains and herds of cattle. Now, there were fences and cattle ranches, antelope, and very occasionally another car. It was certainly a country of wide open spaces. In some places the fields, pastures, lands, I am not sure what to call them, were covered with short trees, but for the most part, it was grasslands as far as the eye could see.

We came to a place where the road started to go downhill fairly steeply.
"This must be the river," John said as we wound our way down into a canyon.
"It is," I said. "Look, over there, water."
"Let's stop at the bottom and take a look," he suggested. We drove down and crossed the bridge that was there and found a place to pull off the road, then walked back to the bridge to look over at the river.
"There's quite a bit of water coming down," I said. "I think more than the Pecos."
"I'd guess about one and a half cubic feet per second," John said, eyeing the river critically on the one hand and the second hand on his watch on the other. I suppose he had had a lot of experience with rivers and water and could at least estimate what the flow rate would be.
"I'll bet this can come up quickly with a good rainstorm," I said.
"It would," John agreed. "Did you see that farm back there on the other side of the river?" A truck came down the hill and passed us, the driver looking at us curiously, probably wondering what we were doing. He waved and we waved back, clearly not in distress, so he left us to our observations and continued on his way.
"I wonder what is farmed in the canyon?" I asked.
"I didn't see any plantings, maybe cattle?" he suggested.
"Rugged country for cows," I thought.
"Well, there's water in the Canadian River, shall we go on?" he asked.

We went back to our car and drove up the road that led out of the canyon, back to the plains and grasslands. We came to Roy. If Wagon Mound was a village, then Roy was a hamlet. It boasted a petrol station and some other stores, that looked to me as if they were related to ranching. The speed limits in Roy seemed to me to be ludicrous, but I noticed that John was being very circumspect.

"You're being very good," I commented.

"I don't trust little *dorpies*," he said. "Too often they're where the local cops lie in wait for unwary people just passing through. This place reminds me of any number of little *dorpies* in the Karoo."

"It's quiet isn't it?" I said.

"*Ja*, if this were the movies, I'd say too quiet," he laughed.

"I suppose there are people here, there's certainly pickup trucks parked all over the place," I commented.

"Welcome to the American West," he said. "Let's go and see if Mosquero is any bigger and if it has anywhere to eat."

As we drove past the buildings, the speed limits went back up until we could once again do fifty-five. A couple of large transport trucks went flying by us in the opposite direction and I realised that they were full of cows. Where they were off to we would never know, perhaps Denver, perhaps places farther afield. We passed a few small collections of houses, then in the distance, we could see another hamlet.

"There's our turn-off to Trementina," John said as we flashed by a signpost. "We'll need to come back to here to pick up the road."

"Mosquero looks even smaller than Roy," I said as we slowed down and passed the outskirts. Well, outskirts was perhaps too grandiose a term. We went round a slight bend and we were there in the main street. It was wide, really wide and I wondered why.

"Looks like towns in the Karoo or Rhodesia," John said. "Room enough to turn a horse or ox wagon around in the street."

"Look, there's a place there," I said pointing to a café that advertised food.

"We'll try it," John said. We pulled over and parked and walked across the road to the café.

"Howdy folks," a lady said as we entered. "Sit anywhere." There were four other people in the place, all men, all dressed alike, jeans, cowboy boots, denim shirts and hats, cowboy hats, white, brown, grey and black. I suppose if they all took their hats off, then there would have to be somewhere to put them, so the easiest thing to do was leave them on. I could not do that, so took mine off and placed it on an empty chair, and also took off my sunglasses. The outside may have been brilliant sunshine and bright, but inside, the light was filtered a little, so no need for sunglasses, except as a fashion statement. The cowboys looked us over and nodded to us and went back to their conversation, which as far as I could tell had to do with cattle and current market prices. The lady came over to our table, handed us a short menu and put down glasses of water.

"I'm Sally," she said. "Let me know when you're ready, coffee?"

"Coffee would be fine, thank you," I said.

"Oh, you're English," she said. "What brings you to Mosquero?"

"We're just passing through," I said. "We wanted to take a look at the Canadian River, so have been crossing it where we can."

"What's the interest in the river?" she asked.

"I've just bought a winery on the Pecos," John explained. "I've looked at other wineries on the Rio Grande and wondered if anyone had ever tried grapes along the Canadian."

"Javier," Sally said to one of the cowboys. "Anyone ever try grapes along the Canadian?"

"Melvin Mills," he said. "Back before 1904, Mills started the settlement of Mills right by the Canadian, he planted all kinds of orchards and he planted grapes. The whole lot went in the flood of 1904, then he rebuilt the settlement of Mills up on the plains where it is now."

"Where is this Mills?" John asked.

"You go north of Roy towards Springer," Javier said. "You can get down to the Canadian from there, but you do need a 4x4, the tracks are not the best. You're the folks I saw stopped on the bridge on the road to Roy?"

"That was us," John said. "We wanted to get some idea of how much water there is in the river."

"Depends on the rain to the north," another cowboy said. This drew the others into the conversation and it quickly settled on rain, the lack thereof, what local rainfall patterns looked like and what grew best where. They were all cattle people so were more interested in grasses than grapes, but they appreciated that a grape grower would also have a lively interest in water, whether from a river, from rain or from a well.

"You buy Dale Black's place?" Javier asked.

"Yes," John said. "Have you been there?"

"Sure," Javier said. "Seemed to me that Dale was always away in Utah with his ski resort, left everything to his winemaker, Audrey."

"That was my assessment," John said. "Audrey is good, she makes some really good wines."

"Didn't get your name," Javier commented.

"John Cillie," John replied. "This is, let's see how to place you, my son-in-law's sister, Fiona Barclay. My daughter and son-in-law will be moving over from a vineyard we have in France to run the Pecos winery."

"Well, at least you're winemakers," Javier said. "If it wasn't for Audrey, Dale would have had a real loser on his hands."

"And you're all ranchers?" John asked.

"All," Javier confirmed. "My place is to the east of here, Josh has a place almost to Logan, Tom's place is west of here towards the river and Fred works on the Bell." We got nods all round but I was really disturbed when I met Tom's eyes. It was the same as when I had first met Ian, we had looked into each other's eyes and felt something. To see that in another was troubling, was I being disloyal to Ian, no, not really, he was dead, had been dead for some months now, was I imagining things, was I just looking for human contact, was I just lonely. I dropped my gaze quickly and drank some coffee to hide my confusion. How could I feel something for someone I had just met and would be unlikely to ever meet again. I peered over the rim of my coffee cup and stole a look at Tom. He was dark, dark hair, dark complexion, as I could judge an inch or two taller than me, I placed him in his late twenties, so had the obvious question, married or not, if not why not. I came back to reality with a start and the realisation that John had asked me a question and was awaiting an answer.

"Sorry, daydreaming," I said.

"Shall we change our plans and go north and look at the ruins of Mills?" he repeated.

"Why not?" I said. "But first some lunch I think."

"Sorry folks, we've all got to go," Javier said. "You should come by again one day, we have a meeting once a month to talk about things, so we'll be here again third Wednesday in October."

"Thanks for your help," John said. "Nice to have met you all." They left and I got a big smile from Tom and could not help smiling back. I saw them all cross the street and the others were clearly teasing Tom.

"You made a big hit there," Sally commented as she brought us our lunch. "Tom's smitten. Not surprised, pretty girl like you, you married?"

"Widow," I said. I am not sure why that came out, it just did, it was an announcement that I had no real attachments, why on earth did I say it.

"Sorry to hear that, what was it?" Sally asked.

"Traffic accident," I said.

"Well, at least you've got family, when your brother moves to Pecos, will you come and visit him?" Sally asked.

"I'm sure I will," I said.

"You come out here and break a few hearts," Sally joked.

After lunch, we turned around and skipped the Trementina turn-off and went back north to Roy, then north again to Mills. There was a sign for Mills Canyon Road, so we took it. It was an unpaved road, but well-maintained, at least for the first part. We took some turns and eventually the road became less well-maintained and we started down the twisting road to the river. In the canyon bottom, it was delightful. There were trees in the bottom, there were shrubs clinging to the canyon walls, that in places were quite steep. The river swung back and forth between the canyon walls and it was easy to see how a flood would devastate anything low lying close to the river. We found some ruins of houses and marvelled that someone had actually built there. I have to admit, apart from the odd devastating flood, it would have been an idyllic place to live, it had water, it was well away from too many people, the summers would be nice, but I am not so sure about the winters, but there were enough trees around to provide firewood. We stopped and paddled in the river and threw twigs in to see how fast it was flowing, we listened to the birds that were somewhere in the canyon walls, we saw some deer on the far bank and even a coyote.

"We should start back," John said. "What was bothering you at the café?"

"Oh, nothing," I dissembled. I might discuss my feelings later with Maman, but until then they were private.

"Are you okay?" he asked.

"I'm fine, really," I said. "I was just wool gathering for a minute back there."

"Okay, if you're sure?" he said.

We drove out of the canyon, and we did need the four-wheel drive that the Blazer came with. The road was steep, rough and twisted and turned as if clawed its way up the slope. Once on top, we could shift back into two-wheel drive and pick up speed again.

"Shall we go north to Springer?" John asked.

"Let's," I agreed. We drove north until we had to make a choice, east or west. West it had to be because the river was to our west, as was Springer. We crossed the river and what a contrast. Now it looked more like a muddy ditch flowing in the fields, with bushes and reeds growing along the banks, that could be no more than a few feet high. Gone were the impressive canyon walls, gone were the echoes of birds in the canyon, now it was more like an English countryside with a quite small river flowing through it. It was, in fact, quite a disappointment. Springer was another village, but it did boast a petrol station and it had a railway line running right through the centre. We filled up at the petrol station, then joined the freeway there to go south to Las Vegas and then back to Santa Fe.

The next day we were up early, not quite with the birds, but early enough. I decided that as this was the closing day and it was to be at a bank, then I would be formal, so wore my grey suit, white blouse and grey shoes. John had put on a jacket and tie, not a suit, but blazer and grey flannels. We drove into Albuquerque with all the commuter traffic and went to the Bank of the West building. We were shown to a conference room and offered coffee while we waited for the others. First to arrive was the lawyer representing John, a rather fierce-looking woman who had probably had to battle her way through the legal profession. She reminded me in some ways of Portia, she was knowledgable, she clearly knew what she was about and probably took no nonsense. The next to show was Dale and finally his lawyer. The two lawyers had met before as they had both been party to the negotiations, I was the newcomer. I was introduced as an investor in Cillie Wines and then they all got down to the serious business of signing papers. When all was signed, a bank official then passed over a cheque to Dale who looked it over, thanked John, thanked his lawyer, thanked our lawyer, thanked me, probably thanked the tellers for all I know. Dale handed over keys to John and we all posed for photographs and gave a short interview to a local newspaper reporter. John wanted it known that the

Cillie family was moving into New Mexico, so had thought it prudent to make the transaction known. So, now I was part owner of a winery. It dawned on me why John had used Bank of the West, it was now owned by BNP. Banque Nationale de Paris, where the family banked in France. Transferring money between the various parts of the bank would be quite easy. All was done by ten, so John and I said our goodbyes to the lawyers and the bankers and drove to Pecos to talk to the people there.

John called a meeting of the staff, meagre as it was, all three of them and handed out new business cards for them, with the notation Old Pecos Wines, and as a footnote, A Cillie Wines Company. We then set about our various tasks. John went with Audrey and her husband, Jeff, who also functioned as the cellarman, to go picking, and I stayed with Maria, the office manager, to introduce her to the mysteries of the Apple computer that John had bought before and had been keeping for this day. I showed Maria how the computer functioned and then loaded the programs we were going to use and spent some time with her explaining how it all worked. We loaded all the inventory data, then fulfilled some orders and debited the inventory as we did so. Maria was delighted and wanted to try her hand at more. So, I gave her the fixed asset listing and showed her where the data should be entered for the balance sheet. I also showed her how the accounting model worked and where to enter all the expenses and incomes. I suggested that for a period of a few months that she maintain her paper system in parallel to the computer system, to safeguard against data loss until such time as we could effectively back everything up. I did take a look at the house that was on the property. It was a log cabin, well, perhaps cabin is an understatement, as it was quite large. Dale had moved out before we even arrived, so the place was quite bare and empty. I thought that before John started to furnish it for Charlize and James, that it would benefit from a thorough cleaning, so I asked Maria to find an industrial cleaning service and get it scrubbed, vacuumed and polished.

I stayed on with John and the crew for another week, helping with picking, helping Maria with the computer systems, I also got an IBM typewriter and some electronic gear and modified it to be able to print from the computer. That took a little work as the typewriter was a mechanical beast and I needed to work out how to send signals and get them translated into the mechanical actions, but in the end, I succeeded and we had a working printer that would give us very nice printed reports, invoices, statements, whatever we wanted. John bought a couple of pickup trucks and had them emblazoned with the emblem of the winery. John also bought a really nice-looking little tractor. It was from Japan, a Kubota, it came with all kinds of attachments, so for new plantings, they could now plough, harrow, dig holes, scoop up stuff, and tow a trailer full of picking bins. I tried it out and it was a super little machine, bright orange and built like a tank. It had four-wheel drive and would go anywhere on the property, up hills, down hills, in mud, and I imagined in snow, and for that, there was even a snow plough, I could see it becoming a fast favourite of the crew. My flat and my work was calling, so it was time to think about going home. I went to the library in Albuquerque and found information on Dundee materials, I also discovered they were a publicly traded company, so got the latest annual report and quarterly report. I was surprised. It was a huge concern, with revenues of almost five hundred million dollars. Richard Berg had started the company quite some years ago and it had grown and grown and then he had taken it public. I gathered reading the fine print that he still owned a good portion of the company stock. His wife was also a shareholder in her own right and was listed as one of the directors. Between them, they held some 45% of the common stock. I called the Dundee Materials people and told them that I had a layover at the O'Hare airport, and suggested that they meet me there. I was a little surprised that they actually jumped at the chance and not only said that they would meet me, but booked one of the meeting rooms that was at the airport, in the American Airlines Terminal. I got John to run me back to Albuquerque and there I rented a car to drop off in Denver. I said goodbye to John and told him that I would be back, probably before Charlize and James moved over.

My drive to Denver took me back through Las Vegas and Wagon Mound and north. Charlize had been right, the drive got quite pretty as I climbed up over the mountains from Raton to Trinidad. Quite why a place in the middle of the United States would be called Trinidad was beyond me, but I suppose there was a reason. Trinidad was about halfway to Denver so I stopped for lunch. That took some searching, I drove up and down Main Street, which seemed to have more than its fair share of property to rent, so perhaps the economy in Trinidad was not the rosiest. I finally settled on a sports bar. When I went in conversation stopped and I was looked over by all and sundry. I caught sight of myself in a mirror behind the bar and saw what they saw, a young woman, probably late twenties early thirties, trim figure, a little under average height, burgundy blouse, well, reddish to them, jeans, suede jacket and a black hat, I suppose I would have looked as well. A blowsy blonde came over with a menu and steered me to a table away from the bar and the oglers.

"Never mind them," she said. "What'll it be?"

"I think just a lemonade and a hamburger with fries," I replied.

"How d'you want the burger honey?" she asked.

"Well, please," I said.

"Just passing through?" she asked.

"Yes," I said. "Just needed something to eat."

"Well, it'll be out in a jiff," she promised. She scuttled off to the kitchen and I looked around. There were probably ten television screens, all playing different games of what type or another. The patrons seemed to have settled back down to drinking and giving running commentaries of the various games. I silently thanked the waitress, she had given me a table with a clear view of all comers and easy access to the door. I cannot say that I felt threatened, but this place did not have the easy-going friendly atmosphere that the café in Mosquero had had, I was uneasy and kept a close eye on all in the place and decided to literally eat and run. I thought about the day that we had gone to Mosquero and even felt a little guilty. Ian was dead, but only about six months dead, so was it too soon to be even thinking of anyone else, and how could I have had the electric spark connection with Tom?

From Trinidad north to Denver, the road roughly paralleled the Rocky Mountains, so they were always on my left, and to the right was grassland. The Denver airport was much larger than the Albuquerque airport and was close to the city, close enough that I predicted that at some time a new airport would be built, farther out with room for expansion. I found my flight, a Continental flight to Chicago and did not have long to wait before boarding. This flight was on a DC-10, back in the air after being grounded for a while as the crash of an American

Airlines DC-10 had been investigated. It was spacious, colourful and the crew were very chatty and accommodating. It, at least in First Class, was not full, so I had the choice of the window seat I had requested, or the aisle seat next to it. I chose the window until it got dark, then switched to the aisle, not being able to see the ground any more. In my jeans and suede jacket I actually felt under-dressed compared to the other passengers, who in the case of men, all had on business suits, and in the case of the women, were dressed to the nines, and many of them were draped around with jewellery. I went back to my mathematics and came up with a really elegant distancing model that was better than the one I had come up with on the way from London and that I thought I could easily write a computer program for.

"What's that you're doing?" one of the stewardesses asked.

"It's what's called a distancing model," I explained. "It's used by shops to work out how far people may go to go shopping, and helps them site new shops."

"Oh," she said. "Are you a university professor?"

"No," I said. "Just in business for myself." I wondered why it was that when people saw mathematical models they assumed you were with a university.

"You must be very clever," she said.

"I hope my clients think so," I joked.

"No, I'm sure you are," she said.

"Thank you," I said. It had been a while since anyone had paid me a compliment, so I took it and was grateful. At Chicago, I said goodbye to the crew and collected my bags then walked through the tunnel to the Hilton Hotel. My flight back to London was the next day, so I was going to spend the night and relax before the next flight.

I met with Richard Berg the next day. We met in a conference room at the airport. With him were Hal Lesnewski and Stuart Kahl. Hal was the finance man, Chief Financial Officer, and Stuart a lawyer, the General Counsel for the company. Richard introduced me and asked me to give them some sense of other projects I had worked on. I apologised in advance for the lack of specifics, but most of my clients preferred that I not make public what I had done for them. That did not stop me from describing the kind of models and computer programs I had created, which were many and varied. Richard then told me what they were

43

looking for, a better model for the economics of sand and gravel than the rule of thumb that thirty miles was the limit for transporting materials. I could do that, but pointed out that a lot depended on where the sources of materials were, so knowledge of geology was important and a soil map would be really useful.

"We have the USGS maps of all the states where we operate," Richard said. "It gives us a good idea of surface deposits and rock outcrops."

"What about climate?" I asked. "I would have thought that the season for construction projects was limited by temperature extremes."

"It is," Richard agreed. "When it gets really cold then concrete setting is an issue and people and machines just don't work well."

"Is there a difference between naturally occurring sand and gravel and manufactured sand and aggregate done by crushing and grinding?" I asked.

"Sure is," Richard said, looking at the others with raised eyebrows. "Sand and gravel that occur naturally have different grain sizes and tend to be smooth shapes, unlike the angular materials we have crushed."

"How much of what is deposited was the result of the last ice age?" I asked.

"A lot," Richard said. "You sure you've never looked at this before?"

"I've never looked at construction materials," I assured him. "It just struck me that there probably would be differences between sand and gravel that you just dig up, versus sand and gravel that you make. Which is preferable?"

"If you can find good sand and gravel, then it's cheaper to just dig it up and sort it than excavating rock and crushing and grinding and sorting," Richard said. "Plus the materials behave differently in concrete, so you have to remember which you're dealing with."

"So, knowledge of what's on the surface is important," I commented. "No naturally occurring sand and gravel means that you'd have to make which drives the costs up."

"Absolutely," Richard said.

"I presume that you can find land ownership easy enough?" I asked. "Does that also include mineral rights, in the US are those rights vested in the land ownership, or do they vest in the State?"

"What did you say your education was?" Stuart asked.

"Mathematics first," I said. "Then economics and computer science."

"Not law?" Stuart asked.

"No law," I said. "I only asked about mineral rights because I did some work for a consortium of metals miners and with them who owned the rights was important."

"Well, it depends on the state, but the rights generally come with the land but they may have been separated in the past and belong to a previous owner," Stuart said. "It takes some research to find that out. Royalties will be a matter for negotiation if land we acquire does not come with the rights."

"Actually, what we're really looking for is a predictive model that looks at leading indicators and gives us a better sense of what's coming and when, we use housing starts and a few others today, but they're not always the best, can you do a model for us to plan five years out, so we know better when to open quarries and pits and other plants?" Richard asked.

"So, you're really looking for a true economic model, yes I can do that," I agreed. "Do you have your own computer or access to one?"

"We've an IBM 3033," Hal said. "We run payroll and accounting on it and we have material reserves on it and we've tried some scheduling programs for deliveries."

"I could create a program that would run the model and let you put in your own data," I suggested.

"That sounds great," Richard said. "How much?"

"Why don't I send you a proposal?" I suggested. "I could do things two ways, either bill you for the hours I work, or give you a fixed price for the project."

"I think we'd prefer a fixed price," Richard said.

"Fine," I said. "I'll write up the scope of work and what I will deliver, it will involve some time at your offices to enter the computer programs, so that will entail travel."

"Great, when can we expect a proposal?" Hal asked.

"Give me about a week to think about it and write it up," I suggested.

"And if we accept, when could you start?" Richard asked.

"About a week after acceptance," I thought. "I have some other things that I am working on now, but I could work this in fairly well."

"Who owns the work?" Stuart asked.

"The computer models I do for you will belong to me but licensed to you for a nominal amount," I said. "Some of the mathematical concepts are in the public domain, and some are mine."

"Can we make things exclusive?" Stuart asked.

"I have a form of agreement that I have used in other industries where competition is an issue," I said. "I'll send you a copy of that, but to make all work in the construction industry exclusive to you will cost you as it may restrict my ability to accept work from others."

"I thought you said that you've never worked in this industry before?" Stuart asked.

"I haven't," I said. "But, I cannot predict the future and would not want to limit my opportunities without recompense."

"Okay," Richard said. "We'll wait for your proposal. You're back off to London now?"

"I am," I said. "I'm on the BA flight tonight."

"Well, good flight back," Richard said. "Look forward to working with you. Look, here's a copy of our latest annual report, and the 10-K and 10-Qs for last year and the first two quarters of this year."

"Thank you," I said. "I'm sorry I don't have anything I can give you, apart from my card."

"We've done some checking," Hal joked. "We're impressed with your qualifications, apart from economics what else do you do?"

"I have a plane that I fly myself," I replied.

"Oh, what do you have?" Hal asked.

"I've a Cessna Stationair," I said. "I bought it recently to replace the Skyhawk that I sold."

"We should take you to a couple of our bigger plants," Richard said. "We can fly out in the Falcon, maybe even let you take the yoke for five minutes."

"Are you the same Fiona Barclay who wrote a paper on bullet velocities back in the late 60's?" Stuart asked.

"That was me," I admitted. "I wrote it before I went to college, it was my first published paper."

"So, you shoot?" Richard asked.

"I do," I said. "I've kept it up, especially when we lived in Kenya, you never knew what might happen."

"You probably should go," Richard suggested. "BA will have the gate open now, you don't want to miss your flight."

"Thank you," I said. "I hope I'll see you all again soon." I left them and went to the gate. I had tried an experiment, meeting the eyes of each in turn, but there was nothing, no spark, no electricity, no disquiet. So, what had happened in Mosquero, why had I felt something when my eyes met those of Tom. Something to ponder on the flight home.

Freya

I busied myself and put together the proposal for Dundee and sent it off with a form of agreement and a confidentiality agreement. I had had those put together for me by Portia, who was still one of the best minds in the legal profession that I had met. I buried into the price of the work several trips back and forth to Chicago, I also included monies for computer time in England as I would have to develop and test the programs there. I talked to the professor at LSE who had been my advisor when I had done my doctorate there in economics, and recruited some postgraduate students for a paid project to research things for me, essentially gathering raw data on a number of industries, commodities and other items that I was planning to use as my leading indicators for Dundee, I asked for the data as far back as could be found, and asked for it annually, monthly or weekly, if possible. For those to whom LSE is one of those mysterious acronyms thrown about by people, LSE is the London School of Economics. It would take some digging as little was available in digital form, it would all have to be culled from trade publications, official government statistics and other sources. I finished up two other projects that I had had in the works and was now in funds, quite a lot actually. I called Maman and talked to her about my trip to New Mexico and about my unsettling experience. We talked for some time and her advice was to revisit the scene of the crime, so to speak, and see if the same spark was there, and if it was go from there and see where things led.

I felt I deserved a few days off and checked the weather forecast. For the next week, things were supposed to be fairly good, a true Indian summer. I called Freya McIntosh on Colonsay to see if it would be convenient for me to visit. Freya had a castle there, a real castle, I know only built less than a hundred years ago by her grandfather, but a true castle all the same with a ditch, drawbridge, curtain wall, battlements, keep, the works. I had met Freya once on the plane from London to Nairobi and again when Ian and I went to stay in what we thought would be a holiday cottage on Colonsay, arranged by my Dad, who it transpired knew Freya. The holiday cottage had turned out to be the castle and the lady of the house had turned up while we were there. Although I had been cool to her on the plane, mainly because she had been a little overwhelming, I had warmed to her a lot while we stayed there, and she had even come out to Nairobi for Ian's funeral. Freya made her living writing romance novels, bodice rippers Ian had called them. She was well-known in publishing circles and worth a penny or two. Freya told me that I was welcome at any time and if I would give her an approximate time of arrival she would be at the Colonsay strip to collect me.

I went out to Biggin Hill and checked my plane. I made sure it had fuel and did an extensive walk-around. I had not used it since I came back from France, so it needed looking over. I checked the engine and made sure that the oil level was correct and looked it over for loose wires, pipes, oil leaks, all the things that might tell me that something was amiss. All in order I went home, packed a bag and called Freya to give her my arrival time, I was going to fly to Prestwick, refuel there and then go on to Colonsay, so two and a half hours to Prestwick, half an hour on the ground for fuel and a loo break at Prestwick, then another forty-five minutes to Colonsay. If I left at seven in the morning, that would put me on the ground in Colonsay at about ten-forty-five. The sun came up right at about seven, so I should have a nice flight north. I was actually quite excited. I had not had an outing just to please myself since Ian died, so this was something to look forward to. I was up early the next day and out to Biggin Hill by six. I did another walk-around, topped off the tanks, filed my flight plan, loaded my bag, then started on the pre-flight checks. All in order, I donned my self-inflating life preserver, then went through the start-up checks, the pre-taxi checks, then the take-off checks and with clearance was on my way at seven on the dot. I wore the life preserver because there was some overwater flying and if I had to ditch the last thing I wanted to be doing was scrambling to find a life jacket. The nice thing about the self-inflating life preserver, was that it was not bulky and as soon as one hit the water it did its thing by inflating with a carbon dioxide cartridge. I also had a life raft in the plane and I had that on the floor behind my seat. I know that overwater time was short, but better to be safe than sorry. My plane was also equipped with an emergency locator beacon, so that if I did go down anywhere, there was a chance that I would be found.

I had to take a circuitous route around London to avoid all the commercial traffic landing at Gatwick and Heathrow, which added time, but I had allowed for that in my flight times, and was fairly soon headed north towards Prestwick. At Prestwick, I bought fuel for the plane, and fuel for me in the form of coffee and a sandwich, and was off over the water to the isles. I was enjoying the flight, the weather was nice, skies clear, not too much wind, no real turbulence, not much traffic in the sky, all in all, it was a beautiful day. Over Jura, I started down and when I got there overflew the Colonsay strip to make sure there were no cows or other planes on it, then went back into land. On the ground, Freya came over to meet me and took my bag while I tied down the plane and stowed my life jacket. The Scottish Islands can be windy and I had no desire to see my plane upside down.

"Fiona, how are you?" Freya asked.

"I'm having a really good day," I replied. "I enjoyed the flight up, it was super just to be back in the air and free to come and go."

"Well, I'm pleased to hear that," she said.

"How are you, how's Kirsty?" I asked.

"Kirsty's away the while, doing a painting for some rich American," Freya said. "The sitting's in Rome, so Kirsty's been gone a week now and I expect her back in about ten days."

"How did Kirsty get that job?" I asked.

"It seems he had seen some of her work and knew that she did my covers, so I think he wants a romanticised version of himself," Freya laughed. "She's being well paid, £15,000 plus expenses."

"That much?" I asked. "He must really like her work."

"I think it's his wife as much as him," Freya said. "I gather she's a big fan of my books and she's the one who discovered that Kirsty does the covers, so they contacted us through my publisher and we set things up."

"Well, good for her, and you, are you well?" I asked.

"I'm delighted that you're here," she said. "I'm fit, well, idle at the moment, so this is a great time to have you visit. We'll have some fun while you're here, how long can you stay?"

"Would a week be too long?" I asked.

"No, a week, a fortnight, whatever you want," she said. "Come, let's away, lunch is calling."

We drove to the north end of the island where her castle was situated. It was a lovely spot, in splendid isolation with a grand view of the sea. Freya parked in her multi-car garage and we walked to the front door of the keep. Inside it was warm and welcoming and Freya showed me to a guest room where I dropped my bag. I went back downstairs to the kitchen where she was busy with lunch.

"So, Fiona, how have you been?" she asked.

"I'm managing," I said. "Good days and not so good days."

"Keeping busy?" she asked.

"I am now," I said. "I took a few weeks off, but am back to work now, I'm an aunt now, my brother, James, and his wife, Charlize, just had a daughter."

"I remember her from Nairobi," Freya said. "What's the name?"

"Fiona Anna," I said.

"You miss Ian?" Freya asked.

"I do," I said. "Sometimes more than others, when that happens it's usually because it's somewhere we were together, or I see or hear something that I would have talked to Ian about."

"That must be hard at times," she said, sympathetically.

"It is," I agreed. "I did have a weird moment a couple of weeks ago, I was having lunch and there was a chap there and when I looked at him and he looked at me, it was electric. I felt really guilty about that, am I being disloyal to Ian, was it just a once-in-a-lifetime thing, does it mean something more?"

"All good questions," Freya said. "First, you're not being disloyal to Ian, you two had a wonderful life, but you're far too young to live in the past, you have to look to the future. Second, the only way you're going to know if it's a once-in-a-lifetime thing is to go back and see him again and see if it happens again. If it does, explore a little, test the waters, find out if he's married, all the usual things. Where did this happen?"

"In the wilds of New Mexico," I said. "I had gone there with Charlize's dad to help with the purchase of a winery, and we took a drive into the country, and when I say country I mean country, miles and miles of grass, some hills and mountains and very few people. We had stopped for lunch at this little café and he was there with three others. We gathered that they were all cattle ranchers. When our eyes met, it was like it was with Ian, like an electric shock, it was very disturbing and I wasn't sure what to do, I felt excited but guilty."

"So, if there's anything there it's going to be a long-distance romance for a while," Freya thought. "You should go back and find out. Do you have reason to go to the States?"

"I think I have a new client in Chicago," I said. "And I can always find a reason to go to the Pecos winery, of which I'm now a part owner."

"Then you should go, go soon, go with your eyes wide open, go to test the waters, go and find out his name," Freya instructed.

"Perhaps I will," I said. "So, what novel are you working on now?"

"The seventh in my series set in Africa," she replied. "There were three in Kenya, two in Rhodesia, and the others in South Africa. The basic plot doesn't vary much, but the characters and the setting does, so each novel seems different. It still amazes me how many people buy them. I keep thinking I should branch out, and I've actually been toying with the idea of a mystery novel under another pen name."

"I'm sure that would sell," I thought. "Look at how many editions P. D. James or Agatha Christie have sold, or Ngaio Marsh, come to that."

"Who dunnits are popular," Freya said. "So, we'll see with the first one whether or not it's worth pursuing. Look, would it be a lot of trouble for us to take a trip tomorrow to Mull? I've almost run out of whisky and have an idea to visit the distillery in Tobermory and get some more."

"That shouldn't be a problem," I said. "How far is it, where's the field?"

"Well, here's a map," she said. "And there's a grass field at Glenforsa and I know the proprietor of the hotel and we could borrow his car to go into Tobermory."

"Well, looking at the map, it's only about thirty miles or so, so say fifteen minutes in the air at the most, so I've plenty of fuel, when do you want to go?" I asked.

"I thought we could plan to arrive in Tobermory at about ten, and it's a twenty-minute drive, so we should leave here when?" she asked.

"Let's say, fifteen minutes to the strip here, another fifteen to untie the plane and do pre-flights, fifteen minutes in the air, another fifteen to tie it down at Glenforsa, so leave here at eight-thirty," I suggested.

"Eight-thirty it is," she said. "I'll call the Glenforsa and tell them we're coming and tell them we want to borrow a car. So, we'll tour the distillery, have some lunch, then come home, how does that sound?"

"That sounds like fun," I thought. It did sound like fun, a short trip outing that would take hours by ferry.

We were up early the next morning and breakfasted then left for the airstrip. There was a little drizzle in the air, but visibility was good, and the winds were light from the west, so not a bad day to go flying. I did all my before-flight tasks and got Freya aboard then did my safety briefing, this time including the life jacket drill and where the life raft was. I gave Freya a headset and told her that the microphone was voice-activated, so that all she had to do to talk to me was speak. We took off to the west then turned to the north and headed for Mull. I chatted on the radio with the local traffic controllers and told them where I was headed. We could see Mull ahead so we would not be long over the water, in fact, I estimated that there was probably only about 15 miles of open water that we had to cross. When we made landfall over Mull, it looked as if that part of the island was largely uninhabited, and the only activity we saw looked like Forestry Commission work with lines and lines of trees growing. Freya kept up a running commentary and where she thought we were and I got an Aha from Freya, as we passed over a small collection of houses.

"That's Pennyghael," she said, pointing down to the houses. They were on an inlet that came deep into Mull from the west. Beyond Pennyghael the ground climbed steeply and we went over some hills, maybe mountains, I am not sure what defines what.

"It may get a little bumpy," I warned Freya. "There's odd wind patterns because of the hills below, so be prepared." It did bump a little, but it was not too bad, not as bad as midday in Kenya where the thermals could really throw you around.

"There's Glenforsa," Freya said, pointing ahead.

"I see it," I said. I changed to the local frequency and called the hotel and talked to them briefly and got the wind direction then dropped down and turned to overfly the strip and looked for a sock to check for myself, I saw two actually, one at each end of the strip. The wind was now out of the east, so we did a circuit and landed that way. We taxied over to the hotel and parked next to two other light planes and close to a Loganair Britten-Norman Islander. Freya explained that it was a summer service that ran from Glasgow to Oban to Mull and then to Coll. While I tied down the plane, Freya went off in search of the hotelier and the car and was back in a few minutes with an ancient Morris Minor Traveller, it had to be from the fifties, but it was free, so beggars could not be choosers. One thing was nice, because it was a Traveller there would be plenty of room in the back for whatever Freya wanted to buy. Our landing fees were waived if we came back and had lunch at the hotel, but I rather think that had been Freya's plan. We motored into Tobermory and parked near the distillery. Freya knew the proprietor there as well, she seemed to know everyone, from the hotelier at Glenforsa, to the postman, and odd people we saw about the town.

The distillery was old, but it had shut down for quite a while following the Great Depression, but was now restarted. We took a tour, and I was impressed with the big copper stills, it all looked so industrial, quite unlike the glass stills that we had set up in the chemistry lab when I was at school. Unlike wine, the ingredients were not grown on the estate of the distillery, the malted barely came from elsewhere, as did the oak casks, but the water was local, water from the peat bogs, that gave it flavour. I had toured a distillery before, the one I had invested in in Fort William, but this one was not the size of that. The Fort William distillery had more stills and a huge ageing building, not surprising as all the whisky was aged for at least three years before being bottled and sold. Our tour terminated in a tasting room, but I declined the samples. They might be small, but I was flying us back to Colonsay and needed to stay sober. The proprietor did take pity on me and actually gave me a bottle of each of their brands, which was very nice of him. Freya went to town and bought six cases, each with twelve bottles. I thought about where I would stow it all in the plane and decided that all the back seats would have a case and the other two could go in the luggage compartment. We said our goodbyes to the distillery and went back to the Glenforsa for lunch.

"Well, what do you think?" Freya asked as we drove back to the hotel.
"It's interesting," I temporised. "I invested in Glen August, so have seen distilleries before, we should fly over and take a look at that one day."
"That would be fun," she said. "What about tomorrow?"
"If the weather's good, let's do that," I agreed. "What would we do, fly into Oban, hire a car and drive up?"
"I can't think of any other landing strips," she said. "I'll call Oban when we get home, let them know we're coming and arrange for a hire car. Here we are, shall we load the booze into the plane before we give the car back?"

"Good idea," I agreed. Freya drove around to the area where our plane was parked, and we loaded the cases. The Loganair plane had gone as had one of the other small planes. There was certainly more traffic than in and out of Colonsay. Over lunch, Freya took me back to how I was faring after the death of Ian.

"It was very hard at first," I admitted. "I went out to Nairobi with him and really enjoyed my time there."

"What did he actually do?" she asked.

"He handled all kinds of things at the British High Commission," I said. "It sometimes seemed to me to be an endless stream of stupid visitors who had either lost everything or got themselves mixed up in things they should have left well alone."

"Did you get to see much of Kenya?" she asked.

"We did," I confirmed. "We took trips whenever we could and flew all over the place."

"Was it safe?" she asked.

"Well, there were a couple of times when war drums beat, but that was mostly from Uganda, so we stayed away from that border," I replied.

"What was Ian like?" she asked.

"He was great fun," I said. "He was clever, well read, had a good general knowledge, he knew the bush and his birds, animals and trees."

"And?" she pressed.

"I know, I know," I said. "Yes, he was good in bed, out of bed too, come to think of it. We were quite adventurous in when and where we made love. What was your husband like?"

"Classic tall dark and handsome. He was a good lover, but he was a bastard," she said. "I was smitten, but should have listened to myself and my misgivings. He got what he deserved when his lover's husband shot them both."

"How did you meet?" I asked.

"I was at a reception given by my publisher and he was there, he was in the booze business, he was charming, smooth, lizard-like now that I look back, and he pursued me," she said. "He could be fun, but while we lived in Paris, I think he reverted to type and found himself a girlfriend. As I look back, I rather think I was meant to be the meal ticket while he lived the high life. I look on it now as a lesson learned. Fortunately, he had no family to speak of and I was his sole beneficiary, not that there was that much after I had cleaned up all his mess, but I did net about

£150,000 out of his booze business after I sold it. Good riddance to him. I can't believe I was that naive and stupid."

"You don't miss him at all?" I asked.

"I did for a while, there were good times, but there were also bad times, especially when I started to get suspicious about his carryings on, so, all in all, no, I don't miss him anymore," she said. "He's featured in a few of my novels as the bastard who just won't be tamed by the heroine and gets dumped in favour of a nicer chap. I'm thinking if I write a who dunnit I'll kill him off in a most unpleasant manner."

"So, no one else?" I asked.

"Kirsty for the most part," she said. "I do have a friend in London who I will see when I really feel the need for male companionship."

"Is that in any way serious, or just casual?" I asked.

"He's a good fuck," she said, then looked around the room guiltily to see if anyone might have heard. Satisfied that she was not overheard, she grinned and relaxed. "John is married to his work translating ancient texts from Greek, Sanskrit, you name it, and I think lives like a monk, but he is available when I call."

"Nothing serious for you or for him?" I asked.

"No, we have an understanding and if he decides that he wants more, I will end it," she said. "In case he ever gets ideas about pressuring me to do anything I have the goods on him, not that he knows that. But he is a good fuck. From what you said, I gather Ian was a good fuck too?"

"He was," I said, and I know I reddened in embarrassment to say so. "God, he was, but I have no way to gauge how good as he has been my only partner."

"Really?" she asked. "No one else, not even at college?"

"No," I said. "I was twenty before I fell in love and that led to my first experience and that was with Ian."

"And this Tom in New Mexico?" she asked.

"I honestly don't know," I said. "As I said, when our eyes met there was electricity, but is that real, is it enough, am I being disloyal? I'm really confused."

"You know what I should do?" she said. "I should go with you to New Mexico and help you check out this Tom. I could charge all the expenses to book research, yes that would make a good romance novel, lonely cattle rancher, rich city girl with a prick for a boyfriend, she breaks down on the road, cowboy helps out, then things go from there. It's almost written, all I need now is a title and a cover."

"Really?" I asked, laughing. "You'd traipse all over New Mexico and charge it all to research?"

"Of course. When will you know about your new client?" she asked.

"Probably next week," I said. "Then, I anticipate making a trip to Chicago to talk to them in more detail about what they really want and how to give them the models they are looking for."

"So, if you go to Chicago, go on to New Mexico and check out this Tom," she suggested. "I'll come with you to carry your bags and take notes, I can review agreements, I'm pretty good at that, and I can do shorthand really well and I can even type!"

"So, not just a pretty face?" I laughed. "I suppose I could pass you off as my associate and have you sit in the meetings with me. I wonder if they'd tumbled to the fact that Mary Stuart, author, and Freya McIntosh are one and the same, is your picture on the back of your books?"

"You mean you don't know, you've never read any of my books?" she said, throwing her hands up in mock horror.

"Well, Ian and I did find one when we stayed with you," I confessed. "But we were more interested in the sex, so reenacted what you wrote."

"Ah, and was that satisfactory?" she asked. "Always good to know if the scenes are accurate or even feasible."

"It was," I said. "But I have to confess we got to laughing at the flowery language so much that it turned into chaos."

"It's what the publishers want," she explained. "Their theory is that it's housewives who buy, and they are torn between wanting to have more than fade to black, but not wanting clinical descriptions, so we have this not-so-happy medium which leads to the flowery language. In days gone by we had to worry about censors, but that seems to have relaxed a lot, Lady Chatterley took care of much of that."

"Makes sense," I thought. "Should we pay and start back to Colonsay?"

"That might be a good idea," she agreed. I paid the account and we left. The flight back was a little more bumpy over the hills as the day had heated up and we now had some warm air rising from the hills. But it was soon over and things calmed down a lot over the water. Colonsay does not have any really tall hills, so no real issues there with bumpy air. Our landing was delayed for a minute or two as we watched another plane land. We followed it in and parked. Freya was interested to know who it was, so she went over to investigate while I tied the plane down. She came back with news.

"They're some wealthy folk from Edinburgh," she said. "They've taken a house for a month and are here to bird watch."

"Is the plane staying?" I asked.

"No, it's a drop-off, they said that they'll be collected in a month, and if they get tired of things before then, then they'll take the ferry to Oban and try something else," she explained. "So, let's get our supplies home and think about dinner."

The next day, we did fly to Oban. Most of the trip was over water, with only brief landfalls over the island of Kerrera, then a little of the mainland until we put down in Oban. There was no getting out of the landing fees in Oban, but they did have fuel so I topped off my tanks before we started off on our drive to Fort William. It was only about thirty miles to Fort William, but Freya told me that before the bridge was built at North Ballachulish, the ferry queue could be terrible and it was sometimes quicker to take the long detour inland to avoid the ferry. At Glen August we joined a regular tour of the distillery. It was all very professional, but it lacked the personal touch of the Tobermory tour. We both skipped the tasting room, but did pick up two cases of Glen August. I offered to swap one case of my Glen August for one case of Freya's Old Mull and the deal was struck.

"So, now what?" Freya asked.

"Lunch," I suggested.

"Where, where?" Freya mulled. "Let's try the Ballachulish Hotel, it's on the way back and it's not bad." We drove there and instead of staying on the main road over the bridge, took the old ferry road that led us down to the waterfront and the hotel.

"So, if you're going to pose as my associate, what do you know about leading indicators?" I asked as we lunched.

"Movements in things like oil prices, housing starts, crop yields that can be linked to other buying patterns later," Freya said.

"Ha, so you do understand," I commented.

"In the short term, my publisher and I have noted a few things that typically indicate improved book sales," she said. "Once we worked that out then we would make new releases at the right time. Of course, there will always be some buying, but it's not worth a big advertising blitz if the sales won't be there. By tracking our indicators we can usually get three to six months notice of future buying patterns and plan our advertising accordingly."

"My mother used to run a lingerie boutique, and we noticed similar patterns, apart from the obvious Valentine's Day and Christmas," I said. "Once we had identified the indicators and put a mechanism in place to track them, she could add stock when she needed to and not carry inventory just for the sake of it."

"So, for your new client, what are their indicators?" Freya asked.

"That's what I need to research," I said. "I've taken a look at all kinds of things, from oil production, to taxation policy, to crop yields, to alcohol consumption, you name it, and I'm thinking about the mathematics of it all now, and what is the best fit to the data."

"You mathematically model this stuff?" Freya asked.

"That's my skill, such as it is," I said. "I look at the data and create models that fit, then start to do predictions, then examine what actually happens and modify the model. It all takes time, so I often have long-term contracts with some clients who want me to keep modifying the models as we collect more actuals."

"So, what does your new client do?" she Freya asked.

"It's a huge construction materials company," I said. "They have mines, stone quarries, gravel pits, cement plants, ready-mix facilities, all over the country and want to know when and where to start new ones."

"That would be a good thing to know," Freya agreed. "Can you do it?"

"Of course," I said. "How good the model is will depend on what kind of data I can get and what kinds of relationships I see and can model. The main problem I see, and it may not be a problem, is that everything is built on history, so if there is a fundamental change in behaviour, then the models could be misleading."

"I know," Freya said. "If audible books ever become really popular, it will change the market for print books."

"Are there other ways to get books, can I get them on my computer?" I asked.

"Not yet," Freya said. "But that's worth keeping an eye on, if that happens then the whole issue of copyright and ownership will need examining. You load a book on your computer from a disc or tape, then you copy that disc or tape and give it to someone and I've lost a sale. So, it doesn't worry me yet, but it needs following."

"And here I thought authors were just writers and all that stuff was handled by the publishers," I said.

"Usually it is," Freya agreed. "But I don't rely on them for my livelihood, I want to be in control of what I do. Do you know much about the Apple II, I just bought one and am trying to see what I can do with it?" "I can help you with that," I promised. "My sister-in-law and her family now use them to track all kinds of things in the vineyards and wineries." "So, I could track my personal finances?" Freya asked.

"That, plus book sales, royalties, demographics of the book-buying public, the only thing I can't do for you yet is get a decent program that will let you create the text easily on the computer, but that's coming," I said. "You could try Word Star, I haven't played with that yet, I'm planning to, and I'll let you know what I think."
"We should probably be getting back," Freya suggested. "I don't like the look of those clouds building over the mountains."
"You're right," I said, looking at the said clouds. The sooner we were back on Colonsay the better. It did start to drizzle as we flew over the water back to Colonsay, and shortly after we landed the clouds really blew in and it turned from drizzle to rain.
"No flying tomorrow, by the look of it," I said to Freya as we drove back to her castle.
"Tomorrow's perhaps a day for staying in," she agreed. "You can help me with my Apple."

I did help her with her Apple. She had a study, writing room, whatever you would call it, it had an ancient-looking desk with the Apple II computer and an IBM Selectric typewriter on it, and around the walls were bookshelves with just about every romance novel I could think of, from Fanny Hill, to works by Anais Nin, Wallace, Lawrence, and many others.
"Do you read these for ideas or style?" I asked.
"I just like to see what the competition has done and is doing," Freya explained. "It's incredible how many are published each year, some of the authors churn out two or three a year, they must just write all the time. I usually have one ready to go, so when the publishers and I think the time is right, I just send it off to them and start on the next one."
"Doesn't it get boring?" I asked.
"I look on it as work," she said. "I have to work for a living, or at least I used to, so have developed disciplines for writing."

"You write under the pen name of Mary Stuart, have you ever written under your own name?" I asked.

"After I got my doctorate in literature, I tried a couple of times with historical novels about the Highlands, but they all got rejected, so I added sex, a lurid cover, and changed my name to Mary Stuart, that seemed to resonate with the Highlands theme, and suddenly I'm the talk of the town," she lamented. "Still, it pays the bills, in fact, it does more than pay and for one of the more serious romances, there's even discussion about a film. Now, that could pay, but I'd need to read any contract very carefully."

"I don't know much about that industry," I said. "But I doubt that the studios got to be rich by being generous."

"That's my impression too," she said.

"Do people ever confuse you with Mary Stewart?" I asked.

"Some," Freya said. "Those that don't understand the difference between Stuart and Stewart, but it probably serves me well as I get unintended purchases."

"Well, don't go really confusing things by writing your own Arthurian novels," I joked.

"You're right, better not," she agreed. "Would you make us some tea while I try this stuff you've loaded onto my Apple?"

"Of course," I said. I went downstairs to the kitchen and made tea, found biscuits and took them back up to the study. Freya was standing by the window looking out.

"The sea looks angry today," she said. "No swim today."

"No," I agreed. She was right, the sea was grey, the waves were big and it looked really unpleasant out there, almost as though Neptune himself was stirring things up. The rain was still coming down in buckets and I could see it sheeting across the sea, bouncing up from the ground when it hit and settling back to puddle on the ground.

"This is good for my cisterns," Freya said. "The more it rains, the happier I am."

"What happens when your cisterns are full?" I asked.

"There is an overflow that takes the water out and runs it to the burn over there," she said, pointing to a small stream. "If the cisterns are full, I have enough water for two years, allowing about 25 gallons a day for drinking, cleaning and washing."

"That's a lot of water," I calculated. "When we were here before we saw some processing equipment, does that circulate the water and keep it fresh?"

"That was the plan," she said. "I've added some charcoal filters to trap any bugs or algae, and the drinking water supply to the taps is filtered again."

"Do you have spare filters?" I asked.

"Plenty," she said. "I think my father was afraid of nuclear attack, because there are enough emergency rations for years down there. I've been replacing them over the past couple of years, so that they're not too out of date. So, if we go off to the wilds of New Mexico looking for Mr Right, do I go dressed as a cowboy, cowgirl, a city slicker, or something else?"

"I don't know," I confessed. "I was planning boots, jeans, a denim shirt and suede jacket, plus a hat."

"I can probably manage that," she said. "Boots, cowboy boots or kinky boots?"

"I think cowboy boots might be better," I suggested. "I think any kind of stiletto heels would not be practical."

"So, we are going then?" she asked.

"Why not?" I said.

"What are you grinning at?" she asked.

"The idea of us off to New Mexico on a manhunt," I said. "I did it once before when I went to Arusha to try and find what had happened to Ian. That time I didn't find Ian, but I found his letters to me and I tracked him down through his sister."

"So, you have a history of hunting down men?" she laughed.

"I suppose so," I admitted. "But only if he's the one, and I need to find out if New Mexico Tom is the one."

"Brilliant," she said. "When?"

"Let's plan for two weeks from now," I suggested. "Then if I do have my new client in Chicago we can stop on the way."

"Where do we have to go?" she asked.

"The closest airport is Albuquerque," I replied. "But Denver has nicer service and the drive down, although long, is really quite nice."

"How long?" she asked.

"It's about 320 miles to Mosquero, so if we're good and stick to the stupid speed limit of 55, then getting on for six hours, if we take a radar detector, we can knock an hour off that easily," I replied.

"And, this Mosquero to where your winery is?" she asked.

"That's about 140 miles," I said. "Some on the motorway and some through little towns, so about two and half hours."

"Is there anywhere to stay in Mosquero?" she asked.

"I'm not sure," I said. "I could call John in Pecos and get him to find out."

"This could be fun, what will the weather be like?" she asked.

"Well, when we go, it'll be mid-October," I thought. "So, would guess at least cool evenings, maybe rain, maybe even snow, the whole area is fairly high up. We'd better take some winter clothes in case. Are your books published in America, will we see any in bookshops?"

"Hopefully," she said. "I have an American publisher and they claim that my books are in the shops, it would be interesting to check."

"I should call my service that handles my mail and calls and see if anything has come in from my Chicago client," I said. "May I use the phone?"

"Please do," Freya said.

I called my service and learned that I had had a response from Dundee. They had accepted my proposal in principle and were looking for an initial meeting on the 9th of October at nine to finalise details. That was possible, so I asked the service to send a Telex back and confirm that I would be at their office at nine on the 9th.

"We're on," I told Freya when I went back upstairs. "We've an initial meeting with Dundee Materials on the 9th of October at nine in the morning. Do you want me to make reservations for you when I make mine?"

"Please do," she said. "I'll pay for my own ticket, but we can settle that later."

"We'll be flying out of Heathrow, so do you want to come down and stay with me the night before, or sooner if you like?" I asked.

"Why don't I come down on the Saturday before?" she suggested. "I suppose we'll fly over on the Monday for the Tuesday meeting."

"That's what I was thinking," I confirmed.

"Brilliant," she said. "What an adventure, let's hope that it leads to something."

"We'll see," I said. I was still unsure about this. Had I read far too much into a single glance, was he married, if not why not, if it led to something, what was New Mexico like, it seemed pretty isolated to me, could I cope with the isolation, could I cope with the winters that I was sure were more severe than British winters, the summer heat I knew I could probably managed, Nairobi had been hot at times?

"A drink to celebrate?" Freya suggested.

"Sounds good," I said.

Back to Pecos

I flew back from Colonsay in heavy weather nearly all the way, only clearing up after I had passed Buckingham, and was thankful to be on the ground again. It was as well that I had got my instrument flight rating, because visual flight rules were out for most of the way. The clouds were low, the winds were variable and the sun was nowhere to be seen. I probably spent more time on the radio than I had for ten trips in Kenya, but there was a lot more traffic in England and Scotland and I had to avoid the airports at Glasgow, Manchester and Birmingham before even getting to London. Still, it was good for me to fly using instruments. I towed my plane into the hangar I rented, took out my luggage and my whisky, probably enough to last me a year or two, and then locked up the plane and went home.

I spent the next few days digging into the data that had been collected for me by the grad students at LSE. I found five things that seemed to climb and peak about a year before the construction industry climbed. I will not disclose them because I made an agreement with Dundee that I would not. I made up charts that showed peaks and valleys in construction and superimposed the items I was looking at, then made slides out of them. I could use those to show the Dundee people what I was thinking and where we might get some good leading indicators. I called Maman and talked to her at length and she told me that James and Charlize were going to move to New Mexico sooner than they had originally planned and were in fact leaving that day, so would be in New Mexico by the time I got there.

Freya came down from the isles by train and I met her at Euston and we took the Tube back to Sloane Square, which is only a short walk to my flat.
"This is a nice place," Freya said when I showed her around the flat.
"It's convenient for London," I said. "It's paid for and big enough."
"Very nice," she said. "So, when do we leave, how long in Chicago and how long in New Mexico?"

"We take the BA flight to Chicago from Heathrow on Monday, stay at the Drake and then go to the Dundee offices which are on Lake Street," I replied. "We'll spend the whole of the next day there, then fly on to Denver on Wednesday and drive down to Pecos and spend a few days at the winery, then drive to Mosquero and explore cowboy country."

"I found a place that sells cowboy boots," she said. "I got myself a pair and a jacket, all I need now is a hat."

"I'm sure we could find one in Denver," I said. "Now, what do you fancy for dinner?"

We flew to Chicago and took a taxi to the Drake. It was an older hotel and it looked as if it were in need of some maintenance and updating. But it was nice enough and we were only there for two nights. Dressed in obligatory grey suits, we found our way to the Dundee offices the next morning and made ourselves known at the front desk. We were asked to wait and shortly thereafter a man came down a lift and asked us to follow him. We were whisked up to the fifteenth floor where Dundee had their corporate headquarters. There was a nice view of other buildings, but little else to make it in any way remarkable. We were shown to a conference room and offered coffee. We had just sat down when Richard Berg and Stuart Kahl came in.

"Dr Barclay," Richard said. "Thank you for coming."

"Good morning Mr Berg," I said. "Thank you for seeing us, this is my associate Dr Freya McIntosh, Freya, Richard Berg and Stuart Kahl."

"Nice to meet you," Richard said. "Good flight over?"

"Good enough," I said. "It was on time, which I like."

"We got your proposal," Richard said. "I agree in principle, there's just one or two items in the agreement that we'd like to discuss."

"Of course," I said. "What do you have concerns with?"

"It's not so much concerns as preferences on our part," Stuart said. "For instance, in the event of dispute, we'd like arbitration, then if that fails then for the matter to be tried in an Illinois court. I have some wording here for you to review."

"Isn't it interesting," I commented. "How all agreements have a fairly short section of what we will do, and then pages and pages of what if and what happens then."

"You're right," Richard laughed.

"What do you think, Freya?" I asked, passing the document to her. She read through it quickly.

"I see no problem with arbitration, the way this is written you get a hand in choosing the arbitrator, as for legal venues, we might suggest New York as an alternate," she replied. "We understand the need for suits to be tried and settled in a US court, but would prefer New York to Illinois."

"Any problem with that Stuart?" Richard asked.

"No, one's as good as the other," Stuart said. "There's the matter of ownership of the product, this language here is our suggestion." I sat back and watched as Freya and Stuart went around and around arguing the niceties of intellectual property. It was clear that Freya had quite some knowledge and experience in that field, probably gained through bitter experience with publishers of her books. In the end, we reached an agreement, whereby I licensed to them the models I would create for one dollar and any other licensees would have to pay considerably more. Freya argued that as I was using tools of the trade so to speak, arcane and peculiar as they may be, they were still tools of the trade and any blanket ownership of the product by Dundee would potentially hinder my ability to do business.

"You're fortunate in your associate," Richard commented to me. "Tell me, Dr McIntosh, are you a lawyer?"

"No, I'm actually a classicist by education, schooled in Latin and Greek," she said. "But, I've had a fair amount of experience in intellectual property matters."

"That's apparent," Stuart said a little ruefully.

"Good," Richard said. "We'll have those changes made and have a fresh agreement shortly." Stuart slipped out of the room and was back with fresh coffee. "So, Dr Barclay, any thoughts?"

"I have some," I said. "Do you have a slide projector?"

"I'll get one," Stuart offered. He was only gone a few minutes then he was back with a projector and an empty slide carousel. I loaded my slides then looked to Richard.

"Is there a screen?" I asked. He nodded and pressed a button and the blinds closed and a screen came down from a compartment in the ceiling. "So, these are some thoughts I had," I said. I went through each slide and discussed what was there and why it was important.

"We need to get Hal," Richard said. "Can you hold there a minute Dr Barclay." Richard picked up the telephone that was on a side table and

66

called a number and I heard him ask Hal to join us. He was with us shortly carrying two copies of the new agreement. Richard handed one to me and then he and Stuart looked over the other. I read through it, noting the changes made and looked to Freya for confirmation, she nodded yes, so I signed the one copy and handed it to Richard who did the same. With both signatures on each copy, I kept one, or should I say I gave it to Freya, and Stuart took one.

"Good, that's done, now Dr Barclay, would you go through what you were just telling us again, for Hal's benefit. Oh, and Hal, this is Dr McIntosh who's with Dr Barclay, don't try and negotiate with her, she's tough," Richard said. "Now, Dr Barclay, over to you." I went through my slides again explaining what each meant and what each implied, and how I would build a model from them.

"Who would have thought?" Hal said. "But there's no reason for there to be any relationship."

"Not directly," I agreed. "It's more of a sociology impact, with this and this it points to a demand for housing and infrastructure, it's certainly held for the past thirty years."

"How much of that was just post War boom?" Richard asked.

"If you look at the numbers, you can see that effect," I pointed out. "Some of these peaks are as a result of government policy, so I would need to adjust a model to accommodate that, it's really noticeable in the year or so just prior to an election. There are also obvious relationships with borrowing rates, the lower the rates, the more inclined people are to invest. There are the town planners, who tend to look at things five, ten, twenty years out, and they all work off population growth predictions."

"How soon can we get a more refined model?" Richard asked.

"I can have a working computer model in a month or so," I said. "Then, it's a question of feeding in data and seeing if the model produces expected results. I'm also going to look for other relationships, be they directly driven by housing need or infrastructure construction, to more esoteric indicators, you never know the demand for Easter eggs may signal a pent-up demand for bridges. Some of that will be purely chance, so the trick will be to sort out what is real, versus what is random. You've all heard of the famous story that if you put enough chimpanzees in a room with typewriters, then eventually they will come up with some Shakespearean work. If there are valid relationships, either economically or socially I will find them and build the mathematics for them. Also, I'm sure that I don't need to point out that natural disasters that cannot be predicted will change the demands. An earthquake in California or a hurricane coming ashore in Texas or Florida would wreak havoc with the infrastructure, but it would create a demand for materials."

We discussed all the indicators I had suggested and why they had either a direct relationship or a more obscure indirect one. I think that idea was new to them as they had not been thinking of generally how societies function and how behaviours might trigger a demand for something. I pointed to the consumer goods hawked at Valentine's Day and Easter and how it was a purely artificial construct within the society that created those demands.

"Right, guilt," Richard said. "If you don't buy your wife a dozen roses for Valentine's Day, you're a jerk, and who created that idea, the florists."

"Exactly," I said. "Sometimes pent-up demand is a purely social construct and not an economic or practical one, but the demand is still there. There will also be seasonality, you must have seen demand go up for do-it-yourself materials in the spring and summer."

"True, true," Richard said. "But, there's a way to mathematically model social behaviour?"

"There is," I confirmed. "One starts with a set of conditions and then goes from there."

"Anything else you guys?" Richard asked of Hal and Stuart.

"No," Hal said. "I need to look at some of the indicators you've thought of and pull up as much data as I can find, I've never looked at those kinds of possible relationships."

"Remember it's not a direct relationship, but an indication of societal behaviour that will create the conditions for demand," I said.

"I get that," Hal said. "This is all new to me, I suppose I should have paid attention in those economics classes at college. Stuart, you got anything?"

"When can we expect to see you again?" Stuart asked.

"I was thinking in terms of about six weeks," I said. "I have some business in New Mexico and then I need to see how to write a program that will allow you to put in data and get some output, either in the form of just numbers, but probably more usefully as a curve."

"Just let us know when and we'll set things up, maybe next time you come we can take a trip to a quarry and hold the meeting there,"

Richard suggested. "Now, let's go get some lunch. I thought we'd go to The Berghoff, Hal, Stuart, you coming?"

"I will," Hal said.

"Sorry, I've got some issues with a property in Iowa that I need to look at," Stuart said. "Dr Barclay, Dr McIntosh, I look forward to seeing you both again."

We walked to the Berghoff, a German-style restaurant that had been in business for decades. It was busy, but Richard was known and treated as an honoured patron and we were shown to a table where I saw Barbara Berg, already seated and apparently waiting for us.

"Dr Barclay," she said. "How nice to see you again, I don't believe I've met your colleague?"

"Barbara Berg, Dr Freya McIntosh," I said, making the introductions. "Freya is working with me for a while."

"She's got the measure of Stuart," Richard laughed. "She may not be a lawyer, but she knows intellectual property."

"Everything go well this morning?" Barbara asked.

"Really well," Richard said. "I'll tell you later, too many ears in this place and I don't want to give anything away. But, suffice it to say that it was an eye opener."

"That's good to hear," Barbara said. "I never asked, Dr Barclay, are you married?"

"It's Fiona," I said. "And, I was until he was killed in a car accident earlier this year."

"Oh, I'm so sorry," Barbara said. "And you, Dr McIntosh?"

"I was until mine was killed in Paris a couple of years ago," Freya replied.

"Oh, you two must be a great support to one another," Barbara said.

"It helps," I agreed.

"And Freya, may I call you Freya, what is your doctorate?" Barbara asked.

"Literature," Freya said. "Not much use in the real world, but I manage."

"We should eat so that Richard and Hal can get back to running the business," Barbara said. "I have an interest," she explained to Freya.

"If you can call holding fifteen per cent of the company just an interest," Hal joked.

Over lunch one of the differences between doing business in France and the States was apparent. In France there would have been wine, in

Chicago, even though we were in a place famous for its beer, there was no beer, just soft drinks or coffee. That was another difference, the Americans liked their coffee watery, not much espresso here. I also took the time to study Barbara a little, with the current market value of Dundee, Barbara was worth a cool $25,500,000 and she had received dividends of over a million dollars in 1978 alone. I know that Dad was worth a penny or two, but it was interesting to see how money in America looked. Barbara did not flaunt her wealth, she did not, at least not at the luncheon, wear expensive design name clothes, any more than I did, she was not weighed down with diamonds and gold, in fact seeing her on the street one would mark her down as an upper middle-class person.

"Isn't that a Rachel Adams?" Barbara asked me, commenting on my suit.

"It is," I confirmed. "I do work for Rachel and we've been friends for quite a while now."

"It's very nice," Barbara. "Very professional, but chic, not plain business, I think what the consultants would call a power suit. When we saw you before, who was that you were travelling with?"

"John, oh, John Cillie is my brother's father-in-law, the Cillies have a family business in wine and we were on our way to New Mexico to finalise the purchase of a small winery," I explained.

"I'm familiar with Cillie wines," Barbara said. "I like the ones from France, but didn't I read somewhere that they had sold the South African winery?"

"They have," I confirmed. "They acquired another one in France in Provence, about the same size as the one in the Loire Valley. The one in New Mexico is much smaller, but if the opportunity to acquire more or plant more arises, I'm sure they will take it."

"Do you do models for them too?" Richard asked.

"I do," I confirmed.

"If they ever go public, let me know," Barbara said. "I have some money in wine already and a little more wouldn't hurt."

"Sorry to break things up," Richard interrupted. "But Hal and I must get back. We're looking forward to seeing you in a couple of weeks."

"I'll be here," I promised. "And Hal, send me the latest specs on your 3033 and I'll make sure I write the program to match your computer."

"I'll do that," Hal promised.

"I suppose I should go too," Barbara said. "So nice to see you again Fiona and nice to meet you, Freya."

70

"Fancy a beer?" I asked Freya after the others had gone.

"Why not?" she asked. "You're not flying us tomorrow and we've the afternoon to kill, so a beer sounds good." We called over a waiter and asked about the beers. He reeled off a list and we picked one, not quite at random, but close enough, he then had the gall, or perhaps I should have taken it as a compliment, to ask me for my ID. I was not quite sure what that meant, but Freya explained that I needed to show that I was over twenty-one. Fortunately, I had my passport with me and showed him the relevant page. Satisfied, he beetled off and was back in less than a minute with two large steins of beer.

"Cheers," I said to Freya. "Thanks for coming with me today, I hope you weren't bored to tears."

"Cheers," she replied. "No, far from it, nice to see a group of men intimidated by you, they just don't know what to make of you. I think they were thinking in terms of some university theoretician and you go and ask them the difference between natural aggregate and crushed."

"Well, it struck me that might be significant," I said. "So, I noticed a huge bookshop when we were on our way to the hotel yesterday, let's stop and see if your books are on display."

"Good idea," she agreed. We finished our beer, paid for them, then wandered off to find the bookshop. It was huge, and we had to find a directory to tell us where the romance novels were shelved. We found them, arranged alphabetically by author, so Stuart was lower down on the shelves, about knee height I would guess.

"This is not the best for you," I commented. "Shelf browsers are not going to crouch down to pick a title, only those who come in with a mission will do that."

"You're right, Freya agreed. "It would be better if they were on a flat surface where a buyer could see all the titles without having to bend down."

"I wonder if you can get yours moved up higher?" I asked.

"Probably only if they're a featured item because I'm here to do a book signing," Freya thought. "I may actually have to do a tour and promote my books, then if people get hooked, then they will stoop down to look at my titles."

"Something to talk over with your US publisher," I said.

"Right," she agreed. "I'll do that when we get back. Now, let's find the travel section and buy a book on New Mexico."

There was no time the next morning to eat before the flight, so we dressed in our best western gear, jeans, boots, jackets and went to the O'Hare airport to catch the Continental flight to Denver. Freya had not flown Continental before. Most of her trips to the States had been to New York to meet with publishers, so for her, this was a foray into the interior. We had seats, row two, K and L. Those seats were very nice because we had extra space in front of us, the row one seats actually looked as if they could turn around to face us, but were separated from us by a table, which gave the extra space. We were served breakfast and then we got down to the serious business of studying our New Mexico guidebook. We read about the history of New Mexico and the huge land grants, about the cattle ranching, the copper mining, the government research facilities at Los Alamos and White Sands. There was only a little about the wines of New Mexico, either the author was not aware of the growing trade, or he, and the author was definitely a he, just preferred California wines and did not want to muddle people's minds with something new.

"Are we doing something silly?" I asked Freya. "Here we are flying off to see if I man I saw only once is of any interest."

"You won't know until you go," she replied. "And, if it turns out to be nothing, we have had an adventure, I will have had the chance to see something more of America than Fifth Avenue."

"Yes, but," I started.

"But me no buts," she said. "When you were there before you told me that there was a spark, was that not so?"

"It was, it was like an electric shock, I was startled, felt guilty, felt curious and uneasy," I confirmed.

"So, now we go back and see if that same spark is there," she said.

"But what if it isn't, what if it is, but he's a complete toad, what if he's already married?" I asked.

"You'll what if yourself to death," she said. "Now, we have to think about my research, I need you to observe as we go and tell me what you see, what kind of mountains, and I've heard that they're big, what kind of trees, what do people wear, how do they talk, what do they eat?"

"I can do that, just don't make your novel about me," I said. "We're starting to go down, so we'll find out soon enough what people are like."

"When we land, then it's officially research time, so I pay for the car, any hotels we might get, now you're my associate," she said.

"But," I said.

"No buts," she said. "This is my research trip and you're along to carry the bags, I hope you can take shorthand and type."

"Shorthand, no, type a little, but I'm sure nowhere near as fast as you," I confessed.

"Well, we'll manage," she said.

We left the plane and joined the throng in the concourse, and I have to say we did not look out of place among the others with boots, jeans and suede or leather jackets. We retrieved our luggage and went to get a hire car. Freya flashed an American Express Gold Card and people jumped. It was funny to watch, but then they became all apologetic, she had made a booking for something with four-wheel drive, but there was just nothing available.

"Never mind," I told her. "Just get something and we'll go to the winery and borrow one of their pick-ups."

"I suppose," she grumbled. "I will complain about this." We took our luggage and found our car, a very ordinary Ford Thunderbird, that still looked to me like a huge boat. We packed our luggage into the boot, sorry the trunk, and set off to find America.

"Look at those mountains," Freya said as we drove south. "Mountains, snow and blue sky, what a sight?"

"We're going to be running parallel to the mountains for a while," I said. "So, you'll have plenty of opportunity to study them, just don't drive off the road while you're doing it."

"Ha, ha," she said. "Now what I want first is a hat, I read about this shop, Rockmount, it's on Wazee Street, can you find that on the map?"

"This map's not good enough for that, we'll need to ask, what about that cop over there?" I suggested.

"Good idea," Freya said. We pulled over and stopped and Freya waved to the policeman who came over to us. Freya posed her question and we got detailed directions on how to get there. We found the shop and there was actually a space to park in the front, so we did not have to go wandering looking for a space. The shop was huge and was dedicated to ranch and western wear, shirts, boots, hats, belts, belt buckles, ponchos, waistcoats, you name it. Freya told them what she wanted and hats appeared, felt hats, suede hats, straw hats and leather hats, brown hats, grey hats, black hats, white hats, almost too many to choose from. Freya spent some time trying on and checking on herself in a mirror until she settled on a black felt hat. We both also bought some gloves, thinner ones in case we had to work and heavier ones in case the weather turned really cold. We paid and got directions back to the motorway, sorry freeway, and were soon on our way south to New Mexico.

"Do you ski?" Freya asked me as we motored south in view of the mountains and the snow, so much snow, which I suppose was to be expected as the mountains were high, so much higher than anything we had in Britain, even the road we were driving on was at a higher elevation than even Ben Nevis in Scotland.

"I had planned to learn when we were posted to Italy," I replied. "But, that never happened. Do you?"

"I do," she said. "I try to take a couple of trips each winter to the Alps, but I've been thinking that they have some nice places here, so maybe I should come here instead. I could fly to Chicago and then to Denver."

"Is it hard?" I asked.

"To just come down a short slope, no," she said. "To swish around between trees, jump moguls and do all the fancy stuff takes some skill and a lot of practice. Lessons are a good idea, you can teach yourself, but you'll get it right much quicker with some guidance."

"Could you, would you teach me?" I asked.

"I could," she said. "But a good ski instructor is worth the money and I'm sure they have them here, and, I'd like to stay your friend and I've noted that when friends or spouse try and teach each other, it often ends in tears and recriminations."

"It says here in the guidebook that New Mexico has ski areas too," I said.

"We should investigate those," she suggested. "Where are they?"

"There's one not far from Santa Fe, there's another couple near Taos, so they're all fairly close to Pecos," I said.

"Let's plan to come back in early December," she suggested.

"What do I need in terms of gear?" I asked.

"I would suggest that you rent boots, skis and poles to start with," she said. "No point in buying the expensive items if you hate it. Get some pants and a jacket, goggles, helmet and gloves, we can go over all that when we get back to the UK."

"I have a client who's a major sporting goods retailer, I should ask them if they sell ski stuff," I thought.

"Ask them if they sell Ellesse, Rossignol or Helly Hansen," Freya suggested. "Those are good brands to start with."

"What do you have?" I asked.

"Most of my outerwear is Rossignol," she said. "I have specialist skis, bindings, boots and poles, but you don't want to spend that kind of money until you've tried it, decided you like it and will go often enough to justify spending the money on your own rather than renting."

"How do you transport skis when you go?" I asked.

"The airlines all know how to handle skis," she said. "Just like they do with golf clubs."

"Don't tell me you play golf as well?" I asked.

"I play, but I'm not that good," she said. "I'm not a fanatic about it, so won't spend hours and hours on courses. Look there's a sign to Trinidad, how on earth did a place in Colorado get to be called Trinidad?"

"I wondered about that too," I said. "The best explanation I could find was that it was named after the daughter of an early settler, her name, believe it or not, was Trinidad, which is also the Spanish for trinity, so, I suppose has religious connotations."

We bye-passed Trinidad where I had stopped before for lunch and was less than impressed, and went over the mountains to Raton, climbing to almost 7,834ft to the summit and marvelling at the signs that could order chains to be put on wheels in bad weather. We pulled off at Raton for something to eat. We must have picked the right place because there were five police cars and a sheriff's car parked outside. We were looked over by the police when we walked inside, and they nodded to us and went back to their lunch. Food was almost entirely Mexican or Southwestern, so we opted for tamales, wondering what we would get. A plate arrived with these things that looked as if they were wrappers of some kind of coarse leaf. We stole looks around the place and divined that we were supposed to remove the wrapper and the dish would then be revealed. They were chicken tamales and were really good. There was a green chile sauce to go with them, and that was hot, as hot as a good vindaloo curry. I thought a beer would go well with them, but we decided that with possibly half the Raton police force watching us that we would stick to coke. The police all left and the sheriff followed, I noted that whereas the police wore the typical peaked cap, the sheriff had a cowboy hat, white, or rather off-white. He had a Chevrolet pick-up and waved to us as he left. We saw him again when we left the diner and made our way back to the freeway. He was parked just off the road, watching the traffic, but we were being good, not speeding, so he waved again and watched us go.

From Raton south we left the high mountains of Colorado, there were still mountains to the west of the road, but they were not the dramatic high snow-covered peaks of the Colorado Rockies. We were now in flatter country with the occasional hill, albeit all at a high altitude, and we passed Maxwell, Springer and Wagon Mound then veered a little to the west and came once again to the mountains, still the Rocky Mountains, but the less dramatic New Mexico Rockies, more tree covered than snow-covered. From Las Vegas we climbed into the foothills and passed through the wonderful scenery that is there between Las Vegas and Rowe, the turn-off to Pecos. We arrived at the winery in time for afternoon tea. The whole family was there, James and Charlize with Fiona, John and Anna and Maman and Portia.

"Fiona," Charlize said as we got out of our land boat. "Have you come to join the fun?"

"Fun?" I asked.

"We've been pressing, fermenting, decanting, and even bottling from the ageing barrels," she explained. "It's been busy."

"We were just stopping to steal one of the pick-ups," I said. "How are you, how's Fiona?"

"We're both fine," Charlize assured me. "Fiona's gaining weight and seems to have adapted to the altitude nicely. I'm sorry but we're short of space, were you planning to stay?"

"I thought we'd stay in Santa Fe," I said. "Do you remember Freya from Ian's funeral?"

"I do," Charlize said. "I hope you have time to tour the vineyard, I can explain what I want to do here. Anyway, come in and say hello to everyone before you steal one of my trucks."

"We won't need it for a couple of days," I assured her. "But, when we take off to do the research Freya wants to do on cattle ranching for her racy romance novels, it would be better for ranch roads than the land boat we have now."

"You're right there," Charlize agreed. "We've had occasion to drive out to look at things and a large pick-up truck is definitely handy, especially one with four-wheel drive and a winch, many of the county roads around here are dirt and in the rains can be interesting, it's like being back in the Karoo."

We caught up with the news, we talked about my visit with the Dundee Materials people, we discussed Freya's latest novel ideas and found out what was happening with the winery. The harvest had been good, so they had been busy pressing and vats were full of red and white wine, busy fermenting away. Charlize had a baby carrier that she strapped about herself and then went about the vineyard lugging Fiona with her. James was delighted with the Kubota and had made fast friends with it. I checked with Maria and she had one or two questions or issues with the Apple computer, but I was able to quickly resolve them for her. Charlize and James were getting on well with Audrey and Jeff. I had wondered how that would work, Charlize had definite ideas about wines and how they should be made and fortunately, Audrey had similar ideas, so there was no clash of ideas or even egos. Charlize and Audrey were already planning out new plantings to double the acreage and the winery model I had done for them told them when they would need to add presses, tanks, ageing barrels, all the physical items that went with winemaking. They were also looking into setting up a distillation process using the pomace from the white pressings to make grappa. That was a simple enough process, the complication was the morass of Federal and State regulations and permits to distil. With the peculiar American attitudes towards alcohol, the paperwork and permits were far more complex than the actual making, no wonder in rural areas moon-shining took off, they simply could not deal with the government, or afford the various licenses that were required. The red wine pomace was being sold as cattle feed, but both Charlize and Audrey were looking into a second fermentation to produce a wine similar to what the Italians would call *ripasso*.

Freya and I stayed the night at the La Fonda Hotel. It was close enough to Pecos that it was no particular inconvenience to drive back and forth.

We shuttled back and forth for the next couple of days while Freya took an extended tour of the winery with Audrey, then James, then Charlize, then Jeff, while I worked with Maria on some invoicing and shipping label issues. We took a quick trip to Taos, and discovered a shop there that sold sheepskin coats, as winter was impending and snow was possible, we each bought one, three-quarter length, suede outside finish and wonderfully woolly inside. I had the chance to talk to Maman and Portia and told them that I was going back to Mosquero to test the waters so to speak.

"I'm uneasy about this," I said. "I keep feeling that I'm being disloyal to Ian."

"I don't think Ian would have wanted you to stay single," Maman said. "He would want you to get on with your life, find happiness, and that might be another man, it might be a convent, who knows?"

"A convent?" I said in horror. "Maman, I'm not that far gone. No, I'm ready to try something else. I was blissfully happy with Ian and if I can find that again I will."

"Well, Tom did," Maman reminded me. Tom was my brother-in-law, he was married to Irene, Ian's sister. Tom's first wife had died and he had met Irene and they had hit it off and were now happily married. Does a brother-in-law stay a brother-in-law when the person around which the relationship is built dies. I wondered what Irene would think if I remarried. She probably would approve and encourage it, because she had seen what a difference it had made to Tom.

"Is it possible to be attracted to someone just like that?" I asked.

"I remember when you called me, quite late at night as I recall, all excited about this man you had met," Maman said. "Then you gushed about this chap called Ian and how your eyes had met and how the spark was there, how did that turn out?"

"I know, I know," I said. "Ian was the love of my life, can it happen again, what does happen anyway?"

"That's one of the great mysteries of life," Maman said. "What did Puzo call it in *The Godfather*, the thunderbolt?"

"So, what are you and Freya going to do?" Portia asked.

"We thought we'd motor to Mosquero than make discreet enquiries about Tom, but given the size of the place, my guess is that anyone asking about anyone is reported on very quickly," I said. "I want to show

Freya Mills Canyon, it's such a pretty place along the Canadian River. I also would like to drive some of the county roads and see what the countryside is like away from the towns. My only real concern is that I will show up on the pages of one of Freya's romances."

"I'm sure that if she uses you as a character you will be well disguised," Portia said.

"Do you have a good road map of New Mexico?" Maman asked.

"I saw a bookshop in Santa Fe, I thought I'd look in there for a road atlas of New Mexico," I said. "What would be good to know is where the petrol stations are?"

"I imagine that there are enough of them," Maman said. "It seems to me that there are a lot of ranch trucks and cars, so there must be petrol stations not too far from each other."

"We bought a guidebook on New Mexico," I said. "But it's singularly quiet about much of the north-east part of the state, and looking at the map that the car hire company gave us, towns are small and are few and far between."

"So, if anything comes of this Tom, would you be ready to move out here to the wilderness?" Portia asked.

"I'm not sure," I admitted. "As romantic as it sounds, it could be very isolated, Nairobi wasn't London, but it was a good-sized city and there was always lots going on. From Nairobi there were daily flights to London, here it's a drive to either Albuquerque or Denver, then a flight to somewhere then another flight to London or Paris."

"Yes, and your little plane can't really take you back and forth across the Atlantic," Portia said.

"No," I agreed. "I also can't afford the kind of flashy jet I'd need to fly myself across the ocean."

"What do you know about cattle ranching?" Maman asked.

"There are cows," I joked. "What kind of cows, how many cows there are per acre or acres per cow, I don't know, I suppose depends on how good the grazing is and how much water there is, but I've not much idea. Ian did tell me that bovids have to drink daily, so a ranch would need a water supply."

"What are you three talking about?" James asked was he joined us.

"Ranching," I said. "We were talking about cows and I was thinking the little I know about them is what transfers over from wild bovids like the buffalo we got in Kenya."

"I imagine a buffalo is a lot tougher customer than your average cow," James said. "Domestication must have altered their behaviour at least a little."

"Well, buffalo are good to eat," I said. "Like beef, but generally leaner than the beef you buy in the butcher's.

"There's certainly a lot of them around here," James said.

"What, buffalo?" I joked.

"No, dodo, I meant cows," he said. "Between here and Raton there are lots of pastures with cows in them."

"I wonder if sheep do at all well here?" I thought. "I've not seen any on the two trips I've made here now."

"So, what's Freya going to write about in her next novel?" James asked.

"She has a plot line already, cowboy bails out city girl when she breaks down on the road, city girl has a toad for a boyfriend, but he does have money, so will she opt for the toad and the lifestyle or the cowboy and a really different lifestyle," I explained.

"So, are you the city girl?" James asked.

"I don't see myself as a city girl," I protested.

"You are by many people's standards," he said. "You live in London, which the last time I checked was a handy-sized city, you wear design label clothes, you drink nice wine, of course, it's nice we make it, you flit around the world hobnobbing with all and sundry, you fly around in your own plane."

"You make it sound so glamorous," I said.

"It's not?" he asked.

"Well, I suppose it has its plusses, the only real minus right now is someone to share it with," I bemoaned.

"I'm sure you'll find someone," he said. "Really, Fi, I know you will. If not you can come and live here and be the maiden aunt who runs after her niece at every turn."

"I'm not exactly a maiden aunt," I said dryly.

"No, I'll give you that, I heard too much from you about the exploits of you and Ian to think you're a maiden," he laughed.

"How are you and Charlize doing here?" I asked, changing the subject away from the sexual proclivities that Ian and I shared.

"We love it," he said. "There's work to do, plenty of it, but the winery is on a firm footing, we just need to expand carefully and get some brand identification going. Charlie is thinking of a tasting event in Santa Fe and another in Taos, to hit the arty crowd. She's also got a couple of the local papers lined up for tours here to tell them all about vines, grapes and wine."

"And how is Fiona adapting?" I asked.

"She's at the age where all that is important is that she's close to Charlie, so they stay attached, Charlie was joking to me the other day that she feels like one of the African women they had working in the Cape. They would come to work with babies strapped to their backs," James replied.

"She's certainly healthy enough," Maman commented.

We were joined by Anna and John and conversation turned to their other grandchildren and the differences between them all. Eventually, Freya and I excused ourselves and drove back to Santa Fe and our hotel. We found the bookshop still open so went in and browsed and found a road atlas of New Mexico. It was quite detailed and showed all the back roads as well as the major roads.

Mosquero

Freya and I traded our hire car for one of the winery's pick-up trucks. It was a beast of a truck, a Ford F-350 Super Heavy Duty Pick-up with a huge V8 engine, it had four-wheel drive, a winch on the front and a big push bar thing on the front as well, and a tow bar on the back. In a locked box in the back, we were shown tyre chains, tow ropes, a shovel, a pick, an axe, flares, jumper cables and other items for rescue and survival. Clearly, when John had bought these trucks he had gone out of his way to ensure that all possible measures were taken to provide the driver all the items he or she might need in the event of problems. I made sure both fuel tanks were full, put two cases of wine in the back, that I did pay for, and we set off to discover the wilds of America. The drive north from Rowe to Las Vegas was simply a retracing of the route that Freya and I had taken coming down from Denver, but somehow it seemed different from the cab of the truck, we were high up, looking down on cars that went by, and had this feeling of invincibility. Past Las Vegas, we continued north past Watrous and at Wagon Mound, we left the main road and took the road to Roy. In Wagon Mound itself, we took the opportunity to top up our petrol tanks, not that we had used that much, but I had no idea where the next petrol station might be. We had only just cleared the environs of Wagon Mound when we saw our first pronghorn antelope. They stood looking at us as we pulled to the side of the road to get a better look at them.

"They're rather pretty, aren't they?" Freya said. "I suppose they can jump these fences."

"I don't know, but look over there, those are crawling under the fence," I pointed out.

"Maybe that's how they move pasture to pasture," Freya suggested.

"Shall we go on?" I asked.

"Drive on," she said. "Makes me feel most superior riding in this beast, don't try and hit anything, but I suspect that if we do we'll come off best, unless it's a big lorry." We drove on and came to the Canadian River, we wound our way to the bottom, crossed the river, then wound our way back up again the other side.

"What's next?" Freya asked.

"Roy," I said.

"Roy, how does a place get a name like Roy?" she wondered.

"Does the guidebook say anything?" I asked.

"Only that it's there," she said, after consulting the pages. "My guess is that it was someone, I wonder someone Roy or Roy someone?"

"It's a small enough place," I commented as we drove through Roy, turned right at the crossroads in the middle of the hamlet, and continued on our way to Solano and Mosquero.

"There's a policeman," Freya said, pointing. "Wave to him." I waved and he waved back, then went back to doing whatever he had been doing. It looked as if he was giving some poor soul a speeding ticket, I filed that away for future reference thinking about something John had said about not trusting little *dorpies* as they tended to be speed traps. Solano was even smaller than Roy and we flashed by it. It looked like its claim to fame was a small building that advertised itself as the post office. My guess was that it served local ranches more than the half a dozen houses there were just off the road we were on. I did notice something that I had not observed before when I had come this way with John, it looked as if we were running parallel to an old railway line. Certainly, there were all the signs, something built up or cut into the slight hills, running as straight as it could, it had to be an old railway line.

We came to Mosquero and pulled up on Main Street outside the café run by Sally.

"Howdy," she said when we walked in. "You're back, ready to break some hearts?"

"I doubt it," I laughed. "Is there a motel or B and B here?" I asked.

"Just down the road," she said. "You want me to call them for you?"

"That would be great," I said. "Two rooms if they have them, for Fiona and Freya for three nights."

"I'll do that," she promised. "Coffee?"

"Please," I said. "Do you serve wine here?"

"Not here, next door at the bar," she said. "You like some?"

"No, I've got a couple of cases in the truck, you might like to try," I said.

"That's right, when you were here before you said that you were buying Dale's place, how's that going?" she asked.

"Well," I said. "They had a good harvest this year and are busy right now with pressing, fermenting and all the other things they have to do. Let me just go and get the cases for you." I went back out to the truck and collected the wine and brought it in and placed it on the counter for Sally.

"What do I owe you?" she asked.

"Nothing," I said. "Just try it and let us know if you like it."

"What can I get you for lunch?" she asked.

"Burger, well done," I said. "Freya?"

"Is it local beef?" Freya asked.

"It is," Sally confirmed.

"Then same for me, thanks," Freya said. Sally scurried off and was back surprisingly quickly with the burgers. They were good, but large, I still had a difficult time adjusting to the sizes of meal portions in the States, it seemed that everything really was bigger and better in America.

"Okay, you've got rooms at the Bunkhouse just down the road, small motel, five rooms, not busy this time of year. So, what really brings you back here?" Sally asked, as she parked herself close to our table.

"My friend, Freya, is a writer and she's looking for background on a new novel," I explained.

"What kind of novel?" Sally asked.

"A romance," Freya explained. "I write under the name Mary Stuart."

"You're Mary Stuart," Sally said, looking as startled as a deer in car headlights. "Really, Mary Stuart, author of *Safari Heartbreak*?"

"Really," I confirmed.

"Would you autograph a couple of my books?" Sally asked.

"Of course," Freya said. Sally hurried off to the back of her café and was soon back with a stack of novels, she must have had ten of them. I watched as Freya talked about each in turn and asked Sally what message she would like inscribed in each. When she came to the latest, she waved it at me and said. "This is the first Kenya novel, *Safari Heartbreak*."

"I see," I said. "I first met Freya on the plane from London to Nairobi," I explained to Sally. "She was on her way there to do some research."

"Were you going there on vacation?" Sally asked me.

"No, I lived there," I said. "My husband was a diplomat there."

"I remember you said you were a widow," Sally said. "So sad, so Freya, Mary, what's the new novel?"

"Cowboys," Freya replied. "Ranchers and cattle and city folk."

"Well, there's plenty of cowboys round here, but you'll have to look for them, they're pretty scattered on the ranches," Sally said.

"Fiona told me that there were four who said that they'd be here the third week of October, so I thought we'd come out and I'd talk to them," Freya said.

"So, what are you going to do for the rest of today and tomorrow before they come on Wednesday?" Sally asked.

"We thought we'd just drive around a little and look at the country and get a feel for it," Freya said.

"You could do that," Sally agreed. "Tomorrow you should take the road here down to Logan and come back on the county road, that'll take you through a few ranches, you'll probably see cows, maybe even a cowboy or two, but you'll get an idea of what the country looks like."

"And this afternoon?" Freya asked.

"I'd take the county road north and explore a bit, it's different country than you'll see tomorrow, flatter, have you got a good map?" Sally asked.

"We do," I said. I scooted out to the truck and came back with the road atlas. Sally opened it to the appropriate page and pointed out the county roads she had suggested. What struck me about them, was that they were straight, straight as arrows, not like British roads that meandered everywhere, except what was left of the Roman roads.

"We noticed between Roy and here what looked like the remains of a railway line," Freya said. "Where did it go?"

"There was a coal mine at Dawson and the line ran from Dawson to Tucumcari," Sally explained. "It was pulled up a while ago when the coal mine shut down. There are some places where the county roads run down the old track, you have to watch out for railroad spikes there."

"We should probably go and check-in," I suggested.

"Down the road, first right, you can't miss it," Sally said.

We found the Bunkhouse, it really did look like a converted bunkhouse, the rooms were all in a line and there was a room for sitting and eating, but we gathered that the only meal served was breakfast. The rooms were nice enough with brightly coloured blankets, pictures on the walls of cowboys, either driving cattle or what looked like branding and other activities around corrals. We dropped our bags in our rooms, and then took off to discover Harding County. The guidebook told us that the county was one of the least populated counties in the United States and that most of the employment was in ranching. We also learned that Mosquero, small as it was, was the county seat and boasted a courthouse.

We drove north up County Highway O and then east and back south on N. The guidebook was right, it was cattle everywhere. We ate dinner that night at Sally's, basking in the newfound celebrity that Freya now commanded. Sally had apparently called friends, because several women showed up with books to be autographed. I think Freya was happy to do so as it showed that she had some readership. The following day we ploughed our way through the breakfast that the Bunkhouse offered, and it was huge. We both of us felt that we would need little else that day until the evening. We then explored further by driving to Logan, another small village, but in a different county. To get there we went east from Mosquero then dropped down an escarpment to the land below. As we wound down the escarpment we would catch glimpses of vistas to the east, vistas that seemed to stretch for miles into the blue-grey of the distance. The terrain did not look overly different from the lands above, except that we were now almost 2,000ft lower. We found a small place open in Logan and had coffee, then started back.

We retraced our steps for a short way, then turned off onto a county road that headed west. The county road was like those we had taken the day before, unpaved, but graded, in better condition than many of the roads I had driven on in Kenya. It started to snow, lightly at first, then quite hard. Visibility was reduced a little so I did actually slow down, and as a precaution engaged the four-wheel drive on the truck. It was quite a way before we saw our first habitation, it looked like a ranch, there was a house and behind it cattle pens, lots of them. We came to a road junction and our way was to the north, not the south as the road we had been on seemed to be going. As we went on we noticed evidence of the old railway line that we had seen between Roy and Mosquero and concluded that we must be headed in the right direction. We saw no more houses, no people, no cars, just cows, cows scattered in pastures, cows clustered around water tanks, and cows sheltering from the wind and snow as best they could with the few taller trees that there were.

"There's someone not far in front of us," I commented to Freya, pointing at the tracks in the snow.
"How do you know they're not far in front?" she asked.

"If you look at the tracks, you can tell by the amount of snow that's falling and the track definition that we're close," I explained. "Ian taught me a little of how to read tracks."

"Well, let's hope we don't run into them, literally I mean," she said, I think only half joking. We did run into them, not literally, but suddenly there they were. They were stuck on a slope, a Cadillac Eldorado with Texas licence plates, a huge boat of a car, even larger than the one we had hired in Denver. We had slowed down and were following their tracks around a corner and the road dived down into a creek bed and up the other side, and there they were sitting halfway up on the other side. I could see where he had skidded as he had obviously stamped on the accelerator in the vain hope that more power to the wheels would propel him out of his problem. I stopped, put on my new fancy sheepskin coat and my hat, and walked down and up to see if we could help.

"Do you need a tow?" I asked a man as he wound down his window.

"That'd be great," he said. "I didn't expect this and we're a little lost, we just came from Amarillo on our way from Dallas to Santa Fe and thought we'd take the scenic route, didn't count on the snow."

"Don't worry," I assured him. "We'll get you out." I looked at the road, tested the ground by his car where I would have to pass him, then walked back to the truck.

"What's the problem?" Freya asked.

"Stuck," I said. "They didn't expect snow and I don't think they took a good enough run to get them through this gully."

"Can you tow them out?" she asked.

"Of course," I said. "I'll drive to the other side and walk back with a rope. I just hope there's somewhere decent to tie it to on their car." I drove down into the gully and up the other side and stopped at the top. It only took a minute to fish out a tow rope from the box in the back, then I hitched it to the tow hook on our truck, then walked back to the car. I peered underneath the front and found what I was looking for, a tie-down loop that was probably used when shipping the car. That would serve very nicely as my attach point.

"Okay," I told the man. "I'm going to slowly take up the slack on the rope, when you see it go taught, then put the car in gear and put your foot lightly on the accelerator, don't try and rev it too much, let me do the work."

"Okay," he said. I walked back to the truck and slowly took up the slack in the rope, then felt the drag as we picked up the car behind. Pulling him out of the gully took less than a minute and when we were well clear, I pulled up and let the rope go slack. I walked back to the car and untied my rope.

"Say thanks," he said. "Don't know what we'd have done if you guys hadn't come along. How far to the nearest tar road?" Freya had been consulting the maps again, so I knew where we were and how far it was to Mosquero and a tarred road.

"About twenty miles," I told him.

"Twenty miles?" the woman in the car complained. "Should we turn back?"

"It's about the same going back," he said. "We'll go on."

"We'll go ahead of you and if there's any more of these gullies, we'll wait until you come to make sure you can get through," I suggested.

"Say, that's mighty nice of you," the woman said. "But, ya'll are not from around here, I just love your accent."

"We're just visiting," I said.

"But, where'd you get the truck?" she asked.

"I borrowed it from my brother," I said.

"Old Pecos Wines?" she said. "I read the sign on the door."

"They have a winery in Pecos," I said. "It's not that far from Santa Fe."

"Maybe when, if, we ever get back on the main road, we'll take a look," she said.

"That would be nice," I agreed. "Look, we'll just take off slowly and we'll keep an eye on you, and as I said, any more of these gullies we'll stop to make sure you're through." I coiled up the tow rope and stowed it in the box, then waved to the Texans and drove on. We had not gone too far when it was apparent that we were driving on the old railway line.

"I hope we don't meet someone coming the other way," Freya joked. "One of us would have to reverse to some passing place."

"Someone has been ahead of us," I pointed out. "But a while ago, we're not likely to run into them."

"The snow's really coming down, isn't it," Freya said. "It reminds me of the time I entered the Monte Carlo Rally."

"You were in the Monte Carlo?" I asked.

"I drove it in 1977 in an Alpine," she said. "I finished, not in the top twenty, but I finished."

"Who was your navigator?" I asked.

"Kirsty," Freya replied.

"How would your Alpine do in this?" I asked.

"Fine," she said. "It would actually be fun, but I might mess up the road a little and I'm sure that the people here would not appreciate that. Are those hillbillies still behind us?"

"They are," I assured her. "Which way?" I asked as we neared some buildings.

"Veer to the right," she said. "It looks from the map as if the county road leaves the railway line here, that over there is the railway line, but maybe it's no longer passable." We drove on and on and on and then came to another gully. I drove through and pulled up and stopped a little way from the top to await the Texans. They came flying into the gully, but failed to make it to the top. This time, instead of trying to get out by spinning his wheels, the man just waited. I backed up a little, then got the tow rope and pulled them out of that predicament. The road now started to climb, we were obviously going back up to the higher plateau. I kept a close eye on the car behind, but he seemed to be managing. Perhaps because I was not going at any great speed he had to keep his speed down as well, which actually gave him better control. We did come to quite a hill and he had trouble again and actually started to slide towards the edge. He did stop and just sit, which was a smart thing to do. I backed down the hill, hitched him up, engaged the low range of gears and pulled them all to the top. From there, there were some ups and downs, some delays as we waited for cows to get off the road here and there, until we saw Mosquero in the distance. Once in town and on the tar, I stopped and went back to talk to them.

"Just down here, turn left on Main and you'll be on the road to Roy," I told them. "At Roy take the turn to the left and follow it to Wagon Mound, at Wagon Mound you can join the freeway."

"I need a drink," he said. "Can we buy you a drink?"

"And a place to stay, is there anywheres in this place?" she asked.

"There is," I said. "There's the Bunkhouse, a small motel just down there where we're staying, and on Main there's a bar, next to Sally's Café, we're walking over there after we drop our things."

"Great, let's go and see if this Bunkhouse has rooms, then we'll see you in the bar," she suggested. We drove in procession to the motel and went to our rooms while they went to the lobby. The snow was still coming down and there was now an appreciable accumulation on the ground, probably four to five inches, so our walk to the bar was through snow, undisturbed snow, fluffy snow, not like the damp sticky stuff we got in

England. As everywhere when it snows, it was quiet, as though the snow dampened all the sounds. It was really rather charming.

We had been in the bar a few minutes relating our experiences to Sally when the Texans came in.

"Hey guys, what can we get you?" he asked. "Name's Elmer, this is Joy, we're from Dallas and where're you guys from? It ain't from around here, that's for sure."

"We're from the UK," I said. "I'm Fiona, this is Freya. This is Sally, she's the proprietor here."

"You know what these guys did?" Elmer asked Sally. "They pulled us out of the mire, three times, didn't even bat an eye, just hitched us up and towed us out. So, what can we get you?"

"Just a glass of wine would be fine," I replied.

"Give them a bottle, the best you've got, I'll have a Scotch, rocks, make it a double," Elmer instructed Sally. "What about you, Honey?" he asked Joy.

"I'll have a Rob Roy," she said. "Make it a big one, I've never been so glad to get anywhere, I thought we were going to have to walk here, until these guys showed up. I'm sorry Honey, I know it was my idea to take the scenic route, but I didn't expect snow."

"No more did I," Elmer said. "When they offered to tow me out I was going to tell them what to do, but Fiona seemed to know, so I just shut up and let her get on with it. A pity we had snow, I bet that if the weather's good, that that would be a nice drive."

"It is," Sally agreed. "But, not many people go that way, mainly just the ranchers that live down there."

"Well, we saw a heap of cows," Joy said. "Cows everywhere."

"You passed through a few ranches on your way," Sally said. "The biggest one is the Bell, about 290,000 acres all told. What do you folks do in Dallas?"

"Oil," Elmer said. "We're into oil, got wells in the Permian, got wells in Pennsylvania, got wells in the Williston, got wells in California. Our company is JET, Joy Elmer Tate, EJT didn't work, so we switched it around to JET, has a nice ring to it, don't you think?"

"So, are you more like Bobby or JR?" Sally asked, making reference to the popular soap opera, *Dallas*.

"Neither," Elmer said. "Maybe a little like Jock, but I've no time for scheming, I just drill wells in and get them producing, then Joy and I can indulge ourselves."

"You said you were on your way to Santa Fe," I said. "Is there anything special there?"

"Nope," Elmer said. "Just had a hankering to see the place, maybe motor on up to Taos, Joy wants to buy some more art and we both like the southwest style, even decorated our home in Dallas that way."

"I'm hungry, El," Joy said. "Let's get something to eat, and let's get these gals something as well."

Sally produced menus and we ordered. She disappeared for a few minutes and was then back with the Rob Roy, the Scotch and one of the bottles we had brought. Elmer picked it up and looked at it. "This is from the place you got the truck from, is it any good?"

"Sally, why don't you bring Elmer and Joy glasses and they can at least taste it," I suggested.

'This ain't half bad," Elmer announced when he tasted the wine. "Where do you say this Old Pecos was?"

"In Pecos," I said. "Turn off the freeway at Rowe and go north."

"We should buy a few cases," Elmer said to Joy.

'We should," Joy agreed. "They don't make a Scotch do they?"

"Not yet," I laughed. "They may do some distilling in time, but Scotch has to come from Scotland, if you fancy some nice Scotch try Old Mull or Glen August."

"I've been there," Elmer said. "We took a tour last year of Scotland and that included distilleries, couldn't bring that much back with us, so I'm looking into becoming an importer."

"So what do you two do that brings to the US?" Joy asked.

"I'm researching a new novel," Freya said. "Fiona is keeping me company when she's not working."

"What kind of novel, have you written others, have I heard of them?" Joy asked.

"Perhaps," Freya said. "I write under the name of Mary Stuart."

"Mary Stuart of *Highland Heartbreak*?" Joy asked.

"That's me," Freya said. "I've written a few in the *Heartbreak* series."

"I love your books, I've got *Safari Heartbreak* along with me to read, would you sign it for me?" Joy asked.

"Why don't you bring it to breakfast tomorrow and I'll sign it then?" Freya suggested.

"That'd be great," Joy gushed. "And you Fiona, what do you do?"

"I create economic models for businesses," I said.

"What kind of economic models?" Elmer asked.

"Either high-level models to look at supply and demand, or operational ones to model the production economics of companies," I replied.

"Are you any good?" Elmer asked.

"The Chancellor of the Exchequer thinks so," I said. "I've done a couple of taxation models for the UK."

"You know anything about reserves?" Elmer asked.

"My first big project was a model for proven, probable and possible reserves for the metal mining industry," I said. "I did it for a consortium that wanted a better model to argue their asset valuation case with the taxing authorities."

"Really?" he said. "We should talk, here's my card, call me if you would in about two weeks' time when we're home."

"I'll do that," I promised. "I'm sorry I don't have a card on me, but I'll give you one at breakfast tomorrow."

"Where did you learn to tow cars?" Elmer asked.

"I lived in Kenya," I said. "The roads there weren't always the best, so we got used to digging out and towing."

"Well, I'm sure glad you guys came along when you did, it looked like it was some way to the closest ranch," he said. "Is this snow usual?"

"We get some," Sally said. "But not that much, it's usually pretty dry here."

"What about the road to Roy tomorrow?" he asked.

"It should be ploughed," Sally said. "Don't leave at six in the morning, give them a little time to clear it, if when you get to Roy you see that they haven't cleared the road to Wagon Mound, just go straight and you can pick up the freeway at Springer, but you should be fine."

"Okay, what about another Honey," he asked of Joy.

"Sure," she said. "You guys?"

"I'm fine thank you," I said. "I think I'll walk back and turn in."

"See you for breakfast tomorrow," Joy said. "And, I'll bring my book for you to sign, Freya."

We had breakfast the next morning with Elmer and Joy and saw them on their way. It looked as if the snow plough had been through earlier, as the road looked fairly clear. At about ten, Freya and I went to Sally's to await our cowboys. They came in as scheduled and nodded to us as they did. We gave them the chance to have their meeting and lunch, and when it looked as if it was about to end, I walked over to them.

"Hello," I said. "I'm Fiona Barclay, I don't know if you remember but I was here a few weeks ago."

"We remember," Javier said. "How you doing?"

"We're fine," I said. "This is my friend Freya, she writes novels and she's thinking of setting one on a ranch and she's looking for background material."

"She's famous," Sally added, coming over with more coffee for the men.

"What can we tell you?" Javier asked.

"Maybe what it's like to work on a ranch, how do you meet other people?" Freya suggested.

"What you should do is meet Tom's Dad," Javier suggested. "He'll tell you stories until the cows come home, he's been out on the ranch all his life, took it over from his dad and he from his dad. The ranch goes back to the 1880s."

"He would at that," Sally added. "What about it Tom?"

"We could," Tom agreed. "Look, why don't you drive out to the ranch, talk to Dad, probably best to stay the night, we're a little out of the way."

"Are you sure we won't be inconveniencing you?" Freya asked.

"Not at all," Tom said. "We've got spare rooms in the old bunkhouse and Mom and Dad like to meet new people. Would you be coming too, Fiona?"

"She's my driver," Freya said. "If you don't have enough spare rooms, we can share."

"That would work," he said.

"How do we get there?" I asked.

"What are you driving?" he asked.

"We have a pick-up," I said.

"Okay, then the smart thing to do is just follow me," he suggested.

"Give us a few minutes to collect our things from the Bunkhouse and we'll be ready," I said.

"Okay, meet me back here in about fifteen?" he asked.

"We'll do that," I promised. I looked to Sally and she nodded, yes, and I took that as an endorsement of the plan.

"Well?" Freya asked as we walked back to the motel.

"Well, what?" I parried.

"Is it still there?" she asked.

"It is," I said. "I'm torn, I want to go with you because I think it will be really interesting, but I'm nervous, but it's still there, the electricity when our eyes meet."

"I understand," she said. "If you need to leave at any time, just let me know and we'll leave."

"Okay," I said. We paid our bill, and collected our things and drove back to Main Street. I parked outside Sally's and went in to see if Tom was ready.

"All set?" he asked.

"All set," I confirmed.

"Just follow me then," he said. "See you guys sometime, see ya, Sally." We followed Tom back past Solano and to Roy where we turned off onto the Wagon Mound road. The road had been ploughed so Elmer and Joy would have had an easy drive to Wagon Mound. Not far from Roy we turned off to the south and followed a county road for a while, then took another turn, this time to the west. This road had not been ploughed, but the snow was not that deep that it made driving difficult.

"We must be getting close to the Canadian River," I said to Freya.

"It looks like it," she agreed. "This place is certainly off the beaten track, there's not much here except trees, grass and cows."

"I don't think there's much in the way of beaten tracks out here," I said. "It looks like we've arrived." Arrived we had. The ranch house was a large stone building with a corrugated iron roof. There were several other buildings around whose purpose and use I could only guess at.

"Come on in," Tom invited. "Mom, Dad, we've got visitors. This is Freya, sorry didn't get your last name, and Fiona Barclay, Freya wants some background on ranching for a novel she's writing, Sally in Mosquero says she's famous, this is my Mom, Maria Ortiz and my Dad, Steve Ortiz."

"It's very nice to meet you," Freya said. "My name is McIntosh, but I write under the name of Mary Stuart."

"You wrote, *London Heartbreak?*" Maria asked.

"I did," Freya confirmed.

"Can I get you some coffee?" Maria asked.

"That would be super, thanks," Freya said. I nodded yes as well and sat back and looked around the room. On the wall were bookshelves, with a vast variety of books, from novels to books on grasses and others on cows and cow diseases, there was also a map with what I presumed were pastures marked and numbered.

"What would you like to know?" Steve asked.

"I think how you got into the ranching business, and what are the issues with ranching today?" Freya said.

"It all goes back to the mid-1800s," Steve said. "There were some huge land grants made back then, from which came today's ranches, like the Bell. My great grandfather, Steve, made a deal for this land back in 1888, and the place has been in the family ever since."

"How big is it?" Freya asked.

"About 40,000 acres," Steve replied. "We run about 600 head at any one time."

"Is that typical?" I asked. "Somewhere around sixty acres per cow?"

"We think of it in terms of sixty acres per cow-calf combination," Steve explained. "The grasses are good, but not that good."

"What kind of cows do you have?" Freya asked.

"Black Angus," Steve said. "They do well here. Other people have tried Texas Longhorn, Charolais, Criollo, Hereford, but we've found that the Black Angus suits us best."

"Do you have many cowboys?" Freya asked.

"No," Steve said. "Our daughter, Linda, runs the place now with the help of her husband Jim, and we've one hired hand, José."

"That's all you need?" Freya asked. I think she had been imagining a bunkhouse full of cowboys all riding off into the ranges to round up cows.

"Over the years we've spent money on fencing, so we've divided the land into pastures, and we move the cattle from pasture to pasture, we don't just let them wander all over the place," Steve said. "Once you get to understand cows you know how they're going to behave and you can move them without a lot of trouble."

"Do you still use horses?" Freya asked.

"Sometimes," Steve said. "But most of the time we use Honda ATVs. You should talk to Linda, maybe get her to take you out on the ranch tomorrow, you are staying the night?"

"I suggested that, Dad," Tom added.

"I'll get Linda and Jim to come over for dinner," Maria said.

Conversation between Freya and Steve continued and my mind wandered, wondering what it would have been like to be raised on this remote ranch. I suppose the schooling would be in Roy, but did not recall seeing a school there, in fact, the only school we had actually seen on our trip was in Wagon Mound, where we had driven right by it. I caught the eye of Tom who was looking at me and smiled and he grinned. I was about to say something, but was forestalled by the arrival of Linda and Jim and their two children, Maria and Hillary, who I would have put at about twelve and ten. Introductions were made and Freya and Linda started chatting away about cows, grass, weather, beef markets and what it was like to grow up on the ranch. Conversation was interrupted by dinner, beef, I suppose naturally.

"Is this your beef?" Freya asked.

"It is," Linda confirmed. "We typically take a steer a year to a plant in Amarillo and have it butchered and jointed for us."

"So, what's your rôle on the ranch?" Freya asked Tom, I think saving me from having to begin the questioning.

"I'm just visiting," he said. "I'm waiting for my visas to come through so that I can go to Cambridge for my doctorate, I'm going to study photovoltaics at the Cavendish labs."

"I would think solar power generation would be useful here," Freya said.

"If you could get the economics to work. So, have you been working in the field?"

"I got my master's at MIT and have been at Hoffman Electronics," he said. "They've been able to boost efficiency of panels to 14%."

"How does education work here?" Freya asked.

"The Roy school takes everyone from Kindergarten to high school. That's where Maria and Hillary go," Maria said. "There's only, what forty-some students there now, but they all get a really good education."

"I'm sure they do," Freya said. "The island I grew up on is really small and we have a primary school and for high school, we would go to Oban and stay there the week going home on the ferry for weekends, but we did get a really good education."

"How far away was that?" Maria asked.

"The ferry would take about two and a half hours," Freya said.

"Where did you stay during the week?" Maria asked.

"The school had a hostel for students like me from Colonsay and those from Coll, it was staffed during the week, but sometimes even over the weekend if the weather was really bad and the ferries could not sail," Freya explained.

"And I thought it was remote out here?" Linda said. "At least here we could come home every night, how big is Colonsay?"

"About ten miles long and two wide, I think about 10,000 acres in all," Freya said.

"That is small," Linda laughed. "Fit about four of those on this ranch and even more on the Bell."

"What do people do there?" Linda asked.

"Small farms, cows, Highland Cattle, sheep, people like me who live there because we like it, but earn our money somewhere else," Freya said.

"And you, Fiona?" Maria asked.

"I grew up in a fairly big town, but my parents got me tutors until I went to high school, then I went to college at fifteen," I said.

"Wow," Linda said. "You must be really bright."

"She is," Freya said. "When did you get your first doctorate, Fi?"

"When I was twenty," I said.

"And the others?" Freya pressed.

"You've more than one?" Tom asked.

"Three," I said. "The first in mathematics, then one in economics and the last in computer science."

"I was right, you must be bright," Linda said.

"So, what do you actually do?" Maria asked.

"I create economic models for companies and governments," I explained.

"Ever done one for a ranch?" Steve asked.

"No," I said. "I've done one for a large agricultural company to predict crop yields, I done one for a coffee farm and do all the models for the Cillie Wines operations."

"What do you know about cows?" Steve asked.

"Beyond that they have four legs, a head and a tail, very little," I admitted. "I know like all bovids that they need to drink regularly, preferably daily, other than that, not much."

"Say, Freya," Linda said. "Why don't you come for a drive tomorrow with me and I can show you the ranch? Fiona, do you want to come?"

"I was going to suggest that I take Fiona on a ride tomorrow, that is if you can ride Fiona?" Tom said. I saw Linda glance at Maria raise her eyebrows a little and smile and wondered if this was a rare or common occurrence.

"I can ride," I said. "I've not used a western-style saddle before, but I've been on a horse quite a bit, I even used to jump when I was younger."

"Okay then," Tom said. "Linda you take Freya and talk ranch stuff and I'll see what Fiona can tell me about Cambridge and living in England."

"If we're going out and about in the morning, I need to get some sleep," Freya said. "Would you all mind if I turned in?"

"Of course not," Maria said. "Let me show you where you can sleep." She led us off to an adjacent building and showed us a room each with a bathroom between. The beds were already made up and there were towels on each.

"Breakfast at seven?" she said.

I got up at about six-thirty the next morning and looked out of the window to see deer wandering by. There were five of them, three does and two fawns. I dressed, navy blue underwear, cotton with lace trim, blue jeans, denim shirt, socks, boots and suede jacket. The room had been heated with a fire, but it was long out and it was quite chilly. Breakfast was similar to that served at the Bunkhouse, and I ploughed through mine until I was full. I went back to our cottage and collected my coat, hat and gloves and went back to await events.

"All set," Linda asked Freya when she arrived at the house. She and Jim lived in their own house about five miles away from the main ranch house, so she had driven over to collect Freya. "Jim's taken the kids to school, so we'll take a drive around the ranch and be back for lunch, oh, and before I forget, Fiona, this is the phone number for us, so if you ever need anything just call me. Okay, Freya, shall we go?"

"All set," Freya replied. "Fiona, will you be okay?"

"I'm sure I'll be fine," I assured her.

"So, let's go and pick you out a horse," Tom said. I followed him out to a corral and there were four there. He picked out two and had them quickly saddled.

"Try Blue," he said, leading a gelding to me. Blue was about fourteen hands, so a little shorter than the mare I used to jump with, who stood at about sixteen hands and always made me look diminutive perched atop her. I checked the girth cinch to ensure that all was tight, then mounted. I have to say that having the pommel horn to hang on to was really nice. It was also the first time that I had been on a horse with a rifle scabbard, with a rifle in it, a lasso tied lightly to the pommel and saddle bags behind me.

"Are we going to need these?" I asked.

"You never know what we may come across," he said. "We've mountain lions, coyotes, even a few bears around. Can you shoot?"

"I can," I said. "Where are we going?"

"I thought we'd ride out and take a look at the river," he said as we set off at a walk. "You can tell me about Cambridge on the way."

"I went to Oxford, then London, so my Cambridge experience is limited to people I know and the times I visited," I said.

"The first time I saw you, you had a wedding ring, now you don't, did something change?" he asked.

"My husband died early this year," I explained. "I had been wearing the ring out of habit, but it's time now to move on with my life."

"So sorry to hear that," he said. "What was it?"

"A traffic accident," I said. "He was near the Kenya-Uganda border and got in the way of a Libyan in a lorry, fleeing the fighting, and you, you're not married?"

"Was going to be once," he said. "Then she decided to go with an oil guy from Texas, had more money than me."

"How do you meet people out here?" I asked.

"Dances in town, mutual friends, college friends," he said. "It's not easy and if you actually live here, it has to be a special person to be able to live isolated like this. Where do you live?"

"I have a flat in London, I was living in Kenya until my husband died, then I had to return to London, he was a British diplomat and the house belonged to the legation in Nairobi," I explained. "Do you know whether you'll be living in college in Cambridge or in digs?"

"Sorry, digs?" he asked.

"Rented accommodations," I explained. "It really is beautiful here, it's peaceful, no traffic, sunshine, clear blue skies, quite different from either London or Cambridge."

"It is," he agreed. "But, we have a problem continuing to live here. Dad and my uncle were both heirs to the ranch, my uncle wasn't interested and moved to Dallas, where, with some cash that Dad found for him from the ranch, he built a successful hardware chain. Now he's dead and my three cousins all want their share of their dad's inheritance. That's why Dad wanted to know if you'd done an economic model of a ranch. We need something to counter the claims of their shyster lawyer, or the only way we'll raise the money is sell part of the ranch, then is it even viable, a pity that Dad never got a loan agreement from Uncle Rick for the cash he gave him to start the hardware business, if he had we could deduct that plus interest over the years from the ranch value?"

"I'm sure I could build a model of the ranch easily enough," I said. "The lawyer your cousins have, is he basing the valuation on pure land value or as a percentage of the income from the ranch as a going concern?"

"Straight land value," Tom said. "Ninety dollars per acre, so all told for half the ranch, $1,800,000, far more cash than we have."

"Have they specified what part of the land?" I asked.

"No, they just want half the value of the land," he said.

"Would the land out near the main road have a higher market value than say this land here?" I asked.

"I suppose it might, it could go for $100 to $120 an acre, while this here could be $70 to $80 per acre, but even at $120 an acre, that would still be 15,000 acres, which I don't think we could lose, I don't know if the ranch would be viable at 25,000 acres, maybe it would, but it would be a smaller operation. We couldn't afford to keep José on and we'd have to rethink the retirement accounts we set up for Mom and Dad and for Linda and her family. Just as well I don't want to take money out as well or there'd be no option other than selling the whole thing, then where would Mom and Dad live and what would Linda and Joe do?"

"I suppose banks are loath to lend?" I asked.

"You bet," he said. "If we take a market weight of a steer at 1,456, that dresses out to 872 and right now carcass prices are $1.37 a pound, which gives us $1,195 per steer and we ship 400 a year, that gives us what?"

"$478,000 a year," I said.

"Okay, that sounds like a lot, but out of that has to come all the operating expenses, the salaries, vehicles, horses, maintenance, house repairs, pensions, health care, taxes, and the rest, so net earnings are way less than that and free cash to pay anyone off even less, we don't have that much room to take on debt, we can't really change the stocking rate, the grazing's not that good, and if we get a drought year with no rain, we may have to buy feed just to maintain the breeding herd we have, so, the banks, if they lend at all, lend at a high-interest rate, because of their perceived risk," he said.

"If you could give me numbers I can see what I can work up," I said. I was already doing mental arithmetic and I could probably come up with that amount. I had a million pounds, which converted to over two million dollars, so, the real question was, was I being fanciful to even think about this, and would Tom and his family countenance an outsider providing funding. They would want to know what my expectations were and on what terms I would expect repayment, after all, LIBOR, the London Inter-Bank Offered Rate, was running at about 14%, so bank lending was going to be far higher than that. If banks would lend, they would probably charge LIBOR plus at least fifty basis points, more likely far more than that, but fifty would do for now, so the interest alone on $1,800,000 was going to be significant, well over $261,000, and if they mortgaged the place to raise the money, then the monthly repayments over thirty years would be over $22,042, just not doable with the current operation, but this was all surely in the realms of romantic musings. "When do they expect an answer?" I asked.

"They know that it's not going to be that easy to either come up with the money directly or find a buyer, so they've at least been reasonable and set a deadline of a year, which is actually eleven months from now," he said.

"How is the ownership of the ranch structured?" I asked.

"Gramps set up the Ortiz Cattle Company and Dad and Uncle Rick each held 50%, then three years ago Dad made over his 50% to Linda and me, so we now have 25% each. With Uncle Rick dying, then each of the rats has 16.5%, with the last half a per cent being held by their lawyer as his fee for managing Uncle Tom's estate, so if they get money from us he gets $3,000 for being a pain, and whatever else he's charging them for his time."

"So, sometime in the next few months, you have some decisions to make?" I said.

"We do," he agreed. "This pisses me off, Linda's doing a great job with the ranch, but we can't pull that much out of it. I don't need the money from it, but Mom and Dad still need an income in retirement and Social Security won't cover everything, it's a pity that when Uncle Rick said that he didn't want any part of the ranch that Dad didn't get that in writing and get Uncle Rick's shares made over to him, also a pity that when Dad gave Uncle Rick the cash for the hardware stores that he didn't draw up a loan agreement from the ranch to cover that cash plus interest on it over the years. It's probably something that a lawyer could argue, but that takes time and money. Anyway, enough rant for the day, we're almost to a lookout where we can see the river."

"That is spectacular," I said as we came up to the view. It truly was and deserved a picture. I had brought my camera with me, so shot off a few frames of the canyon, the trees and even of Tom, posed by his horse. I also got him to take a picture of me, dressed for the part, with my, lariat, rifle, the works.

"Let's walk a little?" he suggested. We dismounted and tethered the horses to a nearby tree and then walked out towards the edge. It was apparent that Tom really liked this place, he obviously knew it well and seemed happy to share it with me.

"Look," he said, pointing down the slope. There were elk walking along towards us, three of them.

"Are they common here?" I asked.

"We see them, but I wouldn't say that they're common," he said. "Some people don't like to have them around because they're grazers, not browsers, so they see them as competition for the cattle."

"This really is a beautiful place," I said. He started pointing other things out, the types of trees, the birds, some deer on the other side of the river, it was like being out in the bush with Ian, a comparison I had to tell myself to stop making. Ian was Ian and he was dead and buried, and I was left to make a new life for myself.

"Coffee?" he asked.

"Thanks," I said. Tom went back to his horse and fished in one of the saddlebags and pulled out a flask and container that looked as if it had cake in it. He also got two enamel mugs and poured us each coffee, after he had brushed the snow off a rock so that we could sit, then offered me some cake.

"So, how is it living in England?" he asked.

"Not many places as quiet as this," I said. "There are a lot more people everywhere and distances are not what they are here. Driving from here to Denver would get you from London to Carlisle which is the other end of England, almost to the Scottish border."

"You said you live in London?" he asked.

"I have a flat in the centre of London," I confirmed. "It's convenient for doing business in London and easy access to Heathrow if I need to go anywhere."

"How far is it from London to Cambridge?" he asked.

"About sixty-five miles," I said.

"Have you ever been there?" he asked.

"A few times," I said. "I've been to conferences there on economics and I just visited a few times. It's a nice city, on the River Cam, full of students, not much industry there, surrounded by countryside which is farms, arable lands, dairy farms and the like."

"I think they have a place for me to stay in college," he said. "At least that's what I took the letter to mean. I got a fellowship to see if we can improve the efficiency of solar panels by changing the substrates."

"I'm sure places like this could use solar," I said.

"We could," he said a little wistfully. "We use windmills already to fill the water tanks for the cattle, and maybe pairing a panel with that would help when we get no wind. So, how are you doing, I mean after the death of your husband?"

"I have good days and not so good days, but I have to say that the good days are now beginning to far outweigh the bad days," I said. "I've even thought about dating again."

"You have?" he said, looking at me questioningly.

"I have," I confirmed. "Freya's been a big help as has my family."

"Who's in your family?" he asked.

"I have one brother, James, he now lives in Pecos with Charlize and their new baby, Fiona, my Mom lives in France with her partner, Portia, and my Dad lives in London with his wife, Felicity, that's it for my close family, I also have some distant cousins in France, you?"

"Well, you met Mom and Dad and Linda and Jim and their two, Maria and Hillary, then there's the cousins, Bert, Dale and Steve, plus their wives and hangers on, there was Uncle Bert, but he died in France flying for the USAAF in 1944," Tom enumerated. "Your Mom lives in France and you have cousins in France, what's the connection?"

"My Mom is French, well French and Tahitian, my grandfather was French and grandmother Tahitian," I explained. "And you?"

"Dad is Hispanic as is Mom, obviously Pops, Dad's dad was Hispanic but Nana, Dad's mom was Anglo, and so was my great grandmother, and I think if you go further back there was some Navajo and even Hopi, but that was quite a long time ago," he said. "So, we're also a bit of a mix. So, you speak French?" he asked.

"I do," I confirmed.

"Anything you can't do?" he laughed.

"Rope a cow," I said. "My life growing up was very academic, but I did learn to shoot, I can get myself out of most situations if I bog my car, I can't cook worth a damn, you don't want to hear me sing, I'm not at all musical, you?"

"Well, I can play the guitar, I can cook some, not restaurant food, but basic stuff, I speak Spanish, I can weld, hunt if I have to and butcher my own kill," he replied. "Oh, and I can rope a cow."

"Are you looking forward to your time in England?" I asked.

"I am," he said. "It'll be different, but MIT was different, I'm sure Cambridge in Mass is not like Cambridge in England, even though those folks back east talk about how old things are there. Look, can I see you when I get to London?"

"I would like that," I said, and he smiled a smile so wide that it was infectious. That was it, I was committed now, to at least one date. What we might do, where we might go, I would have to wait and see what transpired. I felt relieved, relieved that I had taken the plunge and relieved that he seemed as interested in me as I was in him.

"We're expected back for lunch," he said. "We should head back." He packed away the coffee things, brought over the horses and waited until I had mounted Blue. We set off back, not retracing our steps, but taking a slightly different route, which was just as enchanting as the ride out, or was it the company that made it enchanting. We picked up the pace a little from a walk to a trot to a canter, and it was fun. We wove between the trees, scattering snow as we went, they were not very big trees, but there were lots of them, mostly juniper that I could see. I knew that we were close to the ranch when I saw the cottonwood trees. I had gathered that where there were cottonwoods, there was water and the ranch house had been close to a small stream. At the corral, I unsaddled my own horse and rubbed him down before sending him off to roll around and get the itches out.

"Did you enjoy your ride?" Maria asked as we went into the house.

"I did," I said. "It's beautiful out here."

"We think so," she said cheerfully, but I could see the concern in her face, were they going to have to sell up in order to satisfy the demands of the other heirs?

"You've got some mail," Linda said, handing Tom a package.

"It's my passport and visa for England," Tom said. "I'm all set to go now, I've also got the travel arrangements here, I leave in ten days, Denver to Chicago, Chicago London on TWA."

"I'll meet you at Heathrow," I said. "Just give me the date and the flight number." I saw Linda glance at Maria and raise her eyebrows a little.

"So, you two are getting on?" Maria asked.

"We are," Tom said. "Fiona's been telling me all about England, and she promised to see me on my way from the airport to Cambridge."

"I'll drive you there," I said.

"I found out that Fiona's half French," Tom said. "Speaks French too."

"Do you speak Spanish?" Linda asked.

"Not yet," I admitted. "I do speak Italian as well as French, so it's probably not going to be too difficult to learn Spanish, I was going to do that because now that my brother lives in Pecos, Spanish might be useful."

"She's hiding her light under a bushel," Freya said. "She also speaks Swahili and Mandarin and some Tahitian, and she flies her own plane."

"What do you have?" Tom asked.

"A Cessna 206," I replied. "I had a Skyhawk in Kenya, but sold it when I left and bought the Stationair. I'd be happy to take you for a spin Tom when you come to England."

"She was just up visiting me on Colonsay," Freya said. "We went for a couple of quick trips to visit distilleries."

"I hope you didn't sample too much," Tom laughed.

"I did, but Fiona didn't," Freya said.

"Lunch will be about five minutes if you wanted to wash up first," Maria suggested.

"Well," Freya asked as we walked back to the cottage we were sharing.

"I like him," I said. "I'd really like to get to know him better."

"Linda was asking me all about you as we toured the ranch and went to the post office," Freya said. "I told her all the good bits, I did confirm that you had been married and that Ian had died and that I had been to the funeral, so she knows that's not just a story."

"I noticed she and Maria signal one another," I said.

"Yes," Freya agreed. "I think they were both concerned that Tom would ever find someone, he got burned when his first love, Juanita, ran off with an oil man, so he's been loath to date ever since. Linda told me that she doesn't think he even had a girlfriend in LA while he's been working for Hoffman."

"Did she tell you about the cousins and the demand for money?" I asked.

"No, what's that all about?" Freya asked.

"I'll tell you on the plane on the way home," I promised. "Do you want the loo first?"

"Okay," she said. "I'll yell when I'm done, and see you back at the house."

Lunch was a very haphazard affair, with food set out to help ourselves. The ranchers did eat well, I will say that for them. There were a few hot and spicy dishes done with green chile, and by hot, I mean hot, I could only manage very small tastes of them. But there was plenty besides, so I was not going to go hungry.

"What was Kenya like?" Linda asked over lunch.

"It was hot, we lived in Nairobi which is quite a big city, English was spoken by the professional class and the government workers, but out in the villages it was Swahili, Kikuyu and at least fifteen other languages. I did pick up some Kikuyu while I was there," I replied.

"Did you see much game?" Tom asked.

"Lots," I said. "Both on the ground and from the air."

"Did you work while you were there?" Linda asked.

"I used to fly back and forth to London or Paris for projects," I said. "So, I logged a lot of miles on British Airways."

"The Maasai are cattle people, aren't they?" Steve asked.

"They are," I confirmed. "They know each cow and can tell you all about them, they really look after them and work hard to preserve their way of life."

"Were you ever worried living there?" Maria asked.

"There were a couple of times when I thought there might be war between Kenya and Uganda or Kenya and Somalia, but it was mostly hot air," I said. "I kept up my pistol shooting skills in case, and even took up combat pistol shooting. But, fortunately, never had to shoot in earnest. If there had been war the High Commission would have shipped us out before it got too bad. So, Freya, how was the tour?"

"Fascinating," she said. "It's not quite what I expected, but all I had seen before was old westerns on the TV. This is different, much more concern about the cows and less concern with shooting at the neighbours."

"We wouldn't do that," Tom laughed. "Even when some of them deserve it."

"Do you have enough material," I asked Freya.

"More than enough," she said. "Are you thinking that we should go back to Pecos?"

"Go tomorrow," Maria suggested. "Enjoy the afternoon here, take a drive, take a ride, or do nothing. Steve can entertain you."

"Okay," Freya said. "Fiona?"

"Well, our flight's not until three days from now, so if we go back to Pecos tomorrow and collect the hire car we'll have plenty of time to get back to Denver for the flight," I thought.

"That's a plan then," Freya said. "So, what do we do this afternoon?"

"We could take a look around the ranch buildings here," Tom suggested. "See what it takes to run a ranch."

"What's here?" Freya asked.

"We have a workshop, barns, stables, old wood shed, the chicken coop," he said. "And, tomorrow morning there's a rodeo in Roy, would you like to go?"

"A rodeo?" Freya said. "That I have to go to, Fiona, that's something we have to do."

"Absolutely," I said. I had never seen or been to a rodeo, so this would be a first. "Is this a professional rodeo or just local people?"

"This is just local folks," he said. "It's a big social occasion for us, one of the few times we all get together. It's the best time to go speeding through town because the local cop is a member of the committee and will be busy in the arena as a safety rider."

Rodeo

We took the tour after lunch, in time to see Joe and José leave with a truck laden with fence posts, barbed wire and tools. The workshop was an Aladdin's cave. There were tools, anvils, compressors, bits and parts of all kinds of things, spare tyres, wheels, oxygen and acetylene cylinders, rolls of barbed wire, steel fence posts, wind pump vanes, ropes, chains, workbenches and even some open space where one could work. We toured the stables that adjoined the corral, with stabling for six horses and storage for feed and storage for saddles and other tack. We peeked into the wood shed, actually full of neatly stacked logs of wood all cut to the same length. The chicken coop was well populated and when we went there the chickens all came rushing over to see if we had brought anything worth eating. The chickens provided eggs to eat and also some were themselves food on the hoof, so to speak. The barn had freezers, which we looked into and saw packages of beef, all neatly labelled. The barn also had bulk storage of non-perishables, well stocked in case trips to town were not possible. Freya understood all this better than I, for after all, she had to deal with the occasions when the weather was bad enough that the ferry could not sail and supplies not be delivered. We looked into another little shed and that was the water supply system. A large tank was fed by a spring and the header tank kept a pressure for the house. Tom told us that the spring had never failed and that for most of the time, there was in fact an overflow as the tank was always full. He told us that he recalled four times in his life when the levels had dropped to the point that they had rationed water for themselves. We were shown Maria's garden and it was well planted with all kinds of herbs, peppers, onions and other vegetables. Tom told us that Maria was getting to the point that she could not maintain the garden as well as she would like and was facing the unwelcome prospect of having to let it go.

I took stock of Tom, recalling my description of Ian to Maman, he was an inch or two taller than me, that meant that he was perhaps a little under average height as I was short. I guessed that he weighed about eleven stone, so he was lean and slender, he had dark hair, almost black, perhaps that was the old Spanish influence. I could imagine Maman telling me that she was not there to buy him, but to tell her something about the man. Well, so far he had been very nice, happy to attend to my needs, he smiled a lot at me, and seemed genuinely taken with me, which I was thankful for, because it would have been awkward, to say the least, if I had been drawn to him and he had rejected me. I would guess that he loved his parents and his sister and he really loved the ranch that he had grown up on. I could see that having to potentially sell part to satisfy other heirs was going to be difficult in the extreme.

We finished our tour back at the ranch house in time for an early dinner, which was a barbecue. We were joined by Linda, Joe and the girls and by José with his wife, Sofia, and their daughter, Renata, who was of an age with Maria and by the look of it great friends. Before the light faded I imposed on everyone and lined them up in various groups for photographs, I wanted something to take with me to remember this all by. Maria, Hillary and Renata crowded around me and asked what it was like to live in Africa.

"It was warm," I said. "Not really hot, because we were fairly high up, but nice and warm. We had two seasons, wet and dry, actually really three, long rains, short rains and otherwise dry."

"So, no snow?" Maria asked.

"There was snow on the mountains, and they were high enough that the snow was there all year," I replied.

"Were there lions and tigers?" Hillary asked.

"You don't get tigers in Africa," Maria told her.

"We did have lions," I said. "If I went away from the town, there were elephants, lions, wildebeest, zebras, giraffes, all sorts of animals."

"What do the people speak?" Renata asked.

"Some English, some Swahili, otherwise the language of their people, and there were lots of them," I said.

"Did you speak any of them?" Renata asked.

"I spoke Swahili and some Kikuyu," I said.

"What does Swahili sound like?" Maria asked.

"*Jambo*," I said. "*Jambo* means hello, *habari*, how are you, *nzuri*, fine."

"What about goodbye?" Hillary asked.

"*Kwaheri*," I said.

"And thank you?" Renata asked.

"*Asante, asante sana*," I said. "*Asante,* thank you, *asante sana*, thank you very much."

"Did you see many animals?" Hillary asked.

"I did," I said. "I went into the bush as often as I could, I would usually fly somewhere and then have people pick me up."

"They have airlines there then?" Maria asked.

"They have," I said. "But I meant I would take my own plane and fly out."

"You have a plane?" Renata asked.

"I have one, not the same one I had in Kenya, but a new one that's a little bigger. That's how I went to see Freya, I flew to the island where she lives, it was much quicker than taking the train then the ferry," I said.

"What's the Swahili for lion?" Hillary asked.

"*Simba,*" I said. "Elephant is *tembo*, zebra is *pundamilia*."

"Did you live in a big house?" Maria asked.

"It was quite big," I said. "It had a nice garden with grass and trees and a wall all around."

"Why did you leave?" Hillary asked.

"My husband was killed in a car crash, so I went back to London," I said.

"Oh, I'm sorry," Hillary said.

"It's all right," I said. "It's good for me to talk about it. It was difficult for a while, but it's getting better and better. Now that I have met all of you, things look very good."

"We need to get dinner organised girls," Linda interrupted. "You can talk to Fiona more after we've eaten."

Dinner was to be steaks cooked on an open grill with mesquite wood, served with a huge green salad, I had begun to wonder if anything green was served, but it was and in abundance. After dinner, Tom and José got out guitars and played, and as far as I was concerned they were good, really good, but my judgement of things musical probably should not be relied upon. Sofia did sing for us, Spanish songs and English songs. I had warned Tom before not to call upon me to sing, as they would regret it if they did. It crossed my mind that singing was not one of Ian's talents and had to pull myself up again and remind myself to stop comparing Tom to Ian. It was unfair to Tom to be always judged against Ian, they were different people in different times. Freya could sing though, something about her I did not know. She sang some Gaelic songs and the classic stand bye *Over the Sea to Skye*. I did have more questions from the girls about living in Kenya, what did people wear, and they were in hysterics when I told them that the Turkana often wore nothing at all. They also wanted to know what people did for a living and were intrigued by the Maasai and the fact that they were cattle people. I suppose they could identify. They were disappointed that the Maasai did not use horses at all, I told them that they did not need to, they herded the cattle on foot and stayed with them all the time. They wanted to know what I did for a living, and when I told them I did mathematics they wanted to know how anyone other than a school teacher could possibly make a living with mathematics. I tried as best I could to explain, but guessed that Linda and Tom would get a lot of questions after I had gone. Eventually, the evening broke up and the girls went off to bed to get some sleep before the rodeo.

I went to bed thinking about the day, the ride in the morning, the romantic side of ranching, riding off into the west looking at the scenery and enjoying the outdoors, then the more practical side in the afternoon, the fixing of things that will break, the fencing, the gathering of the cattle, the branding, the inoculations, the weaning, the problems of varying demands for beef, and therefore the price that could be realised off each animal sold, all the work that had to go into maintaining the ranch. It was hard work, like any farming enterprise. I admired Linda for managing it, and thought that if ever I had to urge to get into ranching that I would hire a manager to do most of the work for me.

I was up early the next morning, I had been neglecting myself lately and needed some exercise. I put on my Chinese pyjamas, or at least that is what I called them. Loose trousers and a matching top that gave great freedom of movement. I went outside and found a nice clear space near the horse corral and went into my katana routine. It was a mix of the martial arts moves of karate and kung fu with the more flowing moves of tai chi, so lots of moves designed to awaken the body, centre oneself and improve balance. By the time I was done, my mind was clearer and I was ready for the day. I went back in and changed and went to the kitchen, where there was coffee on the go.

"That looked very elegant," Maria commented, apparently she had seen me from the kitchen window.

"It helps me relax, and keeps me in shape," I said.

"Do you do karate then?" she asked.

"I do, I have a black belt at the *hachidan* level," I said.

"That's high isn't it?" she asked.

"I still have a lot to learn," I said.

"Well, after that, you should eat some breakfast," she instructed.

Breakfast was another huge affair, burritos with scrambled eggs, and toast. We had barely time to wash the dishes when Maria chivied us all out to the cars. She had blankets and cushions already set out, and she produced flasks of coffee and cocoa and some snacks to eat. It looked as if we were headed off for an expedition, not a trip to town.

"Why don't you ride with me?" Tom said to Freya and me. "Mom and Dad are driving themselves, and Linda and Jim are taking the kids."

"That sounds fine," I said. "Let me just grab my coat and hat."

"Do want me to sit in the middle?" Freya kidded me as we went to the cottage to collect our coats.

"I'll manage," I said. "Just keep your distance and think about Kirsty."

"All set?" Tom asked as we joined him. He led us to the pick-up and I climbed in the front seat and parked myself in the middle. Freya got in after me and Tom got in the driver's side. The ride into town did not take long and we came to the rodeo arena on the outskirts of Roy. There were already pick-up trucks parked all over, some with horse trailers, some with dogs, some with bales of hay in the back. There were a lot of people there, I guessed many from Roy, but also from the surrounding ranches, I had never seen so many people all wearing hats, it seemed that everyone had a hat on, either a cowboy hat or a baseball cap. There were white, black, brown, grey and even a few brightly coloured cowboy hats and even one or two hats that were like mine with flat brims. The baseball caps for the most part advertised something, John Deere, Caterpillar, Ford, Steiger, and so many more. I reached out and grabbed Tom's arm, I did not want to get left behind or lost in the sea of people, horses and trucks. Freya dropped back to walk with Maria and Steve, which was very nice of her. Tom obviously knew most of the people there, because he waved to many of them and said hello to quite a few. I began to feel like a prize attraction, I was getting looks, comments, and second looks. Tom found us seats on what the Americans call the bleachers, and I saw why Maria had sorted out cushions and blankets. The seats themselves were bare metal and there was no cover, no side walls, nothing, just tiered seats, someone had swept off the snow, probably the day before, because the seats were not only clear of snow, they were dry.

"Will you be okay there for a few minutes?" Tom asked. "I should go and say hi to some people."

"I'll be fine," I assured him. I watched him go then turned to Freya.

"I'm so glad we came," I told her.

"What, to the rodeo?" she asked.

"No, just that we came," I said. "I really like Tom and I'm looking forward to finding out more about him."

"Is he the one?" she asked.

"Maybe, who knows, perhaps, I don't know yet, I'll see what happens, what do you think?" I asked.

"You could do a lot worse," she said. "He's cute, he's not a jerk as far as we can tell, he's not full of himself, looks pretty good to me."

"Hey Fiona, Freya," a voice said. I looked around and saw Tom's friend, Javier.

"Javier, nice to see you here," I said.

"This is my wife, Angela, Angela this is Fiona and Freya, they're the ones I was telling you about, so Freya are you getting what you want from Steve?"

"I am," Freya confirmed. "It's been an education to talk to Steve and to go out onto the ranch with Linda, it's not quite what I imagined. You're not taking part in this?"

"Our daughter, Robin, is riding in the barrel racing," Javier said. "She's in a big competition with Maria, Linda's oldest, and with Renata, José's daughter."

"Barrel racing?" I asked.

"We set up barrels in the arena and you have to ride down the arena, round the barrels in a clover leaf pattern and back, fastest time wins," he explained. "Do you ride?"

"I have," I said. "I used to jump when I was growing up. I think I had about six clear rounds in my jumping career. I did go for a ride with Tom yesterday, we went out towards the Canadian."

"It's pretty country around the river," Javier said. "When do you guys go back to England?"

"We're leaving for Pecos this afternoon, then we'll switch back cars and drive to Denver tomorrow and get the plane to Chicago, then London," I explained.

"Has Tom heard from Cambridge yet?" Javier asked.

"He got his visa and travel stuff yesterday," I said. "He's leaving in about ten days he said."

"Howdy Angela, Steve," Tom said as he joined us.

"Fiona was just telling us you've got all your papers," Steve said.

"Yep," Tom said. "I'll leave soon enough and Fiona has promised to drive me to Cambridge."

"Are you looking forward to it?" Angela asked.

"I am," Tom said. "It'll be different that's for sure. From what Freya and Fiona have been telling us, I'll need to go to the island where Freya lives for some peace and quiet."

"You live on an island, is it big, small?" Angela asked.

"It's small, maybe ten miles by two miles," Freya said. "Two and half hours by ferry to get there."

"I should go and make sure Robin's ready," Javier said. "See you folks later."

"So, what events does the rodeo have?" Freya asked Tom.

"Bronc riding, team roping, calf roping and steer wrestling," Tom said.

"You don't compete?" I asked.

"Not any more," he said. "When I was in my teens I used to, but it's easy to get banged up, so gave it up. Okay, we're about to start."

I was surprised, the whole crowd actually stood and sang the national anthem, if this had been England there might have been one or two, but most would have stayed silent, or even left. Then the announcer took over and launched into a rapid-fire description of each rider as they took part in their events. First, there was the team roping, two riders as a pair, one at the front of the steer and one at the back. The aim was to catch and secure the animal as fast as possible and it seemed to me that a well-trained horse could make or break this event.

"When I competed, I was a team roper," Tom told me. "I would usually take the head rope."

"It looks like a good horse is necessary," I commented.

"It is," he agreed. "You'd better be in sync with your horse, or your time will be way off."

"Who's going to win today?" I asked.

"My money's on Carlos and Edgar," he said. "They've worked as a team for a while now and there's few that can come close." They did in fact win, but only by a small margin, two relative newcomers gave them a good run for their money. Next was barrel racing. It seemed that this was an event for women only, and most of the competitors were teenagers. I was amazed to watch fairly small girls racing around the arena, pigtails flying as they flung their horses into tight turns around the barrels and did not fall off, did not even lose their hats. It came down to Robin, Renata and Maria and it really was neck and neck, but in the end Robin won. I was amazed at the bursts of speed the quarter horses could achieve, they might not be flat racers, but for short distances they were explosive. The barrels were cleared away and calf roping followed. This was another timed event, but with only one rider. Half the Carlos and Edgar team competed and I had to check with Tom to find out which half, it was Carlos. While the calf roping was going on we were joined by Robin, Maria, Renata and Hillary, done with competing, now just socialising and enjoying the evening. As far as I could tell, Maria and Renata bore no ill will towards Robin, they seemed to be best of friends, and they even tolerated Hillary, who as the younger sister was either included or shunned, depending on the day of the week. I understood that from my interactions with James. I gathered from Tom that the winner of the barrel racing swung back and forth between Robin, Maria and Renata and they were running about even for wins and losses.

There was a short break for people to stretch their legs, use the portable loos that were lined up and socialise before the finale, the bronc riding. I needed some explanation of what was to happen. I had not realised that the horse was scored as well as the rider and all the rider had to do was stay on for eight seconds without touching the horse with his free hand. Well, that might have sounded simple enough, but it became clear to me that that was no simple task. I watched men get thrown, I watched them leave the saddle and seem to fly above the horse all the while counting one to eight. I doubted that I would have even made it out of the chute, let alone stay on for eight seconds.
"What do you think, Freya?" I asked.
"I can't believe some of them actually stayed on for the full eight seconds," she said. "I think I would have been off in the chute."
"Will any of this go in your novel?" I asked.
"Oh yes," she said. "This is gold, the atmosphere, the people, the hats, boots, pick-up trucks and horse trailers, the smell of horses, horse poop, the sounds of the cheers, the hooves thudding on the ground, I'm so

glad we came. Be a dear and send me copies of your pictures when you get them developed, it'll help with getting the clothes right."

"I'll do that. Will your hero be a bronc rider?" I asked.

"I don't think so," she said. "I might have a secondary character as a spoiler for the loving couple, to counter the city slicker, no, I think if anything he'll be a team roper."

"Can I get you something, a beer?" Tom asked.

"A beer would be nice, thanks," I said.

"I'll have one too," Freya added. Tom went away and came back with an armful of bottles that he handed out to all, beer for the adults and Coca-Cola for the girls. He made the rounds quickly with an opener then raised his bottle in salute.

"Cheers," he said. "I'm glad you came with us, did you get what you wanted Freya?"

"I did," Freya said. "This has been wonderful, and when you come to England you must come to the isles and stay with me."

"You should go," I told Tom. "Freya lives in a castle."

"A real castle?" Hillary asked.

"A real castle," I confirmed. "It doesn't have cannons, but it's got walls, battlements and a drawbridge."

"Really?" Tom said.

"My grandfather tried to buy one, but no one would sell, so he built one and it looks just like an old castle, but it's got better plumbing," she explained. "Steve, Maria, when you come to visit Tom, you should come and stay with me, so should you Linda, bring the girls, José, if ever you come, you're welcome too. Fiona's been a couple of times, but she does it the easy way, she flies in, most people come by the ferry."

"We should think about getting back to Pecos," I said to Freya.

"I suppose we should," she agreed. "Tom, if you would run us back to the ranch we can get our truck and leave you in peace."

"I'd be happy to," he said.

"Maria, Steve, thank you so much for putting us up," I said. "Linda, Joe, Maria, Hillary I'm glad I met you and I'll be back. José, Sofia, Renata, I hope I'll see you again when I come next time, it has been wonderful and I've enjoyed myself so much."

"I'll echo that," Freya said. "I've got what I need for a new book and when it's published I'll send a boxful for you."

116

We parted and Tom drove us back to the ranch so that we could collect our pick-up. If I have thought about it we should have driven ourselves to Roy, so that we could have left directly from there and not have to drag Tom away from the festivities. At the ranch, we collected our bags and Tom came out with a cooler.

"Here's a little beef for your family in Pecos," he said. "I'll stop by the winery and collect the cooler next time I go to Albuquerque."

"You needn't have done that," I said.

"No, my pleasure," he said. "I'll see you in London?"

"I'll be there, I have your flight number and the date, so I'll drive out to Heathrow to collect you," I replied. Now came the awkward bit, did I kiss him goodbye, did I just wave, shake hands, hug. I decided to hell with it and kissed him on each cheek.

"Thanks for a lovely time," I told him. "I'll see you in London."

"Come and see me when you're in England," Freya reminded him, then she also kissed him goodbye, also on the cheek, but for her only one. We got into our truck and waved goodbye as we left and I watched him in the mirror as long as I dared without running off the road and saw him smiling broadly.

"So?" Freya said as we turned off the county road onto the main road that would take us back across the Canadian River and to Wagon Mound.

"It's worth pursuing," I said. "I've been telling myself to stop making comparisons between Tom and Ian, so I'll see where this leads."

"And?" she asked.

"I like him," I said. "I really do."

"So, sex in London?" she asked.

"We'll see," I said. "The spark is there all right, but am I really ready for it?"

"You'll know," she said. "You'll know when the time is right."

"I can't get over those blokes who were riding the broncos," I said. "They must get really banged up, I wonder if any of them has no broken bones?"

"Makes you wonder about the human psyche that we actually do that kind of thing for entertainment," she said.

"So, what was the ranch tour like?" I asked.

"It was really interesting," she said. "Linda took me through a few pastures, cows everywhere, she showed me pens where they hold them for injections, and for shipping, she talked about grass and water and what keeps a ranch going. It's a hard life, but I think a dairy farmer might even be worse, at least with the beef cows you don't have to milk them every day."

"I'm sure I was never cut out to be a farmer," I thought. "But I'm very glad there are people who are."

"Linda did tell me about Juanita," Freya said. "Apparently Juanita was the local beauty queen and she and Tom had had a thing since high school, they were supposed to be getting married and then Juanita and her friends went on a trip to Las Vegas, the gambling one, not the one we drive through. Apparently, while she was there she met this Texas oil man and he was winning money hand over fist at the poker tables, they made a connection and actually got married then and there in Vegas. Tom was away at MIT at the time and learned about it from the other girls when he came back."

"So, not even dumped at the altar," I said. "Not even a Dear John letter."

"No," Freya said. "Linda also wanted to know about Ian, I told her that I had met Ian and that I'd been to the funeral. I told her that you two had come and stayed at my place and that I liked him and I told her what I knew about you two nearly losing each other when he went back to Tanzania. I heard some of the story from your mother when I was in Nairobi."

"I hope she doesn't think I'm a hopeless case," I said.

"No, I think she was concerned for Tom, that he doesn't get abandoned again," Freya said.

"Well, I don't think I'll do that, I'll see how things go in England, you know I could always rent or buy a place in Cambridge, it really doesn't matter where I live, I'd have to move my plane, but I'm sure there are small fields around Cambridge," I said.

"Could we find somewhere to eat?" Freya said. "I'm hungry, even after that gargantuan breakfast."

"Let's see if Wagon Mound has anything," I suggested. "If not we'll have to go on to Watrous, failing that Las Vegas." We found no places to eat in Wagon Mound or Watrous so went on to Las Vegas and found a place in the centre of town that had the most fascinating machine for making tortillas. The staff prepared the shape and then fed it onto a conveyor and it came out the other end cooked. I could have watched it for hours.

It seemed that tortillas was a common item for people to come, buy, and take away, along with the normal items that one might find in a bakery.

We were back at Pecos by five, in time for a sundowner, before going on to Santa Fe to our hotel. Charlize and James were delighted with the beef and promised to look out for Tom when he came to collect the cooler. Maman and Portia had left that morning to go back to France, but John and Anna were still there. We gave everyone a quick précis of our trip and talked mostly about the rodeo we had been to that morning. Freya waxed quite lyrical about it all and I could see a local rodeo featuring in her novel. We said our goodbyes to everyone as the next day we would be driving north, but we would bye-pass Pecos and go straight to Denver. It was strange driving the land boat of a car again after the beast of a pick-up truck that we had been driving, but it sufficed. The people at the La Fonda hotel were happy to see us again and actually gave us the rooms we had vacated a couple of days earlier. We agreed that all we needed was a glass of wine and a light snack as we had eaten well for breakfast and for our late lunch in Las Vegas. I was tired, I think not so much physically, but emotionally. I was still wrestling with the notion of another man in my life. There was no doubt that there was an attraction to Tom, and I knew that he was attracted to me, but was I ready to let go of Ian, I could imagine a scenario where I was making love to Tom and called out Ian's name, how embarrassing would that be. I know time and all that, but it still bothered me and I was not sure how to deal with it.

We drove to Denver, stopping for lunch in Pueblo, quite clearly a steel town. From the road, we could see the blast furnaces and all the other buildings that went with a steel mill. I presumed that iron ore and coal came in on the railway but had no idea where from and wondered just why a steel mill had been placed in the middle of Colorado. We found a place not far off the freeway, I had learned by now to call them that, that served lunch. We dined on enchiladas, decided to forego the beer that we were offered and were in short order on our way back to Denver. We returned our hire car in Denver and checked in with the Continental people. Our plane was on time, so no issues with making our connection to the overnight BA flight to London. Once on board, in the air and drink in hand, Freya brought up the subject I had glossed over before.

"So, what's the deal with the ranch?" she asked.

"Well, it seems that Tom's father, Steve, had a brother, Rick, and they each held fifty per cent of the Ortiz Cattle Company. Rick had no interest in the ranch and left for Texas and founded a successful chain of ironmongers. Rick has now died and there are three cousins, his heirs, and those cousins want their share of the ranch in cash," I explained.

"Oh boy," she said. "I can see that being a problem. How much, do you know?"

"There's 40,000 acres and Harding County land is going for $90 per acre, so half is 20,000 acres, so $1,800,000," I said.

"Can the ranch afford that much?" Freya asked.

"Not a chance," I said. "They'd have to sell land, which even in the best-case scenario of picking the land to sell with the highest market value, it still means selling off at least 15,000 acres just to raise the cash. Then that would leave 25,000 acres, and the question is that viable as a going concern. That's why Steve wanted to know if I'd done an economic model for a ranch."

"What are they going to do?" Freya asked.

"They've got eleven months left of a year in which to come up with the money or I suppose it goes to court," I said.

"What a shame," Freya said.

"It's also complicated by the fact that Tom's dad gave cash to his brother to start the ironmongers business and that cash came from the ranch, but there was nothing in writing," I said.

"That's a pity," Freya said. "So, lawyers will have a field day."

"The thing is," I said. "I've enough money to pay the $1,800,000 and essentially buy the cousins out of the shares of Ortiz Cattle, but if I suggest that will it kill any chance of a relationship with Tom, and is it something I should even be thinking about?"

"You can come up with that amount of money?" Freya asked.

"I can without borrowing," I said. "That's the real problem, interest rates are so high that borrowing the whole amount incurs a huge debt service amount that the ranch simply can't pay and run as well, without running it into the ground."

"What are you going to do?" Freya asked.

"I think when I pick up Tom at Heathrow, I'm going to tell him that I'm exploring financial options and to do nothing for three months at least,"

I said. "That will give me, and him, time to get to know one another and if we hit it off well enough he may be amenable to me buying the cousins out."

"That's a risky strategy," Freya said.

"It is," I agreed. "But, I can't come up with anything else at the moment, the borrowing rates are just too high to mortgage the ranch and raise the cash. I suppose that this is something all family farms and ranches face, if a family member wants their cash value of the place, what do you do?"

"What indeed?" she mused. "I'm lucky being the only child of an only child, so no others to come claiming their inheritance. All I have to decide is who to leave it to when I die."

"You could always leave it to me," I joked. "I've always fancied the idea of a castle, but I think I'd add a cannon or two, dig a moat, fill it and add a crocodile or two."

"Maybe I'll leave everything to the Battersea Dogs Home," she said. "They could use it as a refuge for unwanted animals."

"Bit far from Battersea though," I said. "No, better leave it to me."

"Would you ladies like some dinner?" a stewardess asked, interrupting our badinage about the castle.

It was dark when we landed in Chicago and we scurried to get our bags and check them in with British Airways, ready for our flight to London. This crew was a little more cheerful than the crew we had had coming over from London, but then if they managed things right all they had to do was feed and water the passengers, turn up the heat and turn down the lights and hope that everyone slept for most of the journey. I did, after dinner, another dinner on top of the one Continental had served. I had asked to be awakened for breakfast before we landed, and was just about surfacing when the stewardess touched my shoulder and asked me if I wanted breakfast. They served it in record time because we were coming in early. The tailwinds had been particularly favourable and we were over half an hour early, not that that mattered because when we landed they were not ready for us and we sat in a penalty box on a taxiway until we had a gate to go into. Freya and I cleared immigration and customs quickly then took a taxi into town to my flat.

"Will you stay a day or two before going back to Colonsay, or have you things that need doing?" I asked Freya.

"Unfortunately I need to get back," she said. "I booked myself on the night sleeper to Glasgow and I'll get another train from there to Oban."

"So, we have the day to kill, take a bath or a shower and clean up after the flight," I suggested.

"That's a good idea," she said. "Then let's go and find some lunch."

"I should drop off my films to be developed," I said. "I'll do that when we go out." Freya showered first, then I cleaned up and changed into clothes perhaps more suited to London than cowboy boots and suede. We debated about where to luncheon and decided that for a complete change to Mosquero and Sally's, we would go to the Savoy. On our way to the Tube station at Sloan Square, I dropped off my films to be processed and then we took the Circle to Embankment which gave us a short three-minute walk to the hotel. A very superior being escorted us to a table and we had only just sat down when my dad and Felicity came in. The superior being was fawning outrageously as Dad was a frequent diner and well-known. Dad waved and said a word to the superior being who snapped fingers and organised a table for four in record time.

"Hi Fi, Freya, why don't you join us," Dad suggested. Dad knew Freya from financial dealings and it had been through him that Ian and I had had use of Freya's castle as a vacation home.

"Why, William," Freya said. "What a nice surprise, and so nice to see you again Felicity."

"Dad, Felicity," I added. "How are you?"

"Middling," Dad said. "I've been having some issues lately, I need to talk to you Fi, when you have an afternoon spare. So, what have you two been doing?"

"I had business in Chicago, then we went on to see James and Charlize in Pecos," I said.

"Pecos?" Felicity said. "What's Pecos like, it sounds so very western, I can almost hear someone saying, west of the Pecos?"

"It's small," I said. "Not too far from Santa Fe, not far from skiing, lots of Spanish influence, or Mexican Spanish. They had a good harvest and were pressing when we left."

"It's in New Mexico, isn't it?" Felicity asked.

"It is," I confirmed. "Freya and I flew to Denver and drove down. We did do a little exploring while we were there because Freya is researching a new book, set in the American West."

"So, cowboys and all?" Dad asked.

"Yup," Freya said. "We met cattle ranchers, went to a rodeo, got cowboy boots, hats the works."

"Did you ride any horses while you were there?" Felicity asked.

"Fiona did," Freya said. "I did my touring by pick-up truck."

"What was it like?" Felicity asked.

"The scenery was beautiful," I said. "Wide open spaces, clear blue skies, some snow on the ground, lots of juniper trees, cows, elk, deer, and it's the only time I've been out on a horse with a rifle scabbard with a rifle in it."

"Why the rifle?" Felicity asked.

"Apparently they get bears, pumas and coyotes," I explained. "As it was put to me, you never know."

"Well, we should think about lunch," Dad suggested. We all consulted the menus and made our selections. Over lunch I chatted to Felicity, I wanted to know what Dad meant when he said he had been having issues. I gathered it was heart-related, which probably explained his lunch selection and his abstinence from wine with lunch. It struck me that he was still quite young to be having heart issues, then the selfish part of us all kicked in and I wondered if the condition was related to his lifestyle or genetics, and if genetics, was I at risk. Whatever the reason he was in an expansive mood and was trying to talk Freya into investing in a sheep station in Australia. How he got mixed up in that, I will never know. After lunch Dad and I compared calendars and set a date for later in the week when I would go to his office to talk about whatever it was he wanted to talk about, perhaps Torrance Aerospace, perhaps one of the other companies we both had an interest in.

Freya and I whiled away the day until it was time for her to go to Euston to catch the night train. I organised a taxi for her and saw her off then went back to call Maman.

"Bébé, how are you, how was your trip home?" she asked.

"Fine Maman," I assured her. "And you and Portia?"

"We couldn't be better," she said. "It's late, what's up, you don't call at this hour unless something is bothering you?"

"I met a man," I said.

"Ah," she said. "Good, go on."

"He's an American, comes from a cattle ranch in New Mexico, but is coming over here to do a PhD at Cambridge," I explained.

"Does he have a name?" she asked.

"Tom Ortiz," I said. "I first met him when I went to Pecos with John, then I met him again a few days ago when we were in New Mexico."

"Tell me more," Maman instructed.

"John and I had gone for an explore," I said. "We went to this little town, well maybe town is generous, let's call it a village, we stopped for lunch and he was there with some other ranchers. It was like with Ian, our eyes met and there was the spark, can that happen twice in one's life?"

"Why not?" Maman said. "So, you went back to this village?"

"Yes," I said. "The ranchers told us that they met monthly, so Freya and I timed our trip to coincide. He was there and it was the same again when our eyes met. Freya told the chaps that she was researching for a book and wanted to know about ranching. The consensus of the group was that she, we, should talk to Steve Ortiz, Tom's dad. Tom invited us out to their ranch to meet Steve and ask away. Steve and Maria, Tom's folks, are really nice and he has a sister, Linda, married to Joe with two girls, Maria and Hillary, twelve and ten."

"So, tell me about the ranch?" Maman asked.

"40,000 acres with a breeding herd of about 600," I said. "It's wild country Maman, I saw elk, deer and all kinds of small birds and animals. I took a ride with Tom and he really likes the place. He's an electrical engineer, into photovoltaics and is going to Trinity to see if he can work out how to improve the efficiency of the panels."

"Are you going to see him again?" Maman asked.

"I said I'd pick him up from Heathrow and drive him to Cambridge," I replied. "I'm confused Maman, I really like this chap, but each time I look into his eyes I feel guilty, like I'm betraying Ian."

"That's to be expected," she said. "You and Ian had a wonderful marriage and the idea of seeing someone else is difficult. It was easier for me because I had begun to suspect your dad and love was turning to hate. I was lucky to meet Portia and rid myself of the hate, now all I have is pity and a little regret. But I have you and James which I would not have had had we not been married, so some good came of it. You were unlucky, no one expected Ian to die so young, but you have a whole life to live yet, so explore this relationship, enjoy it, savour it, and who knows it may work out well."

"I suppose so," I agreed. "I need to find out too what his expectations are as well."

"Why is he not married?" Maman asked.

"Apparently he was going to be, to a Juanita, but she took a trip to Las Vegas, the gambling one, not the New Mexico one, and met this oil baron there and married him then and there. Tom only found out when he came home from MIT, he must have suspected something though, because she didn't call, didn't write, just disappeared into the sunset," I explained.

"Is he bitter about the experience?" Maman asked.

"He talks about it, which I suppose is good," I replied. "I would imagine that if it was all bottled up inside it might be worse. According to Sally, the lady who runs the café in Mosquero, he's smitten, so we'll see."

"Well, be careful, and remember I'm always here," Maman said.

"Maman, what did Grandpa Barclay die from?" I asked.

"Heart attack," she replied. "Why?"

"Dad said that he's been having some issues, he didn't elaborate, but he did say that he wanted me to go and see him in his office, I was wondering if there is a genetic propensity for heart attacks in the Barclays?" I said.

"Only if you include too much high living," she said. "Both your grandfather and father tended to like things that weren't necessarily good for them, and neither exercised much, so it was, is, lifestyle rather than genetics, unless lifestyle choices can be genetic. I think you take after me more, so have less to worry about, James is the one who will have to watch what he eats and drinks, but I think Charlize will take care of that. So, Ortiz, what does that imply?"

"His family is a mix, as he put it of Hispanic and Anglo, and he says that there's Navajo and Hopi in the distant past as well, so a mix," I said.

"Like us," Maman remarked. "Does he speak Spanish?"

"He does," I confirmed. "Rides horses, ropes cows, plays the guitar and sings, knows his cows, animals, birds and trees, and has a master's degree from MIT."

"So, all in all well rounded," Maman laughed. "I suppose tall dark and handsome?"

"Dark and handsome, yes," I said. "But tall, not really, an inch or two taller than me, which probably makes him average for a man."

"I'd like to meet him," Maman said. "When is he arriving in London?"

"Next week Friday," I said. "Coming in on TWA from Chicago."

"Would it make things difficult for you if I came over?" she asked.

"I don't think so," I said. "I was planning to collect him from the airport, come here and then drive him up to Cambridge on Saturday."

"I wouldn't go to Cambridge with you," she said. "But I'd like to meet him."

"Okay, just you, or Portia as well?" I asked.

"I think just me this time, otherwise you'll either have to have him sleep on the couch or with you, are you ready for that?" she asked.

"Not ready," I said. "I'm leery about going that far that quickly."

"Fine, I'll come over on Wednesday, are you busy with work now?"

"I am," I said. "I've got some to do for a big materials company in Chicago, I owe them a computer programme, so will be busy for a while, then I'll need to go back to Chicago to install it for them and make sure it runs properly. But I'm being well paid for it, so can't complain."

"I'll make arrangements and fly over Wednesday morning, don't worry about coming to pick me up, I'll take a taxi into town, I have a key to your flat, so I'll let myself in if you're not here," she said.

"*Bon*," I said. "*À tout à l'heure, je t'aime.*"

"*Je t'aime aussi*," she replied. "*Bonne nuit.*"

I went to Dad's office to see what he wanted to talk about. His secretary, Deirdre, showed me straight in and brought coffee and biscuits and left us to it.

"How are you, Dad?" I asked.

"Well enough," he said. "I'm going to step down soon and retire and I wanted you to take over as Chairman of the company."

"Have you discussed this with your board?" I asked.

"Not yet," he said. "I wanted to talk to you first and see if you'll do it and then work out how to move everything over to you."

"What does that entail?" I asked.

"We'll need to review all the investments we have made and the loans we have outstanding and what the risk criteria are that we use to make lending decisions," he said. "But you already know most of that, because you've helped me modify them in the past."

"An investment banker," I mused. "Do I want to be one?"

"It's interesting," he said. "And I think with your consulting practice you've got more going for you than most bankers I know. They all tend to be a little hidebound and will only lend if you don't actually need to borrow. We've taken a little more risk in our approach and most of the time we've been right. I'll go over the failures with you and what we learned from them."

"We would need to put everything onto a computer," I said.

"I know," he agreed. "I was hoping that you would do that."

"When are you thinking of retiring?" I asked.

"If you'll take over, then six months," he said. "I'd make you the MD while I stayed on as Chairman until I actually go, and then you'd take the chair as well, and at that time I'd also gift my ownership of the business to you and James equally and hope that I live seven years more to avoid inheritance tax for you."

"What does Felicity think?" I asked.

"She's well set," he said. "We'll take our retirement and go and live in the Caribbean. You should know that in my will, Felicity gets a lump sum, and the residue of my estate is divided equally between you and James."

"Felicity won't baulk at that?" I asked.

"I doubt it, she'll have enough to live on even with an extravagant lifestyle," he said. Did I detect a note of cynicism and regret there?

"You said you had some issues," I said. "Are those health issues?"

"High blood pressure, and the stuff you'd expect because, I know, I know, I have been looking after myself," he lamented. "It's the main reason I want to retire, I want to be able to enjoy myself, so I bought a yacht and a villa in the BVI and want to be able to get there soon. So, back to the first question, will you come on board?"

"Who's on your board?" I asked.

"You know them all," he said. "We've made no recent changes, so there's Henry Curtis, no relation to the Rider Haggard Henry Curtis, Henry's in food wholesaling, George Adams, property development, Humphrey Harris, retired cabinet secretary, bit of a wanker actually and I think he should go when we do the next election of directors and officers, Gordon Busby, car builder, Nicholas Brown, furniture factories, Adam Hill, but you know him already, and Andrew McIntosh, chartered accountant."

"All old men," I commented.

"Not all old," Dad protested. "But, you're right, all men and all the wrong side of fifty, but it's typical of non-executive directors."

"How much do they get per year, per meeting?" I asked.

"£10,000 per annum plus meeting expenses, we have regular quarterly meetings and I can call a special meeting if I want," Dad replied.

"Are they worth it?" I asked. "Who has the best mind?"

"I would say Adam Hill, Andrew McIntosh and George Adams are first tier, then Henry Curtis, Gordon, and Nick, and bottom of the pile, Humphrey," Dad enumerated. "Are they worth it? I think on the whole, yes, I've put big positions to them to get their ideas and feedback, and on the whole, it has been useful. How much work have you got on your plate just now?"

"I've a big project for a materials company in Chicago, but should have that done within the month, I can also clear up the rest of my current projects fairly quickly," I said. "Tell me, I never asked, why Thames Cherwell?"

"Well, we couldn't use Barclay or Barclay Capital, those names were taken long ago, so your great-grandfather picked Cherwell, because he'd grown up in Banbury and Thames because he always wanted to live on or near the Thames," Dad explained.

"What's the balance sheet look like right now?" I asked.

"Here," he said. "Total assets stand at £153,576,750, take the balance sheet and the accounts away with you and pore through them at your leisure, here's the latest list of the assets, and here are the analyses of the loans we have outstanding and the equity positions we have taken and my assessment of the risks, and the various projects I have under consideration, some acquisitions and some divestitures, it doesn't matter whether it's buying or selling, there are fees both ways."

"How much will you pay me?" I asked.

"As MD I think we could start at £100,000, plus you'd have a seat on the board," he said. "As Chairman, we would double that, then there is an incentive program based on the long-term growth of the company, there is a formula that is included in the packet I just gave you, the non-executive directors and the staff also share in that incentive. Other than that, there is the opportunity that you and I have both taken to take equity positions in companies and then realise on them at the point of sale."

"Do you have the office space to accommodate a computer?" I asked.

"The rest of this floor has just been vacated, and I've not looked for a new tenant, so the space across the corridor is empty, you'd have to tell me what we need in terms of kitting out the space to handle a computer," he replied.

"When do you need to know?" I asked.

"Well, I was hoping that you'd agree," he said. "I do rather need to start getting myself away from the daily stuff and start taking better care of myself. I had a check-up last month and it wasn't all the best news, so if I want to do any sailing in the Caribbean I need to get out of here."

"Let's go and get some afternoon tea at Fortnum and Mason and you can tell me what I would actually be doing and how to make a success of this," I suggested.

"Good idea," he agreed. He buzzed Deirdre and when she came in told her that he was leaving for the day. We left and took a taxi to Fortnum and Mason and got ourselves a table for afternoon tea.

He talked and I listened. I began to learn what I would need to know to be an investment banker. It seemed that a lot of it was relationships and knowing who to go to and when. Thames Cherwell had a broad portfolio of its own investments and Dad listed many of the transactions he had been involved with, either buying or selling companies. My own background in economics would come in very handy analysing what would be a good proposition and what would not.

"How are you going to sell this to your board?" I asked.

"Well, that's the nice thing about an advisory board, I can if I want overrule things, but I think they'll go along with me, except perhaps Humphrey, who will be horrified that a mere woman should be considered to run the business."

"So, it's essentially a one-man, soon to be one-woman show?" I asked.

"I suppose so," he agreed. "I have six analysts who pore through the financials for me, but in the end, it's my decision, right or wrong."

"When you transfer ownership to me and James, how does he, or me, benefit from that?" I asked.

"You can declare a dividend based on earnings," he said. "I have been playing salary versus dividend based on the tax rates. I need to take another look now that Thatcher has dropped the income tax rate a little. There are also perquisites with the job, car and driver, first-class air travel, clothing allowance, probably other things if you want, like membership to clubs, tickets to the opera or concerts, disguised as customer relations, and James would be entitled to a board seat as a non-executive director and collect his fees and expenses."

"Are there any other women investment bankers?" I asked.

"Not that I can think of," he said. "But, there's no reason why not, except basic prejudice in the industry, not one of us you know!"

"Will people take me seriously?" I asked.

"When you first started consulting on your own, did people take you seriously? No, they didn't, then one or two brave souls took the risk and found out that you've got more brains in your head than a whole bevvy of traditional consultants put together. What about your latest conquest?"

"I met them on a plane," I said. "I was doodling a distancing model and the chap wanted to know what it was. That led to a meeting where I have to say I did rather wow them, then they hired me. I have another prospect that I got by towing his car out of a sticky situation in New Mexico."

"You see, I know that here in the UK you are well thought of and most think they simply can't afford you, but those that do, like Adam Hill, can't say enough," Dad said. "I will take you with me for several meetings and let you do the talking, and we'll see who is smart enough to think and who is so tied up in their prejudices that they would rather go with second best than you."

"Thanks, Dad," I said.

"No, I'm serious Fi, I've not met anyone in the industry as smart, there may be one or two out there, but I've not met them yet," he said. "I know I'm prejudiced, but I've got data on my side to support my prejudice," he added. "Oh, by the way, the Torrance sale has passed all the regulatory hurdles and will close shortly. I've been talking to a tax advisor about leaving money in the US or repatriating it to the UK."

"How much will I get?" I asked.

"Well, based on your equity position, you'll realise, before taxes, five million, dollars not pounds," he said.

"That's nice to hear," I said. "Let me know what the tax advisor says."

"I will," he promised.

"Nice problem to have," I laughed.

"It is," he agreed. "So, what about you, how are you doing?"

"I have good days and not so good," I said. "The goods are outweighing the not so goods and in fact, they are looking up."

"Oh?" he said.

"There might be a bloke," I said. "I met him in the States and he's coming to Cambridge to do a doctorate in electrical engineering, he's been working for a photovoltaic company and he wants to improve cell efficiency."

"Nice bloke?" Dad asked.

"As far as I can tell, yes," I said. "I met his folks, his sister and her family and some of his friends when I was in New Mexico with Freya."

"Will I meet him at some time?" Dad asked.

"I'll see how things go," I temporised.

"So, Thames Cherwell, yes or no?" he asked.

"Yes," I said. It was a whole new opportunity, it looked interesting and who knew where it might lead.

"Good, thank you," he said. "We have a board meeting next Tuesday at ten in the morning here, why don't you join me and I'll give them all the news and introduce you. Can you work from my office to complete your current projects?"

"I could do that," I thought. "It doesn't really matter where I work, I would need to spend some time at Imperial to use their computer."

"I just would like my people to meet you," he said. "You might sit in whatever meetings you would like and give us some ideas. I would also like you to tell me what we need to do to ready the room for a computer."

"I'll do that," I promised. "If you go with IBM they'll tell you what you need in terms of electricity, air conditioning, fire protection and the rest, but as you own the building at least you don't have to get the landlord to agree."

"True, true," he said. "All right then, I'll see you on Tuesday."

"Okay Dad," I said. "Say hello to Felicity for me. Oh, and if you have pictures of the yacht and your villa in the Virgin Islands, bring some with you, so I can see where you're off to."

"I'll do that," he promised.

Cambridge

I attended the board meeting of Thames Cherwell and was reintroduced to the members, not just as an invited guest to give a presentation on some esoteric topic regarding forecasting, but as the presumptive Managing Director, MD as Dad called it. I think it caught them all a little off guard, but the response was on the whole positive. Dad had been right, the only one who seemed to have problems with the idea was Humphrey, who cavilled at the notion that a mere slip of a woman could possibly understand the intricacies of the financial world. Dad in a nice way told him that my knowledge of the financial world was more than adequate and that he had been taking my advice for some years. Dad chaired the meeting, then I gave them all a quick rundown of the deals and transactions that were either closed or pending or being explored. I had been able to pick all that up from the package that Dad had given me. The bank was doing well, despite the best efforts of Mr Callaghan's government over the past few years, and was likely to continue to do well, but I cautioned that Thatcher was going to have to make some decisions that would not be popular. Inefficient and poorly run enterprises, be they public or private would have to be scrutinised and or closed and public funding would probably see some cuts. The country simply could not continue spending its way into oblivion. I touched on the topic of computers and told them that we would be installing a computer system to track our own finances and to model possible transactions. They all wanted to know how much, so I laid out my estimate of what the system would cost, what the kitting out of the room would cost and how many people we would have to hire to run the system, the total coming to some £50,000 for an outright purchase, but I told them that I preferred to lease as we would then be able to upgrade easier as new systems were introduced. When I told them that I was considering an IBM system there was an outcry from Humphrey who wanted to know why I was not going to consider an ICL system. I told them that I saw problems for ICL in the future and reminded them that its success to date was largely due to large government orders being placed for the Ministry of Defence, the General Post Office and other governmental bodies. The buy British idea might sound patriotic, but it was not necessarily sound business practice. Humphrey huffed and puffed about that, but the others essentially outvoted him.

The meeting ended and we adjourned for lunch. Now that I was part of the board they could no longer lunch at the all-boys club that had been their wont until now, so we instead repaired to the Savoy. I think that was one of the reasons some of the directors stayed on, they just enjoyed the benefits of nice lunches and dinners.

"So, Doctor Barclay," Adam Hill said, as we sat down for lunch. "How have you been, I was so sorry to hear about Ian,"

"I'm doing fairly well, thank you, Mr Hill," I assured him. "And you and Mrs Hill?"

"We're about to hang things up," he said. "I'm due for retirement in a few years, but thought that I would go while I have my health and travel the world. I'm afraid that also means that I won't be continuing on your board, but I see a bright future under your leadership."

"Thank you," I said. "It will be different, but exciting."

"You have to be one of the youngest MDs," Andrew McIntosh said. "It's going to shake up the City when news gets out. There will be a lot who will say that you've no idea what you're doing, there'll be requests for interviews from the FT and The Economist, it's going to be entertaining. If anyone asks my opinion, I'll just tell them that you've got a better brain than most, if not all, of them and not to cross swords with you, lest they come off worst."

"Thank you, Andrew, I never asked before, are you in any way related to Freya McIntosh the author?" I asked.

"Cousin Freya," he laughed. "My grandfather was her grandfather's cousin, I know it shocked the family when he came back from South Africa and built his castle on Colonsay. Do you know her?"

"I was travelling with her recently in the States," I explained. "She was researching material for a new book, so I tagged along."

"Did I see you in Chicago recently?" George Adams asked.

"I was there," I said. "I had a meeting with a client."

"Who was that with you?" he asked.

"That was Freya McIntosh the fiction side of the McIntosh clan who Andrew and I were just talking about," I said. "What took you to Chicago?"

"Beef," he said. "I'm looking at beef supplies and am considering the States, Argentina and some other sources. I like that, Freya is the fiction side of the McIntosh clan, Andrew I thought the first question your accountant asked was, what do want the numbers to be?"

"Of course," Andrew laughed. "Tell us what you want and we'll see if the numbers can be presented in such a way as to reflect that."

"See, Fiona, accountants deal in fiction as well, so it's a McIntosh thing," George joked. The banter continued and I began to see the directors more as people, each with their own distinct personality. I agreed with Dad, Humphrey could go without any loss, I was losing Adam, but would replace him with James, who as a shareholder probably warranted a board seat. To replace Humphrey I actually toyed with the idea of Portia, a good legal mind might be useful. I was not sure if Portia would even consider it, but it was worth exploring. Lunch broke up and everyone went their separate ways, leaving Dad and I to take coffee and review the morning.

"What do you think?" he asked.

"I'll manage," I said. "Humphrey's not too bright is he?"

"He went into the Civil Service as basically a member of the club, right school, right college, one of us don't you know," Dad said. "His problem is not that he's not intelligent, he is, he did well at Oxford and came out with a First, but his mind is closed, he's bound to his traditions and thinking and can't imagine a world other than his own limited sphere."

"That's a shame," I said. "What's next?"

"Next week, I have a meeting with Corby Seaton who want to expand their construction machinery business," he said. "You should come with me, the meeting's in Corby, I thought we drive up and see them."

"What day?" I asked.

"Monday," he said. I consulted my calendar and decided that I could in fact do that.

"Okay, do I meet you at your flat or the office?" I asked.

"Why don't I pick you up at seven, is that okay?" he asked.

"Seven it is," I said. "Is this purely an office visit or are we touring factories?"

"No tours yet," he said. "So wear what you have on right now. So, see you tomorrow at the office."

I busied myself the next day moving my files and work materials to my new office at Thames Cherwell. My old office I could sublet out easily. I took time at noon to go and collect my pictures from the shop I had taken my films to and I was quite pleased with the results. I also looked up Corby Seaton and got financials on them, then came up with an idea that I thought intriguing.

"Dad, what if your pals at Corby Seaton buy Metter?" I suggested.

"Is that doable?" he asked.

"I think so," I said. "Didn't I see something about Bob Metter dying not long ago, I'll bet he didn't plan things well and his shares in Metter will pass to his heirs, after the Inland Revenue takes their pound of flesh."

"Why don't you look into that and see what you can find out?" he said. "How much of Metter did Bob still hold?"

"Twenty-five per cent," I told him. "The rest is on the exchange and is currently trading at £1.75 and they haven't paid a dividend in five years."

"You know, that might just work," he said. "Put together some numbers would you and let's see what we might be able to do."

I enlisted the help of two of the analysts, Gerald and Peter, giving them a set of instructions that set out what I wanted to discover.

When I stopped for the day and went home Maman was there, she had arrived from France and taken a taxi into town as she said she would.

"Bébé, you've been busy," she said.

"Dad has asked me to take over at the bank," I said. "He's retiring in six months and will at that time make over the shares of the company to James and me, I just hope he lives for seven years more, or we'll have a hell of a bill from the Inland Revenue."

"Are you happy with that?" she asked.

"It could be fun," I said. "There are things I will change, but not too much, I will probably continue the consulting, but I think I'll start to look for some people to help me."

"As long as you're happy," she said.

"Maman," I said. "Do you think Portia would join my board if I asked her? It would be after Dad was gone, as I need to make some other changes then as well."

"I think so," Maman said. "But, you should ask her. So when does Tom arrive?"

"Friday at seven," I said. "Are you coming with me?"

"Of course," she said.

"Thank you Maman," I said. "Tomorrow I need to go and see Rachel Adams, will you come with me? I need some business suits, I don't like the idea of having to wear skirts all the time, and most of the trousers I've seen are not that exciting."

"I never thought when you were still at school that I'd ever hear you talk about fashions," Maman said, laughing. "Of course, I'll come with you."

"I have some pictures of Tom and his family," I said. "Here, that's Tom, those are his folks, that's his sister and her family, this is the ranch house, the Canadian River and these are the rodeo that Freya and I went to."

"Nice looking," Maman said. "I'm looking forward to meeting him. The place looks rather wild, not many people, I like this one of you all dressed up for the wild west. There was one thing I was going to suggest, perhaps you should take down the life study you have of Ian in your bedroom."

"You're right," I laughed. "Imagine if things do go well with Tom, what's the poor bloke going to think if he's in my bedroom and there's a male nude hanging there, the one of me can stay, because if he makes it to my bedroom he's going to see the real thing anyway."

I took down the life sketch and added it to the treasures that I had in my bank deposit box, it could stay there. Maman and I went to see Rachel, she was one of the premier fashion designers in London and we had a long-standing relationship and friendship.

"Fiona, Brigitte," Rachel said as we were ushered into her studio. "How nice to see you both, what brings you here?"

"I need clothes," I said. "I'm taking over as the MD of Thames Cherwell and I need some clothes that say take me seriously, don't mess with me or you'll be sorry."

"Why don't I just print you a tee shirt that says that?" she laughed.

"I know," I said. "It's a tall order, but I know it's an old boys club and I need them to listen to me, not just look at me."

"So, let's think about a tailored suit with a skirt and with trousers, we can use the same jacket design for both," she suggested. "I'd go with a dark blue, a dark grey and a light grey, you should wear high-necked blouses, white mainly, but red with the light grey, high necked so that they don't leer at you and try and look down your blouse, this has to be all business, you're not auditioning for a theatre part. I'd go for a small heel, not flats, they look frumpy and school maamish, shoe colours to match the suit, and to shake them all up, let's add a dark maroon suit."

"Jacket design, I may need pockets," I said.

"Pockets we can do, on the inside of the jacket and in the trousers," she said. "Let me sketch up some ideas and have you come back and look them over. When do you need things by?"

"Next Wednesday would be super, but if not I can always wear the grey that I already have," I said.

"You don't want much do you?" she laughed. "I can give you one by next Wednesday if we agree a basic design over lunch, and you're buying," she said.

"Fine," I agreed. We gathered up Hermione who was Rachel's principal assistant and went off to lunch at Harrods. I got us a table for six, which would give Rachel and Hermione the room they would need to sketch ideas. I had never watched Rachel at work and was amazed at how quickly she sketched up a design, showed it to Hermione who pointed out issues with the fabrication and then made modifications. She really was an expert. They did not eat me out of house and home, but I had it to spend now, £100,000 a year, even after taxes was still very nice thank you very much.

"Can you come for a fitting on Friday?" Rachel asked.

"Friday about lunchtime," I said. "I have to go the Heathrow early to pick someone up."

"Lunchtime is good," Rachel said. "You can buy lunch again."

"Fine," I agreed.

"I'm thinking of 12oz wool for the winter, 9oz for the summer and we'll add linen for the summer as well, so all in all what about twelve suits say, two with skirts and the rest trousers?" she suggested.

"I can't imagine the bill," I said. "But the MD position comes with perks, and clothing allowance is one, so go ahead, give me nice things that project power, real power, I want those smug old boys to sit up and take note."

"Unfortunately women can't really do that with ties," she said. "But we can add some jewelry that shrieks money without being ostentatious. You want these men to think that you're horribly successful and therefore expensive."

"I'm not thinking of being a lady of the night," I said. "So, when you say expensive I presume that you just mean that I look as if I can create the best deal for them."

"We can do that," Rachel said. "We'd coordinate handbags and briefcase as well, not the frumpy handbags that Liz lugs around all the time, but something a little more chic, with my name on it of course."

"Of course," I agreed. "A little advertising for you won't hurt."

"Thanks for lunch, Hermione and I will have to get back if we're going to have anything for you to try on on Friday," Rachel said.

Maman and I were up early on Friday and drove out to Heathrow in the rain. What to wear, was the big question of the day. In the end I settled on a pair of blue jeans, a sweater and a jacket, to keep the rain off, and on my feet, my cowboy boots. One of the nice things about the Land Rover was that the pedals were big enough that wearing boots and driving was not a problem. The M4 was quiet, but I was prepared to bet that when we returned that it would be the usual chaos, made even worse by the rain and drizzle coming down. We parked and went to the Terminal 3 arrivals hall and watched the exit from customs where all arriving passengers from foreign parts were disgorged. We checked and the TWA flight had arrived, so Tom must have been still either waiting his turn at immigration or waiting for his bags to appear. I finally saw him, or should I say, I saw his hat first, then I saw him, pushing his trolley, laden down with bags.

"Fiona," he said, as I threw my arms around him and hugged him, then gave him a peck on each cheek.

"Tom, this is my Mom, Brigitte," I said.

"Nice to meet you Ma'am," he said. "Is it always this busy?"

"Always," Maman said. "It's really nice to meet you Tom."

"I have my car here," I said. "So, shall we go?" I led the way, while Tom engaged himself with manœuvring his trolley past the hordes of people waiting. We had to use a lift to get us to the floor where we had parked, so I took the opportunity to take his hand. The spark was there, it was still there, I was thrilled and delighted. We disengaged hands so that we could exit the lift and then load his bags into the back of my Land Rover. They fit, just, I had begun to wonder if I would have to use the roof rack.

"Did you have a nice flight Tom?" Maman asked, while I busied myself with finding my parking ticket and the money to pay it.

"Not bad," he said. "A little crowded, but could have been worse."

"Did you sleep at all?" I asked.

"A little after dinner," he said. "But it seemed that almost as soon as I'd dropped off they were waking us for breakfast before we landed."

"Is this your first trip to England?" Maman asked.

"Second," he said. "I had to come over to meet with my thesis advisor, but that was a couple of months ago."

"Did you stay long then?" Maman asked.

"Only three days," he said. "Long enough to get lost in Cambridge, but not long enough to find my way around. Fiona, when were you going to run me up there?"

"I thought tomorrow," I said. "Stay the night here, then we can leave early in the morning and be there by lunchtime. Perhaps by then the weather will have cleared up a little too. Driving in this rain is not that much fun. So, how are your folks and the rest of the family?"

"They're all doing fine," he said. "We've weaned the herd now and we're looking forward to next year."

The M4 was not too bad, but things went bad on the Chiswick Flyover, someone had managed to run into the car in front on them, so we were all held up until the police arrived, ascertained that there were no injuries and cleared the road. We inched past with the stream of other cars and then picked up speed again. We made it back to my flat by eight-thirty, so the delay was not too bad. We lugged Tom's bags upstairs and then took a break for coffee. Personally I was hungry as we had left for the airport without eating anything.

"Breakfast?" Maman suggested. "Tom, would you like breakfast, I'm having some and I know Fiona will too?"

"Thank you," he said. "This is a nice place."

"Let me show you where you'll sleep," I said. While Maman busied herself in the kitchen, I gave Tom a quick tour of my flat, not that there was that much to see.

"Breakfast," Maman called. She had made crêpes, lots of them, but they all disappeared quickly. "When's your fitting, Fiona?"

"I'm going at noon, would you entertain Tom while I'm gone?" I asked.

"Of course," she said.

"I'm sorry, Tom," I explained. "I had a clothes fitting at noon, so will have to leave you in Maman's hands."

"That's fine," he said. "I may just take a nap, if that's okay?"

"Go ahead," I said.

I went to see Rachel for my fitting and have to say that I was thrilled with the design and the fit.

"This is really nice," I said, pirouetting in front of the mirror.

"I think so," Rachel said. "What do you think, Hermione, a little tuck there?"

"A little," Hermione agreed and came at me armed with chalk and pins. Whatever she did it did improve the line of the jacket, which was this lovely soft woollen fabric, dark grey, with just a faint pin stripe. The jacket was lined with a purple silk and was just elegant, there was no other word for, just elegant. Rachel had shoes and a blouse for me to try as well, so I stripped off and donned the whole ensemble.

"You look ready for the City now," Hermione said.

"You do," Rachel agreed. "Now this handbag and this briefcase, yes, looks good to me. You will also need a mac in case of rain. I would suggest an Aquascutum trench coat in navy. What have you worn until now?"

"Marks and Sparks," I said.

"Well, now we need to move you up a little, when you've established yourself, you could go back to a donkey jacket and it wouldn't matter, but for now, you need to play the game and outdo the doers," Rachel said. I appreciated having Rachel's views, I had learned in Nairobi, that once in a while it paid to conform a little.

"So," Rachel said. "Where are we going for lunch?"

"There's a new place just off the Cromwell Road," I suggested. "It's an easy walk from here."

"Good," Rachel said. "Let me just get a brolly and we can go."

"All organised?" Maman asked when I arrived home.

"All done, I pick up the suit on Tuesday," I said. "What have you two been up to?"

"We've just been talking," Maman said.

"Your mother was telling me about your life growing up," Tom added.

"I hope she edited things," I said.

"I did a little," Maman said. "So, at what time will you leave in the morning?"

"I thought we'd leave here at about eight, that will put us in Cambridge in time to find out where Tom will be living, unload his stuff and then go and find lunch," I replied.

"I have the address," Tom said. "It says, Angel Court, on Trinity Street."

"I thought the term started at the beginning of this month?" I asked.

"I got permission from the Dean to arrive later, the visa took longer than expected," Tom explained. "The college was funny, when I told them what I had been going at Hoffman, they almost wet themselves, so I think they would have done almost anything to have me go there."

"Nice to be wanted," I said. "Did Maman feed you?"

"She did," Tom said. "Does it rain like this a lot?"

"Rain, drizzle, showers, storms, we get it all," I said. "That's why the place is so green. If it isn't raining then expect it to later in the day. You'll find that sunny days are to be appreciated."

"No particular time of the year when the rain comes?" he asked.

"No," I said. "The only real difference is that in January to March it could be sleet or snow instead of rain."

"Well, it's a change," Tom said.

"Is there anything you need before you go to Cambridge?" I asked.

"Maybe a bicycle," he said. "They told me that the easiest way to get around was with a bike."

"We can get one for you," I said. "We'll get a cheap one, so that if it goes missing we're not out too much, we'll also get a chain and a padlock."

We went on an expedition to Wandsworth to Halfords and found Tom a basic Raleigh with a carrier on the back to take his stuff, and we also got the requisite chain and lock. Friday afternoon traffic was bad, so it took us a while to drive there and back. We took a detour on the way back to get some dinner and went to an Indian restaurant that I knew in South Kensington, which I knew was popular with students. Tom had had Indian cooking before while at MIT, so knew what to order and how hot he liked things.

"Your Mom reminded me that you've got three doctorates," Tom said. "How did you manage that?"

"The first was simple enough," I said. "I stayed on at Oxford after my bachelor's degrees, and did a PhD in mathematics. I was then offered a funded fellowship which focused mainly on economics, and got really interested in that, so I enrolled as a mature part time student at LSE and got my second there. Then I needed to get some skills in computers, so again enrolled as a part time mature student at Imperial and got my third there. I've also taught at LSE and Imperial and at the University of Nairobi. My Oxford college would like me to go back there and teach full time, but I'm not ready for that."

"How did you manage all that in such a short time?" he asked.

"Well, the LSE doctorate I got in eighteen months, mainly because I had so much done before I even went there, it was research into theory that I did, and it was new ground for them, but simple enough for me," I said. "The same at Imperial, I was developing a language and created an operating system that ran much faster than the existing system. That was all new, so they were happy to work with me."

"You said bachelor's degrees," he said. "You got more than one?"

"I studied mathematics and economics at the same time," I explained. "I didn't find it too much work."

"What next?" he asked.

"I'm going to take over the investment bank that Dad currently runs," I said. "I've done work for him already and he's ready to retire."

"How will that go down in the City?" he asked.

"Probably with great skepticism," I said. "But, I've dealt with that most of my life, so nothing new, I just need to get some successes and I'll be fine."

"You're very confident," he laughed.

"I suppose I am," I said. "But I've learned that when it comes to numbers I can stay with the best."

"That's a bit of an understatement," Maman added. "Even your Dad says that he's never met anyone that can come close to you."

"How did you manage at MIT, that's a long way from Roy?" I asked.

"It was different," he admitted. "The hardest part was getting used to how close everything was. The eastern states are pretty small compared to the western states, from Cambridge I could be in New York in just over three hours, from Roy I might be able to get to Albuquerque in three or to the Colorado state line, the distances are just different."

"Well, get used to even shorter distances," I said. "Three hours here gets you almost to Scotland."

"Look, sorry to put a damper on things, but I'm dropping off here, could we go back to your place?" he asked.

We were up early the next morning and I helped Tom load his things into the Land Rover while Maman prepared breakfast. The only item that Tom and I debated about was the new bicycle, where to put it, on the back, on the roof, in the end we took off the front wheel and put it on the roof. After breakfast I gave Tom a map of London and one of Cambridge and we set off.

"I need to get to the M11," I told Tom. "Which way?" He looked at the map and then started to give me lefts and rights as we went until we came to the M11. Fortunately it was Saturday morning which meant that traffic was light, or passing through the centre of London and out on the A11 would have been tedious. For reasons probably only known to the planners the entrance to the M11 was actually off the A12, not the A11 as one would expect, and we joined it at Junction 3, what happened to Junctions 1 and 2, I have no idea.

"Okay, we're set now until we get to Junction 9 at Great Chesterford, we have to get off the motorway there because they haven't finished it yet, I think completion is supposed to be next year, we'll see," I said. We settled down to the steady drone of the Land Rover and ate up the miles until we saw the signs that told us that we would have to exit.

"We should find Trumpington Street," I suggested to Tom. "That will take us to Trinity Street."

"Okay," he said. "Left here, then stay on this road until we get into Cambridge." We motored on and found our way to Trinity Street and then Angel Court, after navigating around the one way system. We pulled up and Tom got out, went to the imposing gate and found a porter. He wanted to know what we were doing, so Tom explained and produced a letter, which then had the porter, not quite saluting, but certainly being most helpful. He told me where to park while we unloaded everything and then led the way to the room that Tom had been assigned. It was very nice, it even had its own bathroom, which I thought a real plus, sharing bathrooms was never one of my favourite things. The porter also showed Tom where he might store his bicycle. All unloaded we then asked for recommendations for lunch and also a place to park. As Tom had yet to get all his administrative tasks completed for the college, eating in Hall was probably not going to work, so the porter directed us out of town to Grantchester to a pub there. He gave us good directions as to how to get there.

The Green Man at Grantchester was actually on the River Cam, and I suppose on a nice sunny day would be a really nice spot to go for a lunch outside. Sadly that was not the case, it was not raining, but it was just not the weather for outdoor dining, so we ate in.

"Is there anything else you need?" I asked Tom.

"No, I think I'm all set," he said. "I didn't write down your phone number, can you give me it?"

"Here," I said, pushing over a business card. "This has my number and if I'm not there this is my office number, and failing that this number is the service I use for messages and mail."

"Thanks for bringing me up here," he said. "Lugging all that stuff on the train would have been a pain."

"I didn't look, was there a phone in your room?" I asked.

"No, but I saw a payphone downstairs," he said. "When I start at the lab, I'll see if they have one there that I can use."

"What do you fancy for lunch?" I asked.

"What's the steak and kidney pie like?" he asked.

"Usually pretty good," I said. "Very English cooking, some people don't like the kidney flavour."

"I'll try it," he thought. A waitress stopped at our table and took our orders, two steak and kidney pies and two pints of bitter. I could manage a pint and still drive.

"This is pretty good," he said after sampling the pie. "Not so sure about the beer, hard to get used to room temperature beer. I may stick to lager in the future."

"Could I come up and see you next weekend?" I asked.

"That'd be great," he said. "I'll get the lie of the land and call you in the week. What are you up to next week?"

"I've a meeting with my Dad and a client in Corby," I said. "They're looking for money, so we're going to listen and see how much and whether they're worth the risk."

"I'm quite looking forward to getting started now," he said. "I had some misgivings for a while, whether or not I even wanted to go back and do a doctorate, after all what we have been doing at Hoffman is probably as good, and we were doing it commercially, we'd have to make a pretty good breakthrough here to improve on what they've already done."

"Well, my guess is that if anyone can do it, you can," I said.

"Thanks for the vote of confidence," he laughed.

"When you get settled if there's anything you need explanations for, let me know, Brit academic society can be weird at times, they place a big emphasis on tradition, like wearing academic gowns at formal dinners, even having formal dinners in Hall," I commented.

"Okay," he said. "My thesis advisor is a guy called Gerald Prentice, I'd heard of him before I came here, he's written a bunch of papers on photoelectric effects, and specifically photovoltaics, but I'd done stuff at Hoffman that was new to him, so he really wanted me to come here and show him and work with him to see if we can't move things up a notch or two."

"When I was at the ranch you told me about the cousins," I said. "I may have a solution for you, but will need a couple of months to put it together, can you delay any decisions for a few months?"

"Sure," he said. "I think we'd all like to delay it indefinitely, but at some point we're going to have to decide what to do, we have had an appraiser in to get us the current land value and the value of the stock. We expect his report in about a week. Can you give me a hint as to what you might be able to do?"

"It would be an alternate source of funds, not tied to current lending rates," I said.

"Well, when you're ready, we're ready so let me know and we can talk," he said. "Tell me about Ian."

"He was a lovely man," I said. I had known this question might come up, so had been thinking about how to answer it. "His folks were tobacco farmers in Rhodesia until they were killed when they hit a land mine and were then shot. He was an anthropologist, close to the soil like you are with an encyclopedic knowledge of African mammals, birds, reptiles and trees. He had a much better knowledge of music, art and literature than I do, he made me laugh and he grinned a lot."

"It sounds like we would have hit if off," Tom said.

"I think you would have," I agreed.

"Do you miss him?" Tom asked.

"I did terribly for the first few months after his death, but my memories now are all good ones and I was happy and lucky to be married to him," I said. "But now it's time to look to a new life and find happiness again."

"Can you do that?" Tom asked.

"Yes," I said. "Ian's sister is married to this chap, also Tom, his first wife died and now he is married to Irene, and they are happy, really happy, so I know happiness can be found again. Tell me about Juanita."

"We were sweethearts all through high school," he said. "Then I went away to MIT and we wrote and saw each other on vacations, then the letters stopped and there were no phone calls and I found out when I went back to Roy that she'd married this guy from Texas while she was in Vegas. I was really broken up about it for a while, but, like you, I'm looking for happiness now. Happiness that comes with love. I'm so glad we met, it's really made me think that I can find both again."

"So, now what do we do?" I asked.

"Take it day by day and see how we go," he said. "I love being with you and the fact that you're here in England not far from me is great."

"I'll come up again next weekend," I promised. "I'll find somewhere to stay, so don't fret about me."

"I won't," he promised. "We're not at the sleeping together stage yet, so let's take things slow and we'll get there."

"I should run you back into Cambridge so that you can unpack and find your way around," I suggested.

"Probably should," he agreed. I paid the bill and we drove back into town and I dropped him off at the gate for Angel Court. There was nowhere to really park, so it was a quick drop off before I was moved on by the ever vigilant porters. I did kiss Tom on both cheeks and promise to see him the next weekend.

I drove back to London thinking of my first real date with Ian and how I had fretted over everything. I was more confident now, but there was still the unease of getting to know someone new and wondering what I might discover about him. I took stock of the situation, at first glance I really liked Tom, when our eyes met or our hands touched there was that electricity, so clearly I was drawn to him. He was like me being careful about how we proceeded, he had been burned and I had been bereaved, so we had both lost, could we each set aside our losses and find each other. That was the question that I would have to answer in the coming weeks and months. When I got home, Maman had dinner ready and was obviously eager to talk about my day, but left it to me to start. I gave her the travelogue first, then talked about what I felt, what we had talked about, how he had reacted to my description of Ian, how he described his relationship with Juanita. It was good to tell it all, it helped me see things more clearly for myself. It helped that I knew that Tom and Irene were happy and that Maman and Portia were as well. That gave me comfort knowing that finding the so called soul mate twice in one's life was possible.

Dad and I drove up to Corby, or should I say we were driven by Tiffany, to see Corby Seaton who had ambitions to take on JCB, Caterpillar and others, but were a little too small and were looking to expand.

"Good morning Mr Barclay," James Seaton said as he introduced himself. "This is my partner Vincent Edwards, thank you for coming."

"It is our pleasure," Dad said. "This is Dr Barclay, Fiona, my daughter, she is with the bank and has been advising me for some time."

"Doctor, doctor of what, might I ask?" Vincent said.

"Economics," I replied.

"From?" Vincent prompted.

"LSE," I said.

"What do you know about the construction machinery business?" James asked.

"I have gone through your literature and that of JCB, Caterpillar Aveling Barford and a few others," I said. "It's been useful, and I can see that from a specification point of view, your machines are largely equivalent, but I didn't see in your materials how you plan to go to market if you expand."

"I'm not sure what you mean?" James said.

"Well, JCB, Caterpillar, Ruston Bucyrus and others all have established routes to market either their own outlets, or through dealers, how are you proposing to get your machines to market, directly through your existing few outlets or through dealerships?" I asked.

"We'd go directly," James said. "I don't see the benefit of sharing the time and efforts of a dealer with other companies."

"That's what accounts for the significant investment in land, buildings and inventory?" I asked.

"I suppose it does," Vincent said.

"What differentiates your machines from those of Cat or JCB?" I asked.

"Our machines are better built," James said.

"If I am a buyer, let's say a major contractor who has an opportunity to do major work on a sewer system and wishes to buy a number of backhoes, should I buy from you and what support will you give me that I can't get from Cat or JCB?" I asked.

"We know most of the majors," James said. "They'd be happy to buy from us."

"But why?" I asked. "If I think as a buyer, I compare specs, I compare terms and then I look at after sale support, if I have a big contract it probably has completion bonuses and delay penalties, so can I afford to give the business to a newcomer, who I may know personally, but who does not have a proven history of customer support?"

"Not everyone looks at things that way," Vincent protested.

"No," I agreed. "If I'm Lincoln Excavating, a one man company with a backhoe that will do small jobs, I'll look for the cheapest machine I can find and accept that I won't get the support that JCB and Cat would provide, in fact I'll probably do most of the repairs myself."

"You've thought about this," James said wryly.

"I have," I agreed. "You're looking for £10,000,000 to start with to increase your network of owned outlets, so you'll have a lot tied up in land, buildings and inventory, would it not be a better use of cash to recruit dealers and use their existing land and buildings?"

"Perhaps," James said. "But, my numbers don't show that. Here, take a look." I quickly ran through the numbers, which on the face of it looked good enough, but I was more interested in the assumptions that lay behind the projections.

"Tell me about these assumptions," I requested. We went back and forth for some time talking about the assumptions. They had done their homework, but I had issues with some of the fundamental assumptions, most noticeably the overall growth of the market.

"Have you thought about acquiring one of your existing competitors who already has a network and adding your machine line to theirs?" I asked.

"We can't afford to do that," James said.

"Well, perhaps you can," I said. "If you look at Metter, you gain an existing broader network of outlets and you gain a line that does not overlap yours too much."

"We could never do that," Vincent protested. "They're huge."

"You could actually," I said. "Metter is struggling at the moment because since Bob Metter died, they have no effective leader and are floundering a bit, you could provide the leadership to make it work. They also are going to face an issue with the Inland Revenue, because Bob Metter left his quarter of the business to his four children, but didn't do it earlier enough, so they have death duties to pay."

"Us buy Metter, how on earth could we do that?" James asked.

"Here are some numbers," I said, handing over copies of the proposal I had put together.

"Whew," Vincent said. "This is ambitious. Are these numbers real?"

"I laid out the assumptions and the projections," I said. "I think you'll find that it all works."

"But, who do you approach, who's going to make a decision over there?" James asked.

"You talk to the four heirs, none of whom are really that interested in the business, Edwina the oldest is into horses and they are expensive, next is Patrick and he's into fancy cars, then there's Robert, who has a racing yacht and wants to compete in all kinds of offshore events, and finally there's Helen who goes through boyfriends like water and has debts that she needs to clear," I said. "Then, you talk to the current chairman who as I said is floundering a little because he just doesn't understand the business. You currently both buy steel from British Steel, engines from Detroit Diesel and Ruston, hydraulic pumps and components from Abex, so you could benefit from combined purchases. In those towns that you do have an outlet, there's also a Metter outlet, so pick the best location and sell off the others, do the same with sales forces, look at the two factories and decide which machine is best suited to which factory."

"But, it's still a huge gamble," Vincent said.

"Not really," I said. "You get the four heirs to agree to see you, you name a price that's above what's it trading for now, and I have some numbers on that, you go to the board and tell them that you want to merge, so you make an offer for all the outstanding shares, and you land up with the whole. My sense is that the board will be happy to have a plan."

"Won't someone else bid?" James asked.

"They might," I agreed. "So, here are the risks, the highest we could go, if someone pays above that, they'll be in for an unpleasant time, the numbers just don't work out."

"Are you for this William?" James asked Dad.

"It makes sense to me," he said. "It's ambitious, but why not?"

"You really think we could pull this off?" Vincent asked.

"I do," Dad confirmed. "I'd let Fiona talk to the heirs, give them the unpleasant facts about the payment they're facing, then offer them a way out. They might engage someone to look elsewhere, but my sense is that they're lazy and would be delighted if someone showed them how to pay what the Inland Revenue will demand and still leave them with enough cash to indulge their hobbies."

"God, wouldn't it be interesting," James said. He was hooked, I could see that. The whole idea just appealed to him. He just had never thought along this scale before and had no idea what was possible.

"What do we do about the current management at Metter?" Vincent asked.

"That's up to you," I said. "But, I would look at who you have, who they have and pick the best. The one thing I would not do is give them the usual blather about the most important asset is the people, then turn around and get rid of everyone. There have to be good people there that you should hang on to."

"And their board?" James asked.

"Thank them for their service and then decide if you want to retain any of them," I said. "You have to wonder if they have done the best job for the company and wonder if they advised Bob Metter on inheritance matters and what would happen if his holdings in the company were not transferred soon enough that they were liable for taxation upon his death."

"I don't remember," Vincent said. "Who's on their board?"

"I have the list here," I said, passing over a sheet of paper to each of them that had on it the names and pedigrees of the non executive directors.

"Maybe one out of this lot," James said. "Where does the money come from to be able to do this?"

"This is a schedule of borrowing," I said, passing over another piece of paper. "I picked lenders that take a long view, so we're not looking at usurious rates. There are balloon repayments at five years and ten years, but I those would be manageable if you look at the revenue and profit projections."

"What do you think, Vincent?" James asked.

"It's a gamble, but the odds look pretty good, we should give it a try," he replied.

"I think so too," James said. "William, Fiona, let's move forward on this, you'll handle all the necessary?"

"For a fee, of course," Dad laughed. "Seriously, we'll manage everything, what we need you to do is start thinking about your plans for integration of the two companies, what you'll keep, what you'll divest, who you'll keep, and as Fiona said, don't assume that your people are necessarily the best, look at everyone and pick the best no matter whether they're Corby or Metter."

"We know most of them," James said. "I'll get going on that."

"Lunch?" Vincent asked.

"Great idea," James said. "Where?"

"The golf club?" Vincent suggested.

"We can drive you," Dad suggested. "Then, we can drop you back here after lunch and go on back to London."

"Fine," James said.

Tiffany drove us to the golf club and Dad told her to get some lunch for herself and add it to the bill. James ushered us to the dining room and got us seated in an alcove that cut off most of the noise, and also made it difficult for anyone to overhear anything that we might say.

"William," James started. "How did you come up with this?"

"Actually it was Fiona who suggested it and she showed me how it would work, all I did was come along to make the introduction," Dad replied.

"Well, if we do this and people get wind of who put it together there'll be items in the FT and The Economist for sure," James said. "So, what else have you been working on Fiona?"

I gave them a brief résumé of my career to date and listed those clients that I was permitted to and pointed out that there were others who preferred not to be named. I think that they were actually impressed.

"Economics is not her only doctorate," Dad bragged. "She's also got one in mathematics and another in computer science."

"Wow," Vincent said. "What else do you do?"

"I shoot a little," I said.

"What shotgun?" James asked.

"I've used a shotgun, but mainly I shoot with either a pistol or rifle and I took up combat pistol shooting while I was in Kenya," I said.

"Don't mess with me," James laughed. "You don't play golf?"

"No," I said. "I've never tried, but from Dad's bad language at times, it seems that it could be a very frustrating game."

"True," James laughed. "But when you get it right, it's very satisfying, you really should try some time."

"Perhaps I will," I said. We ate, we talked a little more, but kept off the topic we had discussed in the morning, as careful as we might be, walls really do have ears at times, and we did not want anyone to overhear anything about Corby Seaton and Metter. After lunch we ran them back to their office and Dad promised them regular reports as to our progress. Tiffany then drove us back to London.

"Well, Tiffany," Dad said. "Did you hear anything?"

"James Seaton is a scratch golfer," she said. "He's on his second marriage, the first wife lives in Marseille now and he has bills to pay. Vincent Edwards is the operations person, he's apparently quite good, has the reputation of being firm but fair, still on his first marriage with no gossip to suggest any fractures there. Corby Seaton is well regarded as a local employer, they have the usual trade unions, but relations for the moment at least are pretty good."

"Good to know, thank you Tiffany," Dad said. I wondered how long Tiffany had worked for Dad, I knew that she was actually employed by a limousine service, but it seemed that she might be more than that. I did wonder who else she gave information to and if my conversations in the future might be reported to someone. It pointed up the risks of carrying on business conversations in front of someone other than one's known associates. Our route home took us back down the A1, the old road led ran north from London. By a curious quirk the first motorway in England, the M1, did not actually replace the A1, but was so named because it was the first. So, now we had the odd situation where we had the M1 and the A1(M), one can hardly have two M1's. Traffic was not too bad and we were back into the centre of London by four. Tiffany dropped us at the bank.

"So, good day?" Dad asked as we went to his office.

"I think so, what was your impression?" I asked.

"Once you'd shown them the numbers and how they could do it, they were hooked," he said. "I can see them now, plotting and planning, it will be hard to keep them under control for a while. You did brilliantly, enough basic these are the facts to really impress them. I'm still amazed that you put it all together so quickly."

"I wanted to give them something to really think about," I said.

"Well, you did that all right," Dad said. "What's your next move?"

"I go and see the heirs," I said. "Once I've got them to agree, I'll arrange a meeting with Sir John Harding and give him a nice way out of having to try and manage a company he doesn't want to."

"Who's the new MD?" Dad asked.

"Bloke called Francis Bolton," I said. "He was the chief accountant until Bob Metter died. He's not an engineer, all about the numbers you know, can add and subtract obviously but not a marketing chap or a builder of machines. They could do better."

"So, Harding has to stay involved in case Bolton does everything by the numbers and runs the company into the ground?" Dad asked.

"That's how I see it," I said.

"Okay, if you need an introduction to Harding let me know and I'll see what I can do," Dad said.

"Thanks," I said. "I'll let you know. Isn't one of our board a Trinity Cambridge man?"

"George Adams," Dad said.

"Do you think he could get me a place to stay at Trinity for the weekend?" I asked.

"I'm sure he could," Dad said. "He's close to the Master there. I'll call him tomorrow, what arrive Friday afternoon, leave Sunday?"

"That would be super," I said.

I contacted IBM and told them what I wanted, where and when and they sent a couple of men over to see me right away. It seemed you could always tell the IBM people, dark suits and white shirts, with pockets, short haircuts and often some kind of thing shoved into their shirt pockets, known, surprisingly as a pocket protector. I gathered it was to stop pens that might leak from staining their shirts. We looked over the available space and I got details from them as to power supply needs and what other alterations I needed to make to the space. They gave me a set of specific requirements that I could pass on to my contractor. I think at first they had been inclined to give me the sales pitch and gloss over everything else, but after a few questions about the operating system and other aspects of the computer, they realised that I might actually know something about it. We agreed on terms for the lease, after they had made quite some telephone calls to their office and the appearance of a contracts person who was sent around to join us post haste. I do not think they were used to doing things quite this quickly, and with someone who knew what they wanted and could articulate it in their terms. After they had left, I called in the contractor that I knew Dad had used in the past, and gave him the requirements and asked for a price and a date. He promised to have it for me by early the following week.

I picked up my new suit from Rachel and was delighted with it. The rest I could get the following week. I finished the model for Dundee and made arrangements to go to Chicago for my next meeting with them. I also found a tenant for my old office and sublet it to them until the lease was up. Dad and I contacted a law firm in New York that he had previously used and we agreed that the proceeds of the sale of Torrance would go into two US companies that we had previously set up, Thames Loddon for the bank's share and Thames Windrush for mine. In time we could consider what to do with these funds, use them in the US for other investments or repatriate them to the UK.

Dining in Hall

I made my approaches to the heirs of Bob Metter and it was far easier than I had imagined. Greed and avarice are powerful influences and I was offered the opportunity to get signed agreements to sell from all four. It seemed that after I had talked to Edwina, she had called the rest and told that that an easy mark was on the way with money to burn. I made sure that I transferred money to each of the heirs and got the share certificates in return. By Wednesday, Corby Newco owned a quarter of Metter, Corby Newco being a company we had set up purely for the transaction. In time most of the shares held by Corby Newco would be transferred to Corby Metter, another new company, with Corby Newco retaining twenty per cent that would transfer to Thames Cherwell. That made the approach to Sir John Harding simple, I merely told him that I represented twenty-five per cent of the voting stock of the company and would like the opportunity to talk to him. He hummed and hawed and said that he would return my call. He did, ten minutes later. I gather he had called Edwina and she had boasted and bragged about finally getting out of the business and that she had sold her shares to Corby Newco, and that the others had as well. Now, of course, we would have to disclose our beneficial ownership to the stock exchange, but there was time enough for that. Sir John suggested a meeting at his office in the City, which was actually a short taxi ride from the bank offices. For the meeting with Sir John, I wore the grey that I had worn to see James Seaton, all business, no attempt to lure him into anything, no overt sexual come on, nothing but business. I went over there and was ushered into a huge office, replete with art work, and saw Sir John sitting behind this enormous desk.

"Dr Barclay," he said. "Thank you for coming over."

"Thank you for agreeing to see me," I replied.

"You've rather caught us all off guard," he said. "Do you want a seat on the board?"

"Not really," I said. "I represent Corby Seaton and propose a merger between the two companies."

"Oh," he said. "I have to tell you that the company is not for sale."

"I appreciate that," I said. "Let me suggest a way that this may be both beneficial to the shareholders and the employees of Metter."

"I doubt that you could do that, but try me," he said. I talked for twenty minutes after which time he was nodding his head and could see pound signs as he realised on the stock that he owned.

"How would you proceed?" he asked. I knew I had him then. Greed and avarice had hooked him as well. He would salve his conscience by telling himself that his fiduciary responsibilities were properly satisfied by examining my offer and getting the board to recommend to the stock holders that they accept the offer. I was ready for that and had an offering memorandum ready, a copy of which I gave him to review, or more likely his solicitor and accountant to review.

"I will need to present this to the board," he said.

"Of course," I said.

"I thought Thames Cherwell was run by William Barclay?" he asked.

"My father has decided to retire," I said. "He has asked me to take over the reins."

"What prepared you for the job?" he asked.

"I have a doctorate in economics, I have been working as a consultant creating models for various companies, I have created models for the Exchequer and I was abroad for a while, while my husband was part of our legation to Kenya," I said.

"Which companies?" he asked.

"I am bound by agreements not to disclose," I said. "But, I'm sure that a man with your connections can probably find at least some."

"Oh, sherry?" he asked.

"Thank you," I said. He finally got up from behind the battlements of his desk and poured two glasses of sherry.

"What becomes of me and the other directors?" he asked.

"I think that's matter to discuss with James Seaton," I replied. "Do you play golf?"

"Member at Berkshire," he said.

"James Seaton enjoys golf and I have it on good authority that he's a scratch golfer, you may find it advantageous to invite him to play with you one day," I suggested.

"Damned good idea," he said. "You don't play?"

"I'm sorry no," I said. "I can ride and shoot, but never took up golf."

"You said you were with your husband in Kenya, does he have a posting here now?" he asked.

"Sadly he was killed in a traffic accident earlier this year," I said.

"Oh, sorry to hear that," Sir John said. "Where did you get your Phd?"

"At LSE," I replied.

"I'm an Oxford man myself," he said.

"I did my undergraduate studies and my first doctorate at Oxford," I said.

"First?" he said. "What was that?"

"Mathematics," I said. "I then held a fellowship, that was funded by a consortium of mining companies. I examined and modelled the asset valuations of ore reserves."

"I read PP&E," he said, referring to the portmanteau degree of philosophy, politics and economics. "Helped me get prepared for the City, met lots of useful chaps there too. Another?" he asked waving to my empty glass.

"No thank you, Sir John," I said. "I have work waiting for me at my office."

"Well, good," he said. "Look, let's plan on meeting with the whole board next week, I'll get a time and day, and you can talk to them as well."

"Very good, Sir John," I said. "Thank you for your time."

As I left, I heard him pick up the telephone and talk to someone, I heard him say, "Yes she was just here, damn fine filly, bright too, need to find out more about her." I heard no more as I politely walked out of earshot.

When I returned to the office there was a message from George Adams. I returned his call and learned that the Master would be happy to have me stay at the college for the weekend, and had given instructions to the porters to that effect and had also told them to find a place where I might park my car, he had also extended an invitation to me and my host to join him for drinks before the formal dinner on Saturday. I then gave Dad a report on my transactions with the Metter heirs and my meeting with Sir John. Dad thought it might be prudent if he came with me to meet the whole board of Metter. He promised to let me do the talking and to just nod and agree when I needed him to. I also went to see Rachel and picked up the rest of my suits. She had done me proud and I now had a wardrobe that looked like it came from Saville Row. Then I had the big decision to make, what to wear in Cambridge. I knew now that there would be at least one formal dinner where dressing appropriately would be expected, but there were also times when more casual clothes would be the order of the day. I reviewed my wardrobe and made selections. For a formal dinner I had a red cheongsam, which I had had for some time, but had not worn in quite a while. In case there was another formal occasion, I picked a simple French blue dress that I had, it would go with just about anything and had elegant lines to it. For casual, I picked jeans, pullovers, boots, suede jacket, plain shirts and some other accessories. It was late autumn after all, so shorts, mini skirts were largely out, I had no intention of freezing to death just to look fashionable.

Friday, I worked a short day, I just had a few things to clear up, and then I told Dad that I was leaving for the weekend. I went home and packed then went and got my Land Rover and drove back to my flat to pick up my suitcase. I had hoped to get a start out of London before the Friday afternoon traffic, but it was already building and it took me a while to get onto the M11. Once on the motorway things speeded up quite a bit and traffic also thinned. It did get a little more congested when I actually got to Cambridge, but then I did not mind, and just took my time. I went to the gate that I had been directed to and the porter wanted to know my business. I told him who I was, and then the porter was as obsequious as one could be and directed me where to park and even offered to carry my suitcase for me. He led me to a room that was very elegant, lots of woodwork, mouldings, bookcases and other niceties, it even had it's own bathroom, which was well appointed. George must have spun quite a yarn to the Master to get me such a nice room. I deposited my bag then went looking for Tom. I found him in his room entertaining two other chaps.

"Fiona," he said, when he answered the door. "Come in, come in, did you get settled already?"

"I did, thank you," I said.

"Fiona, this is Gerald Prentice, my advisor and this is Patrick Hill, he's another doctoral candidate like me, guys, this is Fiona Barclay," he said, making the introductions all around.

"Nice to meet you," Gerald said. "You're obviously not from New Mexico, how did you two meet?"

"In a small café, in a small town in New Mexico," I said. "I was there buying a winery."

"You were buying a winery?" Patrick said.

"Well, to be accurate, I only have twenty per cent of it, the rest is held by the Cillie family," I explained.

"How are you associated with them, can you get us a good deal on wine?" Gerald asked.

"As to the first, my brother is married to Charlize Cillie, and to the second, I'll see what I can do, I presume you would be looking at the French wines from the Loire and Provence?" I replied.

"Either would be super," Gerald said.

"What do you do that you can buy at least part of a winery?" Patrick asked.

"I'm an investment banker," I said. "I've just taken over the Thames Cherwell Bank from my Dad."

"So, if we needed seed money to start up a fabrication line for solar panels, you'd be the one to talk to?" Gerald asked.

"You can ask," I laughed. "I'm not guaranteeing that I'd fund anything, it would depend on the risk and the likely outcome."

"Are you joining us for dinner tonight?" Patrick asked.

"Tom?" I asked.

"We are," he confirmed. "I hope you brought something to wear Fiona. There's a graduate society group here, the BA Society, and they have a formal dinner on Friday nights, not surprisingly, the BA Dinner."

"I did," I confirmed. "I remember from my Oxford days that dining in Hall required a little more than jeans and a donkey jacket. Oh, I should also give you fair warning that we're invited to drinks with the Master before dinner tomorrow night, and to dine at the high table."

"We are?" Tom asked.

"We are," I confirmed. "One of my board is close friends with the Master and made the introduction."

"One of my board," Patrick said, looking at Gerald and raising his eyebrows.

"What did you read at Oxford, PP&E?" Gerald asked.

"No, I started with mathematics and then added economics," I replied.

"She has three doctorates," Tom added. "Mathematics, economics and computer science."

"Perhaps you could help us with some computer modelling issues we're having?" Gerald asked.

"I'd be happy to take a look," I said. "I've been using the computer at Imperial, but I'm about to install my own at the bank."

"What are you getting?" Gerald asked.

"An IBM 4341," I said. "I'm going to lease it as I know there's a newer model with more memory on the way."

159

"If we going to dine, we should think about getting ready," Patrick suggested.

"If I go back and change will you come and get me in about half an hour?" I asked Tom.

"Where are you staying?" he asked. I gave him the room number and said my goodbyes and went off to change. I decided that it would be the cheongsam that night, so quickly bathed, then changed into the dress. I wore my red shoes that went with the dress and had a gold clutch that went well with the embroidery in the dress. I picked simple gold earrings that looked like little tassels.

Tom collected me at the appointed hour and it was only a short walk, under cover thankfully, to the dining hall.

"Wow," he said, when he collected me, I noted that he was dressed in a nice grey suit, with an academic gown over it, and looked quite fetching.

"What?" I asked.

"I've only ever seen you in jeans, jackets and boots," he said. "That dress is stunning. It'll raise a few eyebrows."

"Why, it's just a dress?" I said.

"Yes, but," he said. "Well, you'll see." We walked into the hall and saw Patrick and Gerald in deep discussion with two others, and Tom had been right, conversation generally paused and people stared, then I heard whispers and murmurs, then conversation generally built up again. I was probably hated by every woman in the place, of whom there were a few, quite a bit less than half the room, perhaps one quarter.

"Tom, Fiona, please join us," Gerald invited. "Fiona, Tom, this is Julia Decker and Mark Decker, Mark is in our lab and we're trying hard to get Julia placed in the languages department. Julia, Mark, this is Dr Fiona Barclay, who's not with us, having been to that other university to the south, and Tom Ortiz who's in our lab and is from the States, an MIT man."

"I love your dress," Julia said. "I wish I could wear things like that."

"I do like it," I said. "I bought it a few years ago from a place in London that had been recommended to me by a friend from Oxford."

"What do you do?" Mark asked.

"I'm an investment banker," I said. Somehow that sounded a lot easier to say than a consultant which usually led to a long explanation into what I consulted upon. Investment banking was generally understood, so no long explanation was required.

"I thought all bankers were stodgy old men," Julia said.

"We're trying to change that," I laughed. "What languages?"

"French, mostly," Julia said. "I've a degree in French and I'm looking to see if I can't get myself into the master's program. I need to do something while Mark is busy in the lab."

"Fiona speaks French," Tom said.

"*Vraiment?*" Julia asked.

"*Vraiment,*" I confirmed. "*Ma mère est française.*"

"Now ladies, no talking behind our backs," Gerald said. "Time enough for other languages. Okay, Fiona, we know you're a banker, we know you have computer skills, we now know that you speak French, what else?"

"Not much," I said. "I don't sing, I can dance a little with a good partner."

"She does ride horses," Tom said. "We went out on my family ranch and she managed rather well."

"We should sit," Gerald said. "Julia, Fiona, please." He indicated chairs that put us opposite one another. I had Tom to my right and Patrick to my left, and Julia was sandwiched between Mark and Gerald. Dinner was actually quite good and the wine served was not bad either, not quite Cillie Wines standard, but not bad all the same. I noticed that I kept getting furtive glances from others at the table and smiled to myself at the comments and ribbing that Tom would get after I had gone. They would probably all want to know how he had met someone so quickly having been in the country only a week. It was fun eating and drinking with the others. Tom was funny, he had a wicked dry sense of humour, not the crass kind that I seen with other Americans, but far more subtle, more like a classic British sense of humour. The others wanted to know a little more about the cattle ranch that Tom came from and I know it was a little difficult for the others to grasp just how remote Roy was, and given its remoteness, and how someone from there could have made it to MIT.

When dinner finally broke up, Tom walked me back to my room and I kissed him goodnight.

"Where shall we go tomorrow?" I asked him.

"If you don't mind driving me, could be go to Boston?" he asked.

"Of course," I said. "Will you pick me up at eight for breakfast?"

"Love to," he said. "Goodnight Fiona, sleep well."

"Night Tom," I replied. "See you in the morning." After he had left, I wondered if I should have just dragged him into the room and made love to him, but then got to thinking that I was not sure yet if it was love, it had all the hallmarks of love, the electric thrill of his touch, the comfort I felt in his company, the way he smiled at me, certainly all the symptoms were there, it just needed a little confirmation. I wondered what Ian would think and decided that he would approve, or was I just putting my own wishes into Ian's voice in my head. I took a long soak in the bath and thought about Tom, his funny accent, his easy manner, his sense of humour, the way he made me smile and the way he smiled at me, the more I thought about it the more I liked it. This looked as if it was working out very well.

Tom collected me at eight, casually dressed now for our excursion into the Fen country. We had to wait a few minutes for the refectory to open to get our breakfast and when we did we found a quiet corner.

"Did you sleep well?" he asked.

"Eventually," I said. "I had a lot on my mind."

"Oh?" he said.

"You, you dope," I said. "I rather think that I love you, I know it's a big surprise, it's a surprise to me too, but, you make me happy, you make me laugh, I just enjoy being with you."

"I love you Fiona," he said. "I was smitten that first time I saw you in Mosquero. I couldn't believe someone like you would walk into my life. I still can't believe you're here, I'm so lucky."

"So, what do we do?" I asked.

"I think let things go where they will," he said. "Perhaps next weekend you could come up and stay with me?"

"I'll come up next weekend," I agreed. "But if you don't mind I'll stay in a hotel, staying with you in your room is a big step for me, and I'm feeling a little apprehensive, and want to take things a little slower, I hope you're not too disappointed?"

"I'm sure I'll manage," he said, with a grin.

"It's a date," I said, committed now. "So, eat up if we're going to drive to Boston."

We walked to where I had parked and drove off to Boston. Sadly it was drizzling again, so the roads were wet, the air was damp, even with patchy fog in places.

"Is it always like this?" Tom asked as we motored out of Cambridge on the Peterborough road, with windshield wipers swishing back and forth.

"More than sunny," I said. "If you want sun, you're going to have to go back to Roy, or to the south of France. Which raises an interesting point, what are you planning to do at Christmas?"

"I was planning to stay here," he said.

"If the weather cooperates why don't we fly down to Cannes and stay with my mother?" I suggested.

"That would be great," he said. "I've never been to France, what do we do fly into somewhere, show our passports and then go on?"

"That's what I was thinking, fly into Le Bourget, clear immigration, then fly on to Nice, what do you think?" I asked.

"That sounds great," he said. "Changing the subject a little, it's flat here."

"This is the Fens, and they are flat, you'll see all kinds of drainage ditches and canals," I said. "It can get really foggy here."

"I'll bet it does," he said. "What do you know about Boston?"

"It's a port on the Wash, that's the funny bit that looks as if someone's taken a bite out of the east coast," I said. "It's where the emigrants that founded Boston in the US came from, bunch of religious zealots if you ask me."

We knew when we were approaching Boston, we could see the church. It stood out on the skyline, visible for miles. We drove into town and found a place to have lunch that gave us a view of the river, not that it was a very exciting view, the banks of the river were all piled, so no grassy banks to sit on, no trees to shelter under, but I suppose as the river ran through the centre of the town, then it had to be managed or erosion and other problems would set in. We ordered and then I steeled myself for the conversation to follow.

"I want to talk to you," I said. "And, I don't want you to get upset with me, but to listen carefully."

"Okay," he said. "I'm almost afraid to ask."

"Well, here goes," I said. "What are your thoughts about your ranch and the heirs who want money, what if someone else were to buy them off?"

"Well, on the face of it, I'd rather owe anyone else than the rats," he said. "But, anyone else that has a stake is going to want something, don't you think?"

"True," I said. "But, there are institutions that will take a position and let it just sit for a while, or for ever, like a land bank."

"I don't like the idea of owing anyone," he said.

"That I understand," I said. "It struck me that one of the problems with family farms and ranches is that often get broken up because the various heirs all want their piece. The Chinese have a saying, rice paddy to rice paddy in three generations. The first works hard and builds things up, the second spends madly and the third is left to go back to the rice paddy and start again."

"There wouldn't be interest payments?" he asked.

"No," I said. "I was thinking, as I said, that there are land banks and other institutions that would put up the money to put the land in trust and avoid or defer any development."

"I couldn't take charity," he said. "As much as the idea of getting rid of the rats appeals, will we just be replacing one problem with another?"

"That's for you to decide," I said. "One thing you might do is have Linda get an appraiser from Dallas to get you a value on the ranch, that way the rats can't say that your local appraiser undervalued the property to assist you."

"Good thought," he said. "I'll do that."

What I did not tell Tom was that I was essentially going to be the land bank, albeit a temporary one, I thought I would surprise him and split the rats' share of the ranch two ways, giving half to him and half to Linda.

"I was thinking that I might fly up next weekend and perhaps we could take a trip on Saturday or Sunday, depending on the weather," I said.

"Sounds like fun, where to?" he asked.

"I don't know, you decide, maybe the Lakes, maybe Wales, maybe Cornwall, what do you fancy?" I asked.

"Have you any idea what the weather's supposed to be like?" he asked.

"I've been looking at the long term forecasts, but they don't tell me too much," I lamented. "Plus, weather here is often very local, so it could be sunny west of the Pennines, but pouring east of them. I'll fly up anyway if the forecasts are in any way decent, then we can see."

"That's right, I forgot that Freya told me that you had your own plane," he said. "I wonder if the university has a flying club?"

"Don't know," I said. "I'm sure they have something even if it's just gliding."

"Ever tried that?" he asked.

"Not yet," I said. "It might be nice, I'm sure it's peaceful once you're up and you really would get to understand thermals and winds."

"I'll check to see if there's a club, and if there is, do they have an introductory ride," he said.

"So, what do you think about children?" I asked.

"They're nice enough, why?" he asked.

"I was wondering if you really want children of your own?" I asked.

"I have to be honest," he said. "I'm happy to be without, Linda has two, and that's enough in the family, do you want children?"

"Not really," I said. "James and Charlize have started their family and I don't really see myself in that rôle."

"Just as well we're on the same page," he laughed. "It might have been difficult if one of us had really wanted them."

"Just as well," I agreed. "Should we be starting back, so that we can gussy ourselves up for the Master's drinks reception?"

"Probably should," he agreed. "It's going to be slow going with the fog."

Slow going it was, I doubt that we got much above twenty-five the whole way back. It was dismal. At least in my plane, I could fly above this kind of muck, or at worst fly on instruments.

I chose the blue for the drinks reception and the Formal Hall Dinner. With it I wore the sapphire set that Portia had given me when I had gone to my first ball with Ian. Tom had hinted that the cheongsam might be too much for young male undergraduates, driven by hormones as they were. The blue was knee length and did not have the slits on the sides that the cheongsam did, so far more decorous for the Master's occasion. I had blue shoes to go with the dress and a silver clutch bag that matched the silver settings of the sapphires. Tom came to collect me, nicely turned out in his suit, and academic gown. We found a porter and got directions to the Master's event, which was but a short walk away, under cover, which was fortunate as drizzle seemed to be the order of the day for Cambridge. We arrived and were met at the door by a chap who looked to me the epitome of academia. He enquired as to our identities, handed us each a glass of sherry and ushered us in and introduced us to the Master.

"Delighted to meet you, Dr Barclay, Mr Ortiz. George tells me that you're taking over the reins at Thames Cherwell," he said.

"I am," I confirmed. "My father has decided that he should retire and enjoy life while he can, so he plans to live and sail in the Caribbean."

"How on earth did you meet Mr Ortiz, I know that he's just arrived from the States?" the Master asked.

"I was in New Mexico buying a winery," I said. "And I had taken a side trip looking for suitable growing areas and water and we met in a café in a really small town, well hamlet really."

"I gather from George that have three doctorates under your belt," the Master said. "But, not one from us?"

"Sadly, no," I said. "But, there's always time."

"And Mr Ortiz, what took you to New Mexico, I thought you were an MIT man?" the Master asked.

"My family has a cattle ranch there," Tom replied. "I was back there visiting waiting for my visa."

"What kind of cattle?"

"Black Angus," Tom said. "They seem to thrive on poor grazing and harsh conditions."

"How many acres?"

"40,000," Tom said. "We're one of the smaller ranches in the area."

"That big? You could drop the whole of Cambridge several times over in that. How many cows?"

"We only run about 600 at any time," Tom said. "The grazing just does not lend itself to higher stocking rates."

"Phillip, come and talk to Tom Ortiz here about cattle and ranching, Phillip is our geographer and is fascinated by land use. Dr Barclay, Professor Phillip Baskerville and one of his protégées, Roberta Spinoglio. Now, Dr Barclay, what will it take to have you join us here?"

"In what way?" I asked, admiring the way that the Master had discreetly separated us, so that he could talk to me alone.

"I'm given to understand that you've done work for the Exchequer, the Chancellor was most complimentary when I talked to him recently."

"That was kind of him," I said.

"Did you know that Professor Hopkins died two weeks ago?" the Master asked.

"I had not heard that," I said. "Professor Hopkins and I were nodding acquaintances at best, we subscribed to somewhat different economic theories."

"That's not quite how he put it when the Exchequer picked you to do their models for them over him, but Gerald had failed to keep up with the times and did not know how to integrate his ideas with computer models, whereas you do it so elegantly," the Master said, in his best butter up manner.

"That's kind of you to say," I said, wondering when he was actually going to get to the point.

"The thing is," he said. "We have a good economics department, but I think we would benefit from an alternate view once in a while, keep us all on our toes don't you know."

"I think that's probably sensible," I agreed.

"So, I was wondering what I might do to persuade you to be a Visiting Professor for us and give us the benefit of your insights?" he asked.

"I may be able to do something for you," I temporised. "It will depend on my schedule at the bank, do you have anything in mind?"

"I was rather hoping that you might do something for us early in the Lent Term and another in the Easter Term," he suggested. "So, two lectures, you pick the subject, but I would prefer your thoughts on economic theory and how to translate that into practical terms for use by governments, companies and other institutions."

"I could do that," I said. "Let me look at my appointments when I go home and see what days I might have available."

"Splendid," he said. "Now, I think we might go into Hall, gather up Mr Ortiz there and, please, this way."

I gathered up Mr Ortiz, who was still in deep conversation with Phillip Baskerville and I noticed that Roberta Spinoglio was hanging onto his every word. I interrupted them and told Tom that the Master had indicated that it was time to go.

We went into Hall and were seated at the High Table, me to the Master's right and Tom to the right of me. There were quite a few stares from the undergraduates who were probably wondering just who we were. Dinner was as good as it had been the night before, but the wine at the High Table was a little better. To my mind, it still was not as good as the Cillie wines, but then I had a bias, wanting the family to flourish. Perhaps in time, I could get to know the Bursar and see what arrangements might be made. The Master and I chatted about banking, ranching, life at college and what it had been like for me to go to Oxford at such a young age. He did draw Tom into our conversation and seemed particularly interested in cattle ranching and the differences between the television and cinema depictions of ranches and the reality. Phillip Baskerville listened carefully to what was said, and I noticed that Roberta Spinoglio was still hanging onto every word that Tom uttered, like a simpering teenager. Dinner over, the fellows all departed and we left with the Master.

"You will give me dates?" he asked.

"I will," I promised.

"Thank you for coming Dr Barclay, and thank you Mr Ortiz for getting her to come here," the Master said.

Tom walked me back to my room, where I kissed him goodnight and asked him to collect me in the morning for breakfast. I bathed then wondered what I had committed myself to. At least it was only two lectures. I thought that I would talk for about an hour, then allow another hour for questions and answers. I laughed to myself over the events of the evening, I should have known that there had been an ulterior motive for the Master to invite me to stay and to High Table. I just hoped Tom had not been put out by the events. I would talk about it over breakfast with him. So, Gerald Hopkins was dead, no more dry as dust papers on arcane aspects of consumer spending or the effects of government stimulus into the economy. I had often thought that Hopkins liked to think that he was a candidate for a Nobel, but to my mind at least, he just was not of that calibre. He was competent enough, just a little dated and not that inspiring. I wondered that the college had kept him on for so long.

Tom collected me the next morning, in time for breakfast, but not so early that we would have to wait for them to open again.

"I'm sorry about last night," I told Tom. "I didn't expect the Master to monopolise my attention so."

"It's fine," he said. "Phillip was interesting and he wants me to go and see him sometime with maps and talk about watersheds, agriculture, raw materials and urban development in New Mexico. I thought you were great last night, you handled the Master just right, and I know now that you'll be here at least twice more. I've also picked up all kinds of points, one for dining at the High Table and two for arriving with the most beautiful woman there."

"Well, how nice of you," I said. "You're biased."

"No, I'm serious," he said. "I had a few comments last night and this morning, they all want to know who and where did we meet."

"I'm sure you can handle the attention," I laughed. "So, what today?"

"Could we go to Duxford?" he asked. "That's where my Uncle Bert flew from in the Second World War. I forget what number mission he was on, but he never came back."

"Of course," I said. "As I recall the Imperial War Museum moved there a couple of years again and they've got quite a collection of planes. So, you never met your Uncle Bert?"

"No, he died before my folks even got married," Tom said. "There are some pictures of him at the house."

"No heirs from him to want their piece of the ranch?" I asked.

"None that I know of," Tom said. "He wasn't married when he came over here, but that's not to say there isn't some Brit around who's a long-lost cousin."

We drove to Duxford and spent a most pleasant day wandering around the collection of planes. I wondered what it would be like to fly one of the fighter planes, so much faster than my Cessna, and far more capable in the air. I imagined myself doing loops and spirals and other aerobatics while Tom looked for and was disappointed to see that they did not have a P-47 Thunderbolt of the type his uncle would have flown. We braved the weather and looked at the larger planes parked outside and both marvelled at how small relatively the airfield was. We found a docent who it turned out had been a British pilot in the War, so I was able to ask him about the various planes from a pilot's perspective. I wanted to know how long the takeoff roll was, what was the stall speed, climb rate, all kinds of things. It turned out that he had actually flown the P-47 a few times and was able to tell Tom about the plane and what it was like to fly. We thanked him for his time and stories and went off to find a late lunch. There was a pub in the village still open, so we grabbed what we could before motoring back to Cambridge. I said my goodbyes to Tom and confirmed that I would be back the next weekend.

"Have you thought any more about where you might like to go?" I asked.

"Would it be possible to go and see a real castle?" he asked.

"I think that could be arranged," I said. "I'll see you next Friday." I kissed him goodbye and drove back to London in a turmoil. Did I really love him, why was I reluctant to jump into bed with him, what was holding me back. Tom was nice, he was funny, he made me laugh, so, what was the problem. Well, it was something I would have to come to terms with, and probably sooner rather than later.

Dad came with me to the board meeting of Metter which was at their main offices in Swindon, we took an early train down from London and arrived before nine, to find the others all just arriving, most by chauffeur-driven cars. I saw Sir John Harding and we waved and he ushered us into the board room, a room complete with panelled walls, windows on the one side looking out over some fields, a huge rectangular table and reasonably comfortable chairs. I presented my case, reviewing the companies, their respective shares of the market, financial performance to date and projected growth of both the market and the companies, with caveats for the unseen and unexpected. I pointed out that Corby Newco now held a quarter of the voting stock of the company, then, I named the suggested offering price for the outstanding shares of Metter and I could see calculations going in either in their heads or on pads of paper.

"Thank you, Dr Barclay," Sir John Harding said. "It would hardly be politic of me to ask you to step outside while we consider this as you represent twenty-five per cent of the voting stock. Gentlemen, I for one am in favour of this merger at the terms offered by Dr Barclay. It combines two well-known companies and brings leadership in the form of James Seaton, who we all know is passionate about this business. Does anyone have any questions for Dr Barclay?"

"Will this past muster with the Monopolies Commission?" a member asked.

"I do not see an issue," I said. "Even with the combination of Metter and Corby Seaton, there is no appreciable market concentration, we still have Caterpillar, JCB, Ruston Bucyrus, Aveling Barford, Volvo, Terex, Euclid,

J.I. Case, Liebherr, O&K, Northwest and other lesser brands. From a customer point of view, there are still plenty of options to go with Metter or Cat or JCB or another."

"What happens to the employees of Metter?" another asked.

"I see some overlap in the sales force and in management," I said. "My advice to the new company is to look carefully at each person and make decisions based on their ability to provide value to the company, whether they be from Metter or Corby Seaton. I would do the same with overlapping branch sales properties, and with the manufacturing facilities it may make sense to transfer products between the two factories to get the best use of the equipment at each."

"Will you stay involved?" a third asked.

"We will," I said. "We will have a stake in this and will work to protect our investment."

"William, you've been silent in all this, what's your view?" Sir John asked.

"I concur with Fiona's analysis, and her recommendations," Dad said. "I think this is a good merger and will succeed."

"Any other issues?" Sir John asked. There was one which I was sure they all wanted to ask, and that was what happens to me. Well, that was largely up to James Seaton. "No other issues, well, I move that we accept this offer. Those in favour?" The hands all dutifully went up. I think they knew that if they did not agree and be cooperative, then I would go ahead with a hostile takeover, which would kill whatever chance they might have of getting James to keep them on as non-executive directors.

"Good, then we are agreed, how do we proceed Dr Barclay?" Sir John asked.

"We issue this statement and this offer to purchase, you will need to have your counsel review the agreement, they may work with ours at Lancaster & Bellows," I said, handing around the relevant documents. "We can do this quickly and have a closing before the end of the year."

"You have all the financing in place?" someone asked.

"I do," I said. "We are putting up twenty per cent of the required funds and I have the balance in place. As soon as we get share certificates, people will get their money."

"My God," a voice said. "I never would have thought that this would happen. How on earth did you come up with this plan William?"

"I didn't," Dad said. "Fiona came to me with the plan and all the details, including the lenders, all I did was acquiesce. I am stepping down from the bank and Fiona is taking over."

"It looks like it's in good hands," Sir John said.

"I think so," Dad said.

"I think lunch is in order," Sir John said. He picked up a telephone and said a few words, then the doors opened and a stream of catering people came in with trolleys. They also came in with wine and that was handed around and I noticed a few glasses disappeared rather quickly. More was served and then place settings were laid out and luncheon plates put out. It was a very nice lunch, these people did well for themselves at the expense of Metter. I had a sense that James Seaton would change that for a while, until he too succumbed to the lure of high living. There were toasts all around and I could see those directors who held stock, either directly or as options, were busy spending the money in their heads. I wondered how many new cars or yachts would come of this. We eventually broke up and Dad and I returned to the station to take a train back to London. On the train, sipping our wine, we reviewed the state of play and concluded that all had gone well.

"Take my advice and sit in on all the meetings with the lawyers," he said. "Both groups will want to justify their fees by making asinine changes, rein them in and keep them focused on the main issues."

"Good advice," I said. "Thanks for the vote of confidence today."

"It was a pleasure to see you take them all on and leave them wondering what had happened," he laughed. "They'll all do very well, but I'm not sure if Seaton will want any of them as a board."

"I wouldn't," I said. "I wasn't that impressed with any of them."

"Get used to it," Dad said.

"So, will someone else make a counteroffer?" I asked.

"It's possible, but I think unlikely," he said. "For someone to do that they would have to either have significant cash on their balance sheet, or have ready access to borrowed funds. If someone loses their minds and outbids us then Corby Newco makes some money, there will be a row with the heirs who will think that they should have had the chance to benefit from a bidding war, but if they read the fine print on the agreement that they all signed, they'll see that that was covered and that they have no standing. One, perhaps two will go to a solicitor and ask for advice, and get the sad news that they have no case, unless the solicitor is an idiot or completely bereft of ethics."

"I was wondering, how reliable is Tiffany the driver?" I asked.

"You mean that because she tells us things, then perhaps she's telling others the same or more?" he asked.

"That thought had crossed my mind," he said. "I've been wondering whether it might not be safer to just have a full-time driver."

"Or, just not talk about much in the car, not that that's easy to do, easy to say, but not so easy to stay mum," I said.

"You're right," he said. "Why don't you talk to Tiffany and find out what her aspirations are, perhaps we could take her on, perhaps we should look at someone else?"

The cynical part of me did wonder if there was more to the relationship between Dad and Tiffany. She had driven for him for a couple of years, and he requested her specifically when he had need for a driver. So, was I being too cynical, or was it just a personal preference on his part. I have to say that she was an excellent chauffeuse, she drove well, she did her homework about routes, parking, current traffic conditions and such. She did wear short skirts and heels, that would probably appeal to a man, but perhaps that was the standard for the limousine company.

I was busy for the balance of the week, supervising meetings with the various lawyers. Dad had been right, both sides kept suggesting minor changes in the language, none of which I accepted. The words stood as they were and left no ambiguity and the meaning was clear enough. The speed at which they all capitulated told me that it had been change for changes sake. By the end of the week, we had gone to press and had issued the offer to purchase. Now the various shareholders would have the weekend to spend money in their minds and accept the offer. The cash offer for the stock was a good offer and compared to the declared dividends would put substantially more in the pockets of the shareholders in a much shorter time.

I then turned to more personal matters. I had committed to Tom that I would go up that weekend and see him. That had been a somewhat spur of the moment thing on my part, but now I was faced with the reality. Was this something I was ready for. I thought that I loved Tom, of that I was fairly sure, so what was the issue. I think partly it was just basic nervousness about being found wanting. My experience had been limited to only one partner, Ian, so how would I find a new partner. Well, the only way to answer that question was to go ahead and see how things went, but I knew I was not ready yet, but perhaps by Christmas I would be. I planned for the weekend and found myself a nice hotel in Cambridge within easy walking distance of the college. I checked the weather, the Met Office was claiming a cold, but clear weekend across the country. So, I would fly up to Cambridge. Next was wardrobe, flying was easy, jeans, a shirt and sweater, and my suede jacket with light boots on my feet, and in case the forecasters were correct my RayBan Aviators. I decided that there would be no eating in Hall, so no fancy clothes were necessary, we could eat out at restaurants or even the hotel for that matter. My thoughts turned again to my first experience with sex when I was twenty. Ian had taken me to a ball, and I had planned out a whole evening, with the bedroom to cap it all. Unfortunately, the ball had been a disaster and we had left early with me in tears. I am sure that Ian thought that the weekend would be a dead loss, but then I came to my senses and decided that a weekend in bed with Ian was not the worst thing to happen. It had all been very magical, and physical, as I savoured the delights of sex with a loving partner, in bed, on the sofa, in the bath, you name it. I thought about the budding relationship with Tom. When would I be ready for that kind of intimacy. As much as I missed it, the idea of jumping into bed with Tom, or anyone else for that matter, still bothered me in a way that I just could not define. I had a difficult time pinning down the reason for my hesitancy, was it some kind of loyalty to the memory of Ian, was it a fear on my part that Tom or another might not measure up to Ian, was it just that I really was not over the death of Ian and was still in some way mourning. I would have to deal with all that if I was going to have a successful relationship with anyone else, and until I did perhaps I was being a little unfair to Tom. I know I was dwelling on it a lot and that I seem to be harping on about the same things, repeating myself again and again, but it was an issue that was on my mind and disturbing me.

I left the office early, went home and collected my bags and then waited for Tiffany. I had engaged her to run me down to Biggin Hill, and would sound her out at the same time.

"Dr Barclay," she said. "Off on another trip?"

"Just a short one," I said. "I've not taken my plane out in a while, and I fancy a ride, the weather is supposed to be good all weekend, so why not?"

"I'd love to take a flight one day," she said.

"I'll take you up for a spin," I promised. "Tell me Tiffany, how wedded are you to the service you drive for?"

"If something came up that was interesting, I'd look at it," she said.

"How good are you are keeping mum?" I asked.

"I can keep my counsel," she said. "Why do you ask?"

"Well, here's the thing, Tiffany, we're looking for a driver to work for the bank and your name came up, but I have a question, I know that in the past you have passed on things to Mr Barclay, how much have you passed on to someone else about us? Forgive me if that seems rude, but it's a question we have to ask."

"Well," she temporised, obviously thinking about her reply. "Part of me wants to be mortified that you would even ask, but part of me gets why you need to. I like Mr Barclay, he's polite and considerate, you wouldn't believe what toads some of the clients are, I suppose because he was nice I didn't mind passing the odd thing on to him. But, if my job depended on keeping mum, I would keep mum."

"So where did you grow up and go to school?" I asked.

"Inverness and Edinburgh University," she said. "I took French and German."

"So, what made you take up the chauffeuse business?" I asked.

"It was interesting," she said. "I didn't want to be a teacher, jobs for linguists are not always that easy to find and I had worked with my Dad a lot when I was growing up, helping him in his garage with his hobby of rebuilding cars. There have been times when the languages have come in handy, but even more times what I learned with my Dad has been really useful when I've been able to fix the car when it had a problem."

"What do you make a year now?" I asked.

"With gratuities about £6,000 a year," she replied, I imagine inflating things a little.

"What if I were to offer you a full-time position at £10,000 a year, but before you say yes, there are conditions, you maintain in confidence anything you may hear, see or infer while driving for us, you should also be prepared to do some weekend driving, I'll try to keep that to a minimum, but it may happen as may evening work? That brings up another issue, I'm not sure if I'm even allowed to ask this anymore, and if you don't wish to answer, then please don't, I won't take offence, any attachments?" I asked.

"Last first, no, just broke up with my partner, other than that, when can I start, what would I drive?" she asked.

"What notice do you have to give where you are now, and do you have a suggestion as to a car?" I asked.

"A week," she said. "The car's the agency's, if you are going to get your own car, what's the budget?"

"I'm flexible," I said.

"Well, I really like the Maserati Quattroporte," she said. "The new version is much better than last year's, it's elegant, comfortable for passengers, drives nicely, and it just has that cachet of a nice import. Jaguars are nice but have reliability issues, the Roller is overpriced for what it is, the Mercedes are good and reliable, but a bit stodgy, the BMW is ugly as is the Audi, there are no Fords or Vauxhalls that I would look at for a limousine service car. The Quattroporte does have four doors, so no clambering into the back like this Range Rover, the only real drawback is that it's expensive."

"I remember that about the Range Rover from our trip to Corby. Have you ever taken a defensive driving course?" I asked.

"No, I've heard about them, that would be fun," she said.

"Okay, here's the offer, a full-time job with me, at £10,000 a year, I'll provide the car and I'll enrol you in a defensive driving course, a skid pan class, and a self-defence class, I'll include a uniform allowance to cover shoes, or boots if you prefer, shirts, suits, gloves, hats, top coats, and sunglasses," I said. "Think about it over the weekend, and give me your answer on Sunday afternoon when you pick me up."

"Thanks, Dr Barclay," she said.

"Have you any self-defence skills?" I asked.

"Yes," she said. "I belong to a karate club and a kendo club."

"Okay, here we are, I'll see you on Sunday at about four-thirty," I said.

"Thanks, Dr Barclay, I'll be here," she promised.

Excursions

I had my plane pulled from the hangar and did my pre-flight checks, then topped up the tanks and did the rest of the checks. Ready, I got clearance to go and taxied out and took off. Flying around London to get to Cambridge was awkward, to the south was Gatwick, to the west was Heathrow, so I was directed east around London and then on up to Cambridge, avoiding Stansted as I went. I had picked Biggin Hill as a place to keep my plane because it would be a simple thing to fly south across the Channel to France. Now, perhaps I should rethink that if I was going to go to Cambridge often and perhaps, move my plane there. I could drive up to Cambridge easily enough, or even take a train. The weather forecasters had been right, at least for that day, it was cold, but it was clear, clear as far as I could see, to the west the sun was getting close to setting, but there still remained a good hour of daylight left. Flying VFR, visual flight rules, was no problem at all, I could see other traffic in the air, I could see the ground clearly and I imagined I could even see Cambridge. I was up at 10,000 feet so technically I could see 122 miles, so the whole vista of southern England was open to me. I was routed via Dartford, Chelmsford and Braintree before beginning my approach into Cambridge. On the ground, I tied my plane down then went looking for a taxi to take me into Cambridge. That took a while as I had to wait for someone to come out to the airport to collect me. I finally got a ride and was dropped at the hotel I had picked. The room was actually quite sumptuous, it looked out onto the gardens at the back of the hotel, so no street noise.

I walked over to Trinity and the porter actually recognised me from my previous visit and waved me through. I made my way to Tom's room and knocked.
"Fiona," Tom said, when he opened the door. "Great to see you. Guys, this is Fiona Barclay," he said, introducing me to the others who were there. "This is Roberta Spinoglio, David Entwistle and Walter Ferguson," he said, introducing each in turn. "I'm working with David and Walter in the lab, and you met Roberta last week at the Master's drinks party."
"We leave you two then," David said. "We'll see you Monday Tom."

177

"Right," he said. The three left and he turned to me and I put my arms around him and gave him a kiss.

"How are you?" I asked.

"Great," he said. "I'm busy, I've met new people, my advisor is happy with what I'm doing and you're here. How's the hotel?"

"It's rather nice," I said. "I was thinking that I'd treat you to dinner, where would you like to go, any preferences?

"Sounds good," he said. "Why don't we try The Eagle, it's been around a while and the food's apparently pretty good?"

We walked to The Eagle, a pub that had been in operation for some years. Tom was right, the food was pretty good, basic but good. To drink I stuck to lemonade, I had a rule about drinking and flying and tried to stick to it, if I was going to fly within the next twenty-four hours, I did not drink.

"So, what did you do this week?" he asked.

"I set up a merger between two companies," I said.

"How do you do that?" he asked.

"Convince them both that it's in their best interests," I replied. "Usually greed and avarice tend to speed things along. What do Roberta, David and Walter do?".

"Well, you met Roberta, she's a geography doctoral candidate, she's working on land use, David is looking into inverters, we use them to convert DC power to AC, and Walter is playing with coatings for PV cells, to try and better protect them from environmental damage but still not attenuate the sunlight too much," he explained. "Roberta's been a help because she really does understand sunshine and what parts of the world get the best sunlight hours and intensity. It's no use putting PV systems in a place that gets weak sun, the efficiency drops way off."

"So, New Mexico would be fine, but Essex would be questionable?" I asked.

"That's about the size of it," he agreed.

"So, which castle do you want to see?" I asked.

"I don't know, you pick," he said.

"Maybe we'll go and look at Caernarfon," I suggested. "It's close to the sea, it's an impressive-looking place and it's fairly intact."

"You're the boss," he said.

"We should start as soon as it's light in the morning," I said. "So, we probably will have to get breakfast somewhere other than the college."

"I know a place," he said.

"Good, well, I'll be at your room at seven," I promised.

I was at his room at seven and he was ready. We went to a small café that opened early and had breakfast, as they say, a full English breakfast, with eggs, sausages, the works, washed down with tea. Then we grabbed a taxi and went out to the airport. I filed a flight plan to Caernarfon, then called them as it was a PPR field, prior permission required. Then I suggested the loo as a sensible visit before we flew off. Too much tea too early in the morning was perhaps not the smartest thing to do in a small plane. I untied the plane then went through all the pre-flight checks and also checked on the fuel level. I actually had enough to get there and back, so that was not an issue. Aboard with Tom, I ran through my safety briefing with him, explained how the voice-activated microphones worked, then ran through with him what I would do in the event of engine failure on take-off. I am not sure quite what he thought of that, he just nodded and looked at me. Then I talked to the controllers and got clearance to go. The weather was still clear, clear skies, no clouds, sunshine and downright chilly, so nice flying weather. Once in the air and on our way there was time to talk.

"How are Linda and the rest of the family?" I asked.

"They're fine," he said. "I talked to Linda about a Dallas appraiser, and she's got one picked out. I'll get you the results when they come out for your discussions with land banks."

"Thanks, I'll get onto the US lawyer we use about talking to their lawyer," I promised. "How are you settling in at the college?"

"Pretty good," he said. "I've found my way around, I know where I'm going now, I'm a big hit already."

"Why?" I asked.

"Because I'm only there a week and I show up with this beautiful woman who just knocks all the rest out of bounds," he said.

"You're just saying that to butter me up and get me into bed," I joked.

"No, really," he said. "I've had tons of guys ask me who you were and how did we meet."

"What did you tell them?" I asked.

"I just told them that we'd met in New Mexico and that you worked in London," he said. Conversation was interrupted for a short time while we were directed around the Birmingham airport, otherwise, we had a pretty straight run to the coast.

"So, tell me more about this merger that you set up this week," he suggested when we settled back down to a quiet flight.

"I put out an offer to buy all the shares of a company," I said. "It should work and by the end of the year that transaction should close."

"I love the way you just casually talk about buying companies," he laughed.

"It's not really that big a deal," I said. "It's just a question of having the right finances lined up. We're coming up on Snowdon, which is the highest mountain in Wales, you should get a good view to your right."

"I can't get over how green everything is," he said.

"It's all the rain," I laughed. "Rain, drizzle, hail, snow, rain, more rain, drizzle again, and once in a while sunshine like today. Once we're past Snowdon, I'm going to start down, we should be on the ground in fifteen to twenty minutes."

We flew over the airport at Caernarfon then entered the pattern and went in to land. It was a windy place, so we wobbled a fair bit coming in, but I have to say that I did touch down very nicely. I taxied over to the hardstand and parked. It was windy enough that I tied the plane down carefully and even added a baffle above the wing. That might have been being overly cautious, but better to be safe than come back and see my plane upside down. The airport manager showed us where the loo was then got a taxi for us and we were in Caernarfon by ten.

"Wow," Tom said. "This castle is huge, I've seen pictures of castles, but when you actually get up close, they're massive."

"Imagine what it was like when there were men here defending the walls," I said. "This was built right before the start of the use of cannons in siege warfare, if it had been built after that the design would have been different."

"Is Freya's castle like this?" he asked.

"No, she's basically got a simple square tower with all the outbuildings inside a curtain wall," I said. "We'll fly up one weekend and take a look."

"What did women wear back then?" he asked.

"No bras," I said. "They hadn't been invented, no knickers either, just a shift, then a kirtle, like a simple long dress, then maybe another layer or two depending how cold it was, people slept in the nude, or in their shifts if it was cold. If you had money you might have some furs to keep you warm in the winter."

"So," he said, looking at me mischievously. "Knickers, yes or no?"

"Yes," I said. "Now, battlements?" We climbed the battlements and looked out over the town, then the Menai Straits.

"What's over there?" Tom asked, pointing over the straits.

"The isle of Anglesey," I said. "Once thought to be the hotbed of the Druids."

"The walls that go over there, is that part of the castle?" he asked.

"Those are the town walls," I explained. "The old town of Caernarfon, then this is the castle itself."

"And how old is this?" he asked.

"There was an old fortification here before this, a motte and bailey, that's basically a hill with a tower on the top of it and a walled enclosure below it, but I think this stonework dates from about 1283 and on. It was besieged and sacked a couple of times by Welsh uprisings and also played a part in the various civil wars that we had in England, there was a much older Roman fort here somewhere as well," I said.

"So, it's been around a while," he marvelled. "Let's see if we can find some lunch that hasn't been around that long."

There was an inn close by the castle and we were able to get a quite decent lunch there. After lunch we found a taxi and had him take us to the Roman fort, that was only about half a mile away, perched higher up with a commanding view of the straits. We had the driver wait for us, then asked him to take us back to the airport to begin our journey back to Cambridge. Once in the air, I asked Tom about his impressions.

"It's hard to image that almost 2,000 years ago there was an active town there, a Roman fort with roads connecting it to other places," he said. "We had ancient people in New Mexico, with the Anasazi and their amazing cliff dwellings, but this Roman fort was just an outpost of an empire that covered North Africa, the Middle East and much of Europe, it makes you wonder what else about the ancient peoples everywhere that we don't know."

"And the more modern castle?" I asked.

"Massive place, but, no central heating, no indoor plumbing, it must have been an interesting place when it was fully occupied," he thought.

"There were a whole line of those castles built to subjugate the local population," I told him. "First the Romans did it, then a thousand years later the English did it."

"What about Scotland?" he asked.

"The Romans didn't really try and subjugate them, they just built a bloody big wall to keep them out," I replied. "I'll take you up there one day to look at Hadrian's wall."

"Were there castles in England?" he asked.

"All over the place," I said. "Each baron had his own castle, so at most old towns, you'll find a castle."

"What's the closest one to Cambridge?" he asked.

"As I recall from my history, there was one in Cambridge, but I think it had been dismantled and all that remains is the mound it was on, for the closest one that has walls, keep, et cetera, I'd have to guess Lincoln or Rockingham, you'd have to check with a historian to find out if there may be one closer, there may be remnants of old castles and forts, but if you want to see walls, towers, a keep and dungeons, you'd have to go to the outlying areas, or the cities where the important barons held sway, places like Warwick," I said. "One I like is Ludlow Castle, it's been around a while, it's a ruin now, but preserved for visitors."

"How far away is that?" he asked.

"I'd guess a hundred and twenty miles by air," I said. "So, well under an hour. The problem will be finding a strip to fly into, England is not like Kenya or New Mexico, not every small town, ranch or game camp has its own strip."

"This was a great idea," he said. "I know my mind was on other things, but I really did enjoy the day."

"Good, the day's not over yet," I said. "Where are we going to eat tonight?"

"I thought we'd eat at a pub in town," he said. "That way we don't have to get dressed up."

"Good, because I didn't bring any fancy clothes," I said. "Okay, let's just talk to the Cambridge people and we'll get set for landing."

I picked the place this time. It was an French restaurant, actually run by a Frenchman. I picked up on his accent and, apologising to Tom, spoke to him in French. He was delighted, clearly I was not just a student trying out my French, mine was Parisian and spoken like a Parisian. He wanted to know what part of Paris I came from and he was surprised when I told him that I did in fact come from Henley on Thames, and it had been my mother's diligence that had given me the accent. The proprietor was so delighted with the conversation that he gave us a bottle of wine, and was puzzled why I did not drink any of it. I explained to him that I was flying the next day and had a rule. That led to another conversation, flying for whom. His eyebrows went up a little when I told him that I had my own plane and was just visiting. The upshot of all this was that he told Tom that he would be welcome at any time and that no matter how busy they were, Tom would always be found a table. I think that impressed Tom more than anything, he was not known at a restaurant in town and guaranteed good service. Tom and I talked about the day, the flight, the scenery, the castle, the Roman ruins, so much had in fact been packed into the one short day. We parted that evening with a goodnight kiss and the promise to meet at the college for breakfast.

I walked over to the college and knocked on Tom's door and asked him if he was ready for breakfast. He was and we decided to eat in Hall. We had just sat down when Mark and Julia Decker came in and asked if they would be intruding. As there was little chance of private conversation in Hall, we waved them to seats opposite us.

"So, what have you two been up to?" Mark asked. "All Tom would tell us was that Fiona was coming for the weekend, but we haven't seen you around."

"We went to Caernarfon," Tom said.

"That's a long drive," Mark commented.

"Ah, but we didn't drive, we flew," Tom said. "Fiona has her own plane, so we took off early yesterday and got back right as the sun was going down."

"You have your own plane?" Julia asked.

"I do," I confirmed. "I got my pilot's licence while I lived in Kenya and fly whenever I have time."

"She promised to take me up to look at Hadrian's Wall at some time," Tom said. "Would you like to come? Is that okay Fiona?"

"It would be fun," I said.

"Is your plane big enough?" Mark asked.

"Seats six, if you include the pilot," I said.

"How long a flight would it be?" Julia asked.

183

"A couple of hours to Carlisle, then a loo break, then fly along the wall and back here, say another two and a half to three hours," I thought.

"Gosh," Julia said. "I've never been in a small plane, is it safe?"

"Safer than a car," I said.

"When?" Mark asked.

"It'll depend on the weather," I said. "To see anything you'd want a nice clear day. Perhaps a cold day early next year would be good, I'll keep an eye on the weather."

"That would be super," Mark said. "So, what now for you?"

"I have to fly back to London this afternoon," I said. "The Biggin Hill runway is not lit, so I have to be back before sunset."

"We'll need to keep an eye on the time then," Mark said. "We'll see you again?"

"I'll be back," I said. "Not next weekend, Tom has promised to come down to London and see me."

"I have?" Tom said.

"You didn't yet," I said. "But, any reason why you can't come?"

"Nothing," he said. "I'll take the train down."

"Just let me know when it gets in and I'll meet you," I promised.

"May I join you?" a woman said. "I looked up and it was Roberta.

"Please," Tom said waving to a seat.

"What are you all talking about?" she asked.

"Tom was telling us that they flew up to Caernarfon yesterday," Mark explained.

"Caernarfon, where's that?" she asked.

"Wales," Mark said. "Caernarfon is the site of one of the main castles that were built to control things out there. It's impressive even today, so in its day it must have been quite a place."

"You flew up, who flies there, surely not British?" she asked.

"No, Fiona has her own plane," Mark explained. "She's just promised to take us some time for a spin and look at Hadrian's Wall. You should come along, didn't you say that there's room for six, Fiona?"

"There is," I confirmed. I was not sure about this, Mark issuing invites to others to ride in my plane.

"Don't you think you should have asked Fiona first?" Julia said to Mark.

"It's fine," I assured her, while feeling that, no, it wasn't fine, but why make waves.

"So, what are you two doing today?" Julia asked.

"I thought we'd find the old Cambridge Castle," I said. "Tom was asking yesterday if Cambridge had one and I recalled that there was one once upon a time, but it had been pulled apart and the stone used to build colleges."

"Can we come along?" Julia asked.

"Of course," I said.

"Why don't you come too, Roberta?" Mark suggested. "The more the merrier."

"That would be great," she said.

The site of the old castle was actually very easy to find, all we had to do was walk up Castle Street, then there was a sign pointing to the mound. That was all that was left of the castle, just a mound where the building would once have stood. There were even steps up the mound, so ascent was easy. The view from the top was not very exciting, but then the mound itself was not that high. I had to explain to Roberta what a motte and bailey castle was and how it differed from Caernarfon Castle. The castle mound was interesting, but I think a bit of a disappointment for Tom and Roberta who had probably been thinking in terms of walls, towers, gates, portcullises and moats. I was beginning to regret my willingness to expand the group visiting the mound, Roberta seemed to be taking an unwelcome interest in Tom and I had to stop myself a couple of times from competing for his attention. I was not going to stoop to that. He had declared his love for me, so why should I be at all concerned just because some other woman looked at him. Luncheon called and Mark knew a place that was quite close to the mound, so we repaired to there and got ourselves Cornish Pasties and beer, I kept to my regimen and took lemonade instead of the beer, but everyone else was happy to try one of the local brews. I think that Tom and Roberta would have preferred a lager rather than the bitter they got, but it was something new that they should try.

We walked back to the college and I said my goodbyes to Tom.

"Thanks for coming," he said. "I had a great time."

"I enjoyed the trip," I said. "I haven't been up in the air much lately, so this was a good chance to take advantage to the nice weather and fly.

Will you let me know what train you're on and which station it will arrive at?" I asked.

"Sure," he said. "What's the weather supposed to be like next weekend?"

"I've no idea," I said. "My experience has been that forecasts a week out are notoriously inaccurate, things change so quickly."

"Well, it makes no never mind," he said. "I'll be there Friday evening."

"Great," I said. "I should get back to my hotel and collect my bag and get out to the airport."

"Do you want me to come with you?" he asked.

"No, it's fine," I said. "You don't want to ride out there, only to have to come back again five minutes later." I kissed him goodbye and walked back to my hotel and collected my bag. The hotel got me a taxi that took me to the airport. There, I filed my flight plan back to Biggin Hill, then untied the plane and went through all my pre-flights. That done, I got clearance and took off for Biggin Hill.

As I flew back I did something that I had sworn I would never do, I started to compare Ian and Tom. They were different people, so comparisons were not really fair, but, it was hard not to weigh one against the other. On balance it was almost a tie. Tom made me laugh the way Ian had done, he was intelligent, he did not push to get me into bed, he was considerate, so all in all, not bad. It was so good to believe that I was in love again, I had not thought it possible, but apparently it was and it was as good as the first time. For the longer term I had given little thought, would Tom want to return to the States after his doctorate, would he be happy staying in England, would I consider moving to the States and would I be happy there. I had been happy in Kenya, but I always knew that that had been a temporary thing, Ian was going to be reassigned at some point, so we went to Kenya knowing that it would be three to five years. If Tom were to stay in England or I were to move to the States it would be a much more permanent thing, was that something either he or I were ready for. All that could wait, for the moment I was in love and enjoying every minute of it. The air traffic controllers brought me back to earth, figuratively and literally as I was directed around London into Biggin Hill, good to concentrate on something else for a while.

Tiffany was at Biggin Hill to meet me, and drove up to the hangar as I put my plane away.

"Dr Barclay, how was the weekend?" she asked.

"We took an excursion to Caernarfon," I said. "It was fun, I hadn't been there in ages. And, how are you?"

"I'm doing well," she said. "I've thought about your offer and I'd love to accept, I'm going to give notice tomorrow."

"That's terrific," I said. "We'll sign you on next week, then we'll visit with Rachel Adams for uniforms."

"Rachel Adams?" Tiffany asked. "But, she's one of the top designers in London."

"I know," I said. "She's a friend and she'll put together something nice for you that will be practical as well, I think trousers would be better, easier to run in, easier to change tyres in."

"What colour?" Tiffany asked.

"I think navy blue," I said. "But, we'll also get a grey, a black and a khaki as well, you never know what might be appropriate. We'll get winter weight for the blue and black and summer weight for the grey and the khaki."

"That's a lot," she said.

"I'm feeling frivolous," I said. "When would you be able to start?"

"As you suggested, a week tomorrow," Tiffany said.

"Okay, I'll set up a couple of courses for you to go on, I'll order the car tomorrow," I asked.

"Really, you're going with the Maserati?" Tiffany said. "I was only joking."

"I've thought about it and decided that the bank can afford it," I said. "So, don't worry about it."

"How hard is it to learn how to fly?" she asked.

"Not that hard," I said. "If you want to try, I'll pay for the lessons."

"Really?" she said. "Wow, now that would be something, if I get through all this I'll feel like James Bond, or maybe Jane Bond, or Emma Peel."

"If you need help, just let me know," I said. "Oh, and I'll get the workshop manuals for the Maserati, we should probably know how to fix it in case it breaks down somewhere."

"I don't know how to thank you," she said.

"Just do a good job and I'll be delighted," I said.

"We're here. Dr Barclay," she said. "Do you need a hand with your bags?"

"No, I'm fine, thanks Tiffany, call me in the week to let me know how things are going and let me know when you can get some time off to go and see Rachel," I said.

"I will," she promised.

For the next week, I busied myself with all manner of things. The Metter offer was now public and the Monopolies Commission, more properly the Monopolies and Mergers Commission, came to see us and asked for information. I went through market data and pointed out the other players in the business and focused, as I am sure they would, on market concentration. The total value of the merger was over the £75 million that would trigger a review, but, even with the combination of Metter and Corby Seaton there was still significant competition and the Corby Metter group still was still only twelve per cent of the total market, well under the twenty-five per cent threshold that would trigger an automatic review. That seemed to mollify them and they went away promising to forward an opinion in a few days. Off the record they said that they could see no issue, but would be gathering their own data for confirmation. As they would get the data from the same industry sources that I did, it would be very surprising if they came up with different numbers. It looked as if that hurdle was cleared. Once we got clearance from them, then we would begin the actual transactions of share purchase from the current holders.

I ordered the Maserati in basic black with tan leather upholstery, and was told that I could have it in about two weeks, if I picked it up in Modena, a little longer if I waited for it to be shipped to the dealer in London. I thought about it and decided that Tiffany and I would go to Modena to collect it. We could fly over Sunday afternoon to Milan, stay the night in Modena, pick up the car early Monday morning, then spend the day at the track that Maserati used near Parma, then drive to Cannes and stay the night there with Maman and Portia, then drive to Calais and take the ferry back. On Wednesday I would take a flight to Chicago for my final meeting with Dundee and the tests of my computer models, then go on to Dallas for a meeting with the appraiser and the lawyer for the rats on Monday morning, flying back to Chicago that afternoon, to spend the rest of that day and Tuesday with Dundee again, to make sure everything was working properly and then overnight to London, or at least something along those lines. That meant two weekends without seeing Tom, so I would have to come up with a plan to make up for that. I also debated with myself long and hard about installing a car phone, it would have been a radio telephone, but for me the biggest drawback was it was just ugly. The designs had improved a little over the past few years, but it was still big, ugly and one had to go through an operator to call anyone. I decided that the potential benefits just were not worth it, so shelved that idea until a new and better technology was available.

Winter & Winter, a sporting goods company that I had consulted for called, they wanted me to go and talk to them. I wondered what they had in mind and set a date to go and talk to them the following week. I watched my contractor go to work on the space where the IBM computer was going to be, then advertised for people to run it, two operators and three programmers. I was spending money like water, but looking over the accounts of the bank, we could afford it, even in lean times. I was also confident that I could build some programs that tracked stock prices and gave us the ability to improve our returns on the holdings we already had. I had other things to clean up, I had to make sure that the models I done for Dundee actually worked, and that meant computer time, which I booked at Imperial for Thursday night. It meant going there late in the afternoon and running things overnight, but that was fine, I could pick up all the results Friday morning. I was busy, I had never been busier, I would have to be careful not to take on too much at once or I would become a basket case. Still, when my consulting projects were all behind me, then some of the pressure would be relieved.

By Friday I was ready for a break. I dropped my briefcase at my flat, changed out of my glad rags into some less formal and took the Tube to Kings Cross to meet Tom's train. It was late, what a surprise, it never ceased to amaze me that the Japanese, the Swiss and others ran their trains with minimal delays, but the British, the Italians and others had perennial problems with delays, be they weather related, as I suspect this was, or problems on the tracks, so some other issue. I waited for about twenty minutes beyond the supposed arrival time and finally the train pulled in. He was there, smiling and happy to see me.

"Fiona," he said. "I'm glad you didn't give up on me, I gather fog was the issue."

"It's always something," I lamented. "I think if British Rail ran on time one day, all day, everywhere it would be a record that would stand the test of time."

"How do we get to your place?" he asked.

"The Circle Line is the easiest," I told him. "We just get on and trundle along until we get the Sloane Square, or we could take the Piccadilly to South Ken, then either take the Circle back one station to Sloane Square or walk, it's not too far, take your choice."

"How about the Piccadilly?" he suggested.

"Okay, let's just get some tickets and then we'll take the escalators down to the depths," I said. I got tickets for us both to Sloane Square, then we took the long ride down to the Piccadilly Line.

"How old is this escalator?" Tom asked. "I've never been on a wooden one before."

"No idea," I said. "The line dates from the late 19th century, but I don't know when they put in the escalators." We did not have to wait long for a train, when it came, it was crowded, but we squeezed in and held on to the straps overhead. I had often been surprised at how fast the trains ran, even when one took into account the illusion of speed caused by the closeness of the tunnel walls. Tom studied the map above the seats.

"So, nine stations?" he asked.

"I was thinking we'd get off at Green Park, switch to the Victoria Line, then at Victoria switch to the Circle and go to Sloane Square that way," I said.

"You're the boss," he said. We made our various changes and finally left the Tube at Sloane Square.

"This station is open to the air," he commented.

"The Circle was mainly cut and cover," I told him. "So, in quite a few places you get an opening to the sky, Sloane Square I think is unique, you see that thing that looks like a bridge over there, well, that's actually a river that they channelled underground and put in an aqueduct over the station."

"Has it ever leaked?" he asked.

"No idea," I admitted. "So, let's go, it's not far from here."

It was a short walk to my flat and we were there in a few minutes. Inside I showed Tom the spare bedroom, I suppose I did not actually really need to do that as he had stayed before and knew where it was. I had debated with myself about crossing the Rubicon of sharing a bed with Tom and had decided that I was not ready yet. It had only been a week since I last had had that discussion with myself and nothing had really changed. I still needed more time. I waited for him to get settled then suggested dinner.

"Great," he said. "Are you cooking?"

"I'm a hopeless cook," I admitted. "So, I have an arrangement with a local bistro just down the road. They've always treated me well. Shall we go?"

"Lead on," he said. "You know you've got the cutest ass," he commented as he followed me down the stairs.

"I'm trying to decide if that's good or bad," I said. "No comments about my anatomy while we're in the bistro, they might get the wrong idea."

"I doubt that," he said. "They'll probably read things just right."

"Well, we're here, so best behaviour," I told him.

"Yes, Ma'am," he joked. We got a table and something to eat and drink and then I told him about my travels that were impending.

"Can you afford to come down here next Friday as well?" I asked.

"I can do that," he said. "And, what go back about lunchtime?"

"That would work," I said. "Then I can get the plane to Milan. But then I won't see you for almost two weeks. I'll find a way to call you at the lab."

"Look, when you come back, we have a Christmas ball, will you come?" he asked.

"Of course," I said. "Of course I'll come, is it formal?"

"I gather it is," he said. "So, I'll have to rent a tux from somewhere. What will you wear?"

"I'll find something suitable," I promised.

"Something to knock the socks off the others at the ball?" he asked.

"That will depend on what the others wear, but, I promise you won't be disappointed," I said.

After dinner we went back to my flat and Tom lingered a little, I think trying to decide if he should make the first move or not. I think I settled it for him when I wished him good night. I do not know whether or was caution or paranoia on my part, but I actually locked my door that night. I thought I heard him trying the door handle some time early in the morning, but I may have been dreaming or imagining things. When I did awake the next morning something was cooking and beckoned me to go and investigate. I wandered through and there was Tom, dressed and busy cooking.

"Morning lazybones," he said. "Have a shower, put some clothes on and come and have breakfast, half the day is gone already."

"What time is it, nine-thirty, nine-thirty, I don't think I've slept this late in years?" I said in surprise.

"There was no sound from your room when I got up," he said. "But, go, shower, dress, breakfast awaits." I did as commanded and returned in quick order to find coffee, and an interesting dish on the table.

"Breakfast burrito," he said. "Eggs, potatoes, tomatoes, chiles, beans and home made tortillas."

"Where did you get all the stuff for this?" I asked. "I'm pretty sure I didn't have any of this in the fridge."

"I found a small store down the road that opened early," he said. "So, eat up, enjoy."

"Thanks," I said, taking a bit, it was good, really good. "You're hired," I said through mouthfuls of burrito.

"Good," he said. "I won't ask if you slept well, I gather that you did. So, how do we get to the Tower of London from here?"

"Circle from Sloane Square to Tower Hill," I said, when I got the chance to say it without my mouth full.

"You can buy us lunch," he said. "I did my bit with breakfast."

"I'll do that," I promised.

We took the Tube to Tower Hill and surfaced just outside the Tower. We made our way to the gate, paid our fees and entered. We were two among a throng, which surprised me as it was a drizzly day, not the best I would have thought for sight seeing. We saw Yeoman Warders, Beefeaters in tourist parlance, we saw ravens, we saw the Crown Jewels and the collection of gems gathered from all corners of the globe, we saw the Royal Armoury in the White Tower, with its vast collection of suits of armour, swords, pikes, pistols, muskets and other weapons of war. We saw the coin collection, walked the battlements and looked at the river and at Tower Bridge, and wondered at the foresight of William in building the first parts of the castle where he did.

"When did this lot get started?" Tom asked.

"According to the book, William started on the White Tower in 1078," I read. "After that it was expanded by various other rulers."

"So, this is where Henry chopped off the heads of his wives?" Tom asked.

"Only two of them," I said. "It's divorced, beheaded, died, divorced, beheaded, survived."

"So, who were the lucky ones?" he asked.

"I think Anne of Cleves, who agreed to a divorce, but stayed in England and did not go back to Cleves to be married off again, and Catherine Parr, who outlived Henry," I replied.

"Who got beheaded?" he asked.

"Anne Boleyn and Catherine Howard," I told him.

"What about the guy who wanted to blow up the Houses of Parliament?" he asked.

"Guy Fawkes, he was supposed to he hanged for treason, but he did the smart thing and jumped from the ladder and broke his own neck, otherwise he was going to be hanged, drawn and quartered, not a nice fate," I said.

"And the Princes in the Tower?" he asked.

"Edward V and his brother Richard, there are theories, but it is known that they weren't seen again after 1483, the most widely held theory is that Richard III had them done away with," I said.

"It all makes the rats in Dallas seem rather tame," Tom laughed. "At least they're not looking to get rid of any of us, just shake us down for money."

"Is there anything else you'd like to see?" I asked. My stomach was growling a bit and I was thinking about at late lunch, or afternoon tea.

"Now, where can we get some lunch?" he asked.

"Let's try Porters in Covent Garden," I suggested.

It was a short Tube ride from Tower Hill to Embankment, and a short walk from there to the restaurant. Porters served English food, not French, not Italian, not Indian, but basic English stuff. It was renowned and it was good.

"So, what do you think of the Tower?" I asked Tom after we had given our orders and were awaiting delivery.

"I like Caernarfon better," he said. "The Tower feels more like a palace than a fortress, Caernarfon has the frontier feel about it, I could imagine sieges and battles going on there. I'm sure that the Tower had its share of action over the years, but I prefer Caernarfon."

"And the armoury, the Crown Jewels?" I asked.

"I liked the armoury, the Crown Jewels probably means more if you're a monarchist, but to me it's just a statement of how much the aristocracy of any nation pillages the colonies and the wealth of the nation," he said.

"Pretty radical thinking," I commented.

"Sorry if I offended," he said. "But, it's like the Vatican, from what I've heard there's a fortune there and yet half the world's Catholics live below the bread line, same here, there's a fortune tied up in the heritage that's there, but we saw homeless people today. I don't know how you balance a need to preserve a heritage and yet see to the needs of the people."

"A bigger issue than one I'm ever likely to solve," I said. "But, food for thought."

We chatted for a bit longer trying to solve the problems of the world until be both laughingly admitted that we could not. So, I paid the bill and we went back to my flat and actually watched a movie that was playing on the television. We turned in late as a result of that and were both up quite late the next morning. While we were finishing off the left overs from the day before breakfast, Tom said that he had to return early to Cambridge as he some experiment running that needed his attention. I went with him on the Tube to Kings Cross and saw him off on the train.

"I'll call you at the lab tomorrow," I said.

"Great," he said. "Look forward to it. Thanks for the lovely weekend."

"It was fun having you here," I said. "Love you."

"Love you, bye," he replied. He boarded the train and hung out of the window waving goodbye as the train pulled out of the station. So, he was gone and I had work to get back to and travels to plan. I did wonder if had invented the experiment as a way to leave early because he was disappointed that we had not shared a bed. He was probably wondering if that would ever happen, but I had only known his for a month or two, and we had only spent a few days together, if you counted them as dates, then only seven or eight so far. For me that was too soon to be giving myself to him in that way. I would know when I was ready, as I had done with Ian. There it was again, those nagging comparisons kept coming up. It was something I was going to have to address, or I would never find anyone else.

The next two weeks were going to be busy. The Corby Metter deal was proceeding and what I needed to hear was that the Monopolies Commission had decided that we were not concentrating the market unduly, so would not oppose the merger. I also needed to make sure that everything was set for my meeting with Dundee and for my meeting with the rats' lawyer in Dallas. It was a shame that there were no direct flights from Dallas to London, so I was stuck with flying back to Chicago, then on to London. That was all in the future, meanwhile, I had chores to do, I had laundry that needed doing and I had a flat to clean.

Travels

Tiffany duly reported to work on Monday morning at nine. I had Deirdre the office manager go through all the usual processes for hiring a new person, then sat down with Tiffany for a chat.

"I see you cut your hair," I commented.

"I like the way you do yours, so had mine cut," she replied.

"I ordered the car," I told her. "We can pick it up next Monday at the factory in Modena, do you have a current passport and would you be free next Sunday to fly over?"

"I just got a passport thinking I was going on safari," she said. "And, I've got nothing on at the weekend."

"Fine," I said. "Get with Deirdre and make us bookings for flights to Milan on Sunday, then a hotel in Modena for Sunday night, a hotel in Parma for Monday night, we're going to spend the day at a track that Maserati uses to learn all about this car. We'll spend Tuesday night at my mother's place near Cannes and drive on up to Calais on Wednesday and get the ferry back."

"I'll do that," she said, making a few notes.

"Then on Thursday, I'm flying to Chicago and I'll be back on the Saturday a week after that," I told her. "While I'm away, I've booked you in at a defensive driving school, an off-road course and a self defense class, here are the details, any questions about all that?"

"No," she said.

"We have garage space under the building, with an office for you there as well," I told her. "We should keep the car there. I normally work from nine to five or six, depending what's going on. We've another meeting in Corby coming up soon, and another one in Swindon. Is there anything else I can tell you?"

"What exactly does Thames Cherwell do?" she asked.

"We are an investment bank, that means we either invest money in companies or properties and we also facilitate mergers, acquisitions and divestitures," I explained.

"So, if I wanted to buy a house I could get a mortgage from you, us?" she asked.

"No, we don't do mortgage lending, but if you wanted a good deal, I could point you in the right direction," I said. "But, if you wanted to buy this building and develop it into flats, shops and offices, we would look at providing the financing to do that."

"Oh, I see," she said. "So your trip to Corby to see Corby Seaton was one of those deals?"

"It was indeed," I confirmed. "You may have seen in the paper the announcement of an offer to buy the shares of Metter, we are looking to merge Metter with Corby Seaton as a new company Corby Metter."

"I can see I'll have to read the Financial Times," she said.

"Good idea," I agreed. "You might also look at The Economist and the Wall Street Journal. We get those in the office here, so no need to go out and buy them. So, if you're ready, we'll go and see Rachel Adams."

We took a taxi to Rachel's shop and were shown into her studio and given coffee.

"Fiona," Rachel said, as she joined us. "How nice to see you again, how are you?"

"In the pink," I said. "Things are going well for me, and you?"

"I'm well and more importantly the business has picked up," she replied.

"Rachel, this is Tiffany MacBeth, she's just joined us as our chauffeuse, and I'd like something for her to wear, here's a list of what I was thinking," I said, making the introduction.

"Lucky you," Rachel said to Tiffany. "Let's take a look at you, Hermione, could you join us with your tape?" Hermione joined us and they measured Tiffany. I remembered the process for myself, but I think Tiffany was little surprised at the thoroughness of the measurements.

"Now what were you thinking of?" Rachel asked.

"I think something professional, easy to run in and bend down in to change tyres if necessary," I said. "Something that breathes so that Tiffany doesn't get uncomfortable on long journeys."

"Something similar to a pilot's uniform?" Rachel suggested.

"What do you think, Tiffany?" I asked.

"I think that would be super," she said. "At my last place we had grey skirts and jackets with frilly white blouses, I'd rather have a simple white shirt with pockets and wear a tie, than have to worry about the ruffles."

"We can do something nice for you," Rachel promised. "I see here we're also talking about blouses, boots, top coat, gloves and hats, do you want me to put it all together?"

"That would be fine," I said, wondering quite why I was going this far, was I just being practical or was there something deeper. I dismissed that notion, mainly because it made me too uncomfortable, it was nothing that Tiffany was doing, it was just me and my own thoughts about Tom, about Ian, but now mainly about Tom, I thought that he was the one, so why was I having any kind of feelings for someone else?

"When, and don't give the usual tomorrow?" Rachel asked.

"Well, we're going to Italy next week to pick up the car, so perhaps when we come back we could see something?" I asked.

"We'll have a first fitting this Friday," Rachel said. "Could you be here at ten, Tiffany?"

"Dr Barclay?" Tiffany said, turning to me.

"That would be fine, and I'd rather you called me Fiona, unless we're with a client," I said.

"Brilliant," she said.

"So, Fiona, where are you taking us to lunch today?" Rachel asked.

"She does this," I said to Tiffany. "Takes my orders, then shakes me down for lunch. I thought we'd go to that place on Brompton Road that's opposite Harrods. Hermione, are you joining us?"

"Of course," she said.

We trooped off for the short walk to the restaurant and were seated quickly, then I brought up the ball gown that I would need. Rachel and Hermione had a quick discussion then Rachel sketched out a dress, that had simple elegant lines, but was rather fetching. She suggested basic black with some silver trim and silver accessories. That sounded fine to me and I asked her to go ahead and start on it.

"So, what's the occasion?" Rachel asked.

"A ball at Trinity Cambridge," I replied.

"So, new bloke?" Rachel pressed.

"Yes," I said. "Tom Ortiz, American from New Mexico, grad student at Trinity."

"Good for you," Rachel said. "Where did you meet?"

"At a café in a really small town in New Mexico," I explained. "We hit it off and are seeing each other when we can."

"So, what's he like?" Rachel asked.

"Funny, smart, single and even good looking," I said.

"Well, as I said, good for you," Rachel said. "And you, Tiffany?"

"Nothing at the moment," she bemoaned. "I had a partner, Alex, but we split not too long ago, Alex dumped me for someone else."

"You'll find someone," Rachel assured her. "Just make sure that Fiona gives you some time off to go looking."

"I'm in no hurry," Tiffany said. "I quite like where I am right now."

When Tiffany and I returned to the office, Dad was there and he welcomed Tiffany to the firm. We watched her go off to inspect her office space in the basement, then he had news for me.

"The Torrance sale closed," he said. "The proceeds are in the accounts in the US, final tally for you, $5,500,775, the same for the firm. We'll get guidance from the tax lawyers on both sides of the Atlantic and then decide what to do, but as the UK rate is 30% and the US rate is 35% it may just be better to move it all back here."

"That's good news," I said. "I'm waiting to hear from Monopolies about Metter, I don't see an issue there and they said as much when I talked to them, so, now it's just a question of putting that in writing."

"Good," he said. "As soon as we get that we'll go ahead with the close. When are you off to Modena and Chicago?"

"I leave for Modena on Sunday, will be back in the UK briefly then off to Chicago the Thursday, finish up with Dundee, then a quick trip down to Dallas and back and finally back here Saturday morning next," I said.

"Okay," he said. "I doubt that anything will come up that I can't handle," he said. "The biggest item on the agenda is Metter."

"I've a meeting with Winter & Winter tomorrow," I said. "Do you want to come?"

"Why not?" he said. "See what they have in mind."

"I'm guessing they want to buy Copper Beech, that would give them the entrée into the high end tennis racket market," I thought. "It would fit with their strategy of having well known brand in each segment of the market, rather like RCA Musical Instruments does."

"That makes sense," he said. "When do we see them?"

"Tomorrow at ten at their place in Maidstone," I replied.

"So, how do we get there?" he asked.

"Hire a car and let Tiffany drive us there," I suggested. "The traffic's a problem, so we'd leave here at about eight, then we can stop for tea or coffee somewhere before the meeting."

"Okay, will you let Tiffany know?" he asked.

"I will," I said. When Dad had gone, I called the lab where Tom worked. He was there and someone called him to the telephone.

"Fiona, hi," he said. "How are you today?"

"Busy, and you?" I asked.

"Busy, look, so sorry about this but I won't be able to come down this weekend, I've got an experiment running and I can't leave it," he said.

"That's okay," I said, a little disappointed, but trying to understand.

"When do you leave for your big trip?" he asked.

"I leave on Sunday, will be back briefly on Thursday, then off to Chicago and I won't get back until the next week, will you call me then?" I asked.

"I will," he promised. "Say, Fiona, sorry to run, but have to go, I've some stuff that needs my attention, also I'm going out of town to Israel for a couple of weeks to see a panel installation, I'll call you when you're back." He hung up. I supposed that he had some experiment that was at a crucial stage and that just had to be attended to. Tom not having a telephone in his room was quite an inconvenience as it meant we often traded telephone calls without actually talking to one another. I went home in a sulk, annoyed that he had rung up so quickly and that I had not had the chance to talk to him properly, but pulled myself out of it by telling myself I was being silly.

The next day Tiffany collected me from my flat in a hire car, then stopped at Dad's flat and picked him up and we set off for Maidstone. After the initial dancing around the London traffic, we finally got out onto the A2 and were able to pick up some speed. Tiffany had us in Maidstone with thirty minutes to spare, so we found a coffee shop.

"Do you know where W&W is?" Dad asked Tiffany, as we sipped our coffee.

"Yes, Mr Barclay," she said. "It'll take me about seven minutes to get you there."

"Looking forward to the new car?" he asked.

"I am indeed," she said.

"What will you do while we're in the meeting?" he asked.

"I'll park somewhere, then just come and sit in the foyer and wait for you," she replied. "I'll see what I can learn while I'm waiting."

"Good," Dad said. "I'm not sure how long this will take."

"It's not important," she said. "I'll just wait."

"The life of a corporate driver or pilot," I thought aloud. "Rush to get you somewhere, then just sit and wait."

"I've got plenty to study while I wait," she said. "I've brought the manuals of the new car with me, so can start going through them."

"Good idea," I said. "Well, shall we go and see them?"

Winter & Winter did indeed want to explore the option of buying Copper Beech. They gave us the pitch as to why it would be a good idea and then asked us if we would make the approach to Copper Beech.

"Why not just call them yourselves?" I asked. "If you retain us to do this there will be a fee, but if you talk to them directly it won't cost you anything."

"We understand that," John Stanley, the MD of Winter & Winter, said. "I suppose what we're really looking for is the wherewithal to do this and advice on how to meld Copper Beech into W&W."

"Well, I would put sales of Copper Beech at about £25 million a year, would I be far wrong?" I asked.

"Right on the money," John said. "So, it's a chunk to add to us, not so much that it overshadows the company, but still significant."

"Well, you're at about £125 million, with before tax of £12, my guess is that Copper Beech has before tax profits of about £3 million, would that be your guess?" I asked.

"It would," he agreed. "So, what will they ask for the company?"

"They'll ask for the moon," I said. "But, if I were you, I'd start at about £18 million and see if they blanch, blink, or walk out, you can always raise your offer. Would you offer them cash, or shares of W&W?"

"We were thinking of shares of W&W," John said.

"Do you have enough treasury shares, or would you have to make a rights issue?" I asked.

"We'd have to make a rights issue," John said. "That's where you come in, we need an offering memorandum for that, provided of course that Copper Beech goes along with us."

"And, if they want cash?" I asked.

"Then we'd look to you for financing," John said. "Or we'd float a rights issues and used the proceeds."

"On the face of it the combination would be good, you'd not dilute your profits with Copper Beech, in fact it would be the other way around, who actually runs them?" I asked.

"Family company, the Baldwins," John said. "Two sisters and a brother. The one sister, Theresa is the MD, the second sister, Allison is the accountant and the brother, George, is the manufacturing man."

"Have you any sense of their likely response to an overture?" I asked.

"Not really," John said. "The only thing I really know about Theresa is that she's a real women's lib person, sorry if I offended, but she's very vocal about it."

"Ah, so you want me to come along to wave the flag and show that women can also be investment bankers?" I asked.

"Well," John hesitated.

"John, if you and I had not had such a long relationship I might have walked out at that, but, I think I understand your hesitation about dealing with Theresa Baldwin, you've always been straight and fair with me, and when I lived in Kenya you were one of the few who had any qualms about me travelling when there were problems, so, I'll come with you and see what happens," I said.

"Thank you," he said. "I had no idea how to approach this, but I'm hoping that you can help us."

"When do you want to meet with Copper Beech?" I asked.

"I was wondering if we could do it on Thursday," he said. "I've made a tentative appointment with them for ten, would you be able to manage that?"

"Where are they?" I asked.

"Northampton," he replied.

"I can be there," I said. "Dad, do you want to come?"

"I think not," he said. "Rather let you handle it all, if you need help with the mechanics afterwards I can do that for you, but I think it would be more politic if you represented the bank, you are the MD after all."

"Fine," I said. "Is there anything else for the moment John?"

"No," he said. "We'll see you at Copper Beech at ten on Thursday, do you know how to get there?"

"I'll find out and I'll be there," I promised.

Dad and I said our goodbyes to John and his staff and went out and collected Tiffany.

"Where to?" she asked.

"Lunch," I said. "Any idea what's around here?"

"There's a nice place in Sandling, not far from here," Tiffany offered.

"Drive on," I said. It only took Tiffany a few minutes to get us there. It was an old inn, had been around for quite a while I would guess. "You've been here before?" I asked Tiffany.

"I have," she confirmed. "One of my clients used to come to Maidstone a lot and I had to find somewhere to waste away the hours while I waited for him."

"So, did you hear anything of note?" I asked Tiffany.

"Not really," she said. "They were mainly wondering why you were there, I didn't know that you'd done work for them before."

"I created some marketing models for them a few years ago, and done a few other projects over the years, they were one of my better clients, never cavilled about the bill, paid on time and actually listened, which is more than I could say for some," I explained.

"I heard that each time you came in the past, there were big changes that followed, so there were curious," Tiffany said.

"I'm sure they were," I said. "Now, Tiffany on Thursday I need to be at the office of Copper Beech at ten, could you find out where and let me know when we should leave."

"Of course," she said. "Mr Barclay, are you going as well?"

"Not this time," he said.

"Copper Beech are the fancy tennis rackets, aren't they?" Tiffany asked.

"They are," I confirmed.

"They'd be a good match for Winter & Winter," she thought. "Are we still on for Modena on Sunday?"

"We are," I said. "We've got the flight you booked for us to Milan on BA at two fifteen, I thought we'd take a cab out to Heathrow."

"I'll get one and pick you up at eleven thirty," she suggested.

"I'll try and be ready," I laughed.

On the way back to London, I sat in the back of the car with my own thoughts, while Dad and Tiffany chatted about I cannot recall what. I thought that I would surprise Tom with a gift of half of the half of the ranch that I was going to buy from the other heirs, the rats, the other half of the half I would give to Linda. I would also get him a new cowboy hat, I was sure that I could find a shop in Dallas that sold such things. Tom had seemed a little off hand when I had talked to him the day before, but, perhaps he was busy and things were at a juncture that he really did have to attend to them. Tom going away for a couple of weeks was disappointing. I recalled when Ian had first gone away to Germany for three weeks while we had been dating and the loss I had felt. I knew now that separation did not mean the end of the world, so just looked forward to the days when we could be back together. I got to mulling over a new hat for Tom, what colour, what style, I knew the size as I had inspected his hat when he had stayed with me on his way to Cambridge. I was ready for my session with Dundee, I had my models done and was happy with the results I was getting from them, but would have to spend a little time with Dundee so that they understood what kind of data needed to be fed into the model to get any results that had value and meaning. They would probably be surprised at some of the data that was called for, but to me they reflected social behaviours that would impact the very commodity that they were trafficking in. I wondered if I would miss in time the variety of projects that I had had to work on as a consultant, I doubted if I we would see such a variety as a banker, but, perhaps I was wrong. I thought that I should go back and look at all the projects Dad had worked on over the years and test them for variety and success.

I spent Wednesday morning trying to get as much information on Copper Beech that I could find. As a privately held company, financial data was hard to come by, but, I had sources and was able to get some. I also picked up a fair bit of background information from the sporting journals and the sports pages of the various newspapers. At lunchtime, Dad came to see me with news.

"It's official," he said. "We've got a written opinion from Monopolies that will not be proceeding further, basically a qualified approval, not that they would ever come out and say they approved, only that they didn't disapprove."

"Good," I said. "Would you handle the close while I'm gone?"

"Of course," he said. "It should all be done by the time you get back. I think Seaton should be happy and I know that John Harding will be happy with the money he'll get for his shares. Is Dundee the last of your projects that needs to be closed out?"

"It is," I said. "I finished all the others and didn't take on any new ones. I may just contact the JET oil chap while I'm in Dallas, you never know what may come of a decent contact."

"True," Dad agreed. "So, what else is new?"

"I met a chap," I said. "An American, Tom Ortiz, grad student at Trinity, researching photovoltaics."

"And?" Dad asked.

"So far so good," I said. "I think I love this chap Dad, I try hard not to compare him with Ian, but when I do, it's mostly positive."

"Good for you," he said. "So, why the long face?"

"He's off looking at some panel installation in Israel for the next couple of weeks and I haven't been able to talk to him," I explained.

"I'm sure he'll be back," Dad said. "He's not going anywhere is he?"

"You're right," I said. "I'm just feeling sorry for myself."

"So, what have you uncovered about Copper Beech?" Dad asked.

"Some," I said, pointing to a folder on my desk. He picked it up and flipped through the pages quickly.

"This gives us a sense of Theresa Baldwin," he said. "This is going to be difficult for Winter."

"If I were them, I'd bring in Theresa Baldwin as the MD," I said. "If I were John Stanley, I'd make myself the Chairman and then retire, he's of an age."

"Just like me?" Dad asked.

"I suppose," I agreed. "It's the only way I see Baldwin agreeing to any kind of deal, she controls what she's got now with no board to answer to, so why would she give that up just for money, I get the sense that she really likes what she does and is driven by passion not money."

"I think I'd agree with that," Dad said. "Will Stanley put his ego aside and consider that?"

"If put to him the right way," I thought. "He'll come up with the usual want to do best for the employees bit, which in John's case is a little more true than most, but in the end it's the comfortable life that he wants. I know his wife wants to travel the world and that hasn't really been possible yet because it's been business first."

"Did you study psychology at Oxford or maths?" Dad asked.

"I learned a lot from you," I said. "Look at the people, otherwise it's just numbers and looking only at numbers can lead to failure, it's the people that make it work."

"Did I ever say that?" he asked.

"Not in so many words, but yes, often," I replied.

"Well, it's nice to know you listened," he said. "So, ready for tomorrow?"

"As ready as I'll ever be," I said.

"Well, good luck," he said.

Tiffany picked me up at seven the next morning, far more time than we would need to drive to Northampton, but better to be out of the London traffic before it got too bad. Tiffany drove us to the small village of Little Houghton and she drove slowly past the entrance to a rather nice looking country house. I noted that on one of the gate posts there was a discreet brass plate emblazoned with the name Copper Beech and a tennis racket. We found a small transport café not too far away and had breakfast and coffee. We were back at the house at five minutes to ten and saw John Stanley, who had apparently also just arrived.

"Come with me," I told Tiffany. "Are you ready John?"

"Ready," he said.

"John, this is my new assistant, Tiffany MacBeth. I had a thought, John, what if the only way to do this is to make Theresa Baldwin the MD of Winter?" I asked.

"If that's what it takes," he said. "Then I can indulge Mary's passion and go off to see the world."

We went in and were expected and shown to a room overlooking a terrace and lawns beyond. We were joined by what I took to be the three Baldwins.

"Good morning," one said. "Theresa Baldwin, my sister Allison and bother George." I put Theresa Baldwin in her mid to late forties and would have guessed that she played tennis seriously, or did some kind of regular exercise. Allison, a year or two younger than Theresa, not quite as fit, but still not gone to seed at all. George, the youngest of the three was the least athletic looking, but perhaps I was being judgemental. All were soberly dress in dark suits and all were all business.

"Thank you for seeing us," John said. "John Stanley and this is Dr Fiona Barclay of Thames Cherwell and her assistant Tiffany MacBeth." There were handshakes all around and then we sat.

"So, what can we do for you?" Theresa asked.

"I'm sure you know all about Winter & Winter," John said. "We think the company would benefit with the addition of a high end tennis business."

"So, why would you think we would want to sell?" Theresa asked. The fencing continued for a little while then John suggested that I add my piece. I talked for about half and hour and ended on the note that the offer of the MD slot for Theresa and equivalent slots for Allison and

George were open, if they agreed to the deal, plus I showed them how they could take the company back private in five years. After that it was just a question of how much and whether they wanted cash or Winter & Winter stock. They wanted cash, but stated that they would use some of the cash to buy Winter shares, which would make it easier for John to step aside when Theresa joined the company, as she would then be a shareholder. When we left, it was with a heads of agreement signed by both parties. John thanked me and asked me to go ahead with the rights issue, then asked me if I would serve on his board as a non executive director. I thought that if the bank was going to be involved financially, then yes I would be on his board to keep an eye on things, That agreed, John took off for Maidstone, probably to tell his board part of what we had discussed. I doubted if he would touch upon the idea I had floated with Theresa of a buy back of the shares to go private in five years.

"So, Tiffany, what about some lunch, do you know anything around here?" I asked.

"There's a really nice pub in Maids Moreton," she said.

"How do you know all these places?" I asked.

"I had a client who used to go to Silverstone a lot, so I explored the area while he was occupied," she explained.

"Well, drive on, let's give it a try."

Back at the office I gave Dad a précis of the meeting and asked him to set in motion the process for a rights issue. He had done that before for numerous other companies, so knew exactly what to do, without me interfering. I spent Friday and Saturday getting ready for my various travels and was quite glad on Sunday to finally be off. We flew BA to Milan, then took a limousine to our hotel in Modena. The hotel was on the outskirts of the town, actually quite close to the Maserati factory. We had arrived quite late in the afternoon, so had a light supper and retired early. The next day we grabbed breakfast then got a taxi to the Maserati factory. We were expected and we ushered into the hall where the car was waiting.

"What do you think, Tiffany?" I asked.

"It's beautiful," she said. Indeed it was. It had nice lines, it shone in the light and the tan leather interior looked so inviting. We both walked around it and the Maserati representative opened the boot, the bonnet, the doors, so that we could see inside. When we looked inside I thought that I had made the right decision about the car phone, it would have ruined what was a very elegant interior. Tiffany wanted to know where the spare tyre was, were the jack was and where the jacking points were. She also wanted to see where the dip stick was and the other items that needed checking on a regular basis. We finally both got into the car. It was unabashed luxury to sink into the comfort of the seats, smell the leather, touch the wood veneer along the dashboard and play with the seat buttons. The Maserati man handed me the keys, and I handed them over to Tiffany.

"Take us to the track," I said. "Do you know the way?"

"No," she admitted. I had a quick conversation with the Maserati man in Italian, which seemed to impress him, and he gave us a map with precise directions. Thus armed we started out. I have to admit, being on the side of the car that faced the traffic and having no control was a little unnerving at first, particularly as Tiffany had to pull out quite a way before she could see the traffic, but we quickly worked out a plan and she relied on my judgement. The test track was a little south and west of Parma, next to a river that seemed to me to be more sand and mud than water.

We spent most of the day at the track, learning about the new car and what it would do, then we were offered the chance to try out two of the cars that the company had there for testing. That turned into a race, which I am sad or happy to say, Tiffany won, she was the better driver. I think we even impressed the Maserati people. I was impressed by the fact that Tiffany did not let me win just because I was the boss. As the light faded we left the track and went back to Parma and our hotel. On the way we stopped at a petrol station to fill up the tank, we had not used too much that day, but I would rather start the day without having to stop for petrol too soon.

"So, what do you think?" I asked Tiffany over dinner.

"It's brilliant," she said. "It drives and handles as well as it looks, it's fast, really fast, it's going to take a lot of discipline to not get speeding fines. You know you're not a bad driver, I was a little concerned there for a bit."

"Thank you, but I'm sorry to say, speeding fines will be to your account," I laughed. "I'll do most things, but not pay fines."

"Tomorrow we're driving to Cannes?" she asked.

"We are, we'll cross through the mountains and drop down to the Med west of Genoa, then follow the coast road to Cannes," I replied.

"What will that be, five hours?" she asked.

"I would think that," I said. "Unless we know where the police are and risk it a little."

"I want to thank you for this job," she said. "It's a dream job, nice car to drive, nice clothes to wear, nice people to work for and lots of variety, not just Heathrow and back three times a day."

"You may not be thanking me six months from now," I cautioned. "There are likely to be demands on your time."

"I don't see that as an issue," she said.

"So, tomorrow, why don't you drive as far as Tortona and then I'll take us to the border, then you take us in onto Cannes?" I suggested.

"Brilliant," she said. "Where's the border between Italy and France?"

"As memory serves the border station is near Ventimiglia," I said. "But the actual border is a little west of that."

"And the speed limits?" she asked.

"Like today, 130kph on the Autostrada and Autoroute, 110kph on the express roads and less in the towns," I said.

"We needed to be in Germany where we could really open the car up," Tiffany bemoaned.

"You didn't get enough fast driving today?" I kidded her.

"That was fun," she said.

"Let's start early tomorrow and see if we can be at Maman's by lunchtime," I suggested.

"So, leave at seven?" Tiffany asked.

"That would be fine, we have to get breakfast on the way, I'm not sure that the hotel will be ready for breakfast then," I thought.

"I'll fix something," she promised.

Tiffany did fix something, she was ready by the car the next morning, coffee and croissants in hand. My greatest fear was making a mess in the brand new car, but I managed to avoid spilling or dropping crumbs. We retraced the route we had taken on Sunday, back towards Milan until we reached Piacenza, then we took the Torino road to Tortona. At Tortona we switched and I got to drive for a while. Tiffany was right, the car handled well and the biggest problem was keeping to the speed limit. We actually saw three police cars with people pulled over, so decided that caution was the watchword of the day. I delighted in the mountain road south of Tortona, pushing the car around the corners, and diving in and out of the tunnels that were frequent along the road. We saw the sea long before we got to it and followed the route that paralleled the coast, but never quite got down to it, we paid our tolls at the stations along the way and passed remarks about the other road users. At the border post at Ventimiglia, we showed our passports and were waved through with little or no ceremony. Just past the border control we stopped long enough to change drivers again, then set off for Cannes. In Cannes I gave Tiffany the directions and we turned left, right, right, left and so on until we came to Maman's villa.

"This is your mother's place?" Tiffany asked.

"It is," I confirmed.

"It's fabulous," she said. "What a view."

"Fiona," Portia said as she opened the door for us. "We didn't expect you quite so soon, you must have set off at the crack of dawn."

"It was dark when we left," I confirmed. "How are you Portia? Portia this is Tiffany, I've taken her on as my permanent driver. Tiffany, this is Portia, my mother's partner."

"Nice to meet you," Tiffany said.

"Bébé," Maman said when she came to the door. *"Ça va?"*

"Bien Maman," I replied. "Maman, this is Tiffany, she's my new driver."

"Welcome," Maman said. "Come in, come in, have you had lunch yet?"

"Not yet," I said.

"Well, we were about to prepare lunch, so come and sit with me while I do that and tell us about your travels," Maman suggested.

While Maman prepared lunch we sat and told them about our trip to Milan, our drive to Modena and our visit to the Maserati factory. I let it slip that Tiffany spoke French and the conversation switched to French. I have to say that Tiffany did indeed speak the language, her accent was a little strange, but then her accent when she was speaking English was fairly marked as well. We told Maman about our race and she laughed when I complained that Tiffany had won.

"So, when do you go back to England?" Maman asked, after we had eaten lunch.

"We're taking the ferry from Calais at seven-thirty tomorrow night," I replied.

"You'll have to leave really early then," Maman said. "You should be away by five, then you can stop for lunch somewhere, perhaps Dijon, and then be in Calais in plenty of time."

"Are you splitting the driving?" Portia asked.

"We are," I confirmed. "I thought that tomorrow morning, I'd take us back to the Autoroute, perhaps as far as Valence, then Tiffany could take us to Dijon. After lunch I'd drive to Reims and then Tiffany can do Reims to Calais."

"That sounds reasonable," Maman nodded.

"So, we don't go through Paris?" Tiffany asked.

"No," I said. "One, it's a little out of the way, and two, getting through Paris would take time, so better to go via Dijon."

"Where did you learn your French?" Portia asked.

"I took French and German at college," Tiffany said. "And, as part of the degree course I had to send a year working in a French speaking place, so worked in a bank in Luxembourg."

"Good for French and German," Portia commented. "Also it explains the accent, I couldn't quite place it."

"Portia," I said. "Would you consider joining Thames Cherwell as a non executive director next year?"

"I thought your Dad ran Thames Cherwell?" she countered.

"He's retiring in May next year and I'll be taking over as Chair and will be restructuring the board," I explained.

"I'd be happy to help you," Portia said. "I suppose the board now is all men?"

"Of course," I laughed. "You don't think women know how to run banks do you?"

"So, Tiffany, have you any plans, aspirations or desires beyond being a chauffeuse?" Maman asked.

"I'm enjoying what I do, especially now," she replied. "I am interested in computers and how they work and would like to perhaps learn how to do programming."

"Well, Fiona can help you there," Maman said.

"Really?" Tiffany asked. "I thought you were an economist?"

"I am," I confirmed. "But, I write programs to help with the economic theories and have a doctorate in computer science."

"Wow," Tiffany said. "So, that's why you're Doctor Barclay."

"She's also a doctor of mathematics and economics," Portia said. "Her first was maths at Oxford, then the next was economics at LSE, then the computer one was at Imperial."

"You must scare the pants off most men," Tiffany laughed.

"I think she does," Maman said, looking at me with great affection. "I'm so proud of her and what she's done."

"Is there just Fiona?" Tiffany asked.

"No, I have a son, James, he now lives in New Mexico, where his wife and he run a winery," Maman replied. "And to finish out the family tree, I have one granddaughter, with James and Charlize, her name is Fiona. And you?"

"My parents live and work in London" Tiffany said. "I've got one sister, Catriona, she lives in Lerwick, she's married to Rory, an oil driller, no children yet."

"What does she do in Lerwick?" Maman asked.

"She's a geologist," Tiffany replied. "I think you'd actually call her a reservoir engineer."

Conversation continued into the afternoon and I excused myself for a few minutes to take the car to a garage and fill it up. It took nine gallons, forty-one litres actually. With the car full we would not have to worry about petrol again in the morning until we got to Valence, even then we would have enough to go quite a bit farther, but as we were changing drivers there, it would be prudent to fill up, go to the loo and get some coffee.

We were roused early the following morning by Maman at four-thirty. Who knew that there were actually two four-thirties in a day. She gave us coffee and a light breakfast and saw us on our way at five. It did not get light until we swapped duties at Valence when Tiffany took over the driving to Dijon. We were in Dijon before eleven, so stopped for an early lunch. Neither of us had been to Dijon before so we had to pick a place for lunch at random, or rather we consulted the Michelin Guide that we had and picked one from there. I am not sure what the owners made of us, I spoke French like a Parisian, Tiffany spoke it with an accent that they had a difficult time placing, we were driving a car with Italian licence plates, but the steering wheel was on the wrong side. We ate a really rather nice lunch, then were on our way to Reims and Calais. We were in Calais in plenty of time to check in for the ferry and actually did not have to wait too long before they started loading the ferry. Car aboard and locked, we made our way to a lounge to pass the time until the ferry sailed. I got us each a glass of wine and we reviewed the day.

"That would be a nice drive in the summer," Tiffany commented. "I really liked the coast road with all its tunnels and odd snatches of views of the sea."

"It would be easier for us with a left hand drive car," I said.

"You're right," she agreed. "Overtaking has been a challenge."

"While I'm away will you take care of reregistering the car in England?" I asked. "Get Deirdre to give you whatever funds you need."

"I'll take care of that," Tiffany promised. "It's a pity the UK doesn't have the vanity plates like the US does, then you could get TC BANK."

"I'm not sure that I would really like to advertise who we are that much, wouldn't that make us more at risk for kidnaps?" I asked.

"It might," she agreed. "Great, we're underway, so what about an hour and a half?"

"That's normal sailing time," I agreed. "So, we should be back in London by eleven-thirty."

"What time do you leave for Chicago?" she asked.

"My flight leaves at two, so I'll go to the office, pick up what I need then take off for the US," I replied.

"Dr Barclay, can I ask you something?" she said.

"Of course," I said. "And, please call me Fiona, or I'll have to start calling you Miss MacBeth."

"Brilliant," she said. "I was wondering about your Mum, she's just gorgeous, but is she just French?"

"No, Maman is half Tahitian," I replied. "My grandfather was French and my grandmother was Tahitian, they met when my grandfather was posted there as part of the French colonial government."

"So, that makes you, what, one quarter Tahitian?" she asked.

"It does," I confirmed.

"So that's why you're such a knock out," she breathed.

"I don't look on myself as a knock out," I laughed. "I'm just Fiona."

"Tahiti, that's the South Sea Islands, isn't it?" she asked.

"It is," I confirmed. "Tahiti is actually a few islands, it's warm there and from what Maman told me and what my grandmother told me the people are very nice."

"You've never been then?" she asked.

"Not yet," I said. "One day I will go to see where that part of the family comes from."

"Do you have any relatives there?" she asked.

"I'm sure there are some," I said. "I'd have to ask Maman. Okay, we should get going, we're docking."

Tiffany took me to Heathrow the next day and I told her that I would call the office and confirm my return flight. The BA flight to Chicago was on time and we landed within a few minutes of the scheduled time. I took a taxi into town and registered at the Drake and planned what I would do for the next couple of days at Dundee. When I went there the next day they were ready for me and I was able to quickly load the program I had brought with me and test run it. Then I sat down with the two analysts that Dundee had provided and went though with them all the inputs. They were surprised at some of the items that I suggested that they follow, but I showed them the mathematics of why they had significance and what the relationships, no matter how peculiar they might seem, would be. Then it was just a question of input data, run the program, review the results, input more data, run the program, review the results and so on. By Saturday evening I was confident that they understood the program and could be left to their own devices. Richard and Barbara had invited me to have dinner them at their house, so I arranged with the hotel to have a car take me there. They had a sprawling estate in a place called Lake Forest, that was a suburb north of the city. I was not the only invited guest, there were five others, two couples that apparently lived nearby and another woman who was introduced to me as a painter. Judging by the conversation it seemed that Lake Forest was a haven for the rich and famous who liked to call Chicago home. Based on what I heard, I estimated that the people there that evening represented about two billion dollars in net worth, so much wealth concentrated among so few people.

On Sunday I took my flight to Dallas and then a taxi to the Joule Hotel. I had picked it because I was intrigued by the name. I had no idea why they had called it the Joule, but it turned out to be very nice, but no evidence anywhere of energy generation, so no joules around except those being consumed by the hotel itself. My meeting with the rats and their lawyer was at the Chase Manhattan bank at ten on Monday morning.

"Good morning," I said to them all when a bank employee ushered me into a conference room.

"Howdy," was the general response. I got introductions to Bert, Dale and Steve Ortiz and to Grant Edwards, their lawyer.

"We understand that you represent a company who is interested in the Ortiz property near Roy," Grant commented.

"That is so," I confirmed. They did not need to know that I was the company.

"How did you pick us?" Grant asked.

"We've been following various ranches in west Texas and New Mexico and particularly probate filings, it often happens when there are multiple heirs that some want a monetary share of the ranch. That often leads to break ups of the property, if we take that share, then the ranch may be held as a contiguous property, not small parcels," I explained.

"Well, my clients are willing to sell their interest in the ranch, based on appraised values," Grant said.

"That is reasonable," I said. "I have had an appraisal done by a firm here in Dallas, and they should be here shortly to give us their view. I have not had the opportunity to review their report, so will be interested to see what they have to say."

"So, let's get some coffee," Grant suggested. "You're British, where's your office?"

"I work in London," I said. "I run an investment bank there."

"Okay," Grant said. "Well, here's the coffee and this must be the appraiser."

"Howdy folks," the newcomer said. "Name's Walt Williams, I do ranch appraisals in Texas, Oklahoma and New Mexico, based in Dallas."

"Great to meet you," Grant said. "Coffee?"

"No thanks," Walt said.

"So, tell us about the Ortiz ranch," Grant said. Walt then launched into his trip to the ranch, all that he saw and measured and counted and then all the other ranches that he looked at for comparable values.

"The appraisal of the whole property comes out to $4,550,000," Walt said. "That's land, buildings, stock, the works."

"Would that appraisal change if the land was considered as available for development?" Dale asked.

"No," Walt said. "There's too much land in that category already, it wouldn't change the appraised value at all. There's no development planned or envisaged for the next twenty years."

"May we have copies of the appraisal?" Steve asked.

"I've got six copies here, so there's five of you, take one each, any questions here's my card, call me," Walt said.

"Who paid for the appraisal?" Bert asked.

"Chase Manhattan," Walt said. "So, as far as I was concerned it was a blind request and I have no idea who the actual client is."

"Thank you Walt," Grant said. Walt left and Grant looked to me and said, "$4,560,000 by two is $2,280,000, what about it?"

"If that's what the appraised value is, then that's what the appraised value is," I replied, a little surprised that it came out as high as it did. "I am willing to go ahead at the value, plus I will pay your fees Grant so that they will not come out of the proceeds from the ranch."

"Guys?" Grant asked.

"Yep," Bert said, followed by similar responses from Steve and Dale. I suppose they all saw dollar signs and had worked out that it meant $760,000 each. "How do we do this?"

"I have here a form of agreement that cedes your claims to the ranch in exchange for cash," I said. "I think Grant should look it over and see that it meets all applicable law, then if you all agree and sign, I can have monies transferred from this bank to whatever account you name today."

"Today?" Bert asked.

"Today," I confirmed.

"Well, Grant, what about the agreement?" Bett asked.

"Actually, it looks pretty good, well written, covers all the issues, I couldn't have written it better myself," he replied, something that I felt was unusual for a lawyer, often they wanted to change something either to put their stamp on the agreement or just to charge fees.

"So, what's the next step?" Dale asked.

"We all sign the document, then we call in a bank official, you tell him or her whether you want the money wired or as a cashier's cheque, then we wait for then to confirm transfer," I said.

"Let's do it," Steve said. I think he was afraid that I might change my mind and his mind he had already spent the $760,000. Grant passed around the agreement and we all signed, then Grant witnessed it and I called in a bank vice president, probably one of many with that title and he collected information from the three as to account numbers, then a signature from me authorising the transfers and left.

"Grant," I said. "What are your fees?"

"$25,350," he said. "I've got an accounting here."

"When Mr Ward returns we'll give him the information and he can make a transfer for you as well," I suggested. We sat and twiddled our thumbs for what seemed like an eternity and thirty minutes late, Ward came back and handed confirmations to the three that the monies had in fact been wired to their banks, and received. All that remained was to clean up the fees of Grant which we did with a cashier's cheque and it was all done.

"Happy to do business with you, Dr Barclay," Bert said. "I'll say goodbye and go home and tell Adele the good news."

One by one they left, then Grant left and I was left cash poorer, but land richer. I now owned 20,000 acres of ranch in New Mexico, but had already decided to find a way to get it into the hands of Linda and Tom. That was it, I was done, I could go home. I thought that I would stop at Dundee the next day for one last review of the model, then take an earlier BA flight home. I asked Mr Ward if I could use their telephone to change airline bookings, and he was happy to oblige. I called American Airlines and changed my Chicago flight to that afternoon, then called BA and changed my Heathrow flight and finally called the Drake and made a booking for that night. It was all over and just in time for lunch, so I went back to the Joule, checked out, then had lunch. I was surprised that there had not been any more discussion, but supposed that the appraisal came in higher than they had all expected, and they were just keen to get their hands on the money. I had one more thing to do before returning, I needed to buy a new hat for Tom. I found an emporium that fit the bill, Wild Bill's Western Store. It had everything, and I quickly picked a hat that I liked, Stetson style, black and the right size. I also found a post office and sent off a parcel to James and Charlize for Christmas. I had brought the box with me all packed up and ready to go, so it was just a matter of paying the postage, no customs forms to fill out, no worries about if it would make it in time. I decided to forego contacting JET. I had no desire at that time to take on any more consulting work. JET could wait until I was next in the US and with a little less on my plate. I still had the Metter transaction to close out and the Winter & Winter rights issue and merger with Copper Beech was still pending. I know I had asked Dad to usher those two items along, but if I was to run the bank, then I needed to take charge and not hive off those items to Dad.

I stopped at the Dundee offices the next day and went through the model results that they had and helped them understand what they were looking at and what the probable confidence levels were. I tried to impress upon them, that the model was just that, a model, and sound judgement was still called for. I saw Richard, Hal and Stuart briefly and they were delighted with what I had brought them and were testing the model against history to see how well it would have played out in the past. So far it looked good, so they were developing confidence in it, but I pointed out to them as well, that experience and judgement still might be better than the model results, which after all were dependent upon certain assumptions and the accuracy of the inputs. I think they truly understood that, but were still excited with the results the model had already given them. Happy that they were happy I called my office and told Tiffany that I would be back early, and to collect me from Heathrow the next morning. That done I went to the airport to await my flight back to London.

Surprises

When I cleared customs and immigration in London, Tiffany was there waiting for me. She had obviously collected her new uniforms, because she was dressed in a new Aquascutum great coat, and underneath I could see new trousers and light boots.

"Dr Barclay," she said as she took charge of my trolley. "How was your trip?"

"Very good, thank you," I replied. "And how are you?"

"Terrific," she said. "I got my new togs, they fit divinely and are really comfortable to drive in. Unfortunately it's raining, so dreary day today."

"Well, I suppose it's to be expected," I said. "We are in mid December."

"Where to?" she asked.

"I think Cambridge," I said. "Let's surprise Tom, I know I wasn't supposed to be back until later this week, so this should be a nice surprise."

"Okay," she said. She led the way, using the luggage trolley a few times almost as a battering ram to clear a path through the throngs waiting to greet arrivals. At the car she loaded my bag into the boot and I noted that it now sported British licence plates. Tiffany took off her overcoat and held out her arm for mine, which she also deposited in the boot, then we were off. Unfortunately at that time, there was no M25 that ran around London in a giant loop, so we had to find our way between towns, across traffic, against traffic and with traffic as we went north then east to pick up the M11.

"So, how does the car handle in all this traffic?" I asked.

"It's fine," Tiffany said. "We do occasionally get a second look from other motorists who notice that its a Maserati and I even had one this morning who seemed to want to race me down the M4. Not that he would have had much chance, his Jag just wouldn't go as fast as this."

"It's a miserable day," I commented. "I'm afraid the car's going to get really filthy."

"I have a car wash place that I go to," she said. "They do a good job and then I'll clean it off myself."

"How are you settling in at the bank?" I asked.

"Super," she said. "I've made friends with the programmers and they're teaching me how to write my own programs. I've already got a simple one to manage expenses with the car, and we've worked it so that it feeds the general ledger of the bank."

"Good job" I said. "I should get you an Apple desktop as well, you should learn about them too while you're at it."

"When we get to Cambridge, where should I go?" she asked.

"I'll give you directions," I promised. I did as promised and when we got to Cambridge I directed her around the maze of streets. Traffic was quite light as all the undergraduate students had already left for the Christmas break, so it was only some post graduates and staff left. I was excited to see Tom and give him my news about the ranch, and to give him his new hat.

When we pulled up at the gate, I asked Tiffany to wait until I checked that Tom was actually there and back from Israel. So, hat in hand I walked up to his flat and knocked, excited to be able to tell him about the ranch and give him his new hat. I was floored when Roberta Spinoglio answered the door dressed only in a short dressing gown and as far as I could tell nothing else.

"Yes?" she said, looking at me as if the cat had dragged me in.

"Is Tom in?" I asked, more than a little taken aback and hoping that what I was seeing was not what I was seeing.

"Tom, that woman for you," she said, which I thought was really rude as she knew my name well enough. Tom came to the door.

"Oh, shit," he said. On that I flung the hat at him turned tailed and ran, well I did not actually run, but stalked back to the car, angry, confused, feeling betrayed and humiliated. The, oh shit, told me everything I needed to know, this was no innocent encounter, this was something he had not wanted me to see or discover.

"London," I told Tiffany.

"Wasn't he there?" she asked.

"He was there all right," I said. "The bastard had another woman with him, and by the looks of it they had been at it this morning."

"Oh, I'm so sorry," Tiffany said. "Any idea who she is?"

"Roberta fucking Spinoglio, a grad student there," I said. "Blonde, boobs, long legs, all I got from him was oh shit, which told me volumes, I wonder how long that has been going on, I wonder if the bastard ever went to Israel, I'm so pissed right now I could hit something."

"Why don't we stop for brunch and you can unload and tell me all about it," Tiffany suggested.

"Good idea," I said. "I need to tell someone what an arsehole he is and how stupid I've been."

We stopped at a small transport café and ordered breakfast.

"I can't get over the fact that he had someone else there," I complained. "I wonder how long he's been seeing her, is this recent or did the bastard start as soon as he got there?"

"Was it serious between you two?" Tiffany asked.

"I thought so," I said. "I thought the arsehole loved me, I'll bet he'll tell me that he does and that that was a momentary lapse. Well, fuck that, there are no momentary lapses where I'm concerned."

"Do you want to go back and confront them?" Tiffany asked.

"No, I never want to see the bastard again," I said.

"What did you actually see?" Tiffany asked,

"Well, she came to the door, shortie dressing gown, nothing else by the look of it, he came to the door, just underpants with a stiffie," I reported.

"No ambiguity there," Tiffany sympathised. "What a bastard, what was she like?"

"She's tall, bigger boobs, long blonde hair, she's American like him from Denver I think," I said.

"So, two timing bastard," Tiffany said.

"Right, and to think that I just bailed him and his sister out of a sticky situation with other heirs to the ranch, God knows what I'll do about that now," I said.

"What's his sister like?" Tiffany asked.

"She's really a nice person," I said. "I like her a lot, I wonder if she knows what he's been up to?"

"Probably not," Tiffany said. "My own experience was very similar, I came back from a job early, I let myself into Alex's flat and the bitch was asleep in bed with one of my friends, well I thought she was my friend, Alex's sister was my friend and she was as surprised as I was that she was screwing Joanna."

"What was her excuse?" I asked, the realisation dawning on me that Alex was a woman, and that probably made Tiffany a lesbian.

"I never found out," Tiffany said. "I got a pan of cold water and dumped it on them, then left. Fortunately we hadn't moved in together, so I threw away her key and closed that chapter of my life."

"Men, and it seems some women," I said, disgustedly. "What really pisses me off was that I thought that he was as nice as Ian, my husband who was killed in Kenya, now he really was a nice man and I never had any issues with him, well apart from the time that we lost touch with one another when he was in Tanzania. There was another bitch who fancied him and she intercepted all our mail so each thought the other had abandoned them. No wonder Maman prefers women."

"I thought that your Mum and Portia seemed very happy," Tiffany said.

"They are," I agreed. "Look Tiffany do you have big plans for the Christmas holiday?"

"No," she said. "I was going to stay at home, my parents are off to Norway to see the Northern Lights and my sister and her husband are off to Portugal, so I was going to spend a quiet time on my own."

"I was going to fly down to Cannes and spend Christmas with Maman and Portia and had invited Tom, but there's no way I'm taking him now, would you like to come and keep me company on the flight down?"

"Gosh, that would be super," she said. "Can I try flying the plane?"

"Of course," I said. "I'll let you take the controls for a while as we fly down."

"When would we go?" she asked.

"If the weather cooperates, then we'd fly down the Saturday before, the 22nd, the Saturday after next, and come back on the 27th," I replied.

"Gosh, that would be so nice," she said. "You're sure?"

"Absolutely," I said. "I've flown it before on my own, but it's much nicer to have someone else in the cockpit So, let's go back to the office and I'll see what needs doing before we shut down for Christmas."

Dad was happy to see me when we arrived at the office. He had all but finished the Metter deal and it just remained to do the final closing, which I could now do as I was there. He had the rights issue for Winter & Winter almost ready to go as well, so he just asked me to review it before we sent it off. That I did over lunch, making only the most minor changes. Then I scheduled the closing with Corby Seaton and Metter for that Friday to be done at the Metter offices. The new IBM computer was in and running and the programmers and analysts were on board busy inputting all the past transactions into a data base. That would make life easier for me in the future as I would not then have to wade through dusty old files to look something up. Dad also sensed that something was not right as I was short with him a couple of times.

"Okay, Fi, what's bothering you?" he asked.

"Tom, Tom's a big fat bastard," I said. "I go there to surprise him and I surprised him all right, there was another woman there, half naked."

"I'm sorry," he said. "Did he say anything?"

"Oh shit, that's what he said, oh shit, well that told me everything," I said.

"What did you do?" Dad asked.

"I left," I said. "I'd bought him a new hat, so just threw the bloody thing at him and left. Dad, I'm sorry, have I been a pain?"

"Not too bad," he said. "But, I was wondering, you're not your usual self, these things do happen and there's always two sides to every story, so don't judge too harshly."

"I'll try and focus on things here and not dwell on things outside," I promised, thinking that it was all very well for Dad to say not to judge too harshly, did he think I would judge him. I had done that long ago when he dumped Maman for Felicity the floozie, maybe I was like Maman and wanted to be too independent for most men. The telephone rang and it was Tom. I mouthed Tom to Dad and he left, leaving me to listen, rant, hang up, whatever I was going to do.

"Fiona, please don't hang up" Tom said. "I'm sorry you had to find out the way you did, but I was going to talk to you when you got back."

"About what?" I asked.

"Well, to tell you that I didn't think it would work for us, I couldn't see you moving to the States and I don't want to stay here past my doctorate," he said. "Plus, we're not really right for each other."

"Why not?" I asked.

"Well, not to put too fine a point on it, you're too controlling, you want things your way, even when it comes to when we might make it to the bedroom, and to top that off, I always had this feeling that you were comparing me to your dead husband, and I didn't see our relationship blossoming into anything in the foreseeable future," he said.

"I see," I said, trying to digest that tidbit. "So, what about her?"

"Roberta, you know she's a grad student here," he said. "She's from Denver and would be returning to the States at the same time as me."

"And that's supposed to make me feel better?" I asked.

"No," he said. "Look, I said I'm sorry, I was planning to call you when you said you'd be back on Saturday. Look, here's Roberta."

"Hello Fiona, I'm so sorry you had to find out about us this way, I know Tom wanted really badly to talk to you," she said. "But, you had your chance and you never took it."

"Well, bravo, you won," I said, and then hung up, probably rude of me, but I had nothing to say to the winner of Tom's heart. So, I was too bossy, too controlling, wanted everything my way, and from his tone, had not climbed into bed with him quickly enough, I wondered how true that all was. I went and found Dad.

"Dad, am I too controlling, do I want everything my way?" I asked.

"Why do you ask that?" he temporised.

"Because that's what Tom told me, told me that I'm too controlling," I said.

"Some might think so," he said. "You are so much smarter than most people that you're on step nine of an issue when they're still trying to get to step two or three, so you see the answers well before most people and you can't understand why they can't see what is obvious to you, even I have difficulty at times, but I've learned over the years to trust that you've already seen through the issues and you've come up with an answer that is almost always the right one."

"Oh," I said. "Well, I suppose I should try and be more patient and try to see that others have to go step by step. It's frustrating at times, there are times I want to scream because others can't see what is so obvious to me. Have I always been a pain?"

"You're not a pain," he assured me. "With the right person you're caring, loving, supportive and patient, you were with Ian."

"Ian was special," I said, a little wistfully. "I wonder if I'll ever find someone else, I thought I had with Tom, but he just thinks I'm too bossy?"

"You will," Dad assured me. "But, it will take time and it'll have to be a very special person."

"Thanks Dad, so, are you coming with me for the Corby Metter close on Friday?"

"I don't think I need to," he said. "It's your deal and you should be the one to see it through."

I went home that night still seething, I was hurt and humiliated. I had been ready to give myself to this man, and what had he done in return, gone off with another woman who had been more willing to drop her drawers for him. I wanted to cry, but unlike with Ian it was not about loss, it was about anger, frustration, humiliation and a host of other reasons. I was even more annoyed in that I now owned half the bloody ranch that he had a part ownership in and wondered what should I do about that. I could hardly try and sell the part that I had, so needed to think about that for a while. I supposed I had been too romantic, conjuring up this situation where I presented the other half of the ranch to Tom and Linda, in a gesture of great generosity. Now, I wondered how intelligent that had been. It might be generous, but it might also be bitterly resented as it drove home the point that I had money and the ranch did not. Well, there was no hurry to decide what to do about 20,000 acres in New Mexico, that could wait for another day. Had I compared Tom to Ian. I had on at least one occasion done that, but Tom had come out favourably in the comparison, or was that a sop on my part to salve my conscience for making the comparison. Was it fair to compare. That was something I was going to have to come to terms with, how not to compare. Tom's perfidy had thrown me into a turmoil and it was going to take a while to sort things out in my mind. Perhaps at Christmas time I could talk to Maman and Portia and find out how they both dealt with similar situations.

On Friday morning early Tiffany arrived to take me to Swindon and the Metter office. Tiffany was in blue that day, suit and coat, I have to say that Rachel did a terrific job of the uniforms, they could probably function just as well as business attire. Tiffany was probably one of the few professional drivers who could boast a true designer brand uniform.
"Good morning Tiffany," I said. "Shall we go?"
"Of course," she said. "What time is the meeting?"
"Nine," I said.
"Well, we'll be there in plenty of time," she said. "How are you today?"
"Better, thanks Tiffany," I said. "I did my yelling and hit a few blocks of wood to vent my anger, now I'm just hurt."
"Well, if there's anything I can do for, anything at all, please let me know," she said. I wondered was that a come on, an invitation, or just a simple statement. I had never experimented with being with another

225

woman, I know it suited Maman and Portia, but it had never crossed my mind until now, or was I reading far too much into Tiffany's anything at all?

"When we go to Cannes at Christmas, take a nice dress with you," I said. "Maman likes everyone to dress their best on Christmas Eve, it's a tradition with her."

"What's the weather like there over Christmas?" she asked.

"Highs in the sixties, lows in forties," I said.

"So, not beach weather?" she asked.

"I don't think so," I laughed. "But, Maman does have a Jacuzzi tub on her terrace that is heated, so nice to loll in and soak away aches and cares."

"I wondered what that was," Tiffany said. "That must be nice."

"How much farther?" I asked.

"Another ten minutes will put us in Swindon," she replied. "Do you want to go straight there?"

"I think so," I said. "We can meet with the Metter people if James Seaton hasn't arrived yet. I don't know how long we'll be."

James Seaton was there, had been there all week in fact, going through personnel files and other documents.

"Dr Barclay," he said as I went into the offices. "Shall we crack on and get this done, I think all the Metter board are here?"

"Fine with me, James, this is my new assistant, Tiffany MacBeth, she's just learning the business," I said. We went to the board room and James had been right, the various directors were all sitting there drinking tea and probably wondering which of them, if any, Seaton would retain.

"Good morning gentlemen," I said. "I have here the various documents that require signatures, we need the signatures of the Chairman and the company secretary, then James Seaton and I will sign." I passed around the documents and they dutifully signed away the company. I added my signatures to those already there and that of James Seaton and Thames Cherwell was now an official owner of twenty per cent of Corby Metter, and by virtue of that James had already asked me to be on his board as a non executive director. I just hoped that Corby Metter prospered under the leadership of James Seaton, but took solace in the knowledge that as a director I would get to see most of what occurred. I was sure that there would be some things that James would just as soon not share too much, and it would be up to me to guess those items and question him about them. Sir John Harding in his last act as Chairman, passed around champagne and we all drank a toast to the success of Corby Metter. Apparently there was to be no sumptuous luncheon as James thanked all the non executive directors for their service and politely dismissed them all, only promising a golf date with Sir John. I had no need to stay, just got the date and time of the next board meeting and said my goodbyes to James and left. I suppose it was all very anticlimactic. The lead up to this had been busy, with the Monopolies Commission, the buying of all the outstanding shares and the formulation of the various agreements. Now, it was all done and all that remained was for James to sort out who he wanted to keep where and what properties might to surplus to his needs. There were actually quite a few as Corby Seaton and Metter both had sites in many towns, so now James had the luxury of picking the best sites and selling off the rest. I had suggested that rather than try to sell off the excess properties, that James look to lease them out and only sell when market prices were substantially better than there were at that time. However, if an attractive offer was there, then James should take it to get the property off his balance sheet as a non-productive asset.

"That's it, all done?" Tiffany asked as we went back out to the car.
"All done," I confirmed. We watched the others leave and either get whisked away by drivers, who I noted were all men, or get in their own cars and drive off to consider what they had done, had it been in the best interests of the shareholders, the employees, the customers. The shareholders all seemed happy enough with their newfound wealth, the employees of Metter who were bright and enterprising would find a good home with Corby Metter, those who had retired in place would probably go fairly quickly, the customers would still have essentially the same choices that they had before, except that Metter was now under a more engaged leader who understood the business.
"Where to, Dr Barclay?" Tiffany asked.
"I have a mind for some lunch," I said. "Where shall we go?"
"Here in Swindon or somewhere else?" she asked.
"Anywhere between here and London," I said. "Let's go and celebrate."
"I've never eaten at the Compleat Angler in Marlow," she said. "I've sat outside it often enough."

"That sounds good, let's go there," I said. "What did you think of this morning's meeting?"

"It all seemed to go very quickly," she said. "They were all eager to sign, I presume that when they did, they'll all be better off?"

"They will be," I confirmed. "Greed and avarice are great incentives to do these kinds of deals."

We made our way to Marlow, getting off the M4 just before Maidenhead, then taking the High Wycombe road to Bisham and then on into Marlow. The Compleat Angler was not overly busy so we were seated immediately with a view of the river, a waitress came and took orders then left us to our conversation.

"I was brought up not too far from here," I told Tiffany. "My parents had a house in Henley."

"So, you've been here before?" she asked.

"A few times," I said.

"I have something for you," she said. She pulled a small box from her pocket and gave it to me. It was a brooch with the initials T and C intertwined. "Thames Cherwell," she added.

"Thank you, it's lovely," I said. "Where did you get it?"

"I made it," she replied. "I have a side business making jewellery and work in silver and gold. I thought for this that silver might go easier with darker suits."

"I don't know how to thank you," I said, a little at a loss for words to properly thank her, it was a most generous gift and one that I would actually wear, not consign to a drawer somewhere to be forgotten about. "I love this design, do you think you could talk to Deirdre when we get back to the office and design some new stationery?"

"I'd love to do that," she said, grinning at me. "You really like it?"

"I do," I assured her. "How does it fasten on?"

"At the back there's a couple of small magnets embedded in the back and there is another magnet that holds it in place, so there's no need to poke holes in the lapels of your suit," she explained.

"And it won't fall off?" I asked.

"None of those that I've made like this have fallen off or been lost," she said.

"Would you fix it on for me?" I asked. She leaned over and quickly attached the brooch to my lapel, then leaned back and looked at it critically.

"That looks good," she said.

"What's the font?" I asked.

"Garamond," she replied. "It's quite an old font, Garamond himself was born in something like 1510."

"Would you make one for everyone in the office?" I asked. "If you will I'll make it a commission."

"I'd be happy to," she said. "I'll do them as an enamel, so leave you with the unique silver one."

"So, what kind of jewelry do you make?" I asked.

"Rings, necklaces, brooches, earrings, some in gold, others silver, or alloys of both," she said.

"Where do you do this?" I asked.

"I was lucky, I found a loft above a large warehouse in Chelsea Harbour and the owner is happy to rent it to me cheaply and I can tap into their power for the furnaces that I use," she explained. "My biggest expense was buying a safe to keep the gold and silver in and the finished items. I also slip the owner a piece or two for his wife at times to keep him happy."

"How do you sell?" I asked.

"I sometimes take a stall in the Portobello Road, otherwise it's word of mouth," she said.

"When you saw Rachel did you mention that you're a gold and silver smith?" I asked.

"I didn't think she'd be interested," Tiffany said.

"Take some of your work and show her," I said. "She may give you some commissions for special pieces."

"Do you really think so?" Tiffany asked.

"I do," I said. "I'm not really a jewelry person, but there are many who are and there's a market out there."

"Excuse me," a voice said. We both turned and looked and there was a lady standing by our table, I would have guessed in her mid forties, brunette, tending a little to middle age spread. "I was wondering, where did you get your suits, they're so smart."

"We had them made by Rachel Adams," I replied.

"Rachel Adams, I thought she only did haut couture?" the lady asked.

"If you talk to her and give her a commission she might make something for you other than evening dresses," I said.

"Oh, I love your brooch, are those your initials?" she asked.

"No, they're the initials of the bank we work for, Thames Cherwell," I explained.

"That's not a bank I'm familiar with," she said.

"It's an investment bank in London," I explained. "We don't do branch banking, but specialise in company transactions."

"Oh, I see, well sorry to bother you, I just had to know where you got your suits, they look so good on you both," she gushed.

"Thank you," I said. She beetled off to her table and got into a huddle with the other three women what were there, probably discussing us and what we were doing in Marlow. "Are you ready Tiffany, should we start back to London?"

"I'm ready," Tiffany said. "If you'd like to see my studio, why don't you come tomorrow."

"That would be super," I said. "What time?"

"About ten?" she suggested. "Here's the address, there's a door at the side with a name on it, Bijoux de MacBeth, I'll leave it open, come on in and up the stairs, I'll be waiting for you."

"I've never seen a goldsmith's studio," I commented. "This will be a first."

We drove back into London and I spent some time with Dad talking about the Metter deal and the Winter & Winter rights issue, then he brought up a new possibility. It was a mining company, Sable Mining, that was looking to open up a new copper operation in South Africa. Dad had managed a share issue for them a couple of years earlier to raise some capital, but I gathered that was for the exploration phase of that project. Now they were into the start up phase.

"What do you think?" I asked.

"You're the metals expert, what should we expect?" he asked.

"The copper price per ton will generally go down between now and 1985, then we can expect a reasonable climb, if they want their economics to work then they need to be able to have operating costs at less than £250 a ton, anything more than that and they'll have losing years," I said. "Do you want me to go and talk to them?"

"It would probably be a good idea," he said. "They have an office in Millbank."

"Why don't we call them and set up a time?" I suggested. Dad did that and had a brief conversation with someone on the other end and the date and time were set, the following Tuesday at nine. "Anything else of note?"

"No, that's it," he said. "How are you today?"

"Still smarting a little, but now more annoyed with myself for getting too involved too quickly, I should have taken more time," I lamented.

"Well, you'll be fine," he assured me. "I'm off, I'll see you on Monday."

I left the office soon after he did, wondering what the Sable Mining people really had in mind and if they could have a workable prospect. I would find out more the next week.

Saturday morning the weather was fairly nice, so I walked to Tiffany's studio, a walk of a little under two miles. I found the building easily enough and the saw the side door and the name plate. I entered and climbed the stairs and on the landing there was a steel gate.

"Hello," I called.

"Fiona," Tiffany said, as she came over and unlocked the gate. "I put this in so that I wouldn't be surprised by anyone coming up the stairs if I was busy. Come on in." The loft was huge, it obviously ran across the entire warehouse that was below. Tiffany had divided it up and there was a living area and her studio with benches, furnaces and shelves with boxes. Tiffany had on a bikini and wooden clogs and a long leather apron. The view from the back was stunning, her bikini did justice to her and more. She saw me looking and laughed. "I know," she said. "It gets warm up here, but I don't want to splash anything on myself, hence the apron, it's very effective at keeping anything off me. Come, let me show you around."

We wandered around the loft as she explained work benches and furnaces, then she showed me her display cabinet with finished pieces. There were a lot, as she had said, necklaces, rings, earrings, brooches, bracelets and chokers.

"You've a lot here," I commented.

"It looks like it," she agreed. "But, all that could go in one morning on the Portobello Road."

"I hesitate to ask, but what's the value of this lot?" I asked.

"Probably about £25,000," she said.

"Is the building secure?" I asked.

"It's alarmed and I have steel shutters that I pull down at night around this area," she said. "The alarms are fairly sophisticated, including pressure plates on the stairs, motion sensors on the roof and a few other devices. I leave a display cabinet near the door with costume jewelry so that a casual thief will look at it and decide that my work isn't worth much. So, coffee, tea?"

"Coffee would be very nice," I said. She pulled off the apron and went to her kitchen area and put the kettle on.

"Could I buy a couple of pieces from you?" I asked.

"Of course," she said. "What do you have in mind?"

"Earrings for Maman and a bracelet for Portia," I thought. "Then I won't go empty handed for Christmas."

"What are their preferences?" Tiffany asked. I wandered over to the display cabinet and pointed out two pieces.

"These two?" I asked.

"Retail, £724," she said, taking the pieces out of the case and giving them to me. "But I could give them to you at cost."

"No, I'll pay retail," I said. "You need to make a living."

"I'm actually doing very well," she said. "Even before you gave me the job, which I love by the way, I'll drive you anywhere and do anything for you, anything at all."

"Thank you Tiffany," I said. "You don't know how nice it is to have someone who you know is there and has your bests interests at heart."

"How are you now with Tom?" she asked.

"I'm more annoyed with myself for getting too involved too quickly," I said. "I should have taken more time, I suppose I was just looking for solace after Ian's death."

"What did he look like?" she asked.

"I have some pictures, I'll bring some into the office on Monday. While I think about it, we have prospect that's looking at a mining operation in South Africa, if I decide that I need to go and look at the site in January, would you come with me?"

"Absolutely," she said.

"It's dry in that part of the world, never much rain, maybe we could get some kind of safari in," I thought.

"Gosh, how exciting, do we need a visa or jabs of any type?" she asked.

"We'll check on Monday and get what we need, we will need malaria pills, but I'm not sure what else if anything, oh, and you might see what you can dig up on Monday about Sable Mining," I said. "Thank you for the tour, the coffee and the presents, I should let you get back to work."

"Thank you for the sales," she said. "Would you mind if I brought the car here in the evenings and over the weekend?"

"Where would you keep it?" I asked.

"There's a lockable garage at the side of the warehouse," she said. "It doesn't look like much from the outside, but it is well set up with a pit, and a hoist, workbenches and the like, and there is a steel gate inside the door, so I think security would be good. The door is also alarmed and tied to my system."

"That sounds fine," I said. "May we take a look?"

Tiffany led me to a corner of her loft and opened what I thought was a walk in closet, it actually turned out to be a spiral staircase that led down to the garage. Tiffany was right, the garage was well set up, with room for four cars. The steel gate inside the door was massive, set into the floor with guide rollers top and bottom and locking into a massive stanchion at the end.

"This almost seems like overkill," I said. "What did the owner keep in here?"

"He had a collection of Ferraris," she explained. "So, he wanted to secure them and built this place, the walls are solid concrete, so is the ceiling, it's more like a bunker than a garage."

"Perhaps I'll give up my rented garage space and move my Land Rover here," I thought. "Could I do that?"

"Of course," she said. "Anything you want."

"Let's look at that in the New Year," I said.

On Tuesday I took Tiffany, armed with the information she had gathered and we went to see Sable Mining and was surprised to see George Robertson there. George was one of James's friends from school and college and in fact he was the best man at James's wedding, the last time I had seen him had been in South Africa.

"Fiona," he said. "What a surprise. How are you, how are James and Charlize?"

"I'm fine thanks, George, James and Charlize have a daughter and they are running a winery in New Mexico now. This is my new assistant, Tiffany MacBeth," I told him.

"Fiona, Tiffany, this is Patrick Bishop, he's the MD of Sable Mining, this is Harry Black, Neville Hall, they're with me on the Klein Copper project, this is Dr Fiona Barclay," he said making the introductions.

"When did you join Thames Cherwell?"

"Recently," I said. "My father has been running the bank and he wants to retire so he persuaded my to step in and take over."

"Fiona has some knowledge of our business," George told the others. "When I was at RSM, she was already an Oxford fellow funded by a consortium of mining companies to create a model for the valuation of ore reserves and the tax implications."

"Nice to know that someone understands reserves," Patrick said.

"So, tell me about your project?" I invited them.

"Well, we done significant exploratory drilling in the area north-west of Prieska in the northern Cape, the hamlet of Kleinbegin is about eighty miles north-west of Prieska. We've identified reserves of 325,000,000 tons at about 0.72% copper, plus the presence of other minerals such as magnetite and vermiculite," Patrick said.

"That's sounds uncannily like the Palabora mine," I recalled from my studies before of ore reserve categorisation and valuation.

"It is," Patrick said. "We also envisage an open pit mine for the Klein Copper project, with a concentrator, plus a smelter and an electrolytic refinery."

"What infrastructure would you have to add?" I asked.

"We put in a temporary road, but we'd have to improve it," George said. "We'd have to expand the generating capacity we've already put in, or convince ESCOM to extend a line out to us, and we'll have to add to the housing that we've already built, and we do have an all weather strip there for light aircraft."

"What kind of blight are you going to leave on the landscape?" I asked.

"There will be some, but probably not as bad as the diamond operations on the coast around Kleinsee, or the iron ores mines near Sishen," Patrick agreed. "But the government is keen to develop resources out there and is pressing us to move forward."

"What is there to see there now?" I asked.

"We've an exploratory pit," George replied. "We've also got all the cores stored nearby."

"How would you get all the equipment there, isn't it a little out of the way?" I asked.

"It is," Patrick confirmed. "But, there's a railway line that runs through Kleinbegin. We've been talking to South African Railways about putting a spur off the main line, that shouldn't be too much of an issue with them, because it would be a short spur, only a couple of miles."

"Have you estimates of operating costs?" I asked. "I ask because my own models for copper prices show them dropping until about 1984, where I think they'll bottom out at about £700 per ton, then start climbing again."

"We could probably weather that," Patrick said. "Our best estimates of operating costs are of the order of £220 per ton. It would be a hard couple of years, but it'll take a while to get everything in place and running, so we weren't expecting much in the way of revenue for a year or two anyway, and we should be ramping up right about the time you see prices start to climb again. Is it possible to get a copy of your copper price model?"

"I'll look into that," I promised. "I have to look at the agreements I have that relate to the model, if I can I will."

"Would you like to visit and take a look?" Patrick asked.

"I might just do that," I said. "What does your return model look like?"

"Here's our cash flow projections over the next twenty-five years," Patrick said. "You can see where we project going from using cash to throwing off cash and we've included the internal rate of return of the project, so expect a complete return on initial capital in five years."

"What assumptions did you use for your DCF model?" I asked.

"Those are listed here," George said, pushing a paper over the table to me. I looked through them and they seemed logical and reasonable.

"Have you run any sensitivity models?" I asked.

"What based on movements in price and cost elements?" George asked.

"Yes," I said.

"We have," George said. "This output here shows what happens with price shifts, and what also happens with shifts in fundamental costs of labour and materials."

"Tiffany, any questions?" I asked.

"What other metals are present?" she asked.

"There's the magnetite that we can probably extract and sell, using the same technology as they do at Palabora, probably also the vermiculite. There's also gold, silver, selenium, tellurium and the platinum group metals," George replied. "They come out in the anode slimes in the refinery tank house, we'd probably sell the anode slimes to a specialist recovery house."

"What about the political situation, how stable is it now?" she asked.

"Our best guess is that the South African government in its current form has another ten to fifteen years, then things will change," Patrick said.

"So, how much are we thinking about?" I asked.

"We started out with an initial share offering that we've used to cover the exploration costs, but what we're looking for now is a share issue of about £35,000,000 for the new subsidiary company, Klein Copper, to cover the actual start up costs," Patrick said. "Would you handle that?"

"When do you need an answer?" I asked.

"Tomorrow," Patrick laughed. "But, perhaps you should take a look first, January's not a bad time of year to go there."

"What would we do, fly into Jo'burg and drive?" I asked.

"Fly into Jo'burg," George said. "But, we'd fly you out to Kleinbegin."

"Well, I'm interested," I said. "If I may take your numbers, I'll run my own analyses and also we'll make a visit in January."

"That'd be terrific," Patrick said. "Look, can we buy you lunch?"

"That would be nice," I agreed.

We packed up and went to a local restaurant and got a table for six.

"Tiffany," George began. "Are you new to the bank as well?"

"I am," she confirmed. "I only started a couple of weeks ago."

"So, what have you seen so far?" he asked.

"The close of the merger between Metter and Corby Seaton, which was all construction machinery and some discussions in the sports ware business," she replied.

"So, mining's a little different," he commented.

"It is," she agreed. "I'm familiar a little with ore deposits, my sister is a geologist, working as a reservoir engineer for one of the North Sea oil people, my Dad is a professor of economic geology and my Mum is a structural geologist, they've all from time to time taken it upon themselves to enlighten me and probably also wonder why I didn't go into what was essentially the family business. I am also a jeweller, so keep a very close eye on precious metal prices so that I know when to buy."

"George used to work at a gold mine owned by Sable Mining," I told Tiffany. "It was one of the bigger ones in South Africa."

"Sorry, can't get you any gold at cost," George laughed. "I also spent some time at a diamond mine."

"I use some precious gems," Tiffany said. "But, mainly for commissioned pieces, I don't hold an inventory of cut stones, most of my work is simple metal pieces from gold, silver or platinum, plus some pieces with semi-precious stones like amethyst or garnet."

"She has a nice workshop," I added. "Plus a big safe."

"Did you ever catch up with the bloke you were looking for?" George asked.

"I did," I confirmed. "We got married later that year, but sadly he was killed in a traffic accident in Kenya early this year."

"Were you there on safari?" Patrick asked.

"No, we lived there," I said. "Ian was part of the British legation in Nairobi. And you George, are you still single?"

"No, happily married," he said. "Married to Anika, you might remember her, she was one of the bridesmaids at James and Charlize's wedding. We're living in Kleinbegin now, in one of the houses we've already built."

"When do you go back?" I asked.

"This weekend," he said. "Didn't want to spend Christmas away."

"So, if we decide to come out and see the site, who do we contact and when do we come?" I asked.

"Call me," Patrick said. "I'll give you all the details you need, just tell me when you're flying in and where, and we'll organise things from there."

On our way back to the office, Tiffany thanked me for taking her with me to the meeting.

"Safety in numbers," I laughed, half joking, without Dad with me, I really did feel more comfortable with her there.

"I feel that I should do more," she said.

"Well, when we have a prospect you could do background research and find out everything you can about the company and the principals," I suggested. "For sources, I'd start with the FT, then The Economist, then just cast around for trade journals, gossip columns, who knows where you might find something. Are you still on for Cannes this weekend?"

"Oh, rather," she said. "What do I need to do?"

"I'll pick you up at your flat at seven in the morning on Saturday," I said. "Bring your suitcase, we'll drive to Biggin Hill and get the plane and then fly to Le Bourget, clear customs and immigration there, then fly on down to Cannes. We should be in Cannes at about twelve-thirty to one. I'll call Maman from Le Bourget and ask her to pick us up at the airport."

"Super," Tiffany said.

"What about South Africa in January?" I asked.

"Gosh, yes," she said. "I've never been there, what would we need to take?"

"Some boots, trousers that you don't mind getting dusty, khaki shirt and a light jacket," I suggested. "I doubt that Kleinbegin is that formal a place. Why don't you get some shirts, shorts and trousers for us, all khaki and some light boots and some safety boots, we might need them? Rachel can give you my size. Get enough for about a week to ten days then we can take a safari while we're there."

"I'll take care of that," she said. "I'll also get us a couple of light matching khaki jackets and bush hats. If we visit companies and talk to them about mergers and such, can I buy shares in them?"

"Better be careful there," I said. "That can be seen as insider trading and can lead to prosecution. I'll let you know if it's safe for us to buy into any of the companies we'll be looking at. For instance, don't go out and buy shares in Sable Mining, we've seen information that is not yet public, so we are insiders."

"I see," she said. "I won't buy unless I talk to you first."

At the office there was a message for me, a reporter from the Financial Times wanted an interview. I called him and suggested that if he really wanted to talk to me, then the next morning at ten would be good. Then I went to talk to Dad.

"Why does the FT want to interview me?" I asked.

"Probably because they've heard that the Corby Metter deal was yours, and there aren't many women who are investment bankers," he said.

"What do I tell him?" I asked.

"Depends a lot on what he asks," Dad said. "He may want to talk about the deal, which you can handle just fine, but he may want to find out more about you, in which case you'll have to decide how much you want to tell. Personally, I've never wanted too much printed about me."

"I think I'd rather not say anything about myself or my personal life," I said.

"I would agree," he said. "But remember that there are sources that he could go to, like the college, people in the business, you are quite well known as a consultant and they must have heard of you."

"Well, I suppose I can confirm what is already public knowledge," I said.

"Be as non committal as you can," he advised. "Neither confirm nor deny, but throw things back as questions. So, what about Sable Mining?"

"Do you remember George, James's best man?" I asked.

"Of course," Dad said. "Is he with them?"

"He's the project manager for a new mine that Sable is starting up, Klein Copper," I said. "It's a big prospect, it'll mean an open pit mine, very similar to the one at Palabora. They have some infrastructure to put in, but the mine could be up and running in a year or so."

"So, should we fund it?" he asked.

"I'd like to go and take a look first," I said. "But my feeling is that it's a good investment, my only concern is political instability. The Sable Mining MD thinks they've got ten to fifteen years, which would be well past the payback period, so even if everything comes unglued, we would have got our money back twice or three times. If we go ahead and make the issue of the 35,000,000 shares at £1 each, then I think we should take 12.5% and float the rest. As far as I can tell, the project conforms to the Knotman criteria." That was a reference to some observations made by an American mineral economist, Arthur Knotman, who in the 1950s noted that two criteria needed to be met for a project to be viable, first that operating costs not exceed one-third of the sell price and second that the capital investment should be full recovered in four to five years. Failure to meet these two fundamentals had led to disasters around the world with failed mining projects. I had come across Knotman when I had been a fellow at my college working on a full funded study of the valuations of ore reserves, particularly as it related to tax policy.

"Okay," he said. "I'll leave it to you, just keep me informed."

"I'll do that Dad," I promised. "What do I wear when this FT reporter comes tomorrow?"

"Something dark and conservative," Dad suggested. "Give him the impression of business only, no sex, no flirting, no flashy watch or jewelry, just business. Smile and be polite, but stay at arms length and listen carefully to what he says and asks, my experience is that reporters will twist words, take snippets out of conversations and build whole stories about one word taken out of context. Yes and no answers are best, but sometimes you actually have to say more, so consider carefully what you do say."

"Maybe I should just invent a cold and beg off?" I suggested.

"Sorry, you're committed now, better to do it now and gain some experience so that when you have to do it again, you'll have a better idea of what to expect. If you finance Klein Copper, you'll have the FT, the trade journals all wanting the scoop and the Guardian and Private Eye wanting to know why you're indirectly supporting the racist South African government," he cautioned.

"Thanks a lot," I said.

"Don't worry," he assured me. "Even if you make a mess of things, they will always be someone else who will follow and steal the limelight."

The FT reporter duly arrived the following morning and after niceties about the weather, and getting some coffee, he started on his questions. It quickly became apparent that he did not really want to talk about the recent Corby Metter merger, but wanted to talk about women in the world of investment banking. I was reminded a few times of things that Portia had told me about being a successful lawyer in what was a man's world and the resentments and snide comments. The reporter I think was genuinely trying to get a sense of how I prepared myself for the business of investing, so I slowly dribbled things out as he revealed what he already knew about me. He had done his homework and knew what college I had been to, what degrees I had obtained, even that I had been in Kenya for a few years. He also had talked to quite a few of the clients I had had as a consultant and expressed surprise at some of them, not the least the Chancellor. Somehow he had also discovered that I was a pilot. He knew that Ian had died in Kenya and I gathered that he had actually managed to secure an interview with the High Commissioner. Well, he would have only nice things to say about me. The reporter tried to draw me out to say things about others in the business, but I was not going to be drawn into that. Anything I said could be, probably would be, taken out of context and quoted by men who were uneasy about a mere woman making inroads into what had been until now their private domain. After an hour or so of fencing, he finally said that he had what he wanted. I wished him good day and asked when something might be in print. He temporised at that and hid behind the editor, so I had no real idea when I might see my name in print. I was glad that was over and hoped that I had not made too much of a fool of myself. I should have called Freya before talking to the FT reporter and had her guide me through the process of granting an interview.

I called Patrick at Sable Mining and told him that we would like to visit the property in early January and asked him if he could set up a tour of the Palabora mine as well. He assured that me both were possible and we set a date for us to arrive in Johannesburg on the 7th of January, fly out to Kleinbegin that same day and return to Johannesburg and on to Phalaborwa on the 8th. We would take a tour of the Palabora mine on the 9th, then I told him we were going to take a side trip for a couple of days of game viewing in the area and would make our own way back to London. Patrick gave the name of the hotel where we would stay in Phalaborwa. That done I contacted a travel agent that I knew in London who organised trips in South Africa. I told them that I wanted a few days in the Kruger National Park. I asked them to get us a hire vehicle from Phalaborwa, then to book rest camps for us. They promised to call me back the next day with booking information. Finally I called British Airways and made bookings for us to Johannesburg and back from Phalaborwa.

The Corby Metter deal done, the Winter & Winter rights issue on the street, the interview done, I was essentially free until the New Year and the potential rights issue for Sable Mining, so was looking forward to my trip to Cannes. I checked the weather and it looked as if it would be reasonable for the trip south. So, I shut up shop early on Friday and told the rest of the staff to enjoy their Christmas holiday. Dad had already left for the Caribbean and would not be back before the New Year. I collected Tiffany on Saturday morning, we had decided that leaving my Land Rover at Biggin Hill was probably less risky than leaving the car. I gave her a present, a pair of Aviator sunglasses, which she was delighted with and wore, even though it was still the morning twilight. At the airport, I borrowed a tractor and towed my plane out of the hangar and Tiffany drove my Land Rover and parked it in the plane's spot. Then we loaded up our bags, towed the plane to the fuelling point, filled up, and then started on the pre-flight checks. All done, I got clearance from the tower and took off for Le Bourget. That would take us just over an hour.

Once we had settled down to a nice cruising speed I told Tiffany to take the controls.

"Use the yoke here to keep this pointer lined up on this one," I told her. "That's the direction we're going. Try pushing forward a little and you'll see that we start to go down, then pull back a bit and bring us back to this number, which is our altitude."

"Okay," she said, a little nervously. She tentatively tried things and soon got the hang of descending and climbing. Then I went through with her gentle turns, so that we were taking a wavy path to Le Bourget. As we approached I took over the controls and chatted to the ground controllers, then took us down into Le Bourget. On the ground a car met us and indicated that we should follow it. We did and when we stopped the immigration and customs man was there. We got out of the plane, presented our passports, then asked for the loo and where we might get fuel and coffee. He was most helpful and directed us to one of the fixed base operators who would be happy to sell us fuel and give us coffee, and it turned out a croissant each. Back in the air, we had a longer run down to Cannes, some two and a half hours. On that leg I went through all the controls and instruments with Tiffany, tapping on each in turn and describing its function. I was surprised at how quickly she picked things up and after about an hour into the flight, if I tapped on an item she could tell me what it was and what it did or indicated. I let her handle the controls for most of the way only taking over when we began our approach into Cannes.

Maman and Portia were there to meet us, and after I had parked the plane on the grass and tied it down, we left for the drive up the hills to their villa.

"Good flight Bébé?" Maman asked, looking at me and at Tiffany and probably wondering why Tom was not there.

"Good flight," I confirmed. "The weather cooperated for once and we had a clear run down. I even got Tiffany to take the controls for a while, so had a nice lazy run down."

"Tiffany, welcome, how are you?" Maman asked.

"Super, thanks," she replied. "I think I may take up flying after today."

"And how are you two?" I asked Maman and Portia.

"We're doing very well," Maman replied. "We've a surprise for you, James and Charlize decided to pay us a visit as well, so if you don't mind we'll put you two in together, is that okay?"

"Of course, Maman, Tiffany?" I asked.

"Of course, I'd be delighted to share with Fiona," she said. I was not sure what to make of that, but let it go at that.

"How long are James and Charlize staying?" I asked.

"Until after the New Year," Maman replied. "And you?"

"We need to go back to London on the 27th," I said. "We've got a trip to South Africa to organise to visit a mine site that we might fund."

"So, Tiffany, how are you enjoying this high finance?" Portia asked.

"It's brilliant," she replied. "I'm learning so much."

"Well, don't let Fiona work you too hard," Portia cautioned.

"I don't think she could," Tiffany said.

"Your family didn't want you to spend Christmas with them?" Maman asked.

"No, my parents are off to Norway to see the Aurora Borealis, and my sister and her husband are chasing the sunshine in Portugal on a delayed honeymoon, so they didn't want me tagging along," Tiffany explained.

When we got to the villa Charlize came out first, carrying Fiona.

"Charlie," I said. "Lovely to see you, how are you how's Fiona?"

"We're doing just fine," she said. "And you?"

"I'm fine," I said. "Charlie, this is Tiffany, she works with me, drives for me and is learning the financial trade."

"Nice to meet you, Tiffany," Charlize said. "James is on the phone trying to sort out some issues with glass, we need a lot more bottles than we had, so he's trying to buy more. Come on in."

We followed her in and Maman set about putting together a late lunch for Tiffany and me. Portia showed us to the room we would be sharing, it was the one that I had used when Tiffany and I had stayed there before. I dumped my bag on one of the beds and left Tiffany talking to Portia and went out to talk to Maman.

"What happened?" she asked.

"There was another woman," I said. "I came back early from the States and thought I'd surprise him. Well, I did, I knocked on his door and this woman, barely dressed, answered it and all he could say was, oh shit. That did it for me, I left, I've spoken to him once on the phone since when he told me that I was too controlling, wanted to be too independent and that things wouldn't work. So, I'm angry, mainly with myself for diving into things too quickly. I imagined I was head over heels, which I suppose I was, or at least thought I was, but, now, I don't know."

"Never mind Bébé," Maman said. "I would never have guessed that he didn't love you, I thought that he was smitten."

"So did I," I bemoaned. "What the hell do I do now?"

"Take your time, enjoy life, explore, try new things," Maman said.

"It's interesting how history repeats itself," I commented.

"How do you mean?" Maman asked.

"Well, Dad went off with Felicity the floozie, Portia's husband left, Tom decided that Roberta Spinoglio was less independent than me and picked her over me and Tiffany's Alex cheated on her too," I explained.

"These things happen in life," Maman said.

"What I can't still get over is that I thought that he loved me, how could he just dump me for Roberta?" I asked.

"I can't answer that," she said. "I was taken in as well, I thought that he loved you and thought that he was a nice man, could we both have been wrong?"

"Maybe," I said. "It rankles, it hurts, it's annoying and I'm not sure if I'm more angry with him or myself."

"Don't be angry with yourself," she said. "You're not the one who strayed he is, what's this Roberta like?"

"She's an American, she's a grad student, tallish, blonde, boobs, legs, the whole thing," I replied. "I met her once before at a hall dinner I went to at Trinity, I should have suspected something then because she was hanging onto every word that Tom said. But I was blind, all I saw was Tom and what he meant to me."

"Well, as I said, take your time, don't condemn all men, there is one out there for you, experiment, try new things, just be careful not to become too deeply involved with someone before you really know them," she said.

"One thing that did bother me, was that I found myself making comparisons to Ian," I said. "I know it's unfair, but I couldn't help doing it, how do I get over that?"

"Probably at a deep level, never," she said. "In time the comparisons will fade, but Ian was your first real love and you lost him not because there was someone else, but because he died, I think that's different."

"Fi," James said interrupting us. "How are you?"

"I'm okay, I saw your friend George the other day," I replied.

"What's George up to?" he asked.

"He's the project manager for a new copper mine near a place called Kleinbegin in the northern Cape," I said. "Did you know he married Anika?"

"He did?" James said. "I wondered, but didn't know that they'd actually got married. What's the story with you, where's Tom?"

"I caught the bastard with another woman," I said. "So, he's history."

"Oh, sorry to hear that," James said. "How are you doing?"

"I'm pissed, mostly at myself for jumping in to something serious too quickly, I should have waited," I said.

"You'll be fine," he promised. "Look at Maman, she's happy."

"How's the winery doing?" I asked.

"Really well," he said. "We had a good harvest, all indications are that it was a really good vintage, so it'll be a good year. We just need more glass, so I'm on a buying spree."

"And New Mexico?" I asked.

"I like living there," he said. "It's wide open spaces, nice people, lots of wild animals, snow on the peaks already, with more forecast. Might take up skiing, there's a resort not far from Pecos. So George is in the northern Cape, *die gat van die wêreld?*"

"I looked Kleinbegin up on a map," I said. "It's between Upington and Prieska, it's on the railway line that runs from De Aar to Upington."

"So what's the next step?" he asked.

"I'm going out there in January to look the place over and decide whether or not to invest," I said.

"Well, I always thought that George would make a good manager," James said. "So, I'd be more comfortable with him running the place than someone I didn't know. So, who's Tiffany?"

"I took her on as a driver, but I'm using her more as an assistant now, she's a good driver, but she's got hidden talents, she's really very bright and picks up things very quickly, she's also a jeweller, makes really nice pieces," I said.

"Are you talking about me?" Tiffany asked, as she joined us.

"I was just telling James that you're more of an assistant than just a driver," I explained.

245

"What's she like to work for?" James asked. "I'll bet she's demanding."

"I don't think so," Tiffany said. "I've enjoyed the job since I joined the bank and I've learned so much already."

"Wait 'til she says, what is that you don't understand, it's so simple," James joked. "I used to get that a lot when we were growing up."

"That's because you were being deliberately dense," I countered.

"Now, you two," Maman cautioned. "No squabbles. Bébé, Tiffany, I have some lunch for you."

Noël

After lunch I asked James if he had received the parcel I had sent them. "Yes, we brought it with us," he said. "We thought it was probably Christmas presents."

"Good," I said. "I didn't want to have to go running around Cannes looking for last minute gifts for you."

"What should we get Tiffany?" he asked. "I thought you might be bringing Tom, so we brought a new belt and spurs for him."

"I doubt that Tiffany would like those," I said. "She's a jeweller, she likes fast cars, she's a linguist, I'm not sure what you might get her."

"What are you giving her?" he asked.

"Flying lessons," I said. "I got her a full course of lessons to lead to a licence. I was pretty sure that she'd like it, and after our trip down here, I'm certain of it."

"Maybe we could get her a sheepskin flying jacket?" he suggested.

"I think that would do down very well," I thought. "If you like we could drive into Cannes and visit the airport, there's a flying school there and I'll bet they have a shop."

"Great idea," he said. "So, what's the story with Tom?"

"I went to his room in Cambridge and there was another woman there, and all he could say was, oh shit, so I left," I repeated.

"Why do you think?" James asked.

"He said I was too controlling, he also said that he felt I was comparing him to Ian," I replied.

"Were you?" James asked.

"If I'm really honest with myself, then yes, I was, I tried not to, but there were times when my mind drifted and those comparisons were made," I said. "I was also reluctant to get into bed with him, something I would guess that Roberta had no qualms about."

"So, what's it going to take in a bloke not to be compared to Ian?" James asked.

"Good question," I said. "I've actually no idea, I should probably talk to the other Tom, Irene's husband and ask him how he managed and did he compare his dead first wife to Irene."

"Good idea, look, would you come with me into town to see if we can get a jacket for Tiffany?" he asked.

"Of course," I agreed. James went and told everyone else that we were going on an errand and would be back shortly, then we borrowed Maman's car and, after a brief squabble about who would drive, went into town, with James at the wheel. The flight school did have jackets, so we picked one out and paid for it. They had no fancy wrapping available but did have a box, so all James had to do was find the paper to cover the box and he would have his present.

"So, how's the winery doing?" I asked as we drove back up the hills to the villa. He gave me a report on the harvest, the vintage they had just made and the number of bottles they had put up, in summary it was doing well.

"Mission accomplished?" Maman asked when we returned.

"It was," James confirmed. "I needed a Christmas present for Tiffany, I had half expected Fi to show up with Tom, so came prepared for that."

"Your father called, Fi, he asked that you return his call, here's the number," Maman said. I looked at the time and worked out that it would be about nine in the morning in the Caribbean.

"Hello," Dad said, when he answered the telephone.

"Hello Dad," I said. "I'm returning your call."

"Good, here's the thing Fi, I've decided to retire now, I'm not coming back to the UK, so I've resigned from the bank effective today and you're the Chairman, chairwoman or whatever you want to call it, effective today. I've called all the current board members explaining what I've done and asking for their resignations as well, so that you can form your own board. Also, as of today you and James each have half of the shares of the bank, and there will be no tax consequences for that provided that I live for another seven years. Would you put my flat on the market for me and also pack up everything and ship it out here, you have the address?"

"What about Gabriela?" I asked, referring to the live in maid that Dad and Felicity employed.

"I've called her and told her the situation," he said. "I've provided her with a package that'll keep her going until she finds another position."

"Why did you decide to pull things forward?" I asked.

"You know, we got here and I was thinking that you can manage things well without me, and there was really no need for me to just hang on, so decided to hell with it and make the move now," he replied.

"What does Felicity think about this?" I asked.

"She's carping a little about being cut off from her friends without a proper goodbye, but she'll get over it," he said. "She's thrilled with the house here and the boat and happy that I'm not in the office all hours of the day and night."

"Okay," I said. "I'll take care of the flat for you, you're sure you don't want to keep it in case you travel back here for any reason?"

"No, I'll make it a clean break," he said. "Where's James, do you know?"

"He's here," I said. "Do you want to talk to him?"

"Please," Dad said. I handed the telephone over to James and left him to his conversation. Maman looked at me questioningly.

"I'm the chair of Thames Cherwell as of today," I explained. "Dad decided not to wait, so he's pulled everything forward. So, now I need a new board. Do you know where Portia is?"

"On the terrace with Tiffany and Charlize," Maman replied.

I went out and joined the others.

"So, Fi, what did your Dad want?" Portia asked.

"He's resigned as of today, so today I take over as chair of the bank," I said. "Did you consider my request?"

"I did, and I'd be happy to serve," Portia said.

"Thank you," I said. "When I can get the attention of the other shareholder we'll have an impromptu meeting and elect at least one non executive director."

"Congratulations, Fi," Charlize said.

"What does it mean?" Tiffany asked.

"Well, it means that she's the boss, the chair of the board, the ruler of the roost," Charlize said.

"So, Mr Barclay is not coming back?" Tiffany asked.

"No," I confirmed. "He decided to just stay in the Caribbean. So, I've got some work to do when we go back after Christmas."

"Have you any other board members in mind?" Portia asked.

"I'll have to have James, he does have half the shares, then I was thinking of Rachel and I need to think about others," I said.

"How many do you have to have?" Charlize asked.

"The bye-laws state seven," I said. "So, me, James, Portia, Rachel and three others yet to be named."

"Someone mention my name?" James asked, as he joined us.

"I was just saying that you should be a board member of the bank and that we need to elect non executive directors," I explained.

"Anyone in mind?" he asked.

"I thought Portia and Rachel to start," I replied. "Then, I'll need three others, any thoughts?"

"I'll think about it," he promised. "How often do you plan to have board meetings?"

"Once a quarter is probably enough," I thought. "But, if there are items that require board approval, we can always have a telephonic meeting."

"Great, just remember that New Mexico is seven hours behind the UK, so don't schedule meetings for the morning," he said.

"I won't," I promised. "So, James, first order of business, how do you vote on Portia and Rachel?"

"Aye for both," he said. "So, what does that give us, law, fashion, booze with me, what else do you want?"

"I was thinking of construction, transportation and agriculture," I said.

"Sounds good," he agreed. "Let me know as soon as you've identified who you want. If I have a real problem I'll let you know."

"I think a glass of wine is in order to celebrate," I said. "I'll be back."

I brought out wine and glasses and Maman joined us.

"Well, here's to success," I toasted.

"Success," they all echoed.

"Excuse me," Charlize said. "Fiona's awake, I'd better go and see how she is."

"I wonder what made Dad decide to move his retirement up?" I said. "Is there something he isn't telling us?"

"He told me a little more than I think he told you," James said. "He said he had been planning to see how you did at the bank before he pulled out, but he's been amazed at the deals you've put together already and he thinks you can manage without him."

"All the same, I'd like to take a closer look at the balance sheet," I thought.

"Probably be a good idea, but I really don't think Dad's pulling a fast one here," James said.

"What bothers me is that he said he's not coming back to the UK any time soon," I said. "Why? Am I just being paranoid?"

"No, you're just being cautious," James said.

"I'm thinking we should have a board meeting early in January, when do you go back to Pecos?" I asked.

"Saturday the 5th," he replied.

"Can you come over to London for a board meeting on the 3rd?" I asked.

"I could do that," he agreed.

"Thanks," I said. "I want to get things moving and start with a new board as soon as I can."

"It's funny, I have no qualms about the bank, but it's a pity I was not more cautious where Tom was concerned," I lamented.

"You weren't alone," Maman said. "I thought he was genuine as well."

"Well, he's history now," I said. "So, do you have anything planned for the next few days that we need to do?"

"No, just dinner on Christmas Eve, Tiffany did Fiona ask you to bring something nice to wear, we traditionally have dressed up for dinner then?" Maman asked.

"She did," Tiffany confirmed. "I brought something that I think is nice."

"I'm sure it will be," Maman said. "Portia, Dear, would you give me a hand in the kitchen?"

"Of course," Portia said. They left, and James then left to see if there was anything he could help Charlize with, leaving just Tiffany and myself.

"Fiona, what does this promotion of yours mean for me?" she asked.

"Nothing changes," I told her. "I was already the MD, now I just run the board as well. I may need you more than ever to watch my back for me, it has been known for bankers to be kidnapped and held for ransom."

"I'll make sure that never happens," she said fiercely. "So, does being the Chairman mean that you can do what you want?"

"In some ways yes, but there are limits," I said. "That's why we have a board, I would be foolish to go ahead with something if the other members of the board all voted against it. If anything went wrong, then I'd be more at risk than the bank."

"So, do we still go to South Africa in January?" she asked.

"We do," I confirmed. "It's a big project and there's a lot at stake, so before we agreed to finance it we need to take a look."

"I didn't bring anything for your brother and Charlize," she said.

"It's last minute, but why don't you and I go shopping on Monday," I suggested. "I know it's Christmas Eve, but the shops will be open and I'm sure we'll find something, I'll help you."

"Thanks," she said.

Maman called us to dinner, which was as usual excellent and we lingered over coffee and drinks talking about fashion, politics, wine, cars, you name it. Finally I had had enough and announced that I was going to bed. I went off and Tiffany came right after me.

"Do you want to shower first?" I asked her.

"No, please, go ahead," she said. I stripped off and showered, glad to feel clean and rosy again.

"Do you mind if I shower while you dry off?" she asked.

"No, go ahead," I said. She stripped off and got under the shower. I stole a look at her and had to admire what I saw. I suppose it was the kendo and the karate, but she was probably the most muscular woman I had ever seen, not in the sense of body builders who pump up before a competition, but just for sheer definition. She really did have a beautiful body and I could not drag my eyes away. She saw me looking and smiled then spun around so that I could get the whole view.

"You're in amazing shape," I said.

"I like to keep trim," she said. "I run, the kendo helps, I do yoga and I sometimes use weights. As someone once told me, look after your body because where else are you going to live?"

"I'd never thought of it that way," I admitted. "So, are you on for a run tomorrow morning?"

"That would be super," she said.

We both retired to bed, and I noted that she wore no pyjamas or night gowns. I had on a pair of panties and a short night gown top, but she just did not bother with anything. I lay trying to go to sleep, but images of Tiffany kept popping into my head. I was feeling things that I had never thought possible and tried to dismiss my thoughts as just musings about a beautiful woman, rather in the way that one can admire a famous painting of sculpture. But, that did not really work, she was alive, alive in a way that I had not noticed before and it was disturbing. I awoke first the next morning, and got up and dressed for a run. Tiffany was still sleeping and she had thrown much of the blankets off revealing her back, buttocks and legs. Part of me wanted to reach out and touch and caress, to run my hands down the curves that were there, but I recoiled in guilt, what was I thinking. I tapped her on the shoulder and she awoke, turned over a smiled at me.

"Morning, Fiona," she said. "What time is it?"

"Seven-thirty," I replied. "Are you still up for a run?"

"Give me five minutes," she said. She slid out of bed and rummaged through her bag and had clothes on in under five minutes. "Are we ready?" she asked.

I led the way out of the villa and its gardens and off away along the ridge and down the hill. I had done this many times before and had a route that I followed. Tiffany was right at my shoulder all the way and when I turned around to go back, she took the lead. She must have been really paying attention when we came out, because she knew which turns to take where and led us back to the villa. I discovered something that I had begun to suspect, I had been leading an indolent lifestyle and was letting myself get out of condition. Tiffany arrived back a good minute before I did and I confess I was fairly winded, and she, well, she was grinning and looked to be hardly out of breath.

"That was super," she said. "Are you okay?"

"I'm fine," I lied. "I've discovered here that I've been lazy lately and have been letting myself go. When we get back to London I need to be more disciplined with exercise."

"I can help if you like," she suggested. "I could stop by your flat and we could run together."

"That may be the only way I'm sure to do it," I admitted.

"Are you two ready for breakfast?" Maman asked as we went into the house.

"Give us about ten minutes to shower and change," I said. "Do you want to go first Tiffany?"

"Thanks," she said. "I won't be long." I sat on the bed and realised that I was going to ache the next day, but it was my own fault, I had neglected my exercise and become lazy, so now would pay the price for that. Tiffany came through drying herself off, and dropped the towel while she picked out clothes to wear. I stole another glance at her then fled to the shower confused, embarrassed, conflicted and intrigued. I was having emotions that were new to me and I was unsure what to do. Well, this was the kind of thing I would usually talk to Maman about, so I would try and get some time with her alone and talk about Tom and Tiffany.

That opportunity came later in the day when Portia took Tiffany, James and Charlize for a drive to the beach. Maman had volunteered to watch Fiona for an hour so I had the chance to talk to her.

"So, Bébé, what do you think happened with Tom?" she asked, direct as ever.

"I'm not sure," I said. "I know what he told me, that I was too bossy, that I wanted things my way and that he didn't see me wanting to go with him to the States. Oh, and that he felt that I was always comparing him to Ian."

"And were you?" Maman asked.

"As I look back, yes I was," I said. "I tried not to, but the thoughts kept coming, how would Ian do this, what would Ian think about this?"

"That's to be expected," she said. "It wasn't that long ago that he died."

"I also think that Tom was expecting me to jump into bed with him after the first date or two," I said. "I suspect that Roberta was far more willing to be a ready bedmate that I was."

"There's a certain logic to that," Maman commented. "So, I'm to gather from that that has been no sex with Tom?"

"No," I confirmed. "I just wasn't ready."

"How are you managing now?" she asked.

"I'm mostly annoyed with myself for latching onto the first handsome face that smiled at me," I said. "He was, is, very charming, he's funny, he's actually got a wicked sense of humour, he's obviously smart, but, I must have been lacking in something."

"So, what now?" she asked.

"Well, I'm having disturbing notions about Tiffany," I said.

"What do you mean?" Maman asked.

"Well, I saw her in the shower last night, and she's got this body that I think anyone would lust after, I kept looking at her, but when I did I felt guilty, guilty over looking, guilty about wanting to look more and guilty about the emotions that were stirring," I explained.

"I understand," Maman said. "The first time that happened to me with Portia, I didn't know what to do. I kept telling myself that it wasn't real, that it was just a reaction to the divorce and that I was looking for anything not related to your Dad or men in general."

"When did you realise that you feelings for Portia were real?" I asked.
"That took a little while," she said. "I think it might have been one time when Portia and I were having a conversation and we both blurted out things at the same time, after that it was easy."
"So, what do I do?" I asked.
"What do you want to do?" she countered.
"I've no idea," I admitted.
"In that case, take your time, don't rush things, don't do anything until you're sure of your own feelings and don't lead Tiffany on," Maman said.
"I'm half afraid that's it just a reaction to the rejection by Tom, you know, I'll show you, I'll go off with this beautiful woman and we'll be happy and you'll regret not staying with me," I said.
"That's why you shouldn't do anything precipitous," she said. "You need to be certain that whatever you do, with Tiffany, with another man, is not just to get back at Tom. My guess is that he wouldn't care, he's already got another woman and they've obviously moved beyond where you were."
"You're right," I agreed. "There's a complication."
"What?" she asked.
"Well, Tom and his sister have the ranch in New Mexico, but there were three other heirs who wanted their share in the form of money," I said.
"Well, the ranch would have had to be broken up and part of it sold to raise the money to pay off the other heirs, so I went ahead and bought out their interest thinking romantically that I would give it to Tom and Linda as a gift when we got married."
"So, now you have a beneficial ownership of something that I presume you really don't want?" Maman asked.
"That's about the size of it," I agreed.
"Do you get on with the sister?" Maman asked.
"I liked her," I said.
"Why don't you call her and discuss it with her?" Maman asked.
"I'm almost afraid to," I confessed. "I'm embarrassed by my actions, it was presumptuous on my part, it's put them, Linda and Tom, in an awkward situation of having at some point to deal with me, whether they like it or not, and if I were vindictive then I could exercise my right and demand my share of the ranch in cash, but that would destroy the ranch, destroy the lives of people, for what?"
"Call her," Mama instructed. "What's the time there now?"
"Seven in the morning," I said. "Is that too early?"

255

"For someone into ranching or farming, I doubt it," Maman said.

I called Linda. Hillary actually answered the telephone and handed it over to her mother.

"Linda, so sorry to bother you so early in the morning, this is Fiona Barclay," I said.

"Fiona, lovely to hear from you, what's up," she said.

"Well, I'm afraid that Tom and I are no more," I said. "He's with Roberta now, she's from Denver and is also at Cambridge."

"I'm so sorry," Linda said. "I've heard from Tom, and he did mention that he was with a Roberta, in fact he's in Denver right now with this Roberta, we'll get to meet her when they come down here for a few days after Christmas. I'm a little disappointed it didn't work out with you and Tom, but he does like things his way, sad to say this isn't the first time he's done something like this, especially after Juanita, but I really thought that this time he'd departed from his norm and that you two were set for each other."

"So did I," I said. "But, that's life. Look Linda I've created a problem with the ranch."

"How so?" she asked.

"Well, I bought the interests of the other three heirs, so technically I own half the ranch," I explained. "I was driven by this romantic notion to take the interest in the ranch and then give it to Tom as a wedding gift."

"And that's not going to happen now, is it?" Linda said.

"No," I agreed.

"So, do you want us to pay you out?" Linda asked.

"Not immediately," I said. "I'm in no hurry, I've no desire to see your ranch broken up, but I'm damned if I'm going to give any part of it to Tom. What if you pay me out, principal only, no interest to accrue, over thirty years?"

"How much would that be?" she asked.

"$76,000 a year," I said. "Or I could extend the term to forty years if you want, that would be $57,000?"

"That would be better, we can manage $57,000 a year, what I may also do is take out a term life insurance for the full amount, so that if I die before it's paid off, then it'll get settled from the insurance and the girls won't have to worry about it," Linda said. "I think what I'd do is put that portion in the name of the kids, so that in time they have half of the ranch between them in their own right, and then they'd have my quarter, leaving Tom's quarter or whoever his heirs may be. Then the girls would have a majority ownership of the ranch."

"Are you sure that's not a problem?" I asked.

"It's unexpected, but we can manage that," she said. "You're sure you don't want interest as well?"

"The interest on the total principal would be ruinous for you," I said. "I've no desire to make you pay for my stupidity and romantic notions."

"I'll figure it out," she said. "Does Tom know you own half the ranch?"

"No," I said. "I floated the idea of a land bank, but then I got all romantic and bought the half myself from the three other heirs. When I was going to tell him was when I met Roberta half naked at Tom's room, so was in no mood for any discussion."

"I can understand that," she said. "Sorry to ask this, but I have to know, is there any possibility of another heir?"

"No, we never had sex, so if there is another heir it will come from Roberta," I said.

"I'll have to follow that," she sighed. "If you have an agreement that I could sign, I'd be happy to, then we can start transferring ownership to the girls."

"I'll have my lawyer in the States come and see you," I said.

"If you're ever here, we'd love to see you again," she said. "Just call first to make sure that Tom and Roberta, or whoever it is at the time, are not here."

"Thanks Linda, and thanks for understanding," I said.

"That's fine," she said. "This is a lot more doable than having to sell off half the ranch."

"Sorry to drop this on you at this time of the year. Have a happy Christmas," I said.

"You too," she said.

"All set?" Maman asked when I joined her and Fiona on the terrace.

"All set," I said. "Linda knew that I was history, so she said she understood about my wanting to be paid out for my share of the ranch, so we came to an agreement. I'll get my lawyer in the States to go and see her in the New Year. How could I have been so stupid?"

"Love makes one do funny things," Maman said. "On the face of it, it wasn't so stupid, it was very generous and a really romantic gesture. It just went wrong when he behaved like a toad."

"Dad asked me to sell his flat, I was wondering whether I should buy it?" I said.

"Is it nice, is it located somewhere with good resale values?" she asked.

"It is, but it's a little bigger than I would need," I thought.

"If I were you, I wouldn't," she said. "Better to just put it on the market and keep your own place."

"Something's nagging at me too about the bank," I said. "Why would Dad not want to come back to England, is he trying to run away from something that he set up at the bank that he's afraid will come out now and cause problems?"

"Your Dad has been known to do things on the spur of the moment," Maman said. "It's possible that he did something at the bank that is not quite ethical, but I doubt that he did anything illegal."

"Well, I'm going to pay for a complete audit of the books when I get back," I said. "I don't want to have something crop up that I don't know about."

"Well, enough about banks and ranches, the others are back, let's see where they went and what they did," she said.

We heard about the trip from each of them in their own way. Tiffany and Charlize seemed to have hit it off well and were talking about featuring some of Tiffany's jewellery at the winery tasting room. I told James and Portia, as non executive directors that I was going to have a complete audit of the bank's finances done as soon as I got back. They were pleased to hear it and just asked to be informed of anything that arose that would be concerning. Dinner that night was a Charlize creation, typically South African, with wines from the Cillie wineries. The next day, Christmas Eve, I went shopping with Tiffany. We hunted around town until we found things that we both agreed would be liked by James and Charlize and that would not break the bank of Tiffany.

Christmas Eve dinner was always an event at Maman's house. It was a tradition with her that we all dressed up. We did her proud, all of us, even Fiona, who was dressed up early, then taken off to bed before the main festivities. Tiffany had taken my advice and brought a nice dress with her. I was a beautiful deep blue, it was a halter top, sleeves, leaving the back bare down to her waist. It was the kind of dress that if she had worn it to a restaurant or bar, it would have stopped conversation for a minute or two, while people just stared. I thought back to earlier days and remembered the first Christmas I had spent with Ian, before he went back to Tanzania and the Olduvai Gorge. Then it had snowed and James and Charlize had spent time building a snowman and sledging. Then there had been a hiatus of a couple of years because both Ian and I thought that the other had dumped them because we neither of us had received letters from the other, all due to the intervention of a third party who had had designs upon Ian. When we had finally reconnected we had married and spent Christmas with James and Charlize in France before going off to Kenya. Then there had been a few magical Christmases in Kenya before Ian had died. Now, I was together again with the rest of the family and I was wondering what might come next in my life. I suppose I was lost in thought because I had to be brought back to the present to join in the toast that Maman was making. She wished us all well in the New Year and thanked us all for making the trip to Cannes. For James and Charlize that was a much longer trip than for me and Tiffany. All we had to do was fly over the Channel and then south, whereas James and Charlize had to fly to a major airport where Air France flew.

James then proposed a toast to the new Chairman of Thames Cherwell and he wondered what in fact I should be called. Chairman did not sound right, perhaps Chairwoman, Board Chair, Chairperson, finally he decided upon The Boss, which made us all laugh. But, it was something I needed to consider, how did I style myself on business cards, Managing Director was sex neutral, but Chairman definitely suggested a man. I suppose all the titles and honourifics in the business world had developed in a society that was male dominated, so why would anyone consider what to call a woman in that job. Political offices were easy, Member or Parliament, Minister, Prime Minister could be used by either sex, but I suppose the issue also showed itself with things like the New Years Honours list. Order or Member of the British Empire could be anyone, but what about knighthoods. One could hardly have Sir Fiona Barclay, which is where I suppose Dame Fiona Barclay would come in, but somehow Dame Fiona did not have the social cachet as Sir John. But, I was getting far ahead of myself, to even imagine any of the classic British honours being conferred upon me, something I assumed that was reserved for long serving civil servants, pop stars and business people who had contributed to the campaigns of various and sundry politicians, or was that being too cynical?

We all retired to bed late and slept in the next morning, except Fiona who was driven by her own clock and not an artificial one. I felt sorry for Charlize, she had to be up and attending to Fiona, come what may, and late nights were not the concern of an infant. After a late breakfast, or early lunch, we got down to the serious business of exchanging gifts. I believe that I made a real hit with Tiffany when I explained the gift voucher to her, all the lessons necessary to get a PPL, private pilot's licence, air time included. We all were thrilled with our gifts, except perhaps Fiona, who was more focused in the basics of life and who was too young yet to grasp the significance of presents and Christmas presents in particular. We spent the balance of the day being lazy and watching the drizzle that was coming down. I wished it would rain and get it over with, or just clear up. That was one of the things that I had really liked about Kenya, when it rained, it rained, it did not mess about like it did in Europe, with mist, drizzle and rain, then sleet or snow. Rain was good, but drizzle was just depressing.

Boxing Day the sun shone, so it was a day to be spent outside. I had steeled myself for another run and had had to endure defeat yet again when Tiffany left me in the dust. One day I would catch her and be able to keep up, but clearly that was going to take a little work on my part. I was delighted that Tiffany got on so well with the rest of the family, I did not have to worry about her feeling left out or excluded in any way. She got an invitation to visit Pecos and she asked me when it might be convenient for her to take her holidays. We did close the bank down for two weeks in August, along with the rest of Europe, so perhaps that was the best time for her to go. Travel to the States was still quite expensive, but perhaps there was a way I could send her on an errand or fact finding mission and therefore pay for the ticket. I spent some time on my own mulling over who I would invite to join the board of Thames

Cherwell. I decided that I would approach Andrew McIntosh and George Adams who had been non executive directors under Dad's regime, and ask them to stay on. That would give me a chartered accountant and a property developer. My final choice was Pierre Garnier, the finance director of a French Airline who I had done work for as a consultant. Those plus the ones I had already decided upon would give me a diverse board, not all men, and not all living in England, so would have different perspectives on things. I noticed that Tiffany had James corralled and from the odd bits I heard she was grilling him about mining methods and the size and type of equipment that might be needed for Klein Copper. She was obviously taking her new rôle as my assistant seriously.

Early in the morning of the 27th Tiffany and I said our goodbyes to the family and Maman drove us down to the airport. I filed a flight plan for Biggin Hill, via Le Bourget, then looked for alternates around London. The weather reports were of fog from the south coast up towards London and I had no idea what conditions would be like when we got there. We said goodbye to Mama then flew up to Le Bourget, clearing French immigration there, taking on more fuel and getting ourselves some coffee and croissants. I also checked the weather again and there was a problem. Fog had rolled in from the south coast and blanketed Biggin Hill, Gatwick and surrounds. I looked at alternates and decided that the best course of action was to file an IFR, instrument flight rules, flight plan to Southend. The weather reports showed light fog over Southend with minimums at about two hundred feet. That was far better than Biggin Hill where the fog was down to the deck and the runway closed. I looked at Northolt as an alternate, but that was also closed, so Southend it was. It meant that we were going to have to talk to the air traffic controllers all the way, once we hit British air space. I filed the plan, and we took off for the Channel. Once we were picked up by British air traffic control we were routed around Kent, across the Thames estuary and then into the landing pattern at Southend. They had been right, we broke through the low clouds and fog at about two hundred feet above the runway, but when we did, there it was stretched out in front of us, lit, clear and welcoming. We landed and taxied over to the hard stand used by general aviation where a chap came scurrying out to see if we needed help.

"Afternoon," he said. "Gareth's the name, are you needing fuel, ground transportation or anything else?"

"Good afternoon Gareth," I said. "We'll just tie the plane down, then a taxi to the Upminster Tube station would be appreciated."

"I can fix that, if you'll just check at the office for landing fees, I'll call up a taxi," he said. "Where are you inbound from?"

"Le Bourget," I said. "We'll need to clear customs."

"Just over there," he said. "I've got a trolley here, let's put your bags on it and go and see him."

Customs was a formality, he wanted to know about wine, and we had our permitted two bottles each and that was it. Gareth got us a taxi and I told him, that depending on the weather that I might be back that weekend to collect my plane and fly it back to Biggin Hill.

"Just ask for me when you come," he said. "I'll see you right." He then pushed the trolley out to the kerb to the waiting taxi. I tipped him and thanked him, then got the taxi driver to take us to the Upminster Tube station. From there we could get a District line train that would take us to Sloane Square.

"So, what did you think about today's adventure?" I asked Tiffany when we were on the Tube train.

"So much to think about," she said.

"Do you still want to go for your PPL?" I asked.

"Oh, absolutely," she said. "There's just more to learn. Are you going to the office tomorrow?"

"I need to," I said. "After Dad dropped his bombshell, there's things I need to do."

"I'll be there at eight," she said. "I want to dig into Sable Mining and also see if there's anything out there about Klein Copper, I might also talk to my dad about the kind of deposit that Klein Copper is likely to be."

"Good idea," I said. The train rumbled on and eventually dived under the street and became a true underground train. Out in the hinterlands it ran on the surface only going underground at Bow Road. Thereafter it was essentially a cut and cover line, running much of the way under roads.

At Sloane Square I asked Tiffany if she would like to have some dinner before going home. She did, so we were lazy and got a taxi to take us the sort distance to my flat, it saved us the bother of lugging suitcases. At my flat I paid off the taxi driver and made it worth his while, so that there was no griping about the short fare. We now did have to carry our bags, up the stairs to my flat.

"This is a really nice place," Tiffany said after I let us in.

"It's comfortable enough for me," I said. "I've got two bedrooms, two bathrooms, this kitchen and dining area and that sitting room. I bought it some years ago and kept it even when we were in Kenya."

"Can I take a look around?" she asked.

"By all means," I said. "A glass of wine?"

"Please," she said. Then she wandered off and looked into my various rooms. "I love this sketch of you," she called out. "Who did it?"

"Kirsty, she's the partner of my friend Freya," I replied. "Freya has a castle on an island in Scotland, we should go up there one day when the weather is nice."

"It's a really beautiful sketch," Tiffany said. "It really captures you."

"I like it," I said. "Here you are, a Cillie Chablis."

"This is really good," Tiffany said.

"They do make good wine," I agreed. "I'm not much of a cook, so I usually go to a bistro just down the road, they know me and have always looked after me well, would that be okay?"

"That would be super," she said. "Flying today was different, not being able to really see anything."

"You have to rely on your instruments completely," I said. "You get the heading and altitude from the controllers and you have to stick to it. I started classes for instrument flying when I was in Kenya, they have this hood thing that obscures your vision, so all that you can really see is the instruments and then you just watch them carefully."

"It seemed you were busy," she said.

"There's a lot to do," I agreed. "You have to watch where you're going, you've got to stay alert to directions that the controllers give you, and you can't forget the aircraft, you have to keep an eye on the engine performance, the wings for icing if it's cold enough, so you're busy."

"I suppose it's a question of knowing what to do, then practising as often as possible," she said.

"That's it," I agreed. "You can get complacent really easily and think you're better than you really are. I've booked a check ride with an instructor each year since I got my licence, just to keep me on my toes and to get some comments on my techniques. I use a different instructor each time, so I get different reports. It's hard to accept the criticisms that come, but I've found them to be valuable. Shall we go and get some dinner?"

Over dinner I asked Tiffany how and when she knew that she was a lesbian.

"I think I always knew," she said. "I tried to do the accepted thing and dated a couple of blokes, I even tried sex with one when I first went to uni, but it didn't work. I was really stupid, I had had too much to drink at a party, got into bed with this bloke that I'd just met, no pill, no condom, really stupid. In the morning, he just pulled up his pants and left, and I was left wondering if I was up the stick. Looking back now, I can't believe how stupid I was, but I also went off men after that because the arsehole was perfectly happy to take advantage of me. After that I experimented with this real dike and that was interesting but not what I was looking for, then I found Helena and we had fun together until she went back to New Zealand. What were your experiences?"

"I really didn't have much or any before Ian," I replied. "I was really young when I went up to Oxford, so didn't go to many parties. I went to one and there was a bloke there who tried it on, so I broke his arm and he left me alone after that."

"You broke his arm?" she said, laughing.

"I know," I said. "A little extreme, but I didn't know what else to do. I never went to another college party after that."

"After my sad experience I gave up parties too," she said. "I also took up karate and kendo. I swore off men completely, admitting to myself what I had really known all my life, that I preferred women."

"Tell me about Alex, if that's not too painful," I suggested.

"Alex was, is, a stew with BA," she said. "We met when she came to my stand on the Portobello Road, she started talking and on thing led to another. With her it was awkward because she flew long distance routes with BA, so her calendar was always up in the air. I really liked her and was royally pissed when I found her with Joanna, I had thought that Joanna was my friend, but friends don't behind your back. How did you meet Ian?"

264

"I went to a dinner in Hall, but by then I was a fellow, and Ian was there with some other post grads, our eyes met and it was electric, we had coffee the next day, and as you said one thing led to another," I explained. "We were really happy in Kenya and I was devastated when he was killed."

"Since then, there's only been Tom?" she asked.

"Only Tom," I confirmed. "And I hadn't slept with him yet, maybe that's part of the reason he dumped me for Roberta, she was much more willing to open her legs for him. I look back now and am disappointed in myself for throwing myself at the first handsome bloke who smiled at me. Like, you, I'm done with men, at least for a while. Do your folks know about you?"

"I told them when I got out of uni," she said. "Catriona knew, she didn't need to be told, Mum and Dad I think suspected but I was never sure if they accepted or not until I talked to them. When I did I was surprised that they just told me that all they were worried about was me being happy, but they did caution me that some people would not be so accepting. Mum told me that she thought it was probably more difficult for men, because of the old gross indecency laws and societal attitudes towards homos. When I think of it there were two older ladies who live down the road, there was never much said about them, I think people enjoyed the fiction that they were just living together for economic reasons, but when these two blokes set up house in the village, there was a hue and cry like you wouldn't believe. They left not long after they'd arrived, hounded out by the bigots."

"Did you ever have any problems with jobs?" I asked.

"I kept quiet," she said. "I didn't tell the limousine service anything, I just dressed like they wanted me to, did what they told me and drove the cars, all the reports they got back about me from clients were that I was professional, so they never asked anything past that, I think I may have mentioned Alex two or three times to other drivers, but they, being men, all assumed that Alex was a bloke, which was a good thing because none of the other drivers ever asked me out."

"What about clients?" I asked.

"Oh, plenty of them did," she said. "But I got very good at politely saying no, without getting them all in a huff. I suppose you've had similar experiences?"

"Not really," I said. "While I was consulting I know there was talk behind my back, but not overt approaches. I think they thought I was super bright therefore a little weird. After I got married and lived in Kenya it was easier because I would be asked why I lived there and would then tell them that my husband was part of the legation there and that usually ended conversations, except for straight business. It's going to be interesting to see how the banking world accepts me, or not."

"I can see where that will be a pain," she said. "I've not met a woman bank manager yet, I suppose there are some somewhere. It's probably even worse at the top of big companies, all men, all members of the same club, all went to the same school."

"Sadly, there's a lot of truth to that," I agreed. "Are you finished, shall we go back to my flat?"

"Thanks for dinner," she said. "It's been an interesting day."

New beginnings

Tiffany spent the night in my spare room and was up early the next morning, knocking on my door and telling me that it was time to be up and out for a run. I moaned and groaned, but did get up and did go for a run, in the drizzle and fog, I might add, but felt better for it afterwards. After a shower and breakfast that we grabbed at the bistro, it was time to let the others at the bank know that Dad was not coming back and that I was the new Chair. I had wondered about the sense of opening the bank for one day, then having a weekend, but I wanted to set some things in motion as soon as I could. At nine I called a meeting of all the bank staff and told them the news. I told them that I would now be chairing the board and that here would be new board members. To most of them, that was interesting but not something that affected them directly in any way. I asked Deirdre to stay as the Company Secretary and was delighted when she not only agreed, but was keen to do so. Then I told them all that I had other things to do, which I suppose as a polite way of telling them to go back to work. I called Rachel and asked her if she would be on my board and was delighted when she agreed, with some enthusiasm I might add. I called Pierre Garnier in France and asked him if he would join my board and he also agreed. Lastly I called Andrew McIntosh and George Adams and asked them if they would rescind their resignations from the board and stay on. I respected Andrew and George and they would provide some continuity between the old and the new. So, that have me three women and four men, still stacked in the favour of men, but they did make up most of the executives and directors in the business world and I was not going to change the world overnight.

The Winter & Winter rights issue had been mostly subscribed by Theresa Baldwin, so I took the ten per cent that was left on behalf of the bank, after a brief round of telephone calls to the directors. Deirdre brought the papers in for me and pointed out the piece in the Financial Times about me.

"Have you read it?" I asked her.

"I have," she said. "It's mostly complimentary but the reporter does question whether you can make it in the banking world, being a mere woman and all."

"Cheeky sod," I said. "Well, I suppose that's to be expected, challenge the status quo and they'll all close ranks to keep the interlopers out."

"Has anyone pulled out of deals that we're involved with since Mr Barclay made the announcement that you were the MD?" she asked.

"Not yet," I said. "We'll see if after this article whether any of them wake up and realise that there's a new leader at the bank and it's not a man. Listen to this bit — *while clearly academically well credentialed one wonders whether Mrs Hartley has the intestinal fortitude for the exigencies of the banking world* — what a load of rubbish, and why did he call me Mrs Hartley, Ian's dead and I've gone back to Barclay, it fits better with the bank, first Grandpa Barclay, then Dad, now me, and why didn't he call me Dr Barclay?"

"So annoying," she said.

"It is," I agreed. "But if you think about it, it wasn't that long ago that women got the right to keep their own property if they married, and even more recently they got the right to vote, and more recently than that that Cambridge University finally conferred degrees upon women. It's been a long struggle and it's not over yet. Could you send out a formal notice of a board meeting to be held next week on the 3rd? I'm going to South Africa on the 7th to visit Klein Copper. I'm taking Tiffany with me, she's surprised me, she knows more about the mining business than I ever suspected. I rather think that whether she knew it or not that she paid a lot attention to her father as she was growing up. I learned from my brother James that Prof MacBeth was good but also a hard taskmaster."

"So, you're taking a ringer with you," Deirdre said. "I like that. Oh, you should know that Vincent Davis has given his notice, he's leaving us and going to Andersen."

"What does he take with him that could be used by someone else?" I asked.

"Obviously what we've been looking at," she said. "But, Andersen is more in the accounting and consulting business, they don't finance deals, if he was going to Morgan Stanley or one of the banks I'd be more concerned."

"So, probably little risk to us?" I asked.

"I don't think so," she said.

"Pay him his notice period and walk him out today," I said. "I think in this business once you've said you're going to go, you should go. I know that if he were going to steal company secrets he would have done it long ago, but why take the chance."

"I'll do that," she said.

"There is something else we need to do, Deirdre," I said. "I'd like an audit of the bank to be done by an outside company."

"Oh, is this a matter of routine?" she asked.

"Yes, I think we should start the new year with a fresh look at things and make sure there's nothing out there that we don't know about," I said.

"Do you suspect something as being amiss?" she asked.

"No," I said. "I'd just like to have someone other than me look things over and give me an opinion. Who should be use? Who have we used in the past?"

"Field & Rowntree," she replied. "They're a pretty good second tier firm, not one of the Big Eight, probably as good but half the price."

"You think the Big Eight overcharge?" I asked.

"Just my opinion," she said. "But, yes, I think they just park junior accountants who sift through stuff, then a senior manager, or if you're big enough, a partner comes along and makes the big pronouncement. It seems to me that that is more often linked to some effort to tie up future business."

"That's very cynical," I laughed.

"It probably is," she agreed. "But, the Big Eight didn't get to be the Big Eight by being nice chaps."

"So, should we call Field & Rowntree back in?" I asked.

"Either them or Black Knight," she suggested.

"Tell me about Black Knight," I said.

"They're a family business, actually started as two family businesses, the Blacks and the Knights, they merged in 1968, specialise in finance houses, I think the Black Knight name is their attempt at humour, but they're good, they don't mess about and they seem to have a knack for pinpointing issues, if there are any," she said.

"What does Andrew McIntosh think about them?" I asked.

"He likes them," she said. "He was singing their praises a couple of months ago."

"Does he have a financial interest in them?" I asked.

269

"I don't know," she admitted.

"Let's find out," I suggested. I called Andrew and after pleasantries asked him about Black Knight.

"Good outfit," he said. "They looked at me as an acquisition a year ago, I wasn't ready to sell, but if I did, they'd be good."

"What about using them to audit the bank?" I asked.

"They'd do a good job," he said.

"Do you have any financial ties to them?" I asked.

"None," he said.

"Thanks Andrew," I said. "I'm going to go ahead and engage them to do an audit of the bank."

"Probably a wise thing to do," he said. "I saw the piece in the FT about you, nice enough, but you're obviously going to face some opposition."

"I had expected that," I said. "I'm used to it, I've faced it all my life."

"If I can help in any way, just let me know," he offered.

"Thanks, Andrew, I'll see you next week," I said.

I called the Black Knight people and was told that a Geoffrey Black would call on me the following Monday. Lunch was in order, so I asked Deirdre if she was busy. She either was not or decided that an invitation from The Boss, as James had styled me, was not to be turned down. We went to a small place we both knew on the Embankment. Over lunch I asked Deirdre about her aspirations.

"I want to be a banker," she said. "I've been taking economics at the Open University and should graduate this coming summer. I think that with the law degree I already have could be of value."

"Good for you," I said. "How can I help?"

"If you have a project that you'd like me to look at, I'd see what I could make of it," she suggested. "I know you've got Tiffany busy with the Sable Mining people, but perhaps there's something else?"

"Why don't you take a look at Glenavon property?" I suggested. "I think they're underfunded, but with the right funding, I think they could really increase their share of the commercial properties in Hastings."

"I'll do that," she said. "What put you onto Glenavon?"

"There was a piece in the Times that talked about the lack of available commercial premises in Hastings and there was another piece in the FT that talked about Glenavon struggling with their debt. I think we could restructure their debt and put them on the track to success."

"Gosh," she said. "I'd missed that, I'll start on Monday."

I busied myself for the rest of the afternoon and then closed up the office and sent everyone home. I sorted through the post that arrived that afternoon, but there was only one interesting looking item, so I took that to open at home. Tiffany came back with me to collect her belongings and I was left alone. There were things to be done at my flat, cleaning for one and laundry. I used the laundromat down the road and wondered if it would not just be better to buy a small washer and dryer and have them installed. There was room in the linen closet for a small set, all that needed to be addressed was the water supply and drains. That was easy for me to say, but I wondered how complex a task it would be to actually do that. I went to an Argos that was not too distant and found a washing machine that would fit my needs, but it looked as if I would still have to hang my clothes out to dry somewhere. To find a plumber I consulted the Yellow Pages and found a couple in my area, and wrote down theirs numbers to call them on Monday. The weather was still dreary so it looked as if my plane was going to have to stay at Southend for a day or two longer. The other complication was that my Land Rover was at Biggin Hill, so I debated about travelling down there to collect it, or just living without a car for a day or two. I suppose I could have called Tiffany and asked her to bring me the company car, but that seemed a little beyond the pale.

The post that I had brought from the office beckoned, it was a very fancy looking envelope from a banking society. I opened it and found an invitation for Dr F. M. Barclay to attend a dinner, dinner jackets to be worn, at the Cymric Club on January 5th, the dinner address to be given by the Chancellor. Well, it would be interesting to hear what he had to say. There was an address and a smaller envelope with an RSVP card. I ticked off that I would be there and dropped it in the post. I knew nothing about the Cymric Club, but suspected that it was associated with the Isle of Man, and therefore perhaps a tax haven of some sort. That was something to look forward to in the new year, and just before we left for South Africa. I looked at the address in my A to Z and decided that it would be convenient if I asked Tiffany to drive me there. Thinking about that, that would be one of the occasions when a car phone would have come in handy, when I was done I could have just called Tiffany to come and get me, as I doubted that there was that much parking near the club. London street parking was limited at the best of times and places, and the closer one got to the City the more of a problem it became.

Monday was New Year's Eve, so we had a short day. I called a couple of plumbers early in the morning and got a commitment to come and have a look at my flat on January 2nd. That was just done when Geoffrey Black arrived. I think he was surprised that I was not only the person who had called them, but also the Managing Director. I rather suspect that he had been expecting to meet the man behind the bank. I told him what I needed and gave him basic financial numbers to give him a sense of the task and he gave me an estimate to be confirmed. The start date, should we agree on the assignment, I set for January 20th, we would have been back from South Africa a few days then and caught up with whatever would be active at the time. There was a call from James Seaton who wanted free calendar dates from me so that he could do his best to schedule board meetings when most of his directors would be able to attend. I asked him how the merger was actually going and he said that for the most part it was going well, there were one or two small issues, but nothing that he saw as insurmountable. He had already given notice to a few managers and sales representatives, both from Metter and from the old Corby Seaton. He was in the process of evaluating all the premises that they now had and deciding what would be consolidated where. He also had a plan to move certain manufacturing around to make best use of the two factories that they now had. It sounded to me as if he was doing the right thing and streamlining his company based on sound analysis and not emotional ties to people or places. I also got a call from John Stanley to let me know that he was retiring from Winter & Winter as of that day and that Theresa Baldwin would be the new Managing Director and Chairman as of January 1st. That was quick, but it made sense, Theresa now owned a significant number of the shares of Winter & Winter and she could now meld Copper Beech into the company. I was sure that as time went on she would start the share buy back process until such time as she could take the company private again and de-list it from the exchange. Then she would be less hampered by the rules and regulations surrounding publicly traded companies. After

Theresa had wished me happy New Year, I sent everyone home to enjoy the festivities of the New Year and told them that I would see them all on January 2nd.

New Year's Eve, I confess, was not a good time for me. I got distinctly maudlin and wallowed in memories of eves gone by. The one I recalled best was the first one I had spent in Kenya. Ian and I had gone out there just after Christmas and we were expected to attend an official event held by the High Commissioner. We were asked to socialise, mix and mingle, but not to get into deep philosophical questions of politics. Mixing and mingling were never my strong points, but to Ian it all came naturally, but in the end, I had actually enjoyed myself and made useful contacts. I hauled out photographs I had of Ian and Kenya and cried a lot. His death seemed to hang heaviest on days like Christmas and New Year, I suppose because they were also days for reflection where memories would be dredged up. Loneliness weighed on my mind, and it was clear that I would need to be careful or depression could follow. I really needed someone to share things with and the episode with Tom still rankled. How could I have been so misled, or was it my own fault for seeing a relationship there that was actually not there at all, just a figment of my imagination. I actually toyed with the idea of calling Tiffany to see if she was busy, but dismissed that idea, reasoning that a single young woman would have probably invitations aplenty for the evening. Sleep caught up with me at about eleven, so I actually missed the New Year.

New Year's Day was quiet. I actually had to cook for myself as my bistro was closed for the day. They only closed a couple of days a year, and New Year's Day was one. I had bought groceries, so had the makings of meals, and was quite surprised when they turned out quite well. But then I had been following a recipe and instructions carefully, without branching off into my own modifications, so things should have gone well. By the next day, I was ready to get back to work, but first I had to wait for plumbers to come. I showed them where the washer would be going and where the existing hot and cold water lines were. It turned out to be far easier than I had thought, just a simple case of extending two lines and putting in shut-off valves. I got prices from the two plumbers and picked one, actually the slightly higher priced one, they seemed more professional than the other. We set a date and arranged for them to come and do the work. I then called the property management firm that Dad had used for years and asked them to send a representative over that day to babysit the plumbers and see them on and off the premises. That might sound a little paranoid, but I wanted someone there I could trust while there were strangers in the flat. The property management firm kept clients by being trustworthy and in all the years that Dad had used them, he had never had cause to regret his decision. At the office, I called the estate agent that I had used to buy my flat and told them that Dad's flat was now on the market. I had keys for it, so promised to meet them there after work that day. I also wanted to see if Gabriela was still there, or if she had moved out already. The rest of the day I sat with Deirdre and Anthea, who was my accountant, and we put everything together for the board meeting. It was to be my first, so I wanted things to run smoothly.

After work I had Tiffany run me over to Dad's flat on Park Lane. The estate agent was there, so I let him in and we went through the flat. There was a note on the table from Gabriela addressed to me, along with a set of keys. She had received her notice from Dad and the pay he had given her in lieu of any notice and she had gone back to Genoa. The flat was being sold furnished, so there was no need to clean anything out, except to make sure that the refrigerator and pantry were both empty. There was quite a bit of wine left in the flat, so I asked Tiffany to take it all down to the car. The estate agent measured, paced, hummed and hawed, then came up with an asking price. I instructed him to go ahead and make all the necessary arrangements, then I gave him a key to the front door and got all the contact information we needed sorted out. Dad had sent me a power of attorney that had arrived that day by courier, so I could sign on his behalf to complete the sale when a buyer was found.

James and Portia came over from France on the same flight as Pierre, so I had Tiffany collect them from Heathrow. When they got to the office I asked Tiffany to entertain Portia and Pierre briefly because I had something I needed to discuss with James.
"So, what's up?" he asked after the others had left.

"Well, I was thinking that it might be a good idea to provide a way for the people who work here to become part owners of the bank," I replied. "How do we do that?" he asked.

"At the moment, we each have 10,000 shares of the bank, what if we issue 5,000 more and allocate them to the employees that they can earn the right to own if they stay for say five years?" I suggested.

"So, that still gives us a very clear majority," he thought. "What will it do to dividends?"

"Obviously over the next five years, the dividends would be split among an increasing number of shares up to 25,000, rather than 20,000, so a slight reduction, but I'm betting that if we provided a path to some ownership we'll get extra effort by everyone and see increased earnings, therefore increased dividends," I replied.

"So, announce it today, meet with the staff and tell them that if they stick around for five years, then they own part of the bank and can enjoy the rewards?" he asked.

"That's about it," I agreed.

"Not a bad idea, I wonder if we shouldn't do the same at Old Pecos?" he mused.

"That's up to you and Charlize," I said.

"What do we need to do?" he asked.

"Have the board approve the issue of the shares, and approve the scheme that I've outlined here," I replied, handing him a document. He read through it quickly and nodded. We then joined the rest in the board room. They had introduced themselves and Deirdre and Anthea were there as well.

"Good morning everyone," I said. "Thank you for coming. I gather that you have all introduced yourselves but perhaps you don't all know James, James is my brother and the other principal shareholder of the bank. James is part of Cillie Wines and currently lives in Pecos, New Mexico in the US where he and Charlize are running the Old Pecos Winery and looking to expand the Cillie operations in the States. James, you know Portia, this is Rachel Adams, a couturier here in London, Pierre Garnier you met at Heathrow, Pierre is with UTA in France, Andrew McIntosh is a chartered accountant with his own firm, George Adams, property developer with the same name, Deirdre Donlin, our company secretary and Anthea Wilson our chief financial officer."

"Nice to meet you all," James said. "This all came a little earlier than we had expected, but I'm sure Dad had his reasons."

"Thank you James," I said. "Anthea, could you give us a brief look at the financial position of the bank?"

"Of course," she said. She then handed out screeds of paper that included the profit and loss statement for the year and the balance sheet. "These are preliminary numbers for 1979, we'll need to go through them more carefully to see that we've captured all the year end items, but I don't see anything changing materially."

"You got these together remarkably quickly," Andrew commented.

"The new computer system we installed has made that much easier," she said. "Providing we keep the inputs up to date, the results are quick to extract. Now all we have to do is look at items and make sure that we've put them into the appropriate category, and any reserves or other allocations are made properly."

"Does it put you out of a job?" George asked.

"Far from it," she replied. "We now have easy access to tools that let us look at things and do analyses on the data. We can also run simulation models on potential investments and test them for risk."

"So, you'd suggest that we all do something similar?" George asked.

"If you have not already done so," she agreed.

"I think you'll agree that the bank is in an excellent place," I said. "We turned a handsome profit in 1979 and our assets are up significantly over 1978. Anthea, do you have the list of the companies in which we hold a position?"

"I do, Fiona," she confirmed, and handed out another print out.

"These holdings look pretty diverse," Andrew commented. "The major new ones I see are Corby Metter and Winter & Winter, so construction equipment and sporting goods."

"What are we looking at in the near future?" Rachel asked.

"We've been asked to finance the start-up of a new copper mine in South Africa by Sable Mining, it's about the same size as the Palabora mine and has reserves for at least twenty years. I plan to visit the site next week and review the reserve calculations and the financial projections. James knows the project manager and has given his support," I replied. "I have had Tiffany MacBeth, our newest staff member look at the project and I'd like to call her in to give you some sense of how big it is"

"Good idea," Andrew said. I nodded to Deirdre and she make a quick telephone call and a minute later Tiffany joined us.

"Good morning," she said. "Dr Barclay asked me to give you a run down on the Sable Mining Klein Copper prospect." She then went on, with charts, pictures, maps and drawings, to describe the project, quantify the reserves and the talk about the mining method proposed and the likely processing plant that would be required to yield saleable copper. I was actually surprised at the depth to which she had gone, she had given me the overview, which I had thought would be information enough, but she had been very thorough. When she threw it open for questions, there were a few, and those she handled with ease.

"Thank you Tiffany," I said. "We'll call you back when lunch is served."

"Excellent work," George said. "So, what £35,000,000 you said?"

"That is what they are looking for," I confirmed. "We'll float the issue and pick up 12.5% ourselves. But, I want to take a look before we commit, so will be calling you all for a telephonic board meeting when I get back from South Africa."

"We'll be waiting," James said.

"I thought you'd taken on Tiffany as the driver?" Rachel asked.

"I did," I confirmed. "Then I discovered that she'd been hiding her light under a bushel and that she is in fact a very competent analyst. She has done a very good job on the Sable Mining project."

"I'd concur with that," James added. "She did a brilliant job on this Klein Copper project."

"We are also looking at Glenavon, Deirdre will be delving into them to see if they are a company we could do something with," I said.

"Glenavon," George said. "You know, that's not a bad idea, they're well positioned in the market, but suffer from, lack of funds and from poor leadership, I might take a look at them myself. If I did, would you manage the financing for me?"

"That's what Thames Cherwell does," I laughed. "Portia, any legal issues with that?"

"We're not a public company, so the usual constraints don't really apply," she commented. "Although George is a director of the bank, because the bank has as yet made no overtures to Glenavon, this is merely early exploration. It would be a good idea for George to keep Deirdre informed as to his proposed actions."

"There is another matter I would like your approval on," I said. "James and I have talked about this. We're thinking that we'll issue some more shares in the bank, then allocate those to the employees who would earn the rights to then by staying with us for five years."

"That's interesting," Andrew said. "It's done in public companies, more so in the States than here, but why not? How would you do the grants?"

"I have here a proposed allocation," I said, handing out pages to the directors. They all read through the preamble and the grant language itself, then looked through the chart of allocations.

"Who are all these people?" Pierre asked.

"Deirdre and Anthea here, you've met, Tiffany MacBeth, Adrian White, Giles Forester, Helen McBride, Gerald Alford and Peter Stanley are the analysts that we have, digging into companies and their background for any deals we might want to do. Simon Hoppes, Cynthia Green and David Robinson are computer programmers, and Eleanor Hammer and Karen Dean are the computer operators," I replied.

"Thank you," Pierre said. "I think this is a very good idea and I propose that we approve the plan."

"I'll second that," George said.

"All in favour?" I asked. There were nods and ayes around the room, so I told Deirdre to record that as passed. "Is there any other business?" I asked.

"Just a comment," Rachel said. "I read the FT piece on you the other day and I have to say that I was a little put out by the suggestion that you might not be up to the job. I would like it on record that I have full confidence in your abilities to run this bank effectively."

"I'll second that," Andrew said. There were more nods around the room and I wondered how they would all feel the first time I made a mess of things. But, that was possibly in the future, or possibly not.

"There being no other business, I move to adjourn," I said.

"Seconded," James said.

"All in favour?" I asked.

"Aye," came from around the room.

"I've had lunch catered in," I said. "And, I've invited all the staff, so that you can get the chance to meet them. Deirdre, would you let everyone know that we're ready?"

The meet and greet went well. There were no wallflowers among the group, so no-one to rescue from a corner. I notice Pierre had corralled two of the programmers and was deep in conversation about how to write programs to manage crews and aircraft. George and Deirdre were busy talking about Glenavon, Helen, Cynthia and Karen were talking to

Rachel and there were more conversations going on. When we broke up I had Tiffany take Portia, Pierre and James back to Heathrow, then sat down with Deirdre and Anthea and went through the share ownership plan. We agreed that we would have a general meeting of the company the next day to tell everyone about the plan and what it meant to them. I had made the allocation of 500 shares to each of Deirdre and Anthea, then asked them about the balance of the staff, should I treat the programmers and the computer operators the same as the analysts or should I allocate differently. There was quite a lively discussion between Deirdre and Anthea and the upshot was that they recommended granting 350 shares each to the rest. The argument was that the programmers and operators were in the position to make as big a contribution to the company as the analysts, and it would remove any stigma of being less value to the company just because you ran the computer and did not study companies all day. I concurred with their reasoning and asked Deirdre to type up the list in that way, and to create letters that would be sent to each of the staff outlining the scheme and telling them the number of shares that they had been allotted. Anthea would make the appropriate adjustments to the balance sheet and note who held actual shares, and who had rights to shares. All that being done, I quit for the day.

The meeting with the staff the next day brought smiles and tears. I think both for the same reason. It was nice to be appreciated and to be given the opportunity to benefit from the success of the bank.

"Vincent should have stayed on," Giles said. "He may think he got a better position at Andersen, but with this I doubt it."

"What happens if we stay for six years then leave?" Helen asked.

"Then the bank will buy back your shares at market at the time of your departure," I said.

"So, we keep the shares as long as we're with the bank?" she asked.

"That's right," I confirmed. "If you leave the bank, then you're no longer contributing to the success of the bank and the whole idea behind this is that you benefit from your contributions, not just because we exist."

"That's fair," Giles said.

"There is a vesting period," I explained. "Each year you will vest in one-fifth of your allocation, and will receive dividends on that vesting."

"So, we'll get some dividend after the first year, so this time next year?" Karen asked.

"Providing we make money and that there is money to distribute," I said. That caused a laugh around the table, but I could see them spending money in their minds.

"So, all things being equal, what might we expect per share?" Karen asked.

"Going on the record here that this is an indicative number and is not to be taken as a promise or in any way a commitment, then about £50 per share," I replied.

"That's a lot," Karen said, doing the mathematics in her head and multiplying even one-fifth of the shares she had been allocated by 50.

"If there are any other questions, let Deirdre know, and if she can't answer them, then I will," I promised. "There is one more thing, Tiffany has made brooches and badges for everyone with the bank's emblem. If you have dealings with the public I would like it if you would wear them as I wear mine."

Tiffany handed around the enamelled brooches that had the initials TC intertwined as they were on my silver brook. The enamelling was white and there was a very thin black surround to each of the letters. Like my brooch, she had provided magnetic fastenings, something that fascinated everyone in the room. I also told everyone that I expected them to meet a certain dress code when dealing with customers, but that they should not be out of pocket for that, so I had set up an account at Rachel's studio for the women and at a tailor on Saville Row for the men and they would each get two suits a year, one summer weight and one winter weight. Tiffany had also found a place that made ties, so had had some made up with the TC emblem embroidered on them, these she handed out to the men in the team. When there were no customers I did not mind what the staff wore to work, but asked for nothing too risqué in case some customer did call upon us.

On the 5th I spent the day doing laundry at my flat. The plumbers had been in and installed the machine and it worked brilliantly. The airing cupboard came in handy to hide away the dampish clothes, perhaps one day I would think about a dryer. I got ready for the dinner to be held at the Cymric Club. I had decided that as dinner jackets were called for, then a long dress was in order, so went with the cheongsam, plus the matching accessories I already had for it. The evening was typical of January for England, cold and damp, so I took with me the nice topcoat that I had. Tiffany collected me at six-thirty and drove me to the club. She had worn the blue uniform that we had got for her, hat and all, and she insisted I sit in the back like Lady Muck, I think so that she could make a show of opening the door for me at the club. We drew up at a colonnaded door and I noticed a brass plate set in one of the columns with the triskelion emblem of the Isle of Man and the words Cymric Club etched beneath it. Tiffany opened the door for me and held up a large umbrella. She walked me to the door and I went in.

"Can I help you Madame?" a man in what looked like a uniform jacket with the crossed keys of a concierge asked.

"I have an invitation to dinner here?" I said, proffering my invitation.

"This invitation is for Dr Barclay of the Thames Cherwell Bank," he said, stating the obvious.

"I am Dr Barclay," I said.

"I'm afraid there has been a mistake," he said. "This is a gentlemen only club, I am afraid that no ladies are permitted."

"But, I have an invitation for dinner here," I protested, waving it under his nose.

"The invitation must have been sent in error," he said. "As I said, this is a gentlemen only club no women are not permitted."

"Is there a problem here?" a voice said. I turned and looked and saw that it was Sir Bernard Carlisle of the Chancellor's office.

"I am invited to dinner," I said.

"I am sorry Dr Barclay, but you cannot enter, the rules of the club do not permit women," Bernard said.

"Then why was I invited?" I asked.

"I can only assume that it was not appreciated that Dr F. Barclay was not a man," he said. "I am afraid dear lady, that you have made the trip in vain."

"I see," I said. I stalked out, annoyed and humiliated, I do not know what stung the most, the assumption that Dr Barclay was a man, the idea of men only clubs, or the supercilious dear lady by Bernard, probably getting back at me for charging what he thought were fees that bordered on the outrageous for my consulting work that I had done for the Chancellor's office. Tiffany was still there outside the club, waiting for traffic ahead of her to clear. I tapped on the window and she saw me and leapt out in alarm.

"Are you all right?" she asked. "What's happened?"

"I am denied entry," I said, flatly.

"Why?" she asked.

"It's one of those men only clubs, probably the only women they let in are the cleanings ladies and the strippers and prossies," I complained.

"Why did they invite you then?" she asked.

"The typical assumption that the MD of a bank is a man, I would guess," I said. "So, when you can get us out of here, let's go and see if the Savoy wants our money or not."

"I'm not really dressed for that," she said.

"You look fine," I said. "Just leave the hat in the car when we get there."

We finally managed to get through the traffic backed up as the fancy cars that brought the cream of British banking to the club cleared out of the way. It did not take Tiffany long to get us to the Savoy. When we pulled up at the front door, a man leapt forward to open the doors for us.

"Would you like to leave your car just over there?" he asked. I think he was happy to have the Maserati on view near the door or the Savoy as it suggested wealth on the part of at least one patron. Tiffany moved the car and we went into the hotel and the Savoy Grill.

"May I take your coats?" a young lady said. I surrendered my coat as did Tiffany, then we made our way to the restaurant itself.

"A table for two?" the maître d'hôtel asked.

"Thank you," I said. He led us off and ushered us to a table for two. I smiled to myself as our progress was followed by nearly all the people already seated. I wondered what they saw and what they assumed. I caught a glimpse of us in a mirror and we made an unlikely couple, me in a red cheongsam and Tiffany in a finely tailored blue suit, I was sure that many would leap to the conclusion that we were a lesbian couple and that Tiffany played the rôle of the dominant partner, after all she was wearing the trousers.

"Tiffany, excuse me for a minute," I said. "I won't be long, get me a Kir Royale if you would please." I left her to it and went to the front desk.

"Can I help you madame?" the clerk said.

"I'd like a room for the night," I said.

"Of course," she said. "We have a selection available, what did you have in mind?"

"Something with two beds," I said.

"Of course," she said. "We have a luxury double room with a river view."

"That would be fine," I said.

"What name shall I register the room under?" she asked.

"Dr Fiona Barclay," I said, handing over an American Express card.

"Thank you Doctor, shall I have your luggage sent up?" she asked.

"No, we have it in the car and will get it later," I said, stretching the truth more than a little, but I had no intention of telling her that we had no luggage.

"Very good Doctor Barclay," she said, then she handed me back my card and the key and a small card that showed where the room was located. I went back to the grill and Tiffany had got us both a Kir Royale.

"I got us a room for the night, so don't worry about drinking and driving," I told her.

"Thank you, that's brilliant," she said. "Cheers, I'm sorry things didn't turn out well."

"I suppose I should be used to it," I said. "But it still irks when they won't let me in somewhere just because I'm not a man."

"I need to go to the loo," she said. "I'll be back in a minute"

Tiffany returned and we talked, we ate, we drank and had a wonderful time, probably a much better time than I would have had at the Cymric Club with all the stuffy bankers. By the time we were ready for bed, I was a little tipsy and so was Tiffany. We found the room and it was actually quite nice, almost as big as my flat, or so it seemed. There were three bags on the end of each bed, matching canvas bags.

"What are these?" I asked.

"They're our clothes for South Africa," she said. "There's everything in there that we might need, clean underwear, shirts, trousers, boots, brushes and combs, toothbrush, the lot. They were in the boot of the car, so I just had then sent up."

I kicked off my shoes and plumped down on one of the beds.

"That's brilliant, do you want to shower first?" I asked Tiffany.

"I was thinking I'd like a bath," she said. "They've got a nice big bath here."

"Go ahead," I told her. She did only what Tiffany would do and undressed there and then, hanging her suit up, then peeling off her underwear to her bare nothings, and then she went off to the bathroom and I heard water running. "Would you mind company?" I asked.

"Please," she said. I went in and she was lying in the bath, looking as desirable as ever, a thought that filled me with curiosity and guilt.

"Maman and I used to have the best conversations while we bathed," I said, as I sat down on the lid of the loo. "We started when I was very small and never gave it up."

"That seems like a nice idea," Tiffany thought. "I wanted to thank you for the share program you told us about yesterday, everyone was thrilled at the idea."

"It seemed to me to be a good idea," I said. "It makes you all more part of the bank and not just employees."

"I'm finished here," she said. "Would you like me to run fresh water?"

"I'll do that," I said. She dried herself off while I ran clean water, then I undressed and climbed in. It was good to soak for a while and let the cares of the evening fade away from the stupidity that is the masculine need to keep women out, hence the private members men only clubs. I got out when the water temperature started to drop and dried myself off and wrapped myself if the very plush dressing gown that was hanging behind the bathroom door. Tiffany had taken the bed closest to the door, leaving me the one closer to the window. I dropped the dressing gown and climbed into bed and had hardly said goodnight when I dropped off to sleep, the alcohol and the bath had done wonders and I slept the sleep of the innocent.

I awoke to the aroma of coffee.

"Good morning," Tiffany said. "I had coffee sent up, would you like some?"

"Thank you," I said. I got up, picked up the dressing gown from the floor and put it on and went and sat with Tiffany and the coffee.

"Did you sleep well?" she asked.

"I died," I said. "Booze and a hot bath did it. You?"

"Like a top," she said.

"I need to take a closer look at the stuff you got us for South Africa," I said. I took the smaller bag, which I had already raided for a toothbrush, and found in all the things one might want in the way of personal care. So, facecloth, toothbrush and paste, hairbrush and comb, sun screen, a small first aid kit, and various and sundry other items. The bag was of a sturdy canvas, khaki in colour and with the initials FMB embroiled on it. I looked over and saw that the larger bag had similar initials and that the other two were emblazoned with TEM. I knew from Tiffany's job application that the E was for Elspeth. I then examined the larger bag and it had beige underwear, khaki shirts, shorts and trousers, tan suede boots, brown socks, in short all the clothing we would need for ten days in the wilds of South Africa. The shirts had breast pockets and epaulettes and had the Thames Cherwell emblem embroidered above the left breast pocket. The shorts and trousers both had substantial deep pockets, in which I felt I could store anything. I was like a child at Christmas time, I had to unfold everything, try it on and check in the mirror to see what it looked like. The third bag had padding in it and was clearly set up for a camera, plus lenses, or binoculars.

"This is super," I said. "Thanks for organising this."

"It was fun, Rachel helped me a lot," she said. "More coffee?"

"Thanks," I said. "I'm still annoyed that those idiots didn't let me in last night, I suppose no-one ever thought about an invitee not being a man, after all banking is a man's world, at least in their minds. So, I haven't looked outside yet, what kind of day is it?"

"Clear and sunny," she said. "But I also think cold, looking at the river I'm sure I can see little patches of ice."

"So, clear and cold," I thought. "Why don't we have breakfast, then drop the car and the luggage back at your flat, then take the Tube out to Upminster and get a ride over to the Southend airport and get my plane?"

"That would be fun," she agreed. "It's eight now, if we have breakfast, then drop the car off, we can be at the Southend airport by about eleven, noon at the latest."

"Let's do that," I said. I picked out some clean underwear from the clothes bag and then selected a shirt and long trousers, this was definitely not a shorts day. That done I started to fold up my dress, but Tiffany stopped me and handed me a dress bag in which I could hang it and then only fold it over once.

"I had these in the boot of the car," she explained. "You never know when you might need one."

"Thanks, Tiffany," I said. "Good, that's all done, let's go and see what we fancy for breakfast."

We were at the Southend airport by eleven-thirty, having dropped off the car at Tiffany's flat and picked up leather jackets each, and as a joke I had also acquired epaulettes for pilots, so gave myself four stripes and Tiffany three stripes. At the airport we were shown out to the plane, not by Gareth who had the day off, but by Sydney, who was helpful and willing to do anything for us, and apparently who thought that we worked for a charter company. I filed a flight plan that would take us by a circuitous route to Biggin Hill, that would give us ninety minutes in the air. It did not take long to get ready for the flight, and we were soon lined up ready to take off. I handed the controls over to Tiffany and guided her through the take off and once in the air told her what heading and altitude we should take as we were directed around on our flight plan and eventually into Biggin Hill. I even talked her down so that she landed the plane. Because we had not taken the shortest route there, we did not arrive until one-thirty, but there was still plenty of daylight left to drive home in. We moved my Land Rover out of the hangar and towed my plane in and stored it away.

"I landed the plane," Tiffany said, excitedly. "I've booked lessons to start as soon as we get back from South Africa, do I show them the logs of this flight and the ones to Cannes?"

"Of course," I said. "It all counts, just make sure that they're properly recorded in your log book. Today's flight alone is ninety minutes, so it all adds up, and you can record both a take off and landing for today's flight."

"Why did you let me land today?" she asked.

"Well, the weather is about as good as you can get, Biggin Hill is not a major airport with lots of traffic and I felt that you had a handle on everything you needed to land," I said.

"I was exciting, but I felt nervous," she said. "I was really thankful when the wheels touched down and we were able to taxi to a stop. Taking off is much easier than landing."

"It is," I agreed. "All you have to do is get going fast enough and the plane will lift itself into the air. It's much quicker and easier into the wind, that's something you learn very quickly, where possible always take off and land into the wind, it reduces ground speed."

"Do you want me to drive us back toLondon?" Tiffany asked as we went to my Land Rover.

"I think I'll drive," I said. "I like my old Land Rover, it's fun to drive, one thing I miss here is driving on dirt roads, there's so little chance to get off the tar, unless I become one of those annoying townies who goes green laning on Sundays."

"Not all green laners are annoying," Tiffany said. "Sometimes it's good for a car or two to go down a lane, otherwise it might get overgrown and difficult for a walker or a horse to use."

"I hadn't thought of it that way," I admitted. "Should we go one weekend, find somewhere in the Dales or the Lakes and just go and see what we can see?"

"That would be fun," she said.

"Are we all set for tomorrow?" I asked.

"I have the tickets, we have our clothes set, you have the information for our trip to the Kruger National Park, I've been taking my malaria pills, I think we're all set," she said.

"Are you taking a camera?" I asked.

"I got a new Ricoh earlier this year, so I'll take some films for it, are you taking a camera?" she asked.

"I got myself an Olympus," I said. "What about binoculars?"

"I hadn't thought of them," she said.

"We might get more use out of them than the cameras," I said. "I have a second pair, why don't you just take those?"

"Thanks. This is all so exciting,"she said. "My first trip to Africa, a trip to a new mine site and a safari thrown in."

"We should go one day on a tented safari," I thought. "I would think that it's a completely different experience to the camps of Kruger."

"Did you just camp in the open?" she asked.

"Sometimes," I confirmed. "The very first safari I went on was in Kenya and we slept under canvas."

"No fences or anything?" she asked.

"No, just the tents," I said. "The people I went with had done it a lot and were very professional, so I never felt concerned at all."

"Gosh, how super," she said.

"We're here," I said. "Could I leave my Land Rover in your garage?"

"Of course," she said.

"I'm planning to go to the office in the morning, then we should leave on the Tube at about two," I thought. "So, why don't we stop at lunch, go home and change and meet at Sloan Square Tube station at two?"

"I'll be there," she said.

Kleinbegin

The next morning I dutifully went into the office. There was not a lot to do, I attended to the correspondence that had come in. I checked on the progress of capturing all the historical deals, loans, investments and other items, met with Deirdre and Anthea to ensure all was in order before I left and provided Deirdre with whatever telephone numbers I could in case something truly catastrophic happened while I was away. To me that included the deaths of any of my family and little else. Any other issue could wait until I returned. I left at noon, grabbed some lunch at my bistro, then showered and changed for the journey. I met Tiffany at the Sloan Square Tube station and we took the Tube to Heathrow, changing at South Kensington for the Piccadilly line. We had decided not to wear overcoats to the airport, it would have meant lugging heavy coats around Africa in the middle of their summer. So, we had been glad to get into the warmth of the Tube. At Heathrow we checked in with British Airways for the flight to Johannesburg and got seats assigned to us. Tiffany had not been on a Boeing Jumbo Jet before and was amazed at the size of it.

"Can this thing actually fly?" she asked.

"Same as my Cessna," I said. "All it takes is bigger wings and bigger engines, but the physics is still the same, remember, thrust, weight, lift and drag."

"I can't get over how big it is," she said. "There's even stairs in it."

"You'll see, the upper deck will get stretched in time and eventually there'll be a plane that is two stories all the way down," I predicted.

"Heaven help the ground staff if you get a cancellation then," she said.

"You're right, what a mess that would be," I agreed. "Did you look through the numbers that Sable Mining gave us?"

"I did," she said. "I understand most of it, it's just like my business, only on a much bigger scale, I have furnaces, they have furnaces, I have other equipment, so do they. In my business I have to guess at what sales I might make, particularly if I'm going to buy an expensive new furnace or more gold, so do they, but in some ways theirs is more predictable, they're working off predictions of future copper price and demand, I get all that."

"So, what do we look at while we're there?" I asked.

"We listen to their pitch to see if they believe in the project and we try and get a sense of the difficulties and challenges they're going to have, not only starting up, but keeping things running," she thought. "I'd take a good look at the people leading the project, all the money in the world will be of no use if they can't manage the place."

"Good," I said. "We'll compare notes after our visit."

"It looks like we're the only ones not dressed up," Tiffany remarked as she looked around the First Class cabin.

"It does, doesn't it," I agreed. She was right the men in the cabin were all wearing jackets and ties, and the women, well they were generally dressed to the nines. So, we did rather stand out in our khaki shirts and trousers. But they were quite smart looking clothes, almost like uniforms as Tiffany had had the TC emblem embroidered above the left breast pocket. We also had on the same kind on light brown boots and both had the same light khaki jacket, two peas in a pod as it were.

"They're probably wondering who we are and why we're here, probably think we're off on a safari somewhere," Tiffany commented.

"Dr Barclay, Miss MacBeth, what would you like to drink before dinner?" a steward asked. That put paid to our conversation about our trip and the other passengers so, we instead turned our attention to the food and wine offered by BA.

As we ate I thought how lucky I was to have found someone to do things with, not just work with, to fly planes, talk about going green laning and possibly all kinds of other things. Since Ian had died, I had missed that, missed having someone to share a moment with, someone to see the same sunset I saw and remember it, someone to share a drink and a meal with a talk about the day. Tiffany did all those things. I had hoped that it might have been like that with Tom, but he had devastated me with his actions, I was going to say with his infidelity, but I suppose that was a little of a stretch on my part, we, neither of us had made any real commitment to the other, beyond saying, I love you, but was that not commitment enough. To say I love you and to hear it, surely signalled an intent, so yes, it was infidelity. I was getting over it now, and as I got over it I warmed more to Tiffany, she was funny, she was much brighter than she thought, she was willing to turn her hand to anything and she was really good company, and I knew that she liked being with me. As they cleared away the dinner things and we settled down to try

289

and sleep for at least some of the journey, I looked at Tiffany and those uncomfortable stirrings came again. She really was attractive, not just good looking, but beautiful, at least to me, she had an amazing body that I kept wondering about, even though the mere thought of her that way made me feel guilty. That I puzzled about, why did I feel guilty. Was it a fear of upsetting societal norms. I had been doing that all my life, I had been faced with discrimination and condescension as long as I had been out of academia, even there it had been there. So, why the guilt now. Guilty because I felt desire for another woman, guilty because I would be replacing Ian with a woman not a man. The more I thought about it, the more irrational it seemed. Maman and Portia were very happy together, and I was not at all offended or repulsed by their being together, so what was my problem. I gave up trying to understand and resigned myself to sleep, promising myself that I would come to terms with my feelings at some point.

We were awakened in the morning by the crew who wanted to know if we wanted breakfast. As we had no idea when we might eat next, we elected to eat. Then the captain made an announcement that to the left of the plane one could enjoy a really nice view of the Victoria Falls.
"Gosh," Tiffany said, as she gazed out into the distance. "Look at that, it's amazing."
"Let me take a look," I said and leaned over her to peer out of the window. She was right, it was amazing, the river meandered along, then dropped into a gorge and was carried away to the east. The spray from the falls almost obscured them. We were passing over the border with Zambia and Rhodesia, now well on its way to becoming a new state with elections scheduled to be held in a few months that would herald a new beginning for the country after years of white rule. We did not linger long over Rhodesia, but apparently crossed over into Botswana, a brown and dry looking place. Then we started to descend on our approach into Johannesburg. Tiffany grabbed my arm and pointed, "There it is," she said. "It's a bigger town than I thought it would be, there are tall buildings, lots of funny looking yellow heaps and even motorways."
"It is one of the bigger cities in the southern hemisphere," I said. "We'd better get ready for landing, we'll be on the ground soon."
I was right, we made our twists and turns as we got into landing pattern and we soon on the ground and taxiing up to the terminal.

In the terminal there was a man with a sign, obviously detailed to meet us off the plane.

"Dr Barclay?" he asked, as he approached us. As he had ignored all the men and only approached women, he must have been told who to expect.

"That's me," I confirmed.

"I'm Piet Dupree, welcome to Jo'burg, I'll run you over to Rand and put you on the plane to Klein Copper."

"Thank you," I said.

"You've got all your bags?" he asked. "Let me take them." He led us out of the airport to the car park where he had a small minibus parked. He loaded our bags then drove off to the Rand airport, a small airport that handled general aviation.

"First trip to Jo'burg?" he asked.

"Second for me," I replied.

"First for me," Tiffany said.

"It'll be a little bumpy going out," he cautioned. "It's getting hot."

"What's the altitude here?" I asked.

"A bit over 5,000 feet," he said.

"What are those big yellowish-looking dumps?" Tiffany asked.

"Those are from the gold mines," he said. "No gold, no Jo'burg, the whole place was built up because of the mines. Okay, here we are."

He parked and walked out with us to a plane on the hard stand. I looked it over, it was a Britten-Norman Islander, I'd never flown in one before, but they had a good reputation.

"Do you need the loo before you go?" he asked. "It's going to be about a two and a half hour flight." That sounded like a good idea to both of us, so he led the way to a building that served as the offices, waiting room and assembly area for charters. All done he walked us back out to the plane and there were two others there. Piet handed our luggage to the pilot and he stowed it away.

"You for Klein?" one of the other passengers asked.

"We are," I confirmed.

"Simon Webb," he said. "This is Tony Edwards."

"I'm Fiona Barclay and this is Tiffany MacBeth," I said. "Do you work for Sable Mining?"

"We do," Simon confirmed. "I'll be running the concentrator, and Tony will be working in the mine, and what brings you to Kleinbegin?"

"We're here to assess the project and decide on funding," I said.

"Oh, you're with the lender, I thought that was Thames Cherwell?" he said.

"It is," I confirmed. "We're with Thames Cherwell."

"Oh, I thought a Dr Barclay was coming?" Tony asked.

"I am Dr Barclay," I said.

"Oh," Simon said. "Sorry about that, shall we get aboard and go?"

The pilot went through his briefing and then we were off. It was bright, a few rain clouds on the different horizons, but generally sunny and hot, I was very glad that we had decided on lightweight khaki shirts and trousers, and even more thankful for my sunglasses. It struck me that it was a short runway, given the altitude and summer temperatures, but we cleared the end of the runway fine and climbed out on our way to Kleinbegin. Simon took on the rôle of tour guide and pointed out places and landmarks as we went. We passed mines, we passed farms, we passed towns and villages then abruptly the landscape changed. There were very few towns or villages, there was little in the way of farming and the ground looked dry, barren and uninviting. We were now over the northern part of the Cape, a huge expanse of land with very few inhabitants, and those that there were struggled to survive in the arid desertlike land. We passed over a mine, that Simon told us was an iron ore mine, we crossed the Orange River, then we started down and circled the hamlet of Kleinbegin and came into land. George was there to meet us.

"Fiona, Tiffany, thanks for coming," he said. "You met Simon and Tony, how was the trip?"

"Pretty good," I said. "A little bumpy here and there, but it's the summer and it's hot here."

"Let me take your bags," George offered. "Simon, why don't you take the other *bakkie*, here's the keys. Okay, Fiona, Tiffany, are you ready?"

"We are," I said, after I got nod from Tiffany.

"Okay then," he said. "We've put you up in our guest house for tonight, I thought that we'd get some lunch then go over the project, then tomorrow morning we'll take a drive around and have a look at the exploration pit and the surrounding area, then we'll fly back to Jo'burg and go on to see the Palabora mine. I've fixed up a tour there with a friend of mine of mine."

"I think Simon and Tony were expecting someone else," I said.

"My fault," George said. "All I told them was that a Dr Barclay from Thames Cherwell was coming out to review financing, I forgot to tell them that Dr Barclay was Dr Fiona Barclay."

"Kleinbegin is not very big, is it?" I commented.

"No," he laughed. "Mines tend to be in out of the way places unless they're big enough to have a town grow up around them, like Jo'burg. Kleinbegin is essentially a halt on the railway line, my guess is that it's here because it was a watering stop for steam engines."

"How big is the guest house?" I asked.

"Two bedrooms, bathroom, kitchen and living room," he said. "We'll drop your stuff there and go to the mess and get some lunch, then after lunch we'll get together with the team and review the project."

George was right, the guest house was basic, but quite adequate. They had given us a room each but we had to share the bathroom.

"I was thinking that we'd get everyone together tonight for a *braai*, is that okay with you?" George asked.

"Of course," I said. George chattered on as he led us to the mess. There were a couple of others there, but they were leaving as we arrived. George helped us to lunches and drinks, then we went outside and sat in the shade, it was still hot there, but at least there was a breeze that provided some relief. George talked as we ate, he told us about the initial find and then the exploratory drilling that had defined the ore body. I asked what methods they had used to interpolate between drill holes and he told me that that was a question to put to their geologist.

Lunch over we went to another building which was probably going to serve as the mine offices. There we found other men assembled.

"Okay," George said. "This is Dr Fiona Barclay and Tiffany MacBeth, they're with Thames Cherwell to assess the viability of our project and, if we convince them that it's a good prospect, then they'll provide the financing. Before we start, I should tell you that I've known Fiona for years, I was at school and college with her brother, she's got a Phd in maths, and another in economics and a third in computer science, so don't try and snow her with technical stuff. Tiffany is the daughter of Professor MacBeth who some of you may remember from economic geology, so, again, don't assume that they're not going to understand or not ask good questions. So, going around the table we have, Henry Grant, our geologist, Simon, you already met, he's the concentrator chap, you also met Tony, he's the mining type, Gerald Williams is the smelter, Roger Lowe is maintenance, you met Harry in London, he's running the infrastructure and environmental issues and Neville, you also met in London, he's the personnel wallah. So, Henry, over to you, Fiona was asking me about the methods you used to interpolate between drill holes."

Henry gave us some maps and drill logs and pointed out where the holes were drilled and the results that were observed. He then talked about the methods used to interpolate between holes and the confidence levels he placed on the results. Based on that he showed us a map of the deposit itself, how far it stretched, how deep it went and so on.

"What level of oxidation did you find and how far down does it go?" Tiffany asked.

"Not too far," Henry said. "We saw a shift from oxides to sulphide at about thirty feet."

"Is the oxide ore usable?" Tiffany asked. "I remember Dad talking about treating oxide ores at Rokana in Zambia."

"Yes, the TORCO plant," Henry confirmed. "We'll probably strip the oxides and store them and then decide whether to try reducing it ourselves or try doing a deal with Rokana." He and Tiffany then had a longer discussion about the ore body and its structure, and the minerals that comprised the bulk of the reserves. She had obviously done her homework, or had been well coached by her father. I added my bit by talking about the interpolation methods that had been used to get an estimate of the total reserves from the diamond drill holes. To bore you with the technicalities they had used a Kriging method that was well recognised and now in common usage. It had advantages over linear regression and Gaussian distribution methods and I was happy to see that that had used it.

"Tell us about the mining method?" I asked of Tony. He produced plans and talked about the overburden stripping then the ore mining and the bench methods they would use as the pit deepened. He talked about production levels and the equipment necessary. All had to be purchased, probably from the US. Roger chimed in there and talked about the maintenance facilities and procedures they would need. Then came the turns of Simon and Gerald who had the job of converting the ore to a saleable product in the form of copper wire bars. Gerald showed us a large chart that was a project planning chart and had listed all the things that needed to be done and when. It was certainly comprehensive enough, covering everything from getting the money to shipping the first product.

"Harry, what do need to put into place to make this all possible?" I asked.

"Well, we can get everything here by road from Prieska if we have to," he said. "But, it would make life easier if SAR put in a spur for us. Kleinbegin already has a crossing point and a siding, so adding a short spur shouldn't be that difficult. Power will be a bigger issue. If ESCOM will put a line out to us, then we'd be better off than if we had to put in our own generating station. We're waiting to hear from them, but if they decline, then we'll add more diesel sets to our power house, and then add more fuel storage."

"What about water for the plant, the houses, and effluent from the plant and the town?" I asked.

"Water is not a problem," he said. "We found that out when we were drilling. We'll put in a bigger treatment plant for the incoming water, and we'll put in treatment plant for effluent. We'll also need to plan the dumps, the settling ponds and the slag heaps. I have plans for all those here."

"Housing, housing for how many?" I asked.

"We have a manning chart here," Neville said. "And, based off that I'll build houses as we need them, we plan to locate the village here."

"Which way is the prevailing wind?" Tiffany asked.

"Basically from the north from March to September and from the south from September to March," Harry said.

"So it should be fairly simple to locate your workshops so they are not downwind of your crushers?" she asked.

"We've taken that into account," Harry assured her. We carried on for a while, both throwing questions at them and I have to say that they seemed to have thought of everything and had plans for all eventualities. It looked like a well planned operation. Well, James had said that George would make a good project manager. Eventually at about five-thirty we ran out of questions and then I asked them if they had questions of us.

"I suppose the one uppermost in our minds, is will you finance?" George asked.

"I take this back to my board and present the case, my recommendation will be to support the project," I said. I might have been sticking my neck out a little, but there seemed little point in doing further analysis. I had already been through the numbers and run my own calculations, all I was really doing was checking to see what level of confidence I could place upon those numbers. That was what this visit was all about, looking the managers in the eye and checking to see if they hesitated at all.

"What happens now?" Neville asked.

"I have here a list of documents that I need from you," I said. "When my board approves the project, then from those we'll put together a prospectus and make a public offering. The bank will probably take 12.5% and any shares that are unsubscribed. I am confident that within a month you should have the financing in place to begin the processing or ordering equipment, building buildings, and the rest."

"That's great," Simon said.

"On that note, we'll call it a day," George said. "Tomorrow I'm going to take Fiona and Tiffany around the site, beginning with the core shed. If any issues come up that I can't answer, I'll call on whichever one of you will know the answer."

"Sounds good," Tony said. "Now, I could do with a beer."

George explained to us where the *braai* would be and suggested that we take our belongings back to the guest house and join them when we were ready. Well, I was ready for a glass of wine if they had one, or a beer if they did not. So, Tiffany and I walked back to the guest house and dropped our briefcases, visited the loo in turn and then went to join the others.

"Fiona, Tiffany, this is Anika, Muriel, Janet, Elizabeth and Helen," George said, making the introductions.

"Nice to see you again, Fiona," Anika said. "How are Charlize and James?"

"They're both well, they have a daughter now, Fiona, and they're running a winery in New Mexico," I replied.

"So, they moved from France?" Anika asked.

"Yes, the family sold the South African properties and bought another one in France and the one in the States," I explained. "I think they're looking at other sites in New Mexico, apart from the one they bought. We saw them at Christmas when we were all visiting my Mom in Cannes."

"What would you like to drink?" Anika asked. "We've got wine and beer."

"A white wine would be nice, thanks," I replied. "Tiffany?"

"The same please," she said.

"Is this your first trip to Africa, Tiffany?" Anika asked.

"It is," Tiffany confirmed. "It's not quite what I expected, I thought I'd see more jungle and animals."

"For jungle you need to go to the Congo," Anika said. "Africa is so big and varied, it has most climate zones, except arctic."

"What do you do here?" Tiffany asked.

"Muriel and I run the mess," Anika replied. "Janet and Elizabeth both work in the mine office and Helen is our nurse."

"Isn't it a little difficult living out here?" Tiffany asked.

"It has its challenges," Anika admitted. "We go into Prieska for shopping, we fly to Jo'burg when we can, we're busy and it's going to get busier."

"So, Fiona, how do you want your steak?" George asked. That broke up our conversation with Anika and we made the effort after that to try and talk to everyone there. I got the impression as I talked to each in turn that they were universally keen about the project and were all talking as if the financing was already in place and that they could proceed with ordering equipment, construction materials and start building. It was quite a project. Apart from digging the mine, they were going to have to erect sheds for the crushers and grinders, erect more sheds for the smelters and more for the refinery. Then they were going to have to build a town to house all the people needed, and, to top it all off, they were going to have to find people to do all the work. I wondered where the Prieska Copper mine had found all their people, had they recruited locally and trained people, or had they brought them in from outside. With a town of the size they would have, they would also need a school, a clinic of some size and other amenities to keep the workforce happy. It was quite an enterprise. It would be interesting to come back in five years and see what had changed. I saw Tiffany in conversation with Henry, talking about minerals, gems and precious metals, then she was buttonholed by Anika who heard that she was a jeweller and then the conversation switched from minerals in the raw to wearable minerals.

"So what do you think Fiona?" George asked, when he found me in a quiet moment.

"I like your people," I said. "This is a good team, but you've got quite a challenge ahead of you. Can you get it done?"

"I think so," he said. "We've got the project plan that you saw, it looks like a formidable challenge, but it you take each task in turn, it's doable."

"This must be exciting for you to start up a new operation?" I asked.

"It is," he agreed. "I learned at lot at the gold mine and the diamond mine, but they had both been running for a while, this has to start up from what you see here, essentially bare ground. So, how's James liking the wine business?"

"He's enjoying himself," I said. "He and Charlize did a great job in France and now the family is looking for investment opportunities in the States. The winery they bought there is quite small, but they're already looking to expand it and maybe buy more land."

"When will you see him again?" George asked.

"I've some business in the States, so will tack on a trip to New Mexico and go out and see them," I said.

"How do you get there?" he asked.

"Either fly to Albuquerque or Denver," I replied. "Denver's a longer drive, but has better connections than Albuquerque."

"Where did you find Tiffany?" he asked. "She's a whizz at asking just the right question to make you sit back and ask yourself why you hadn't thought of that?"

"Actually she was a driver for a limousine service that we used," I said. "Then we took her on as our driver, then we discovered that she had hidden talents."

"Did you know that she's a kendo champion?" he asked.

"I knew that she did kendo, but I didn't know she was a champion," I admitted.

"Roger is into kendo and he recognised her," George explained. "I think that if he had had equipment here he would have liked a match."

"Well, she can certainly drive," I said. "She beat me handily in a race we had at the Maserati test track last month. She's really good at picking things up, probably make a really good secret agent."

"So, tomorrow, we'll start out with the tour early, then we can get away to Jo'burg and on into Phalaborwa before it gets too bumpy," George suggested.

"That's fine with me," I said. "I think I'll turn in, I didn't sleep that well on the plane last night."

Tiffany had been apparently waiting for my lead, because she came over and joined me as I walked back to the guest house.

"What do you think?" I asked her.

"It's exciting," she said. "They all believe in the mine, they can see it in operation already. It will be a challenge for wives out here, they better find something for them all to do."

"You're right," I agreed. "Do you want to shower first?"

"Okay," she said. We gathered towels from our rooms and went to the bathroom. There was a shower, a handbasin and a loo, so I put the top down on the loo and sat while Tiffany showered and chatted. When she was done, I showered while she dried herself, then we said good night and turned in.

We were awakened in the morning when Anika knocked on the door and brought us both coffee.

"Breakfast?" she asked.

"That would be nice," I said.

"We're serving it in the mess," she said. "If you'd like to come with me, we'll get you some." We followed her to the mess and got breakfast. They might have been out of the way, but they ate well. I think all the people that we had met the night before came and went and different times, all intent on their missions for the day. George came and collected us and we set off on our tour. We did go to the core shed first, where Henry was waiting and he explained what we were looking at the drill cores and what the various indications in the core meant. Then it was on to the test pit, where we drove down into the pit then got out and wandered around looking at rocks and minerals. George had a map and he showed us where the test pit sat in relation to the projected actual pit. Then we toured around to where the dumps would be, the tailings ponds, the workshops, the crusher and grinder buildings, the smelter and the refinery. It all seemed so odd, we were looking at bare ground, but in George's mind he could see buildings, trucks, a pit, houses, everything that made up the mine. We drove back to the guest house and collected our luggage, said goodbye to everyone and drove to the airstrip. There we saw Anika, Muriel and Janet waiting for us. Anika was coming with us to the Palabora mine and Muriel and Janet were taking the chance to get to Johannesburg for an outing. George was our tour guide on the flight back to Johannesburg. He pointed out very much the same things that Simon had the day before. In Johannesburg, we stopped long enough to use the loo, drop off Muriel and Janet, fuel up the plane and then we were off to Phalaborwa. That was a much shorter flight, only about an hour and a half. We landed and it was hot, much hotter than it had been at Kleinbegin. It was also much more humid and there were storm clouds gathering. George rented a car and drove us to the hotel.

Over dinner that evening, I asked who Hans Merensky was.

"He was the *ou* who predicted diamonds along the Namaqualand coast, he discovered the platinum reef, the Merensky Reef, he founded Foskor, which mines phosphates here adjacent to the copper mine," George explained. "When he predicted diamonds along the Namaqualand coast most other geologists at the time said that he was full of it, but he was proven correct and got a huge prospectors find fee for it."

"So the Foskor operation is why he's recognised here?" I asked.

"I presume so," George said. "Anika, do you know any more?"

"No," she said. "I'm from the Cape, I've never been to Phalaborwa before. When we would visit Kruger we'd go in at the south end."

"Have you been to a copper mine before?" I asked Anika.

"No, this is a first, when George set this up for you I told him that I would be coming too," she said.

"I'm looking forward to seeing what a big mine looks like," I said. "This is a first for me, what about you Tiffany?"

"I've been down old copper and tin mines," she said. "Dad took us into all kinds of old mines, he even took us to the open cast iron ore mines near Corby, but I think tomorrow will be different."

"Who do we meet tomorrow?" I asked George.

"Danie van Zyl," George replied. "I've known Danie for years, he was at college the same time James and I were, but in the year ahead. I played rugby with him."

300

"What time are we due at the mine tomorrow?" I asked.

"I said we'd meet Danie at nine," George said. "He'll then give us the royal tour of the mine, the concentrator and the smelter, and he even said that he'd throw in lunch along the way."

"So, I'll see you tomorrow for breakfast?" I asked.

"We'll be here at seven-thirty," Anika said. "Then we can pay the account and George can drive us to the mine."

Danie was waiting for us when we arrived at the mine the next morning.

"Hey, George, howzit man?" he asked.

"Good, thanks, Danie, this is my wife, Anika and these are my bankers, Dr Fiona Barclay and Tiffany MacBeth," George replied, making the introductions.

"Welcome to Palabora," Danie said. "Is James Barclay your brother?"

"He is," I confirmed. "He's running a winery in the States now."

"Lucky bloke," Danie said. "We should get you some safety boots and hats."

"We have safety boots," I said for myself and Tiffany.

"I'll need some," Anika said. Danie took a quick look at her feet and came back with two sizes, Anika picked one and they fit. Danie then handed out hardhats and led us out to a minibus. We climbed aboard and he then took off first to an overview where we could see the whole operation and then down the mine. He gave us a running commentary as he went and a few times he stopped and suggested that get out to look at something. It was fascinating, the equipment in the mine was huge, far larger than anything I had seen at Corby Seaton, or Metter. I think Tiffany would have loved to have had a go driving some of it, but that opportunity did not arise. The mine tour took all morning and we stopped for lunch.

"Well, what do you think?" Danie asked.

"Everything is big," I commented.

"It's quite different to the iron ore mines I've been to in England," Tiffany added.

"I'm like Fiona, I can't get over how big everything is," Anika said.

"There are even bigger machines used elsewhere," Danie said. "Even we may go to larger trucks as we go deeper and they become available."

"Are they easy to drive?" Tiffany asked.

"They are," Danie confirmed. "You just have to get used to how big they are."

We had lunch then went on to the crushing, grinding and concentrating processes, then the smelter and finally the refinery. I was fascinated by the concentrator, watching the bubbles and seeing the metallic sheen on the bubbles that told of metals. It seemed to me that this part of the operation was conveyors, pipes and pumps, then the hot areas of the smelter. That was noisy, smelly and reeked of hazard, or at least it did to me. Tiffany talked to Danie about liberation, recovery and recirculating loads which made me wonder where and when she had learned all that. I think Danie was surprised by her questions, but happy to answer them and even dragged in one of the concentrator managers for a better explanation. I had a clear picture now of what the Klein Copper mine would look like in the future and the challenges that lay ahead building all of it, then operating it. I just hoped that James was right and that George was the man for the job. I saw nothing, nor did I hear anything that would cause me to change my mind about financing Klein Copper, it seemed as if the fundamental technologies were well understood, so it was really a matter of execution. We finished our tour watching copper being loaded into a truck for shipment to market and Danie gave us each a copper symbol, cast in copper. I had not appreciated that the old symbol for copper was also the symbol for female. George explained it. He told us that the Greek's symbol for Mars was the one for iron and the one for Venus was copper and that Linnaeus had standardised male and female to be represented by Mars and Venus respectively. We thanked Danie for the tour and went back to our hotel to marvel at what we had seen.

Over dinner that night, George had another gift for us. He gave Tiffany and I a small display case each that had all the common ores for copper. "So, now you've got the raw materials and the finished product," he said. "Henry puts these together, he scours the outcrops for samples and he grabs other samples for the test pit to make these up. I'm not sure where he gets the cases made."
"Thank him for us, will you?" I asked. "And thank you for arranging this, it's been most helpful."

"So, what do you think about Klein Copper?" he asked.

"Well, it's clear that there are no new technologies to be discovered or invented," I said. "So, it really comes down to how well you and your team manage the project. My sense is that you'll do fine."

"Thanks," he said.

'What do you think, Anika?" I asked.

"It's going to be a challenge just to see George for the next year or so, which is why I moved out to Kleinbegin as soon as I could, but, it's exciting to be part of something new," she said.

"Well, if George ever decides to go on holiday, make him take you to the States and go and see Charlize," I told her. "They live in this tiny town called Pecos, surrounded by forest and vineyards. Fly into Denver and drive down the front range of the Rockies, it's worth the trip."

"I may just do that," she said.

"This is their business card," I said, passing over a card from the Old Pecos Winery. "Those are the best phone numbers to call."

"Thanks Fiona," George said. "Anything else?"

"No, perhaps you could take us to the airport tomorrow so that we can collect our hire car?" I asked.

"Of course," he said. "Our flight leaves at eight, is that too early for you?"

"No," I said, speaking for both of us. "If we get an early start we can take our time driving to Letaba."

"You'll love it," Anika assured us. "Kruger really is a nice park, it's got a huge variety of animals, and you should be able to see most things. The rains are not that far advanced that the grass it too high yet."

"Great, well, I'm for bed, thanks again for the day, George, we'll see you in the morning," I said.

I lay in bed thinking about the day and was satisfied. The project was in good hands, Tiffany was measuring up nicely, as George had commented she had this uncanny knack of asking just the right question. I heard a distant rumble, then another and realised that I was listening to a building thunderstorm. I got out of bed, opened the curtains and the windows and watched. I lost count of lightning flashes, and waited in anticipation for the thunder that followed. The storm was coming our way, even as I watched the time lag between the flashes and the sound grew shorter and shorter, until it had to be almost overhead. Then the rain came, that beautiful tropical rain, that comes down in deluges. I loved the smell of it, it took me back to Kenya, evoking all kinds of memories. There was even a word for the scent of the rain, petrichor, a word invented by the Australians, I suppose they had had the same experiences of heavy tropical rain and the smell of the damp earth that followed. It was to me wonderful and I went back to bed listening to the rain on the roof, beating down, coming down in buckets and washing clean everything. The centre of the storm moved away and I could again count the delay between the flash and the bang. It would have been really nice to go outside and just stand naked in the rain that poured down, but the local authorities would probably take a dim view of such behaviour. I had done it in Kenya, but that had been in our own back garden, space that was effectively screened from viewers, both by foliage and by topography, so I gave up on that notion and went to sleep lulled by the sound of the rain.

Kruger

When I woke up the next morning, the storm had long passed and it was back to hot sunshine again. I went for breakfast and Tiffany was already there with George and Anika.

"Did you hear that storm last night?" Tiffany asked. "It was amazing, I couldn't believe the thunder and the amount of rain that came down."

"I enjoyed it," I said. "It took me back to Kenya. Thinking of rain George, how many days of production at your mine do you estimate that you'll lose because of rain?"

"Not that many," he said. "The northern Cape doesn't get the amount of rain they get here, so a day or two at the most."

I was satisfied with that, they had obviously thought about it. So, I ate breakfast, collected my belongings and went to meet the others in the hotel lobby. George and Anika took us to the airport, we said goodbye and they left to fly back to Johannesburg, then pick up the charter to Kleinbegin. We got our hire car, a Volkswagen Golf, we loaded our luggage in the back and took off for the park, a short drive from the airport. My travel agent had given me a whole booklet of coupons that covered just about everything for our trip to Kruger, one even covered the entry fee, so I tore it out and handed it over and we were waved through to start out on our safari adventure. Before we drove off, I dug in my bag and pulled out a bird book, mammals I knew quite well, but only a few birds, so had purchased a book on the birds of South Africa and brought it with me.

We had only been on the road a few minutes when we had to slow down almost to a crawl as there were several zebra trotting down the road in front of us. I had learned in Kenya that the animals used the roads as well as humans, the roads being nice open thoroughfares that offered easy transit and not much cover on the sides for predators to lurk.

"Aren't they fat?" Tiffany said, delighted with the encounter.

"I don't think I've ever seen a skinny zebra," I said.

"I suppose all the stripe patterns are different," Tiffany said. "I wonder if you photographed them all if you could pick out individuals?"

"Probably, but that would take a lot of work, unless I could develop a computer program to scan images and look for patterns," I mused.

"Look, look," Tiffany said, excited by something. "A giraffe, over there."

"I see it," I said. The zebra left the road and went off into the bush and the giraffe just nibbled away at leaves on some trees and watched us warily, but did not amble off. Clearly we did not represent a threat.

"Can we go on?" Tiffany asked. I drove on slowly, looking left and right to see what there might be. There was a small road that went off to the right, so I took it. The track had had no other vehicles yet, so we were the first for that day. Not far along the track there was a waterhole, so I pulled up and we just sat and looked.

"Look there," Tiffany said, pointing and aiming her binoculars at animals that were there. "Elephants, my God, is that what I think it is?"

"It is," I confirmed. "They're a group of males, so that is the biggest dick you've ever seen."

"It is," she confirmed. She turned to me and grinned, delighted with what we were seeing. "Thanks so much for bringing me, this has been amazing already and we're not even half an hour from the gate."

"I'm sure we'll see more as we go," I said. "Look, down there, to the right of the elephants, those are impala, and a couple more zebra."

"Let's drive on and see what else there is," she suggested. I drove on, back around the loop and onto the main road again. We motored slowly along the road, stopping for animals, birds, more animals and more birds. Finally we came to the Letaba Rest Camp. We went to the office and they could actually accommodate us immediately, as occupancy was low because we were in the rainy season, not the height of the tourist season. The receptionist accepted another of my coupons and we were given a little bungalow, facing the river and as far as I could tell the next four were unoccupied. The bungalow had two beds, plus a bathroom. It was perfectly adequate for us. We went to find lunch and were pleased with not only what we found, but also the prices, which were very reasonable.

"So," I said, when we were finishing up our lunch. "Maybe a short siesta in the heat of the day, and then we'll take another drive this afternoon?"

"That sounds brilliant," Tiffany replied. "How hot do you think it is?"

"Well over a hundred," I guessed. "Just too hot to be rushing around, and most animals tend to be more active in the early morning and late afternoon."

Back at our bungalow, I stripped off to my underwear and stretched out on one of the beds. Tiffany did likewise, but she went a little further and stripped off completely, so I thought, why not and did likewise. It was good to get my bra off as I had been sweating, no, according to the old adage, I was not sweating, I was glowing, horses sweat, men perspire and ladies glow. As I had done at Maman's villa at Christmas time, I admired her body and felt the same uncomfortable stirrings. Was I really attracted to Tiffany, was it plain lust after such a beautiful body, or what. She turned and faced me.

"Fiona," she said. "I just wanted to tell you that I'm having the time of my life. I have a job with you that I'm really enjoying, I can't thank you enough for bringing me on this trip and giving me this safari. Please don't hate me for what I'm going to say now, but, I love you. When we first met I was attracted to you, but as time has gone on and we've spent more time together, that attraction has turned to love. It doesn't matter to me if you don't love me, I just want to be near you. I know it might make things awkward because I work for you, but I can't help it."

"Tiffany, I'm not sure of my feelings right now, I look at you and I get stirrings deep in me, I look at you and wonder and I'm not sure what to do, on the one hand I want to just throw all societal constraints out of the window and romp on the bed with you, but on the other hand I feel guilty about longing for you," I admitted. "I won't send you away, I like that you're with me, I look forward to seeing you every day, I get a thrill from your touch, you make me laugh and feel happy in a way that hasn't happened since Ian died. I don't compare you to Ian, which for me is good, because I was doing that with Tom. Can we take some time and see where this leads us?"

"Of course," she said. "I just wanted you to know that I love you, I think your Mum and Portia guessed when we were in France, your Mum told me to make sure that you wouldn't be hurt. I also want you to know that if you ever need me for anything I will be there for you."

"Gosh, Tiffany, thank you," I said, in some ways glad that it was now in the open between us.

"Do you really get stirrings when you look at me?" she asked.

"I do," I confessed. "And it confuses me, I thought that I was absolutely straight, men only, but when I look at you, I wonder what it would be like. Give me a day or so and perhaps we could find out together?"

"I'll be here," she promised. "It feels so good to have finally broached the subject. When you want to try things, just let me know."

"I will," I promised. Then we both settled back, looking at the ceiling, each lost in her own thoughts. I know I drifted off to sleep, because I had a strange dream about huge trucks, probably recalling what we had seen at Palabora.

I awoke to Tiffany gently touching my arm. "Fiona," she said. "It's two, should we get the car and take a drive?"

"Good idea," I agreed. "Let me just get dressed." I found my panties and bra and put them back on, then grabbed my shorts and shirt and dressed. We got into the car and left the camp following the river.

"Look, warthogs," I said. We watched as they ran across the road and disappeared into the grass beyond. We drove on, past herds of impala, more zebra, some wildebeest, some waterbuck and all kinds of birds. We circled back and went north again towards Letaba, then cut back east on another side road. "There," I said, stopping and pointing.

"Lions," Tiffany breathed. "Lions, oh how wonderful, Fiona, how can I ever thank you enough for this?"

"I'll let you know," I laughed. "But just sharing this adventure with someone who is really enjoying it is thanks enough. Look there, that's what the lions are interested in, those buffalo over there."

"They look mean," Tiffany said.

"They're not to be taken lightly," I agreed. "My guess is that when dark comes the lions will start hunting, and they'll probably go after one of those buffalo."

"I suppose the lions have to eat," Tiffany said. We moved on and slowly wended our way back to the rest camp. Over dinner that night we listed what we had seen that day, both animals and birds, in all thirteen animal species and forty-one bird species. "I wonder what we'll see tomorrow?" she asked.

"I wonder?" I echoed. "Whatever comes along will be a treat, are you having a good time?"

"I am," she confirmed. "It's so wonderful to be here, wonderful to see all these animals and birds, wonderful to have you tell me what they are and just wonderful to be here with you. I'd kiss you but I imagine they're pretty conservative here and that would not go over well."

"You're probably right," I agreed. "Now, a shower before bed?"

We slept apart that night, I think probably both wondering whether or not to make the advance. Tiffany was good, she was leaving it to me to make the advance. I was churning over in my mind the complications of a possible relationship with Tiffany. She worked for me and how would that affect her work, my attitude towards her and so much more. How would we be able to cover up feelings in the bank, how soon before others in the bank found out and would that information leak out and make me vulnerable to innuendo and gossip in the banking world. I suppose the real issue was, did I care. Now that was something I was going to have to think long and hard about, did I care. If all else turned against me, I actually had enough money to tell the world to go to hell and just enjoy my life, like Freya was doing. She did not care what people thought about her, she lived and loved in her castle, comfortable with her feelings towards Kirsty.

After breakfast the next day, we left the Letaba camp and wended our way north to the Mopani Rest Camp, taking a side road that was unpaved. I saw some ground hornbills and stopped and pointed to them.

"What are those?" Tiffany asked. "They're as big as turkeys."

"They're ground hornbills," I said. "They make this lovely booming sound."

"What does the book say about them?" Tiffany asked.

"Turkey sized birds, monogamous pair for life and long lived," I read.

"I wonder if outside the park if people eat them, a bird that big would be a lot of eating," she thought.

"The book doesn't mention that, but it does say that people hunt them for rituals and traditional medicine," I read.

"Listen, they're talking," she said. They were indeed calling, the deep booming sound that they make. While Tiffany was watching the birds I was looking at the road ahead and the tracks in the road. There were elephant ahead of us, quite a few of them and all sizes. I wondered how far ahead of us they were and opened the door slightly to peer down at the tracks that I saw next to the car. Based on the clues that Ian had taught me, I gauged the tracks to be very new, less than an hour old, so the animals could be fairly close. I closed the door and looked over in time to see the hornbills disappear into the thick brush.

"Shall we see what's ahead?" I asked.

"Let's," she said. We drove slowly on and I studied the road ahead and the tracks. I saw where they left the road and pulled up and stopped.

"What is it?" she asked.

"Elephant," I said, pointing towards the river off to our left.

"Oh look, there's little ones," she said, excitedly. It was indeed a small herd of about fifteen, all sizes from the matriarch down to one who had to be only a month or two old. "Is that the male in the herd?" she asked.

"No, that's grandma," I said. "They have a matriarchal society and the herd is led by an old female and then there are sisters, daughters and youngsters, male and female, when the males get to be older teenagers they go off and join the male groups."

"Brilliant," she said. "A society led by women, with the male called in every now and then to do his bit."

"Don't get too excited," I laughed. "Most of the other herbivore species have male dominated herds, or pairs."

We watched the elephants for a while until they moved off into the bush and out of sight. It struck me as very different to the plains of Kenya and Tanzania, in Kruger there was much more in the way of trees and bushes and one had to work to see animals. We drove on stopping at times to look at birds, crocodiles, terrapins, and other animals, we even saw some kudu trying to hide from us by standing still and hoping that we did not see them. When we came to Mopani it was getting on towards lunchtime and also time for a break as the day was heating up nicely.

I liked Mopani, it was perched up on a small hill and there were rocks and trees everywhere. Our bungalow was set among some rocks and placed so that it looked out onto the bush, and neighbours were not really evident. We dropped our bags in the room, then went looking for lunch. We sat and ate lunch looking out from beneath the wooden beams and thatch to the rain teeming down outside. The shower did not last long and the sun came back out and steam started to rise from the heated surfaces. It was hot and humid, not the kind of day to be rushing around. But, from the terrace of the dining area we could look out over a dambo and watch birds and animals.

"Having fun?" I asked Tiffany.

"I am," she confirmed. "This is brilliant, the animals and birds, it's all so new, so exciting, do different. When you lived in Kenya, did you go on many safaris?"

"As often as we could," I replied. "We would often fly off for a weekend and juts see what we could find."

"Gosh, that must have been nice," she said. "To be able to just flit about as you like."

"Well, there were times when we stayed away from the borders," I said. "Kenya and Uganda traded insults and threats for a while, so we were careful to stay away from that border."

"You know, what makes this extra special is that you're here showing it all to me," she said.

"I was just thinking the same, what makes this trip special is that I am sharing it with someone I care about, that makes it all the more fun," I said.

"I know I said this before, but thanks so much for bringing me," she said.

"I'm glad I did," I said. "You've made the trip memorable, in more ways than one."

"I'm glad," she said. I had been looking at her and watching her and her excitement and obvious delight at being there and more to the point being with me, and emotions just welled up in me and I felt desire, want, longing and made a momentous decision.

"I think a siesta or something is in order before we go wandering off again," I said.

"Or something?" she asked, breathlessly.

"Or something," I promised.

We tried not to run back to the bungalow, but we made it in short order. I took her hands in mine and leaned in and kissed her. She responded, gently at first then with more passion.

"Wow, Fiona," she said when we broke for air. "Wow, that was lovely."

"It was, wasn't it," I said. The die was cast now, the decision made, the Rubicon crossed, I was going to do this, all qualms set aside, all notions of guilt tossed out of the window, I was just going to enjoy the moment and revel in the intimacy that being with Tiffany promised.

"Why don't we have a shower together?" she suggested. That sounded like a good idea, get rid of the travel dirt and the perspiration of the mid day and start fresh and clean. Tiffany took charge and we went to the bathroom and turned on the shower. The shower was basic, but had the real benefit of being quite large, so it looked as if two could actually fit. I undressed quickly and watched as Tiffany peeled off her clothes as if they were on fire. She entered the shower and turned the water on and played with the taps a little until it was tepid, not too cold that we would shrink from the water, but cool enough to make it comfortable in the heat of the day. She held her hand out to me and I joined her in the shower. To be next to another body after so long was wonderful. We embraced and held each other close and the feel of her all the way down me was just so nice and oh so exciting and stimulating. From there things got hot and heavy fairly quickly and continued in the shower and on the bed. I think once the dam was broken, then I could not get enough. It was like it had been with Ian, once we had made love the first time and I had realised what was possible it had been a weekend filled with adventure, romance, exploration and delight. The same was now true with Tiffany, now that the shackles had been removed and my concerns about social mores and prohibitions had been thrown away, I was free to enjoy the moment, enjoy being with another person and free to explore my sexuality. I must say, Tiffany was an excellent teacher, and I loved every minute of the experiences that we had together. At some point I heard her breath in my ear, *tha gaol agam ort*, what that meant I had not idea, but no doubt I would find out soon enough.

"My God, Tiffany," I said, when we took a break. "Why did I not do this sooner, what have I been missing?"

"I'm here now," she said. "I'm yours, only yours."

"Come lie next to me, hold me and tell me what else we could try in the next few days," I suggested. She lay next to me, close so that I could feel her body pressed against mine, such a lovely feeling, such comfort and security. Then we talked. We talked bluntly and frankly about the afternoon, what we had liked, what we had liked more, and what we might try next. The conversation led to questions and experiments and we were soon back in each other's arms, flesh pressed tightly against flesh and writhing in ecstasy. I had not had so much fun since Ian died. I gave myself up completely to the moment and regretted nothing.

"You know," I said, as we lay back, arms around one another. "One of the biggest benefits of being with you is there's no risk of getting knocked up, so no need for pills, condoms or all the other things."

"That's true," she agreed. "I love you Fiona, *mo leannan, tha gaol agam ort*, I adore you, I want to be with you."

"What does that mean?" I asked.

"*Tha gaol agam ort*, I love you, *mo leannan*, my sweetheart," she said. "It's Gaelic, the language of my family, we speak it at home in preference to English."

"*Ua here vau ia oe*, I love you Tiffany, *te tiare*," I said contentedly, and I did, I was not just saying it. It had hit me at lunch, that I was happy, and the reason that I was happy was that I was with someone that I loved. What matter that that person was a woman not a man, and what a woman. I had not felt so content since when Ian was alive, I felt a contentment that washed over me pushing away cares, worries, even concerns about what world might think. I was not going to advertise the fact that I was with Tiffany, but I was not going to shy away from it either. I had enough money that if the world of banking disapproved and found fault and reason not to do business with me, then that was their loss.

"Well, are we going to lie here all afternoon and make love to each other, or shall we take a drive around?" Tiffany asked. "We can return to love making in London, but we can't see lions and elephants in the wild there."

"We'll go for a drive and see what else I can show you," I said.

"Brilliant," she said. "Let's get dressed and have an afternoon out." She reached for her clothes and dressed, as did I, then we took binoculars, cameras and water and got the car and went off for an adventure. I was off in a daydream as I drove, I had wondered whether things might come to a head with Tiffany on this trip, had half hoped it would, had half been nervous about how we would handle the situation, and it had all worked out better than I had hoped.

"Shall we take this loop?" Tiffany asked, bringing me back to reality. We meandered our way around until we saw a sign that told us that we were crossing the Tropic of Capricorn. "So. we're in the tropics now," she said. "Tropic of Capricorn, wasn't that also a book?"

"It was," I confirmed. "A chap by the name of Miller wrote it in about 1939, published it in France because it was banned in the States, too explicit I think, then the US decided that it wasn't that bad after all and allowed it to be published."

"Like Lady Chatterly?" Tiffany suggested.

"In style if not subject matter," I said. "Look, over there, wild dogs."

"Aren't they pretty?" she said. "Looks like someone went mad with a paintbrush."

"*Canis pictus,*" I said. "Painted dog, so obviously someone had the same idea you did."

"There's lots of them," she said. "Look, they're all going off that way into the bushes."

"When I first went to this one place in Kenya, all I saw was backsides disappearing into the bush," I laughed. "I wondered if I'd ever see the front end of any animal."

"But, you can tell from the back what they are?" she asked.

"I got good at that," I confirmed. We drove on, stopping to look at birds, animals and more birds, then the pilot in me told me that it was time to get back to the camp, it was going to rain again. It did, we had barely parked when the heavens opened and it poured down. We waited for a brief lull, then ran to the main building and the bar.

Over a glass of Chablis, we watched the rain come down. I was surprised that we were the only ones in the bar area, I had expected the rain to have curtailed everyone's drives and that the bar would be quite full. But then it was not the height of the season, so perhaps things were just slow.

"When we get back to London, what are we going to do?" I asked.

"I think keep this between ourselves," Tiffany replied. "I'm not sure how the others at the bank would accept us. I think there was talk about favouritism before I made the presentation about Klein Copper, then Anthea and Deirdre spread the word that I actually knew something and should be on this trip."

"I hadn't realised that. I'll have to be more careful in the future," I said.

"Would you like to move in with me?"

"Gosh, yes," she said. "I'd keep my flat for the studio, but I'd love to live with you, it would be so much fun. Have you ever had a flat mate other than your husband?"

"No," I replied. "I stayed with Maman and Portia for a while before I married Ian, but then they helped me go and find my own way in the world. You?"

"No," she said. "I was going to move in with Alex, but when I found her in bed with Joanna, I dropped that idea."

"What do your parents think about your lifestyle?" I asked.

"They love me, so they accept it. I think if Catriona has a baby at some point, then they'll be happy, do you want children?" she asked.

"Not really," I said. "If Ian had really wanted children, I might have gone along with the idea, but I don't really want any, you?"

"No," she said, quite definitely. "I've never had any maternal feelings, so don't want to have any or adopt any. How would your dad accept us?"

"I'm not sure," I admitted. "He's pretty bigoted when it comes to what he would call queers, and Maman and Portia getting together bothered him, even though he's the one who left. How he would accept us? I'm sure that James has already told him his suspicions, so we'll see."

"Where do we go tomorrow?" she asked.

"The Punda Maria Rest camp, it's all the way to the north of the park, so a bit farther to drove than today," I replied.

"Should we get some dinner?" she asked. We did, we dined in style, or in as much style as one could there. Then we repaired to our bungalow for a shower and bed. We shared a bed that night, not the one we had rumpled earlier in the day, but the other one, so that they both looked used. I was wonderful to be able to sleep with someone else again, to drift off in another's arms and be happy and contented.

Punda Maria was in fact a little over eighty miles from Mopani and we were constrained about where we could go because the park people closed quite a few of the dirt side roads because of the rain. So, we stuck to the main road and lunched at Shingwedzi before going on north. Just because we did not go off on the side roads did not mean that we did not see animals, we did, we saw them by the score, zebra, wildebeest, hartebeest, impala, eland and on and on. We were held up for a while by an elephant who was just ambling along the road, in no particular hurry, just taking his time going wherever he was going. Eventually he turned off into the bush and what amazed both of us was how quickly we lost sight of him. It was hard to imagine that something so large and grey, could just disappear. Even with the binoculars we could not find him as soon as he got about ten yards off the road. I imagined a few times that I saw the flap of an ear, or the twitch of a tail, or even his trunk as he sought browse to eat, but it may have been just imaginings, or leaves and branches in the wind.

Punda Maria was almost deserted. There were a few guests, but the staff outnumbered them. We were given a bungalow that was actually a semi-detached place, but we had no neighbours. In the bedroom there were candles and a notice that explained that the camp generator was shut off at ten at night and therefore there would be no electric lights. Fortunately we had brought torches with us as part of our travel kits, so there would be no need to fumble for matches if we had to be up in the night. There was no rain that afternoon, so we took a drive on the loop that ran around the hill that the camp sat on. I almost missed them, but a twitched ear caught my attention so I stopped and there they were six hyæna, lurking in the long grass just off the road. We sat and waited and eventually they all got up, crossed the road and went off on their afternoon hunt, or we presumed it would be a hunt. So, now we had seen lions, dogs and hyæna, the only major predator that we had not seen was a leopard, but as they were solitary and most active at night, that was not going to be a simple thing. We had dinner that evening talking about music, about which I was still woefully ignorant, except for the limited amount which I enjoyed. Tiffany also told me about kendo, the Japanese art of sword fighting, but with bamboo swords, not metal ones. I learned about the strike zones that scored points and the rules and constraints. It was not just a case of hitting the opponent, it had to be done in a certain way, and there were referees to scrutinise the matches. She told me that when next she had a match, then she would ask me to come and watch. We talked about Kenya and what little I had seen of Tanzania. Memories of living in Kenya came flooding back and I have to say that they were good memories, with the occasional issue that arose when troubles with Uganda roiled and I had thought that we might have been caught up in a war. That never happened, but there were conflicts in the neighbourhood, between Tanzania and Uganda and Somalia and Ethiopia, there were also squabbles between Kenya and Tanzania that caused the border to be closed and I told Tiffany about our mad dash to fly out of Arusha before the plane was impounded. Bed that night was shared and I revelled in the comfort of getting close to

Tiffany and feeling her down the whole length of me, it was hot and we could feel perspiration between us, but that mattered not, the sheer pleasure of being with someone you love was worth all that minor discomfort.

The next day we had to leave Kruger to fly back to London. So, we had the long drive back to Phalaborwa to catch the plane to Johannesburg. We essentially retraced our steps, staying only to the main road, back past Shingwedzi, stopping at Mopani for an mid morning break and then after Mopani taking the alternate road that avoided Letaba, but instead took us almost straight to the Phalaborwa gate. We did have delays upon the way as various and sundry animals used the road as their thoroughfare. We lost count of impala that we saw, or zebra, but we did add some of the smaller antelopes to our count of species that we had seen. We were sorry to leave the park, it had been a wonderful trip, made all the better by our discovery of each other. I think I knew every curve of Tiffany now, every mound and dell, every area that caused arousal in her, as she did me. It was thrilling to be with someone again with whom I could share anything, including myself, and who clearly loved me, loved me to distraction, I hoped not to the extent of obsession that would show as jealousy and a want to control who I saw or associated with, but I did not get that impression, just love.

Our flight from Phalaborwa to Johannesburg was uneventful, which as I pilot I always took to be a good thing. We had some time to kill so wandered around the airport until the BA counter opened and we could check in for the flight to London. When the BA flight finally took off, we were in seats 2A and 2B and it was all I could do not to hold hands with Tiffany. The steward came and asked us what we wanted to drink before dinner, and we both opted for a Chardonnay. He was chatty and wanted to know of we had been on a safari, I suppose our khaki clothes did rather give that away. He told us about one he had been on in Zambia, and the more he talked about it the more interested we became. It sounded as if it would be really interesting, with only a few people, and with some walking through the bush. That had not been possible in Kruger, so that in and of itself sounded like a reason to go. After dinner we settled down to sleep and Tiffany did lean over and rest her head on

317

my shoulder and put her arm around me under the blanket that I had draped over myself. That small gesture of intimacy meant so much to me. We were awakened by the crew who wanted to rouse everyone before we touched down and who served us a small breakfast while we began our descent into Heathrow. On the ground we cleared customs and immigration then took a taxi into London to the office. I had work to do, particularly a telephonic board meeting to confirm the funding for Sable Mining.

"Good morning, Dr Barclay," Deirdre said when I got to the office. "How was the trip?"

"Wonderful," I said. "I'm not sure that I would want to be a mining engineer, Kleinbegin is miles from anywhere, it's hot, dry and there's nothing there yet but a small hamlet and a railway line."

"But the project is still on?" she asked.

"Definitely," I confirmed. "We toured the Palabora mine and could see what the Klein Copper project would look like, and the reserves all are what they talked about, so, yes it's on, let's set up a call this afternoon at two, that will not get James up too early in the morning."

"Of course," she said.

"Have you had any thoughts about Glenavon?" I asked.

"Oh yes," she said. "George and I have been to see them, and we were right, a little judicious funding and better management and they will thrive. George is making an offer next week to buy them and I have a funding proposal here for us to review, when we do and it goes to the board for approval, then George said that he would recuse himself from the meeting."

"Good," I said. "I think we should get everyone together and talk about who looks at what."

"We could go that at lunchtime," she suggested.

"Good idea," I said. "Have lunch brought in and we'll talk while we eat."

At lunchtime, I went through the assignments. As a group the analysts had to date looked at projects as they arose, or had been assigned them by Dad in a haphazard fashion, I wanted a more structured approach, so gave them all particular fields to follow. So, Tiffany got mining, Deirdre, property development, Anthea, banking and finance, Adrian, sports and recreation, Giles, the motor industry, Helen, food production and distribution, Gerald, heavy industry, Peter, energy both fuels and generation, Simon, electronics, Cynthia, entertainment, David, computers and computer services, Eleanor, fashion and Karen, air travel. I asked them all to follow those fields carefully and note anything that might be of interest to us, and if they found something to research it and bring it to the rest of us as a proposition. We would meet weekly to talk about prospects. There was excitement among the group as they now all had something particular to look at, and their ideas might lead to a deal being made. If someone came to us, then we would look at them and if they fit into any of the fields we had assigned, then that person would take the lead, if it did not fit, then I would decide who best could handle it, including myself in the mix. I asked Simon how the computerisation of the past activities was progressing and he surprised me by telling me that it was all done. We could now call up the details of any of the past deals that the bank had either initiated or had been involved with, and more to the point there were financial statements that showed how those deals had progressed, either to success in varying degrees or to failure. The failures I wanted to look at carefully to see what had been missed or misinterpreted, there was always something to learn from experiences, both good and bad. I emphasised to the staff that projects that did not go as planned, should not be regarded as a condemnation of whoever proposed them, but should be looked at so that we all could learn from what we had missed. Simon and Cynthia chimed in to say that they had culled through all the past projects and had a list of those that had failed to meet expectations. They also had put together a set of likely reasons that that had happened. I suggested that we take one or two of those each week and review them so that we all could learn.

At two I had my telephonic board meetings, rousing James out of bed in New Mexico. I went through the visit, my observations and then told them all that I was recommending that we proceed. There were a few questions, but nothing that either I or Tiffany had not thought of, so the motion to fund was passed, without demur. I told James that he might expect a visit from George and Anika at some time, but not in the immediate future, there was too much to do at Kleinbegin. I also got Deirdre and George Adams to talk about Glenavon and make their pitch, then George left the conversation and we debated funding his acquisition of Glenavon. Deirdre made a compelling argument and the numbers all worked, so we decided that we would fund the acquisition. I told the others that I would call George and let him know. I asked Portia to stay on the line after the meeting, so when the rest hung up, she was still there.

"What's up?" she asked.

"Well, I received an invitation to a dinner and a speech the other day and I was denied entry because it was held at a men only club," I told her. "How did you deal with that kind of thing?"

"I would look at the venue, call them if I had to and find out if there were any dress codes or other restrictions," she replied. "They usually assumed that I was calling on behalf of a man and I would quickly find out if it was a men-only place. Typically hotels and restaurants are fine, but they may have dress codes, any kind of private club is suspect in my book, most of them are men only as members, but some will allow, big deal, allow, women as guests, usually of a member. Where did you try and go?"

"The Cymric Club," I said.

"Don't know that one," she said. "Did they turn you away at the door?"

"They did," I confirmed. "They annoyed me, first they suggested that the invitation had not been sent to me but to Dr Barclay, then when I said that that was me, then they said, sorry lady you can't come in. What's the big bloody secret, why this men only crap?"

"I've never really understood why," she admitted. "I can't decided if they're afraid of us, if they just want someone to go and act badly, or what, I really don't know. There are women only places, but only a few, and again I'm not really sure why, except that perhaps it's a counter to the men only."

"So, if I get another invitation to a club, check it out ahead of time, then what?" I asked.

"Send a regrets that you can't attend and point out that you can't attend because you'll be denied admission, and make sure that you copy whoever is the head of the organisation that is hosting the event, and send a copy to the speaker, telling them why you won't be there," she said.

"I like that," I said. "Thanks Portia, how are you and Maman?"

"We're very well," she said. "And you and Tiffany?"

"We've got together," I said. "It happened while we were in the Kruger Park. I'm happy Portia, I haven't been this happy since Ian died."

"Good," she said. "I'll tell Brigitte the news, she will probably call you tonight."

"I'll be waiting," I said. "Thanks again Portia, *adieu*."

I then called Patrick at Sable Mining and told him that we were going ahead with the funding package for them. He was delighted and said that he would talk to the team in South Africa and give them the news. We also agreed upon a press release that we would send jointly to the Financial Times and the other major newspapers. This was the fourth major deal I had done since joining the bank and was quite pleased with myself. So far all had gone remarkably well, but I did not expect that to last, sooner or later there would be one that was less than successful, the trick was to try and keep those to a minimum and do enough research that the likelihood of a disaster was reduced. As far as we could tell from the numbers, Dad's success rate was about 85%, not bad, but if any of those 15% were really bad then it could have wiped out the bank. I doubted if we could afford to continue with those kind of odds, so we would have to look carefully at the problems and see if there were patterns there that we could look for in the future and avoid poor choices. I finally called it a day and went home. I needed to get back, I had not given Tiffany her own key yet and I expected Maman to call me that evening.

Bravo

I went with Tiffany and we had collected most of her clothes and personal belongings and brought them to my flat. We looked through the Yellow Pages and found a place that duplicated keys, so resolved to get a couple of spares cut the next day, one for Tiffany and another just as a spare. We had not been back long when Maman called.

"Alors, Bébé, quoi de neuf chez toi?" Maman asked, looking for what was new in my life. Clearly Portia had told her how the land lay, and she was now looking for the rest of the story. We carried on our conversation in French, which was usual for us, but it would be tedious in the extreme to translate every word, so I give the English version.

"Maman," I began. "I came to realise on our trip to South Africa that Tiffany made me happy, I haven't been this happy since Ian died."

"Good for you," she said. "And Tiffany, how does she feel about you?"

"I think she's just happy," I said. "Happy to be with me, she loves me, that's clear, she's moved in with me."

"How are you going to manage things with the bank?" she asked.

"We're keeping things quiet," I said. "The banking world has a difficult time just dealing with the idea that a woman invaded their precious domain, let alone one who lives with another woman. It may leak out in time, but I have enough that if it becomes untenable, I'll do what Dad did and drop out of the world, but I don't see that as necessary or likely yet."

"So, tell me when?" she asked.

"It was in the Kruger National Park, it just hit me one day when we were having lunch," I said. "I had been getting these feelings and had been disturbed by them, I wasn't sure that I wanted to admit to myself what they meant, but over lunch I just looked at her and the realisation hit me, I loved her, for what she was, for her company, for her love towards me, so I decided to just admit it and enjoy my life without feelings of guilt."

"Bravo for you," Maman said. "And is she a tigress in bed?" That was a reference to a remark she had made to tease me when she had first got together with Portia.

"I've no idea," I laughed. "How are tigresses supposed to be? I will say that she has an amazing body and we've explored each other a lot in the past few days."

"Keep exploring," Maman said. "I am still learning about Portia, even after these many years. It is still exciting to discover new things about her and the joy she brings me. Does your father know?"

"As I told Portia, James probably suspects and he may have passed on those suspicions to Dad, but Dad will have to live with it," I said.

"He'll be torn," Maman said. "On the one hand he has deep issues with same sex relationships, but on the other hand he loves you, I think love will win."

"That's good to know," I said. "How are you and Portia?"

"Both in the pink," she said. "We are planning a trip to Tahiti soon, it's time I went back to see if there are any relatives of Mémère there, and to see it again for myself and let Portia see it as well."

"When are you going?" I asked.

"Next month, I think," she said. "We'll fly from Paris to Los Angeles on Air France, then pick up UTA for the trip to Pape'ete, then we'll come back the other way around through Djakarta, Singapore, and Bahrain."

"A true around the world trip," I thought. "How long are you going for?"

"A month," she said. "That'll give us time to sail to the smaller islands and explore a little."

"I'm jealous," I said. "That sounds like fun."

"I think it will be," she agreed. "We might as well enjoy travelling while we can."

"Let me know when you're actually leaving," I said. "Do you need anyone to look after your villa while you're gone?"

"We've got that arranged," she said. "I've become friends with the local police chief and he's committed to keep an eye one things for us."

"Nice to have friends in high places," I laughed.

"I should let you go," she said. "Say hello to Tiffany for me."

"I will, Maman," I said. *"Je t'aime, bonne nuit."*

"Was that your Mum?" Tiffany asked when she came through after unpacking one of her bags.

"It was," I confirmed. "She told me that she and Portia are going to Tahiti for a month soon."

"That sounds exciting," Tiffany said. "Perhaps we could go one day?"

"I'd like that," I said. "Now, shall we go the bistro for dinner, or do you want me to see what I can do here?"

"I'll cook," she said. She set about dinner, she examined the contents of the refrigerator, then assembled things and started. She cooked and I watched and chatted. I was surprised at how quickly she put together a meal and how good it was when we ate. My contribution was the wine, which fortunately I had a plentiful supply of from Dad's flat.

"So," she said, between mouthfuls. "Would you rather shower or bath?"

"Bath," I said. "Showers are fine to wash off dirt, but baths are for relaxing and talking about the day."

"I've never bathed with anyone else," she said.

"Well, there's a first time for everything," I said. "What's the adage, save water, bath with a friend?"

"I like that," she laughed. "Are you done, if you are, I'll run a bath and we can soak and relax." Soak and relax we did, but the relaxing turned to touching, which turned to caressing, which led to even more intimacy. We followed that with more when we went to bed and sleep came as I nestled into her back and draped my arm over her. It was so nice to be that close and to feel the rise and fall of her breathing and revel in my love for her.

I was up first the next day and got up and made tea. Tiffany was a tea drinker, at least first thing in the morning. She came through, naked as a babe and gave me a big hug and kiss. Unfortunately work called at the bank, otherwise I would have been tempted to drag her back off to bed and enjoy the morning. She grinned at me and scampered off to dress, while I made breakfast. I did at least have the makings of breakfast in my refrigerator, but would have to go shopping soon for food. At the bank there was work to do, putting together the offering memorandum for Sable Mining and the financing package for the Klein Copper mine. That took quite a while, a couple of days in fact and I was glad to finally get it out onto the street. Now it was time to see what else was out there in the world. We had our first meeting as a bank where each of the staff gave a quick summary of the industry that they were following. Out of that came four definite possibilities and I asked them to check further and see what else they could learn. After work I would join Tiffany at her studio while she worked. Sometimes I sat and read, sometimes I watched her work and sometimes I was given small jobs to do. It did not matter to me, all that mattered was that we spent time together. I was amazed by her ability to create things of such intricacy and beauty, she had an eye for detail and a truly artistic talent. In the mornings we would run or go to the dojo that she belonged to and spar and work out with the other members. I even got to watch some kendo matches. The speed and aggression which Tiffany displayed was terrific, I had never seen anyone else move so fast. Although the matches were supposed to be for ten minutes, when she competed the match was usually over in just a few minutes, just long enough for her to score her three hits.

In mid February there was a call from the Master at Trinity reminding me that I had made a commitment to give a lecture on economics before Easter. I had not forgotten and had a lecture prepared and was ready to go, my only hesitation was running into Tom and Roberta again, not that I thought that they would have any interest in economics, at least the kind of theoretical economics that I would talk about. The Master and I agreed upon a date at the end of the month and told him that my assistant would be bringing me and that I would require accommodation for her as well. He told me that that was not a problem and all would be taken care of. My lecture would be for an hour, with another hour for questions, followed by drinks with the Master and invited graduate students and then dinner with the Master and the professor of economics.

Tiffany was thrilled at the idea of driving up to Cambridge, not quite so thrilled at the idea of staying apart from me overnight, but sensitive to the need to keep our relationship as private as possible. I put together the lecture and prepared slides that I would use and was ready to go. The lecture was set for three in the afternoon, so by five we would be done, and then there would be sherry and mix and mingle before dinner. I thought about what I would wear and decided upon the blue suit that I had, the dinner was not in Hall, so no need for academic dress. Tiffany put together overnight bags for each of us and had the car washed and polished before we went. The drive up to Cambridge was damp, drippy and dismal and I think that annoyed Tiffany more than anything, because it meant that the car got dirty again. She pulled up at the gate of

Trinity and told the porter there who we were and he directed us to a place to park and also called another porter to show us to our rooms. We were housed in two very nice rooms, not adjacent, but across the hall from one another. The porter also told me that he would let the Master know that we had arrived. I had barely begun to unpack when there was a knock at my door and our guide for the afternoon, a Professor Harold Creek introduced himself. I knocked at Tiffany's door and she joined us with the slides and my notes. Harold Creek had replaced Gerald Hopkins as the head of the economics department and was working his way up the ladder of hope that he thought might take him one day to a Nobel, something that had eluded Hopkins.

The lecture theatre was not as large as thought it could be, perhaps with seats for fifty. Tiffany loaded my slides into the carousel tray of the projector that was already set up in the back of the room and we tested things. Harold chatted away, he had heard of my work from the Chancellor's office and was as fawning as a man could be, perhaps he thought that I had some influence in Downing Street. He had tried to suggest that Tiffany would not be needed during the lecture, but she made it quite clear that where I was she was. Harold asked me about the substance of my lecture and I gave him a quick précis of my remarks and even showed him some of my notes and the arcane mathematics that were included. He frowned, he puzzled and enlightenment hit a couple of times as he studied the expressions that I had written. He shook his head a couple of times, whether because he disagreed or because he just did not understand, or in wonderment I did not know. He asked for a copy of my notes and I had come prepared for that and gave him one, but told him that I would not be handing them out generally before the lecture as I wanted people to listen not read ahead. He nodded agreement to that.

At about a quarter to three people started to drift in and take seats. In all I counted 33, some with notepads, some not. Sadly of the 33 only two were women, either my lecture was not well advertised, or there were few women interested in what I might have to say, or few taking economics as a subject. I would have thought that there would have been more people at the talk, given the number of students who I am sure were taking PPE, Philosophy, Politics and Economics. At five minutes to the hour the Master came bustling in.

"I'm so sorry I was not able to welcome you before," he said. "I've been tied up in the most tedious meetings."

"Master, this is my assistant, Tiffany MacBeth," I said, making the introductions. "She is one of my analysts and she also looks after my safety and welfare."

"Oh," he said. "I hadn't realised that banking was hazardous?"

"It can be in certain countries," I said.

"Well, glad that you're seeing to the welfare of the doctor," he said. "Shall we begin?"

"Please do," I said. The Master then made his introduction, pointing out my multiple doctorates, but lamenting that none was from Cambridge. He told the audience that I was now the Managing Director of a bank and had been in the news lately as the architect of several major deals. With that introduction, I launched into my prepared remarks. I talked about macro economics and social behaviours and how they related. I had developed some mathematical models that represented all this and flashed those up on the screen. Some of the audience made notes, some looked confused and one or two even fell asleep. I could have gone on for much longer, but did hold my remarks to the hour, after which there were questions. It became clear that only a few who were there grasped the mathematics, so most understood that there were relationships between social behaviours and macro economics, but had a difficult time with the mathematics. I think that there were perhaps six in the audience who had some understanding of what I had presented, and it was from them that I had most questions.

The Master thanked me for my presentation and asked Harold Creek if he had any remarks to make. Harold thanked me and went on to give me a bravo for a brilliant piece of thinking and exposition. He did wave my notes in the air and told the audience that if anyone wanted a copy of them, that they should see him. He told those present that the graduates among them were invited to drinks with the Master at which time they could ask me any other questions they might have. I noted a couple of the students trying to make conversation with Tiffany. She was polite, but was focused on her task of recovering my slides then joining me to watch my back, figuratively if not literally. We were then ushered off to drinks with the Master and collected professors and graduate students. Tiffany excused herself for a few moments while she ran my notes and slides back to her room. She was back in a remarkably short time and collected her wine as she re-entered the room. She was approached by a couple of the students, whether because they wanted to know what she did at the bank, or because they were looking to chat her up I had no idea, but I was confident that either way she would acquit herself well. Harold wanted to know what Tiffany did as an analyst and I told him that she had recently done all the research on the Sable Mining project, I think he would have enquired further, but my attention was sought by a couple of others, the only two women who had been at the lecture. They had both read the piece in the Financial Times and wanted to know how I had got involved with the bank. That was simple, I just inherited it. They both commented quietly that they felt poorly done to by the university and asked how things had been at Oxford. I told that it was very much the same, antipathy towards women intruding into what was regarded as a male domain. I had just been fortunate that I had just excelled so quickly that they had had no real choice but to tolerate me. I told them about my recent experience of being denied entry to a dinner I had been invited to, merely because the venue was a men only club. They both understood and asked if I had openings at the bank. I suggested that they both finish their doctorates, then to come and talk to me. Further discussion was interrupted by the Master who thanked all, but then told them that I would be leaving in his company. So, the party broke up and Tiffany and I went off with the Master and Harold Creek to a restaurant in town.

Over dinner Harold quizzed Tiffany or her rôle at the bank and she launched into a dissertation about minerals and the mining industry. I think that quite took him aback, he had not expected such an erudite description of the industry. That led to questions about her education and the fact that she was a linguist rather confused him. She finally relented and told him that much of her knowledge came from her father who was a professor of economic geology. The Master tried again to get me to think about joining the faculty, but I told him that the bank had all my attention at the moment, and I was happy to just continue with a couple of lectures a year. The dinner ended early and we were back in college before nine-thirty. We said good night to the Master and to

Harold and went to our rooms. Tiffany came with to my room and told me that part of the reason for her trip back to her room to drop off the slides and notes had been to rumple the bed so that it looked as if it had been slept in. We bathed together and slept together, happy to be in each other's arms. The alarm awoke us early in the morning and Tiffany went back to her own room and dressed and packed, so that when Harold came to take us for breakfast he had to knock on both doors.

We breakfasted in Hall, with Harold chattering on about the lecture and how he might incorporate some of the ideas into his own lectures. I saw Tom and Roberta come in and there was obviously some debate between them and Roberta won as they came over to say hello.
"Dr Barclay, Professor Creek," she said.
"Roberta, Tom," I replied.
"You know Dr Barclay?" Harold asked.
"We have met a couple of times," Roberta said. "What brings you to Trinity, Dr Barclay?"
"I was giving a lecture on economics," I said.
"She gave a most interesting and deeply insightful lecture," Harold said. "I'm going to include some of her thoughts into my syllabus."
"I'm sorry, we don't know your friend," Roberta said.
"This is Tiffany MacBeth, my assistant and one of my analysts," I said. "Tiffany, this is Roberta Spignolio and Tom Ortiz."
"Good morning," Tiffany said coldly.
"We should leave you to your breakfast," Roberta said. They left without having breakfast, probably uncomfortable being in the same room as me. After they had gone, Harold returned to his discussion about economics and I finally had to tell him that we were expected back in London and would have to leave. He thanked me again and told me that he was really looking forward to the next lecture that I had promised. We went back to our rooms and collected our bags and left.

"So that's Roberta and Tom," Tiffany said as she drove us away.
"It is," I confirmed.
"What was his problem, she did all the talking?" Tiffany asked.
"Probably embarrassed," I guessed. "But, looking a them together and looking at you, I won, I got the best of things."

"I think so too," she said.

"What I really wanted to throw in his face was that you're my partner, my lover, my friend, my reason for getting up in the morning, but I think that would have shocked poor Harold," I said.

"Maybe, maybe not," she said. "He may be more enlightened than you give him credit for."

"Anyway, again, I won," I said happily.

"I have something for you," she said.

"You do?" I asked.

"I made us each matching pendants," she said. "Look in the glove compartment, you'll find them there."

I did as asked and found a small box. The pendants were a Celtic design, intertwined strands, done in silver. They were beautifully crafted and came with delicate silver chains, and they were so designed that they actually meshed together one stacked on top of the other to make a larger single piece.

"We should stop somewhere so that we can put these on," I said. We did stop at a lay bye that we saw and I took one of the pendants and hung it around Tiffany's neck, then let her put on mine. I was thrilled and kissed her a big thank you and promised myself that I would not take the pendant off except for rare occasions. The nice thing about them was I could wear mine beneath my blouse so that it would not be seen by all and sundry and advertise that was anything between us, but as long as I wore it I was tied to her.

London was damp and dreary, but at least it was warm at the bank. I called Deirdre and Anthea in and we went through the mail and sorted things out. Then we sat with Geoffrey Black who went through the audit findings. I had been wrong, Dad had left no unpleasant surprises, in fact the bank was in a very sound position. That was gratifying to hear, and relieved me of some of the worries I had had since taking over. I was still puzzled as to why Dad just decided to chuck it all in so quickly and stay in the Caribbean, perhaps one day I would find out. We thanked Geoffrey for his time and Anthea left with him to take care of the account. Deidre gave me what was probably more personal mail and also left. There was an impressive looking envelope in the mail and I had a sense of what it was before I opened it. It was another invitation to a dinner, this time the speaker would be Sir Walter Edgar, the High

Commissioner for Kenya. I knew him well, he had helped me when Ian had been killed, and had been a good friend to me. He was to talk about investment opportunities in Kenya. I checked on the venue, Brown's on Albemarle Street, well at least with that there would be no issues of entry. The invitation was for me and a guest and dinner jackets were requested. I toyed with the idea of getting a dinner jacket made, but decided that that was too much of a dig at male society, so opted for a dress instead. I went home and waited for Tiffany to come in and then gave her the news that we were going to a fancy dinner at Brown's and we needed to dress up. That led to much discussion about what to wear and we both concluded that the easiest thing to do was spend money and have Rachel put something together for us. She suggested a forest green halter dress for Tiffany and a French blue a-line for me. The sapphire and silver necklace would go well with the blue and I loaned Tiffany my emerald earrings, to go with her dress. We each then got a simple clutch bag, to match the shoes we picked out. I also booked us a room at Brown's, then we did not have to worry about how long the event went on for.

When we went to Brown's we took a taxi, so did not have to worry about where to park the car. The event was in the Clarendon Room, so we checked in at the front desk, got our room key and asked for our bags to be sent up, and then asked directions to the event. Essentially it was as simple as follow the signs. At the door an imposing looking individual took our invitation and our names, then gave us each a card that showed us where we would sit. It was at a table in the corner of the room, about as far away from the speaker's podium as one could get. There was a receiving line and we joined it. The first person we met was George Blake, the president of the British and Kenya Trade Society, then his wife, Anne, then there was William Baskerville also of the Trade Society, and his wife Alison, and finally there was Sir Walter Edgar and his wife Chloe.

"Fiona," Sir Walter said. "So nice to see you, how are you?"

"I'm doing well thank you Sir Walter," I replied. "This is my associate Tiffany MacBeth."

"Delighted to meet you," he said. "Fiona, I will find the time to come and sit with you and catch up. Chloe, look who's here."

"Fiona," Chloe said. "This is a lovely surprise, you must come and have lunch with just Walter and me tomorrow, who is this?"

"Chloe, this is my partner, Tiffany Macbeth," I said in Swahili.

"Partner, oh, good for you," she replied, also in Swahili. "I will find you later and you must tell me more. Are you living in London?"

"I am," I said. "But, we're staying here the night."

"Oh, in that case, not lunch but breakfast, come to our suite at eight and we'll catch up," she said. "I'm so happy for you my dear, I worried about you after you left us, but I did get reports back, so knew you were busy."

"We shouldn't hold up the line," I said. "Lovely to see you again Lady Edgar." She grinned at that and punched me lightly on the arm. Then turned her attentions and her charm onto the next person in line who was pushing himself forward. We wandered off to find ourselves a glass of wine. I looked over the crowd, there were Kenyans there, black and white, there were even a couple I recognised and waved to.

"She seems very nice," Tiffany said of Chloe.

"She is," I said. "She's fun, takes her position very seriously and was a great help to me when Ian was killed."

"Was that Swahili you were speaking?" Tiffany asked.

"It was," I confirmed. "I told her that you are my partner, now she wants all the details, we'll have breakfast with them tomorrow in their suite."

"Fiona," a voice said at my shoulder. I turned and looked and it was Julia Conway.

"Julia," I said. "How lovely, are you here officially or just here?"

"I'm in England drumming up business," she said. "So, Walter told me to come and promote the safari industry."

"Tiffany, this is Julia Conway, she and her husband, Henry, took me on my very first safari in Kenya," I explained. "Julia, this is my partner, Tiffany."

"Partner, well good for you," she said. "When are you and Tiffany going to come out and see us?"

"I'm not sure," I said. "We were just in Kruger, we tacked a short trip onto the end of a business trip. Where's Henry?"

"He died three months ago of complications from malaria," she said.

"I'm so sorry," I said. "How are you managing?"

"Surprisingly well," she said. "Henry and I were drifting apart and we had differences about how the business should be run, and his death rather brought things to a head, and now I can do things my way without a lot of discussion and argument."

332

"If I can help, let me know," I said.

"What are you doing now Fiona?" she asked.

"I run a bank, Thames Cherwell, it's an investment bank," I replied.

"So, if I decide to build a lodge instead of running mobile safaris, you're the one to talk to?" Julia asked.

"I'd be happy to talk to you," I said. "I'm not guaranteeing funding, but I'll always talk to you."

Our conversation was interrupted by the master of ceremonies who asked us all to take our seats, so that they might serve dinner. Tiffany and I made our way to the back of the room and the table in the corner, where there were three others, like us banished into outer darkness. Our table mates were all from a shipping company that organised freight forwarding to Mombasa and beyond. We introduced ourselves as being with the bank and quickly got into a discussion about financing for a new ocean freighter. I suggested that they come and see us at the bank and make their proposition. Between the fish and main course, Walter came over and talked to me. He asked if I had a business card with me, I did, and he took it with him, back to his table. Dessert and coffee served the master of ceremonies then stood and made the introductions of the dignitaries that were there and introduced Sir Walter as the speaker.

"Thank you, George for that kind introduction and thank you all for coming to hear about investment opportunities in Kenya," Walter said. "Before I proceed with my prepared remarks, I would like to recognise an extraordinary person who is here tonight. Several years ago a young man joined us at the High Commission and he brought with him his wife. We were quite unprepared for the level of intellect that she had and over the years came to appreciate that we were privileged to know her. I may be the one to tell you about investment opportunities in Kenya, but she is the one who can quickly tell you if your ideas are feasible and now as the Chair of the Thames Cherwell Bank, she can provide financing. Dr Barclay, I am delighted that you are with us tonight. Dr Barclay is a mathematician turned economist and computer expert, who also numbers among her talents several languages including Swahili and Kikuyu, and to cap it all she is also a pilot and a crack shot. I read the piece in the FT about her and can assure the reporter that Dr Barclay does have the intestinal fortitude for the exigencies of the banking world. The bigger question is, are our current crop of bankers smart enough to keep up with her. Chloe and I are delighted that she is here tonight and suggest that if you have not already met Dr Barclay, that you take the opportunity to do so."

I had never had such a ringing endorsement in all my life and was grateful to Walter for giving me such a public endorsement. After the fiasco at the Cymric Club I had wondered what it might take to break into the closely guarded world of private banking and finance, and here I was being lauded by a High Commissioner with all the room looking to me and suddenly wanting to make my acquaintance. After Walter's speech I did have a steady flow of people who wanted to meet me, or so they said, the cynic in me said that they wanted to be seen to be meeting me. Fortunately Tiffany had brought extra business cards, so that when I ran out of those that I had brought, she was able to give me more. When the evening broke up, Chloe stopped to make sure that we would be the next morning for breakfast at the Dover Suite. Then Julia asked us if we would like a nightcap. That sounded like a good idea, so we went with her to the bar. Tiffany excused herself to go to the loo, leaving Julia with me.

"So, Fiona, tell me how you and Tiffany met?" Julia said after we had got our drinks and were seated in a quiet corner.
"We first met when she picked me up at the airfield and drove me back to London," I said. "Then I decided that she should join the bank, since then things have quietly progressed."
"Good for you," Julia said. "You were lucky with Ian, but it looks like you've lucked out again, she's a stunner."
"I think I'm very lucky," I said.
"What are you lucky for?" Tiffany asked as she rejoined us.
"I was just telling Julia that I'm lucky to have you in my life," I said.
"No, I think I'm the lucky one," Tiffany said. "It has been wonderful Julia, I've had opportunities that I'd never dreamed of and I've been able to do them with someone I love."

"You know," Julia said. "There's a whole market out there of women, single, attached like you or just wanting to travel with a companion and I'm thinking that that could be a good business opportunity."

"That's a great idea," I said. "How would you staff the camp or lodge?"

"I'd pick my staff carefully, no religious fanatics, no politicians, just people who want a job and who will just accept the clients for who they are," she said. "Look, if I came to see you on Monday next, could we talk about my idea for a lodge?"

"Of course," I said. "The idea is interesting and I'm sure that there's a market there, but you'd have to really counsel your clients about not only attitudes in many of the African countries, but laws as well. You don't want your clients locked up."

"No, I'd thought of that," Julia said. "I'd probably start with mixed couples and then see how things worked with women who just wanted to travel together and not go somewhere new on their own."

"Is it that bad?" Tiffany asked.

"Oh yes," Julia said. "There are laws in most of the African countries, they're generally very conservative, but that's not to say that same-sex relationships don't exist, they do, if people are discreet and careful, then the locals look the other way, unless they're religious nuts, politicians or just bigots."

"So, we were lucky when we were in Kruger?" Tiffany asked me.

"We were careful," I said. "If we go again, we'll be careful."

"Anyway, Fiona, I think you've succeeded where most thought you wouldn't or couldn't, you head a successful bank, you've got a loving partner, all in all, you've come out on top, bravo, you've won!" Julia said.

"Bravo, I won," I laughed raising my glass to her.

www.ingramcontent.com/pod-product-compliance
Lightning Source LLC
Chambersburg PA
CBHW071048250626
47159CB00002B/406